THE *Persia Café*

ALSO BY MELANY NEILSON

Even Mississippi

MELANY NEILSON

THE *Persia Café*

THOMAS DUNNE BOOKS
St. Martin's Press New York

THOMAS DUNNE BOOKS.
An imprint of St. Martin's Press.

www.stmartins.com

Library of Congress Cataloging-in-Publication Data

Neilson, Melany.
The Persia Café / Melany Neilson.—1st ed.
p. cm.
ISBN 0-312-26219-1
1. Missing children—Fiction. 2. Race relations—Fiction.
3. Women cooks—Fiction. 4. Mississippi—Fiction.
5. Racism—Fiction.
PS3564.E348 P4 2001
813'.54—dc21 00-064477

ISBN 0-312-26219-1

First Edition: January 2001

10 9 8 7 6 5 4 3 2 1

To Fred, Leland Nicholas, and Noel Lafleur,
with all my love

How unsearchable are his judgments,
and his ways past finding out.

—Romans 11:33

THE Persia Café

Prologue

THE STORY BEGINS IN MY nose. A smell of smoke, of blackening crust, of something in the oven too long. I was wiping the counter, refilling cups. I was accustomed to this since I was a young girl, the clink and brush of white china cups, their simple geometry. And the coffee's boil, the smell of blood, mud, and weather, ham bone, spillstain and sour armpits, the tickle of fries in hissing oil, the porcelain stove aged yellow. A customer raised his cup and I refilled it with one hand; my husband, Will, pushed back a plate and I took it with the other.

But the smoke. Smell of it like a gash on the air. So I pushed open the kitchen door. Smoke was rising from the grill; beyond it I could see my help, Mattie. Opening the back door slowly, as though in hesitation. Holding a knife. And what she did was run headlong into the parking lot toward the back of a car. Stabbed the knife into the back tire. A black boy was driving the car, I could see that much; I could see a piece of his forehead just above the wheel. And when he peeled from the parking lot, a white girl lay curled on the pavement.

Now I insist to this day that what was to happen later was in no way Mattie's fault, but I knew the moment I saw that girl there was trouble. The boy's name was Earnest, but the girl slowly stood and drove hands into thighs and stared with wild, wild eyes and hollered, *"Earnie!"* There was liquid in her voice I recognized as sadness, something curtained, something dangerous.

I remembered the kitchen, ran back inside. Smoke was streaming from the grill. Burn forcing the edge of a pancake up like the nose of a bird dog. I slid a spatula under the cake, tossed it in the garbage. Men were passing, their noses up.

Then I watched Will pass without looking at me and slip out the back door.

So I listened to engines starting now, footsteps beyond the kitchen. Sound is magnified through this café and travels loose, the ceilings are so high, the linoleum so wide. I seemed to hear even the crumpling of napkins on the counter, the squeak of counter stools, grit of spilled sugar under the toe of a boot. I could hear a woman out back, one of the few in the breakfast crowd, calling her husband's name. Then another called, then another, and as I went back outside, trucks were already fading down the road.

It was high summer, 1962. A summer when folk looked up from their lives. These few women stood in the parking lot, calling their husbands' names, touching fingers to a throat, to a rib, to a damp spot on their cotton dresses. Flies buzzed the garbage can beside us, and the quality of their voices reminded me of those flies—high-pitched, thin, frantic. It was a sound I had never heard coming from them, a sound much like that girl's, but I was already turning away. A story is a mirror you hold at an angle you choose. For a long time I tried not to look.

My name is Fannie Leary. I run the Persia Café in Persia, Mississippi. I am a cook. I know every white face in this town. And I know who killed Earnest March.

The Wedding Cake

I CAME TO COOKING EARLY on. I should better say I went fishing one Saturday, brought home a mess of catfish, maybe the size of your finger, and my mother praised them to the nines, like they were Fisherman's Paradise. I stood on a chair by the kitchen counter, hands yellow-gloved in cornmeal. We fried them and sat down to the table and ate. Lastly she looked at me across the remains of crust crumbs and devastated fish bones and said, "That's my little girl, bringing home the bacon."

Persia's librarian was Mrs. Nadine Thistle, a woman in her mid- or late sixties when I was a child. Her library held nearly a thousand books, and she claimed to have read every one. Fast-fingered, interested, she could mention a title and know its exact location on a shelf. The library was the old train depot, though the books themselves were housed in half the depot, Mrs. Thistle in the other. It was also one of the first places in Persia to be air-conditioned, in addition to the Persia Café. Mrs. Thistle went before the town board and argued that in a place where literacy was devoted to cattle and weather reports, *Farmer's Home*, and the sports page, the library was Persia's toehold on civilization, and that civilization should be preserved. Mrs. Thistle was a sure-minded woman, somebody to be reckoned with, so the board granted her request. She drew up library cards with a single rose on them, covered in thistles, a comment, I suppose, on her name. At the bottom of each card in tiny print, in the right-hand corner, was the word AIR-COOLED.

I found several books on cooking in the library, including the Magnolia Club's local collection and a yellow-eared *Confederate Receipt Book*, published in 1863. But the books I really fell for came from Mrs. Thistle's private collection. A large green edition of *Good Housekeeping Favorite Recipes* filled with color photographs of chocolate éclairs, racks of lamb, flaming cakes topped with holly. Oranges scooped and made into little baskets, filled with orange sherbet and decorated with mint leaves, with perfect little orange handles. A duck made from pastry. A pie made from a duck. And M. F. K. Fisher's *Serve It Forth*, in which the author describes a sky raining potatoes and fifty million snails, Greek honey and the Hon-Zo, the social status of a vegetable, and folk in France who washed in wine, which they made in enormous lakes throughout the countryside.

I sat on Mrs. Thistle's couch, in the main reading room, many afternoons after school. I would open my three-ring notebook and copy recipes, occasionally brushing my hand over the porousness of paper, the crease at the corner of a page that someone had folded over as a mark. Now and then she would look at me over her glasses. Behind her desk was a framed certificate of library science, earned in 1915. One day as she was featherdusting books she paused and looked over my shoulder.

"Fisher," she said. "A follower of Brillat-Savarin."

"Who's that?"

"Another great food writer. 'Only wise men know the art of eating,' he said. Yet he was very democratic. A lover of all foods."

"Did he love fried chicken?"

"Truth be told, I don't know. He never tried it in Persia."

She laughed, swished her duster along another shelf, then left me alone until I headed home, in time for supper.

My mother shared Mrs. Thistle's love of books, and so approved of my reading habits. She thought it would help with my schooling.

I was not the most studious in my class, but I did stay in school. Mama was determined about that. She had never gone to college, "and you see where it gets you," she said. "Folding underdrawers for every Tom, Dick, and Harry who can spare the dime." Which she did. She took in laundry and sewing, and had done so ever since she left school to have me. But this part she did not mention, only swearing up and down that my father was nobody I knew and long gone besides, and then she would steer the conversation to subjects she preferred. She had books by Dickens and Emily Dickinson, LPs of Mozart and Debussy's "Claire de Lune," and a little reproduction of Rodin's *The Kiss* embracing itself on the table by her Singer sewing machine. Mama was an example of someone who would scrape to beat hell and cultivate high taste but still not have much money. So, of course, she was all too glad when I took over the cooking. We had our share of biscuit and gravy meals, yes, but sometimes I would copy down a recipe from the library and repeat it at home. One day at Mama's suggestion I carried a banana cake to Mrs. Thistle. She thanked me and invited me back to her kitchen, pulled two plates and a knife from the cabinet. She cut two thick slices and as we sat at her table eating, she nodded her approval.

Through the years Mrs. Thistle's approval, offered on one other visit, echoed in my head. "Just *cook*," she said. "God gave you that desire for a reason." Before she died, when I graduated from high school, she gave me her collection of cookbooks. Cooking was what I loved best. It had been from the beginning.

Besides Mama and Mrs. Thistle, I cooked for Will Leary, beginning when I was fourteen. Will was the same age as me, the same grade. He lived on the houseboat *Elvira* with his father, Amos, who owned a small construction business. The houseboat was named for Will's mother, who had died when he was born. Will had, I was told, some of her dark looks, which were Choctaw, and which directly contradicted his father's redheaded Scottish coloring. There were no Choctaws left in Persia after the year we were born, 1941. Not long before her death, the story goes, her name was painted down the side of the boat, in cursive green swirls. This appealed to my romantic side, and is what I count as my earliest memory: the river, crickets, the late evening diminishing and stillness, where all colors ran and melted, green dissolving into the lavender of shadows, and Will and his father, on the *Elvira*, Will riding on his father's shoulders; Mama carrying me past on the levee, saying, "Wave! Wave!" I must have been no more than two. Later I liked to fantasize a time when boatmen named their boats after names of lovers rather than themselves. A woman seen pulling water from a well, holding a tin cup. Some would-be poet's woman, whose bare throat makes him cover a boat with her name. The tin cup drizzles water down her chin, and old Amos sweeps a paintbrush over the wood.

This was the way it was for me, growing up, with cotton rows and slow open country and the town on the edge of the river. And seeing it, as I did, makes me remember how, years later, Will found me fishing on the levee. I had been sitting there for some time. I would sit at the water and listen to the hours, lapping and dissolving on the rocks, and smell the amber honeysuckle of a fine Saturday morning. The world was floating on a white haze of distance, and Will looked as though he might sleep. He was tan and handsome and fourteen. He didn't say anything. He just took a seat beside me. Then he picked up a rock. Rubbed its flat side curiously with his thumb. There was some sense of strength in his hands magnified by his holding a thing as slight as the rock. He threw it across the water. It skipped five times, then sank.

"You want some lemonade?"

He said sure. I handed him my thermos. He took a sip and said, "That's exactly right. Not too much sugar. Not sour either." He offered me the rest but I said I'd had plenty, and so he leaned back and drank it down. He finished it in one breath. Licked his lips. There was a speck of rind on the corner. He slid one of his hands over mine along the fishing pole and pulled it toward him and moved my hand to his stomach and pressed it there for a moment. Then he got up and walked toward town.

Well, after he left I put my lips on the thermos, where his had been. I could not later explain exactly what made that encounter *the* one, but I would remember the way the undissolved crystals of sugar had slid from the bottom of the thermos to the silver lip, glistening with that same luminance I felt on my tongue, the ghost of sweetness. So, for many Saturdays afterward, I squeezed lemons. I went back to the same spot, looking. I thought Will would put my hand on his stomach again, but he did not.

For several years in deer season he would take me hunting with him. There was a stretch of woods bordering the river just north of Persia not given over to farmland. I brought a feeling of nervous mystery to these hunts: What would Will try next? At five one morning we headed out, this time the dead of winter. It was bitter cold. A band of electric blue on the horizon, and a half moon made the path bright and clear. The woods so silent we didn't say a word, all the way to the deer stand. The air made clouds of our breaths. Even after we climbed into the stand Will said nothing, while I tried to think of things warm. I had on three layers of clothes; I was sipping black coffee from my thermos to keep my teeth from chattering. We were sitting like that for a while when the silence began to slow down so I could hear the smaller noises. I could hear Will's breathing. The shift of a branch. Dry leaves crackling as he whispered, "Take the gun, take it! Look through the sight, look!" That was just like Will, startling me in the quiet. His sudden shift reminding me of a passage I read once about the peculiarity of southern weather: *For breeze is the soul of a storm testing itself in hollow places*. A few years later, for instance, after I had begun to work in the café, we were sitting in this very spot when Will, out of the blue, set his gun down as if interrupting himself and whispered, "I saw y'all's help talking to the Jones girl—"

"Hunh?"

"That colored boy. Who delivers milk to the café. The March boy."

"Earnest."

"Right. Well, I saw him yesterday afternoon, talking to Sheila Jones like he knew her."

"And where were you, to see this?"

"At the Piggly Wiggly."

"At the front of the store, or on an aisle?"

"At the front."

"Outside the counter, or in line?"

"In line."

"And—"

"And I was getting some Juicy Fruit. She had a couple of Cocolas and some stockings."

"They got stockings at the Piggly Wiggly?"

"Or leotards or something. Hell, I don't know. But he was talking to her like he knew her. He was bagging her groceries and talking."

"Well, that's his job. Maybe he was being courteous."

"Courteous ain't the word."

"Sounds to me like it is."

"Yeah but it's what he did then. What he did was, he handed her the bag. And she dropped it. So she stooped down to get it and he did too. A bottle rolled loose and he put it back in. Then, when he handed her the bag, before they stood back up—I was there at the counter, I saw this—he reached up and touched her hair. I swear. Right then and there. I *saw*." By the look of Will's eyes I was pretty sure he was pulling my leg, but I was taken with his story anyway. I was at the time. I looked at him, open-mouthed and fascinated.

"Naaw," I said. "Naaw!"

"Sshh," Will said. "It was just for a second. A wink of an eye. Then Clarice Lytle walked up behind the Jones girl and says, 'Hey Sheila.' And you know what? That girl almost dropped the bag again. She says she best be going and then she shot out the store. Like a frightened deer." Will frowned. "Like the one we've already scared away."

"And Earnest?"

"Says, 'Will that be all, sir?' He took my Juicy Fruit and bagged it, quick as a whistle. He was squinting down at the bag but I didn't say nothing."

"I don't know," I whispered, after a minute. "Something doesn't quite wash. Maybe, you know, you thought you saw him touch her hair. Or maybe he just slipped. Maybe there was a bug in her hair."

"Maybe."

"Or maybe you're flat-out wrong. Maybe we're gonna sit out here and rattle our teeth for nothing. Those deer long gone before we started talking. Why, they're back there laughing at those two frozen fools. Sitting out here half the morning and not see a thing."

"Maybe so." Will shrugged. "Wouldn't be the first time."

In my courting days with Will, I felt an answer looking for me. What? When? The green of the world was breathing out the questions. They followed me in waking moments and blanketed me in sleep. Then one evening, after my sixteenth birthday, Will took me for a walk. We walked for a while aimlessly, without saying anything. We walked down Levee Road on the edge of the bluff, overlooking the river, with the spires of the courthouse and First Baptist behind, and Hardin Hardware, Huit Drugstore, Piggly Wiggly, Ardor Department Store, the two-store buildings, brown brick, water dripping in an alley, and the Persia Café, which was then the only place that served food to white folk in town. The café's housed in an old white frame home, its downstairs converted, robbed of its juice in drought, warped by damp, swollen by rain, frozen and cracked by frost, so that its mildewed exterior had settled, slightly crooked, a fact demonstrated by a marble, which when placed on one end of the porch, would roll all the way to the other end.

As Will and I passed, the neon light of the café sign flickered on, for it was getting toward night: The outline of the café sign kept bursting into ruby light, and every time it went out the vertical letters saying PERSIA CAFÉ faded, but the letters could still be made out as a ghostly shadow teasing the eye before its next ruby wink.

"Where we going?" I said.

I looked down at his feet clomping out *one-two, one-two*. He was wearing brown leather boots, very heavy, very square, and the frayed fringe of his jeans flickered, *one-two, one-two*, hypnotically.

"Just walking," he said.

We had left the block of stores and the café, and the faint sound of voices. We passed down the street where tall trees fronted houses, the fleshy leaves touching, a branch jostling as a cat climbed, eyes glowing, claws scratching wood. The windows were open on these houses, with here and there a crack of light, the faint clinking of forks. Against the sky the misty rooftops darkened. Somewhere off a dog barked, and a child laughed. A truck rumbled down the street, then idled, then turned off the motor. At once, a vast silence fell over the street and over the town. Then the sound of water could be heard.

We looked at the river below, visible as a wide dark motion, flecked with evening shimmers. A denser, still darkness, far beyond, blurred the beginning of the other bank. By looking fixedly, though, we could see in the distance the blackish outline of a barge barely visible against the darkening sky. There were the steps down to the pier and we stopped and leaned against the railing. We leaned for a while. Then Will glanced up and over his shoulder. "Daddy's at the café," he said. And let that sink in.

"It's Friday," he added. "He won't be back till late."

As he said that, I was suddenly aware of the emptiness out on the river, the boats floating before us, the dew that would dampen the ground still hovering in the warm air, intensifying the silence and immobility in the space all around. As I looked ahead there wasn't a sound from the town. Below there was the *slap-slop* of water against boats, now subsiding. Maybe just stand here. Just don't say a word. Finally I said, "You about to get me in trouble."

"You already in trouble."

Then we turned and walked down the steps to the pier. At the end, where the *Elvira* was tied off, he didn't even pause or look around. He pulled the rope that tied the boat to the pier-post and held the side of the boat flush to the pier. He reached for my hand and helped me in. Then he jumped in himself. He seemed unconsciously in love with his body, his physicalness, slipping foil from a stick of gum, his jaw working over it slowly, his eyes working over me slowly, when he thought I wasn't looking. He went to the door of the cabin and opened it. He stood to one side while I walked down. Then he closed the door. He took a few steps. Just stand here, Fannie, just don't say a word. When he came up behind me, I turned toward the little cabin window. I pretended to be watching something out there, but I was not. I don't think either of us was watching anything. We were standing in the middle of the shadowy room staring out across the water toward the darkening tops of trees that all at once began to stir with breeze coming up from the Gulf.

Then Will said, in a low tone, "Have a seat." I turned and looked to see if there was any place other than a bed he meant. He didn't. There were twin beds and a wall covered with nails to hang tools on, their shapes outlined in yellow paint apparently so each could be put back into place without anyone having to think about it. I looked at these as I took a seat on a bed. I leaned carefully against the pillow. Watching, Will moved around the bed in a way that was not at all like the easeful way he had jumped into the boat and took out his gum and dropped it in an ashtray. Then he stopped. He looked at me, eyes toward me in a straight line and our faces found each other and I was dropping into the quicksand of a kiss, and I didn't think about it or consider—this was going fast—I didn't think about anything, even waiting for the answer.

There is Mississippi light and Mississippi summer. It is deep as emerald but poor, a kind of thick mute clouded sky, with the river of silver-brown, which the land holds as a hand holds a satin ribbon, the humming of mosquitoes, crickets.

The last light was tingeing the window and for some reason I noticed this. The clothes damp and clinging that were hard to peel away and our breaths coming on top of us and the button torn from my dress that I heard, at a simultaneous pause in our breaths, fall to the floor with a tiny *click*. And again the window light sliding silver threads along our bodies. Will crouched over me. Silver thread along his cheek. I felt the *bite* and then the fall, his falling from me, like a dead man. I saw the light to the cabin slowly fade, hearing the drop of wind into windlessness and then the *slap-slop* of water as it rocked the boat. And all the delicate noises of the river.

"It's all right," Will said, afterwards. He might have been sleeping when he said this. I thought maybe I should say something, but the words were suspended in such a luxurious nonchalance that I just lay back my head. I thought of salt and green onion. Lapping grass, by a pond. That loosed-from-your-skin feeling, when the cats are turning into toms.

When I awoke it was to footsteps overhead. The knob on the cabin door began to rattle just as Will said, "Close your eyes." The door swung open. Then it closed quickly again.

"Hell's bells! Your daddy!"

Will nodded.

"What we gonna tell him?"

"We gonna tell him nothing."

"Nothing?"

"He's a big boy. He can take it." Will pulled back the sheet. "We're gonna tell your mama first."

"My mama."

"Yeap."

"And pray tell you got anything in mind?"

There were freckles of blood on the mattress and I nudged the sheet back over them.

"How about just walking up to her doorstep? Holding hands. She'll get the idea."

"She'll get it, all right. I'll get it too."

Will practically never smiled but he almost did now. "Well," he said, "just get dressed now. You go on up. Just act like it's no big deal."

So I did. Fortunately Amos was busy tying off rope and he said, without looking at me, "Morning."

"Morning."

"You know, young lady," he said, without missing a beat. "Will's come a long way since he was a boy. And he's better on the woodwork than I am. Than I was at his age anyway. An eye for cabinetry, for line. To see the form before it's done. Just thought you'd like to know that. Bet you didn't know that?"

"Nosir," I said.

From the summers of 1955 through 1959 I worked at the Persia Café, full-time. Not cooking, not at first, but waiting tables, washing dishes, cleaning bathrooms. My great-aunt Eugenia was the owner then, but her real name was Mrs. Eugenia Dare Mary Claire Boatwright, a name that fit, for she went on and on. She could talk the hind legs off a donkey. And she gave me as much work as I could handle. Seven to five on weekdays, later on Fridays and Saturdays, when I was not out with Will. Eugenia would work the cash register and turn a lunch crowd into a prolonged visit, though the true cook and influence on my work was Mattie Boyd, the one always in the kitchen, and from the start I thought the three of us worked well together, considering our differences: Mattie black, skinny as a matchstick and twice as hot-headed; Eugenia, widowed aunt of my mother's and the color of faded teabags, a patient intelligence; me a young white long-boned girl, stumbling along, eager to get somewhere.

Mattie saw beyond the present, got quick flashes of coming events like radio waves briefly connected. She had been born with pneumonia; at three, witnessed a tornado uproot a giant oak; dreamed of cherry tomatoes the night before her brother got the measles. She believed in Jesus our Lord. She could make a perfect biscuit. Luna moths stopped on the back screen door to watch her on their annual flight.

The café, as I have mentioned, was air-cooled; the lettering on the door shows the word capped with aqua and white glaciers melting down like cream. Inside, the cold air smelled first of deodorant powder and warm coffee. There was a string of Christmas bells on the doorknob, left year-round, to announce your entry, a cigarette machine, a jukebox that didn't work, a dozen tables, the counter with ten stools, and a dozen skin-colored Naugahyde booths covered in plastic, like loosely nyloned feet. The tables were topped each with salt and pepper shakers, a canister of sugar, a cruet of pale green finger-sized peppers pickled in vinegar. As you entered there was always the seemingly faraway echo of clinking silver and popping grease. There was the sense, particularly behind the counter—with its pictures of high school football heroes and basketball teams, beauty queens, wedding pictures, and pictures of Eugenia's old dog, Earl, long dead, well missed—of a public place trying for an hour or so to be a place to call your own, matched only in my memory by the picture show, before it closed.

Or so I liked to think.

Though work tinged my view. I learned of late deliveries; icebox breakdowns; the battles with roaches, ants, mice; folk who can't hit the toilet; folk who stop up the toilet; folk who forget to leave a tip. To forget all this I would daydream of my future, of one day going to Paris, to chef's school at the Cordon Bleu, Saturday mornings sitting at a sidewalk café wearing a Marilyn Monroe dress and drinking café au lait. And there always seemed to be accordian music as well. *More, mademoiselle? Oui*. To the tables I hauled more fried chicken. More baked ham. Delicate corn pudding. Fresh greens flavored salt-sweet, bacon-rich that slid from your tongue to your blood, singing. Blackberry cobbler. Caramel cake. And Mattie's biscuits, so airy and transcendent that each time I hauled them out to customers they made me want to give up cooking. More, they made me want to try. Anyway, by the second summer Eugenia let me into Mattie's kitchen and I began to watch. Her secret? Baking powder. Single-acting baking powder lends more delicacy to a biscuit than store-bought double-acting, so make your own.

Other secrets: Store milk in glass. Freeze fresh berries, but never meats. Put home-rendered lard in your piecrust.

Mattie's instructions were quick and elliptical. They kept to subjects such as flavor, temperature, when to taste. She taught me about instinctively denying certain seasoning the chance—as she put it—to dominate rather than feature a dish. "If it wasn't already dead," she said, when I dropped too much cayenne on catfish, "you'd burn the life out of it." She had hot, juggling hands that were difficult to follow, and I tried to tell her this. "Well, catch on, Missy," she had a habit of answering. "I ain't gonna slow down on your account."

"Missy" was what Mattie called me whenever she thought I was getting too big for my britches, as black folk were supposed to call all white folk then, including the folk they worked for, Miss this or

Mister that. But all her reproofs were like that, a matter of rush and implication, so that much later I would realize this added up to unique instruction: her harmony with the seasons; her refusal to be bound by the imperative of smother or fry; her demonstration that food can be respected as much as desired. The fresh vegetable, for instance, which wants to be left alone. "Don't cook cabbage till it farts," she said. "Don't boil green beans till they shred to tweed."

"Flavor," she said, "is everything. Add one right ingredient to a recipe and it's yours." I put rosemary in the fried chicken. Garlic in the mashed potatoes. "Mmm-hmmph," she said, tasting, skin of her cheeks caving, tilting her head to the side as though listening. Her praise I could go on for days and days. I would try a recipe, and try again. Learning, I felt I was guessing piece by piece.

And one day Mrs. Viola telephoned Eugenia at the café with an odd request: a blue cake. It was her grandson's fourth birthday. He wanted blue.

"Blue," Eugenia said, the skin around her mouth gathering. She might have been asking me a question. By this time, I think, she knew that in her presence I was butter of easy-spreading consistency.

My own eyes roved over to Mattie. She was standing by the kitchen door. She said, "Well, come on."

I made a cake, seven-minute icing; dyed each with two drops of blue food coloring; went over to Hardin Hardware and bought some tiny toy sailboats and tilted them on the blue frosting waves.

Well, Mrs. Viola thanked me with such a brimful voice we started a little sideline. Other folk had birthdays. Others heard. Eugenia even bought me a cake-decorating book and as orders continued my cakes gradually took on more sophisticated designs. A cake that looked like a fish. A basket of candied flowers. A fiftieth-anniversary cake soaked in bourbon and shaped into a Wild Turkey bottle, complete with label. I charged two to four dollars for those cakes, in addition to hourly wage and tips. By the summer before my senior year I was making enough to pay half Mama's rent and save besides. I was squirreling away money to flee. I would spin the globe at the Thistle library and imagine cooking in France, Italy, Australia, anyplace really. Mama talked of college but I already considered cooking my profession. In June 1959, one month after I graduated from high school, I went to work at the café full-time. And though I was stuck in Persia for the time being, I considered the café the next step in my education.

Anyway, I had been earning money from cooking and was proud of it.

In 1959, I still had a steady hand and did not have to put aside personal torment for an entire day of cooking. I could concentrate on the finest cake, attend to customers, and had not yet fallen into the habit of eating a quarter-pound of chocolate a day. That happened soon after I discovered Earnest March's body and holds true to this day. I never had much of a taste for hard liquor, though I did drink it with Will. Which he did, often enough. On the other hand, chocolate is another cheap magic, its own amnesia, a float in a warm river. Skin on the back of a wooden spoon, and memory twitches, a bowl and a spoon to lick, an opening oven door. What does God smell like, you wonder. God smells like a freshly baked chocolate-chip cookie.

Perhaps it's true that we all need our diversions, but there I go. So much to tell. Though I, for one, have been cooking for much of my life, I have never gotten famous. None of my recipes has made it into a book. My three-ringed notebook from school gathers dust in the café kitchen. Clarice Lytle, who went to work for Will after high school and, to hear the town's version of it, got involved with him after we got married, may still have the floral recipe box I gave her; I don't know. It was a graduation present.

I had bought the recipe box at Ardor Department Store, but that was before the recognition. Clarice Lytle was not much older than Sheila Jones, and I was not much older than either of them. I think of this again as I look back at our years as a whole. That summer was like both an end and a beginning to our lives, longer and full of different meaning, when the drought broke heat lightning and the news broke about Sheila Jones, so the entire town found out about her and Earnest March. I can look back and see a particular day before all hell broke loose. I can see a day before rocks pummeled the café windows and all our white customers threatened to leave the café, and I wonder if we were plain naive. Or is trouble all of a piece only in the remembering?

The days were all alike and ran into one another, and the mind is a sort of sieve, but the day I remember was during my second year at the café working full-time. Sheila Jones had come in after school, as girls did, for Cocolas and shakes. Then Emma Magee and Lynn Hardin followed and took seats at the counter next to her. At the start, it wasn't exactly a gay gathering. In the first place, the typical day didn't make for much chitchat. In the second place, there was the heat, and folk coming in to the air-conditioning took a minute to revive. In the third place, Sheila wasn't particularly chummy with Emma or Lynn, or any of the girls, for that matter. So she sat sucking on her straw and gave herself over to her thoughts. I reckon she had a lot to think about. For one thing, she could think about all that had happened since her father died while she was still out in California, and her mother had packed up all their belongings and brought her back to Persia, back to the old family home that had belonged to her mother's side for years. She would have a lot to think about over a tall, cool milk shake, for there had been a lot of changes.

I noticed Sheila, first and most, maybe because of her father. But I felt there was something childishly sequestered about her looks, and I connected her with that feeling. The straight brown bangs, gray-green eyes, crescent of freckles across her cheeks. Nary a curve to show under a tight shirt, or a short skirt, like the other girls. She wore baggy rolled-up Wranglers and saddle oxfords. No makeup, like the others. She had a space between her front teeth faint as a pencil line that showed just enough for her to hold her top lip down when she smiled. She leaned her head low over her shake, cheeks hollowing over her straw. When her bra strap slipped out of her shirt, she lowered her shoulder just under the counter, still sucking the straw, and quickly pulled it up.

I remember Eugenia saying how Sheila had shaken as if she would convulse during her father's funeral. How on the trip to the cemetery she and her mother had been driven by the preacher himself. Most folk stood politely through the service waiting for it to be done with, until they saw Sheila rush the coffin. They saw her paw wildly at it before Brother Works had even managed to come to a real stop and heard her call her daddy, who was a good three days dead, as she ran out of the cemetery and down the street.

Why Sheila would eventually choose me to talk to, I don't know. Maybe the café was a nice diversion. The cool counter, the tall, frosted glasses. Or maybe I wasn't threatening. When you work in a café, folk often have a habit of punching a hole in the air where you are. Later, when folk started chalking up reasons for her involvement with Earnest March—a mind skidded on grief, all those years in California—I could attest to the fact that they were wrong. I was the one, maybe the only one, she took time to explain it to.

Now Mattie at the kitchen door, in armhole apron. A pea hull stuck to the front.

"Milk delivery," she said, and I left the girls sipping their shakes at the counter. I followed her back to the kitchen. She nodded to Earnest March, who was her cousin; he nodded back. Then she took her seat by a basket of peas. Earnest had deposited a crate on the table along with a pink receipt slip. I hollered "Much obliged!" as he headed out the back door.

For a second I watched Mattie as she picked up a peapod and snapped it. The light hit her on her brown face, which was damp now with sweat, and her chopped-off black hair was spongy and wild, and her black eyes burning right out of her face at me. I could tell she was riled. She presented a profile stiff as a tin duck in a shooting gallery.

"What's got you?" I said.

She kept snapping. Her right hand twisted over and back and she snapped a little curl of string off the end of each pod and rolled out the peas with her thumb. She could snap about four peas to every one of mine. Finally she said, "None of your business."

"Aw now," I said and grinned. Then, "What is it?"

"A dream I had. You satisfied?" Another snap. The symptoms seemed to be running true to form. We'd get started like that over nothing, me waiting and grinning and Mattie working up her black eyes to a glitter and a coil of her hair would separate from the rest and hang down by her forehead so she would have to wipe it back with her forearm. She would say plenty and I would grin, for when I wasn't concentrating on cooking, it was kind of interesting to see Mattie riled. Unless she hit one of my sore spots, and she was one of the few who could. One of the few who knew how. Then the circus would really start. But this was not one of those times, and so I kept grinning.

"What kind of dream?" I said.

"You think it's so funny, oh yeah, so funny. But you won't think it's so funny when you hear what it's about." She stopped, then said, "Part of it's about you."

"What about me?"

"I saw you, I don't know, surrounded by, hubcaps."

"Hubcaps?" I looked at her. "What am I, one of Sikes Daughtry's rosebushes?"

"Oh it's so funny, yeah, yeah." And she started snapping as though she might snap a button off her starched white dress.

After a minute, I said, "I'm sorry. What's the rest of the dream?"

"Oh. So now you want to hear it?"

Another snap.

I watched her.

"Well, I'd really like to hear it but I hadn't got all day. I got to go back out front, to the counter, all those girls—"

"The rest was foggy—you satisfied? I was walking along. Couldn't see a thing. Then, in the middle of that I saw something."

"What?"

"I don't know." She shook her head. "A shadow. Four-legged. Like an animal but—I don't know." Then she returned to the snapping.

At the corner of the kitchen, a scurry, like a mouse.

"Hell's bells," I said. "Hell's bells sonofabitch. You better not be what I think you are." I went to the corner and grabbed the broom, and pulled out the crates of potatoes and onions. There, sure enough, was a new hole above the molding, eaten through fresh plaster.

"He's back," I said. "Monsieur Bigbutt after the potatoes."

"It ain't the potatoes. It's the pecans."

"They all wrapped up."

"I don't care. He can smell them."

"Well he's back." I grinned again at Mattie. "You sure he ain't the one in your dreams? Creeping at you through that fog?"

"Say what you like, Missy. Say what you like and I'll put your tongue in that pickle jar."

I checked the mousetrap by the icebox. A piece of cheese, dried the color of clay, untouched. So I got a fresh piece and reset it, washed my hands, put up the milk, picked up the receipt on the table, and copied the amount in Eugenia's ledger. It was a thick book I added the figures to, the binding cracked, bowed out slightly on the sides so the receipt was cradled within the text of pages. A pink slip stamped Piggly Wiggly, signed in blue ink: "Sweet milk. Ten gallons. EM."

I looked at the small, gnarled handwriting.

The only closer look I had at Earnest March, before the close look at his murdered body, came the night before I got married. Eugenia threw a dinner party for me at her house, just outside Persia on Huit Road (which we called in high school "Do It Road"—it was that secluded). In part, Eugenia saw this dinner as a wedding present.

So we sat down to the dining room table, with Eugenia at one end. Eugenia tamped down at her temple one blue-tinted curl and gave a last look around the table to see if anything was missing, and then she bowed her head for the prayer and blessed these children and the food and the table and all the folk sitting at it. She went on at some length and blessed the café and the county and the state and the country and the president, and she spoke about the poor and the hungry and the weather and other problems with particular reference to the farmers and she asked it all in Jesus' name amen and looked up and reached for the dinner rolls.

"Amen," said Brother Works, who was the only one there not kin. The dinner I am referring to was on a hot evening in July, back in 1961, and I sat next to Will. Mama was there, and Amos, just as Eugenia had planned.

"Commence! Commence!" she cried, a little too eagerly, once the prayer was done. Eugenia, by this time, was around seventy, and she was starting to show her age. Her hands shook all the time when she lifted the meat platter and her head shook all the time, very slightly, as though trying to signal "No" to someone behind my back. She was starting up the talk and keeping a sharp eye for a vacant space on any plate and her face seemed to smooth itself out as she looked around at the group sitting before her burgundy rose-border china; a platter of the same pattern hung on the wall just behind her, along with a large print of some other, unidentifiable flower. Candlelight flickered; thighs shifted; Mama sat in scrutinizing silence as Will and I passed platters. There was reason for tension. I could feel the sweat behind my knees. The general overwhelmingness of the occasion was reinforced by the feeling that the implication of theft, as Mama initially saw our engagement, had somehow taken on an inevitability of its own, for there had been, between Will and my family, a lot of water under the bridge.

Throughout this dinner Mama would glance questioningly at me. She wore a green dress she had made for the occasion, which showed off the color of her eyes, and it amazes me to think how young she was then. Thirty-nine. I watched her pick up her napkin and delicately dab the corner of her lip. Eugenia would tease her about it, as she teased her about everything: her notions of culture, her love of classical music, her fear of getting fat, and her encounters with various men, about which she was apt to hold forth with sharp humor, including her own brief husband by the name of Jefferson Bell. He was named for good measure after Thomas Jefferson and Jefferson Davis, though his mother was said to have died of a broken heart by the time he hit puberty. He had a reputation for taking dares, for diving off the river bridge and selling moonshine in mayonnaise jars, and he told Mama never to pull anything smart like getting pregnant. Mama confided that trading Jefferson for me was the best deal this side of the Louisiana Purchase.

But now Mama put down her napkin. She frowned openly at me

as Eugenia flowed at the swelling and silent Will, "Nonsense, nonsense, son, you haven't begun to eat yet! Now what's the matter with you? Now you just pass your plate for another helping."

"Yessum," he managed. "This is awful good." He sat there, pressed to his chair, his face held a certain way, as always with the hint of held-back, keyed-up intensity, though the expression was hidden under the smooth surface of the face. But the intensity was more than usual, which I could tell. Once in a while I caught Eugenia glancing soberly and consideringly at Will, and he would look to his plate. He had used Amos's Brylcreem, so the black hair was clean-parted and slicked back like an eight ball on a pool table. The black eyelashes very long. The brown eyes that, I remember noticing then, were shaped like Amos's eyes, but in which the Scottish blue was replaced by the circle of dark brown inside of which was a smaller circle of coiling troubled amber. He had on a shirt and tie. He had what must have been the cleanest fingernails in Persia County.

And old Amos, hair slicked back too and stubbled chin razor-nicked, fumbling his fork with tool-hardened hands. And Brother Works, the only person I knew who could outtalk Eugenia. Indeed, he had a voice that was to his ear like a face slow to leave a mirror. I was not a regular churchgoer, but as Eugenia said, he was a necessary part of this function. Having made my own private connection between God and food, I felt moral enough not to pay close attention. Besides, I had already passed my own judgment on Brother Works: I had seen him at the café smothering the contents of an entire lunch plate with ketchup.

"Say, Brother Works," Eugenia said, "I hear you been blessing the cows, you been laying on the hands?"

"Yes ma'am."

"Burl Magee says you lay hands on the fence, the barn, the salt lick."

"He speaks the truth."

"Well, I don't profess to know all these things myself, like I was a high-toned preacher. But I do remember a preacher coming here back in the great flood, back in 'thirty-six, some of you weren't even yet in this world, oh well, but there were a lot of problems connected with that preacher. Folk expected a lot. He cured some folk and offered to pray over their fields and lay the hands on their kin and their livestock and was apparently kicking up his heels in the pasture so to speak like a good brother in Beulah land and I don't like to say it but it got bad. I think it did."

We ate. She looked at Brother Works.

"They brought dead cows," she said. "Put them in the back of their trucks and brought them right up to the church. It got out of hand."

"You can't do nothing with a dead cow," said Amos.

"Here, here," sniffed Mama.

"Personally I'm inclined to agree with you both." Brother Works nodded. "Folk do expect a lot from a minister of God. But we can leave it to the higher mercies to sort out the wobblers and cowards from those making a simple reach in their faith. It's the way you start—just like folk always want to know how I got started. When I first heard the Word I knew what it was for and there wasn't no mystery about it neither! I heard it first on the radio. Brother Joseph Shane. My mother had bought a crystal set. Bought it through the mail. It come wrapped up in a box and you put it together. We lived in Black Fork and we'd heard about Brother Shane, of course, we heard him on the radio. But we'd never actually seen him in the pulpit with our own eyes till he come for revival. Then I knew what the pulpit was for! Because there could be no delays, you see. A man might harden his heart to the Word, but you stand a few feet from a pulpit? Well, hardness of the heart won't do it there, unless you stone-deaf besides. And the laying of the hands is an extension of this. The laying of the hands is a tactile extension of the Word—"

Brother Works loaded his plate as he talked and then he stopped talking and ate. So we sat around the dining room table at Eugenia's, one hot evening in July, back in 1961, waiting for Brother Works and Eugenia to outlast one another and listening for the silence in the pauses as the night air hummed through the open dining room windows. Twice Will opened his mouth and closed it. But Eugenia was already overwhelming him with regeneration and third helpings. Roasted quail, for instance, new potatoes, black bottom pie. Salted pecans served in a silver dish like a tiny birdbath and black, black coffee. I felt glad for the folds of linen in candlelight as Mama moved frugally and Will continued in silence and Eugenia went on and Amos glanced out at it all from under his rust-colored eyebrows. Brother Works went on too, about the flood of the Delta and the flood of Noah and the glory of sunsets and God's carelessness in creating the female leg.

Anyway, it went like that and during dessert I got up and excused myself. Eugenia had one of those old houses with a detached bathroom and kitchen connected by a little porch. Once outside, I paused to let my eyes adjust. The light from a window fell on part of the porch and withdrew again down the edge of the garden in deepening shadow and damp and a bird chittering somewhere in the dark brush. Then I walked toward the end of the porch. It was there I saw him. A flashlight—like something sprayed out of a hose—lit up the edge of the garden, and I stopped in midstep.

A big-bellied man.

The moonlight revealed his shape in the darkness. Doing what looked to be some odd dance, running a few steps, leaping forward, his legs smashing down, bending and moving a hand along the grass, standing. He was very quick; his shoes made squidging noises along the damp grass.

"Howdy?" I said.

The light leaped up and turned in midair toward my direction. It moved around the garden and through the yard, over the porch steps, and then touched and slid toward me. I couldn't see him for the light. Then he dropped it quickly. The man became just a boy, a skinny one, actually; the big belly became a basket tied to his belt.

"Earnest."

"Yessum."

His eyes on me a second, round and dark as coins. He was just outside the porch steps and did not walk up. He stood sideways to me, not facing.

"Nice night."

He nodded and looked down at his basket.

"You catching crickets?"

He nodded again and slid one foot back in the direction of the garden. He stood that way a moment, feet apart and leaning somewhat to offset the bulk of the basket, from which came cavelike cricket sounds. In the misty sky the stars flickered. I looked off toward the distance and then finally back at him. He stood with his hands composed and motionless over the lid of the basket. In the dropped light of the flashlight, I could see his black high-tops, grass sticking to the rubber soles.

"Well," I said, "good luck." That he took as his release; he did not want conversation and in fact seemed as fierce in his solitude as Sheila Jones, whipping the air back toward the garden in long fervent strides. And from that moment until the last time I saw him alive, we said not a word to each other. Which was all well and proper. Earnest March I knew only by the cold milk bottles or the sound of his feet running.

Early the next morning I went out to Tchula Gaze's for eggs. I was making my own wedding cake, of course, and I wanted the freshest ingredients. Leaving town, I carried a basket out Levee Road a bit past Eugenia's house, past Avery Jones's cotton field, and all of a sudden I was on the steep slope by the river.

A timid, tender band of pink caught on the horizon. Mosquito whine and the smell of manure rich as meat. I wasn't sure if it was too early or not. But the feet carried themselves and it felt almost like relief after the flurry of Eugenia's dinner just to walk the path with the dew-taste and croaking frogs that began and then stopped. Then, far below, the sound of the river could be heard. With the lack of light it was almost visible, or at least a few of its glints showed intermittently. A barge moved slowly down the water. Everything moved slowly as it got toward light and I went down the path past the fields, where off in the distance I could see the first field hands. Three tall men, almost black, wearing nothing but cotton trousers and broad straw hats. Side by side they walked carrying hoes over their shoulders, and then they melted into the cotton rows. I went past another pasture, where silver-faced cows questioned my presence and twitched tails over caramel hides. A sign that said POSTED. A twitter of a bird that shot down the slope. It was impossible that time of day not to watch. The path was dirt, puffs of dust at my feet, but there was no real movement. The barge hardly advanced on the water. Finally I reached the slope toward a narrow peninsula, at the beginning of which was a little cemetery, some church ruins, a square of crumbling bricks. Just past it was Tchula Gaze's shack, walled with pine and sod. In 1961 she was ninety, one of the oldest black women in the county, and since her house was next to the church ruins, I thought it looked something like a church. The cool moth smell of it. The way it sat out on the edge of the bluff. To the back was her chicken coop and garden. She had taken a nine-foot crucifix from the church ruins and used it to build a scarecrow, hanging empty Vienna sausage cans that clankled whenever the winds shifted. Straight below, two hundred feet down, was the base of the peninsula; considered a point of danger for barges, it fed a batch of sandbars that had to be carefully navigated. Though fishermen and riverboatmen alike said they got fair warning from Tchula: They could hear her scarecrow before they saw it, high on the air, like a slowed-down sound of chimes.

Then I heard Tchula herself, talking to her chickens. She stood so she was just in the shadow of the coop, bending toward them in their nests. She wore a faded blue dress with gaping armholes that showed her long brown breasts, and her hair was thin and white and tied with one of those strings off a snuff pouch. Tchula couldn't hear too well, but she could pick up on your presence in other ways. Nor was she an easy person to surprise, but then nobody would ever want to surprise Tchula. Not anybody who knew her and had seen the stunts she could pull with the old double-action Colt Lightning that jutted in her right pocket like a hipbone.

"Morning, Tchula," I said, loud enough so she could hear me, so as not to startle her. "Fine morning."

"Best keep away from my eggs," she said in her briny voice. "Don't be tainting my eggs."

"Why surely no. I'm just here for a little purchase. I'm getting married today and I'm making my cake."

"Good weather for marrying. Good weather for practicing, too. Like you and Will been doing. Practice. Practice. Practice."

When Tchula laughed, as she did now, her face cracked into a thousand wrinkles and her mouth bared twisted, darkened teeth. "I always liked that Will," she said. "He never bothered my eggs."

"I like him too."

"I just remember when he was a talker. Talk, talk, talk. He daddy'd bring him out here, to see his mama's grave, he was knee-high to a jaybird. But that was before the accident. You ask me, that accident was the start of that boy's troubles on this earth."

On his eighth birthday, May 14, 1949, Amos bought Will a Red Rider BB gun. There were plenty of BB guns around Persia, usually given to boys that age the way girls were given bicycles or training bras. You could see Will playing with his on trails by the edge of the bluff, high above the water. He would shoot at the river off the houseboat. He would set up empty cans on the end of the dock and take aim, or charge blindly at them with the gun held like a battering ram and knock them in the water, one time falling in himself.

One afternoon I had just come into the café when I noticed something under my foot. A fork, its tines turned upward. Silverware scattered everywhere, and an egg turner on the counter. I stepped over a smashed plate and a broken ketchup bottle and saw several dimes on the seat of the chair. A still, muffled quality held the room, an invisible kind of energy. I picked my way across the floor and, seeing two men at the kitchen door, walked around the counter. They were all but blocking my view. Then I heard a voice cry out "I'm sorry," followed by a loud slap.

At first I didn't recognize the voice. And I couldn't see past those men. Then Burl Magee turned and saw me and leaned down and said, "Well, hey, little lady," in a sudden, tripping whisper.

"You know Sheriff Wade," he said. "Sheriff, meet Fannie Bell."

The sheriff bent down and shook my hand. I felt his hand and waited, but at first he did not speak. I looked up at him, hesitating in Mr. Magee's hesitation, and saw his bald head, unexpectedly close and huge in the light, and a single mole on the side of his nose, like a second, tiny bald head.

"Pleased to make your acquaintance," he said. "But I'm sorry about this accident."

"What the sheriff's saying is . . ." said Mr. Magee, and the words settled a certain way in his lips, in the lines around his mouth. "What the sheriff's saying is, that's Will Leary in the kitchen. Poor boy, he ran into Lawrence Boatwright while playing with that BB gun of his on the bluff. The boy was running and apparently—tripped. Your uncle Lawrence was standing near the edge and was apparently—startled. I wish I could say different, Fannie, but your uncle Lawrence—fell to his death."

Uncle Lawrence, who had been married to Eugenia for thirty-five years, was just recovering from a stroke.

"Uncle Lawrence," I said. "Nunh-unh." I shook my head.

"I'm sorry," said Mr. Magee.

"But it was BBs."

"No, hon," said Mr. Magee, "he fell."

Then the sheriff turned to Eugenia and said, very sharply, "I'll have to ask you not to strike the witness."

I stopped between the two men and saw Will, curled up on the floor and crying. Eugenia was standing next to him. Staring at her hand. She was holding her palm and staring at it like a map of hell, and then she put it down. Then her eyes lost focus.

"My husband was just getting better," she said. "He worked so hard to get back on his feet, and now this?"

To answer, Sheriff Wade seemed to switch direction and walked toward her. He gently placed his hands on her shoulders. At that moment Mama appeared at the door, flush-faced and open-mouthed.

"We know, we know," the sheriff said. "You need to get on home now. We're mighty sorry." He patted Eugenia's shoulders rapidly four times and then led her over and handed her to Mama as though she were a vase he might drop.

"Come on, Fannie," Mama said.

But I was looking at Will. He was holding his arms around himself and rocking. Sitting on the floor and rocking and staring downward through his loosed hair at the shards on the linoleum, his own eyes like splintered glass, and I thought of the word I'd heard for men who'd come back from war: shell-shocked. I could not stop looking at him.

"Come *on*, Fannie."

Years later, I came to believe that Will would look through a thick whiskey focus straight toward Uncle Lawrence. And that no amount of liquor could visit enough punishment on himself. But in that moment, I simply turned to my mother and left the café.

Afterward Sheriff Wade questioned Will for more than an hour. Will had a small cut on his chest from the butt of the gun in the collision, and the sheriff took him to the doctor for stitches. Then he had Will take him to the exact spot on the bluff where the accident had happened. Amos went along too, but Will did not say anything. For some time after that, he did not speak.

I was eight at the time, and I remember the funeral, Brother Works's voice, the closed coffin, and Eugenia, who looked too small for her navy dress, her face falling in pleats. The body had landed on a rock at the bottom of the bluff, which some commented on as fortunate; had the fall been wider, the river would have taken Uncle Lawrence's body and it might never have been found.

And I did not see Will for an entire summer. It was May of that year, the start of school vacation, and talk went that he'd gone off to the mental ward at Whitfield State Hospital. Folk, as usual, set their plots in motion; few guessed when he actually returned, and holed up, for being a recluse in Persia is an act of pure creativity. I even heard Mama use the word *breakdown*. What did it mean? I wondered. Was she talking about Will or Eugenia? Breakdown to me sounded like a temporary inconvenience, a flat tire or a hot engine, something to be fixed and not worried over. And I heard Eugenia say, not too long afterward, "No, I won't hold it against him. I won't hold it against him." As though trying to convince herself. "There's enough blame in this town. And that boy's gonna have to live with the God-awful stupid thing he did."

Tchula sweet-talked one of her chickens and cajoled an egg from its nest. "Well, you newlyweds now, you stay away from my eggs."

"We will."

"And do as you will." Tchula sighed deeply. "Do as you will. Folk don't like me, see, 'cause I remember. You see down there? Down there, just past that willow, I saw a pirate once, sitting on those rocks. Just sitting there, eyeing me. Like he wasn't in a hurry to go nowhere. But folk nowaday don't want you to remember."

She looked out over the river. A breeze picked up and brushed her dress into a stubborn crookedness; then she turned back to the nest and reached in and took another egg and placed it in my hand. It was warm to the touch and I knew that inside the yolk was warm and floating. I held it for a moment, then set it gently in my basket. The chickens rearranged themselves in the face of this, panicking and fluttering just a little.

"Yes, well, thank you, Tchula," I said. I paid her for the eggs. "Much obliged."

She turned back to her chickens.

And I turned back toward town. As though just remembering. For this is the day, I thought, this is the day, and found myself walking, picking up speed, holding the basket just so, in order not to jostle the eggs. I was going faster then; it was almost full light, and I felt the dew-swelled air in the arms of my shirt and all the colors—the pink-streaked sky, the fuzzy deep green cotton rows, brown-skinned eggs, blue-pooling river shadows—seemed to acquire gel and substance streaking from my fingers like transitory paints.

At the café, closed for the wedding day, I made the cake. It was a Saturday, still early, and there were no folk in sight. Closed signs on the storefronts, empty sagging porches. It was one of those days, opening up the café, you got the feeling you were the only person in town. It was one of those days you tried to imagine what might come along the road under the tall hood of old trees.

I looked at the AIR-COOLED sign on the café front door and thought of old Mrs. Thistle. Then, moving inside to the kitchen, I whipped up cake batter and baked and spent the better part of three hours decorating.

When I finished I carried the cake out to the counter. I set it there for a moment. I was pleased to think of myself as the chef of the establishment and I walked around handling Eugenia's worn and cracked and cupboard-crammed possessions. I turned the lights on and off. I felt the coin-cold of the icebox and heard water trickling into the pan underneath. I tried a button on her black NCR cash register and jumped a little at the noise. Finally, I squared my shoulders and took a deep breath and moved back from the cake to take a look. Then I held up my hands and made a little square, looking through the square the way you might see the cake in a photograph. And whispered, *"Yes."* And it was then I felt, at the heart of me, a hush and gratitude, for being in this world. White cake on the light counter. Sunlight through the window. A pair of wooden salad forks, propped in a jar, backs to one another and bending outward like the wings of brown geese. Happiness has its way of seeing. Happiness like none I had ever known or have known since.

Mama had made my dress, pale blue lace, with a deep V in the front. I was big-busted before it went out of style and I looked damn good if I do say so myself. Eugenia and Mattie were there; Mama stood up with me; Will almost smiled. And the cake, of course, was perfect. Not one of those tacky haystack cakes with the plastic hand-holding couple. But a two-layer double ring. A fine cake. Tasteful. It said on top, in delicate cursive, amid candy rose-vine swirls: *Will & Fannie, July 11, 1961.*

Clarice Lytle

CLARICE LYTLE WAS THE FIRST to teach me about jealousy. In high school she began picking at Will in the halls. If he said anything at all, she'd make a comment and toss her hair and walk away. Or she'd shove Will playfully and the minute he so much as shifted a finger in her direction she'd move what was the business and drape against him like soft curtains. She acted helpless, but I knew what she was up to. It took a lot of looking the other way to hold myself in. And another thing: Will didn't seem to be able to fend her off as quickly as I thought he ought to. When I asked him about it he would just look at me, much the way he had looked at Clarice when she was coming up to him and moving what was the business. It wasn't denial and it wasn't surprise. It was an ambiguous, speculative look. Then he said, "That skinny thing?"

He said it in a tone that implied he had settled the subject. But he kept on looking that same way.

Though Clarice was two years younger than me, she was the first on my street to hit puberty, the first to wear short skirts, and skinny is not exactly the word I would use. She was one color, one plane. The pale straight hair. The pale straight skirts. She wore pancake makeup and black eyeliner that itself was lined with white. With her skirts she wore thin, usually sleeveless sweaters in some material like Ban-Lon or rayon, each in a pastel tight enough to show the outline of her brassiere and her small, boyish breasts. She wore bangle bracelets and, for a time, Eddie Sandifer's silver ID bracelet and a thin gold chain on her ankle, under her stocking. She carried a black purse shaped like an oval. When she wore jeans, she kept a teasing comb in her back pocket, the two spikes of its handle pointing toward the ceiling.

In the September afternoons of 1960, I would look up at the mirror above the shake machine and see her coming through the door. Or rather, the image of her coming through the image of the door. For an instant I did not turn to face the actuality. Instead, I looked at the image, which stood there in reflection like a memory caught in a frame of the mind—you have seen, on a wall held in a frame, some pressed fern leaf that makes you think suddenly of the time when that feathery green leaf was on a plant slowly growing and you walked right past it without noticing. But it wasn't a memory, it was Clarice Lytle herself, who turned slowly to survey the room. I caught the flash in her eyes as she looked.

Then she spotted her friend Lynn Hardin and went her way. It was what Clarice Lytle did on those afternoons, after school. She and her friend Lynn Hardin, wondering listlessly what to do, wishing, as high school girls were always wishing, that there were college boys or a city somewhere nearby. Voices twanging gum, Ambush cologne floated one end of the counter as men sat on the other, hunched over coffee, in sweaty khakis and boots, cigarette smoke dissolving in the cloud from the fryer. I swung through the door to pass an order to Mattie, whose stained apron fluttered like a moth caught under a jar. I went back out. Then I turned to face Clarice Lytle, now poised, arched, and waiting on the counter stool.

"Fannie," she said. "Hey."

"Hey," I said.

"I'll have strawberry," she then said, and I turned back to the shake machine. I had scooped in ice cream and poured in milk when I saw her, in the frame of mirror, glance up and down at my back. I attached the silver chrome cup to the shake machine. I punched the button. Then she said, " "How's We-ull?" making two pink cotton-candy syllables out of his name, glancing over to Lynn Hardin with eyes beaming.

"Fine," I said, over the grind of the shake machine, detaching the silver chrome cup. I poured into a glass and sank in a red-and-white swirl-striped straw. I set a paper napkin and the shake in front of her. Then I went to help Eugenia tend to those at the other end of the counter.

That day, I remember, there was the usual crowd coming in. The Christmas bells rang on the front door, opening to allow several flies to take aim at the meringue pie. Sikes Daughtry was the first, but then Sikes Daughtry was always the first, pulling up his rusted pickup with his gun rack and his hound dogs in the back. You would see him pause and walk around to the back of the flatbed and with his good arm reach out and scratch under their stretching chins. The bad arm he had got in Germany during the war. So you might see him reach around in the fur and pick off a tick and squeeze it so blood burst between his fingers. Saying, "Uza a good dog." He would reach into his pocket and fish around and pull out a handkerchief and wipe his fingers. Then he would come inside. Sikes Daughtry was as rickety and stain-toothed as one of his old hounds, asthmatic and leathered and leaning crooked on his cane with his bad arm held close to his side, and his sad eyes watered. He came in every day. He was the most regular of regulars.

And Montgomery Aston Ardor, short, blond, bookish, with acne-scarred cheeks and eyes the color of money. Montgomery Aston Ardor was mayor and lawyer and owner of considerable acreage of farmland and the half the town besides, including Ardor Department Store and the house where my mother and I boarded and his own columned house like a movie set. He had a putting green in his backyard. His wife was head of the Magnolia Club. And his store employed my mother to do alterations, for as long back as I could remember.

And Burl Magee, coming in just off his postal route and dabbing his face with a napkin. He folded the napkin into triangles of decreasing size and dabbed again. There were broken blood vessels in his cheeks and the sweat ran down into his collar. Burl Magee was one of two uniformed regulars, the other being Sheriff Wade, who looked wide and hippy in his gun belt with his bald head and the mole on his nose and his yellow eyes raking the room. He put his hat on the counter. He took out his Camel cigarettes and lit one and put the pack on the counter and put the lighter on top of it and leaned back and looked around. Then he nodded and said another's name. Eugenia flirted and called them all hon. And Burl Magee said he'd seen Brother Works that morning, standing by the cemetery, and Brother Works had shaken his head and said it was a good thing they hired a boy to do the trimming before Avery Jones's funeral because the way this kudzu was growing it was gonna take over.

Burl Magee laughed silently. "A hitchhiker when he come through went to sleep in the ditch too close to the kudzu there and by the next morning he disappeared."

Eugenia poured coffee. "Here you go, hon," she said. "I got a few figures to put down in the books. I won't be too long—I know you boys gonna miss me—but I'll see y'all in a few minutes." She winked and took off her apron and, passing behind me, touched the back of my head. "Fannie'll have y'all a fresh pot." Then she went back into the kitchen.

"Coffee, Mr. Magee?"

"And tea too, Fannie."

"Lots of ice, hunh."

"You read me."

They all smoked. I stood and watched them. Then I waited a spell as the words died away as though they hadn't said anything. Then Sikes Daughtry touched the tip of his cane and said, "Yeah, I seen one of those hitchhikers."

And Mr. Ardor said, "Up to no good."

And Sheriff Wade said, "You can count on it."

And Sikes Daughtry said, "Yeah." Then he looked at Mr. Magee. "And this one, you saw him, Burl. Looked to me like he was passing for white."

"What a thing to say," Eugenia scolded saucily as she pushed open the kitchen door, walked to the cash register, and picked up an ink pen.

"Well, you should have seen his lips: the size of them. And his hair."

"Where'd he say he was from?" said Mr. Ardor.

"Indiana," said Mr. Magee.

"Indiana," the sheriff repeated. "I heard a fellow tell that they don't got them up there. They don't let them in. You can go for miles, I swear, all the way across the state and never see a nigra face. *Not a one*."

Eugenia said, "Me, I'm crazy for Ray Charles. I'd drive across the state to see him."

Then she went back to the kitchen.

I waited, then said to the sheriff, "A little warm-up?"

"Just half this time. Yeah, thank you, that's perfect, hon." Then, to the men, "You don't know what this world is coming to." He looked to them for agreement.

They were shaking their heads.

Mr. Ardor hitched a pants leg higher before he spoke. He reached for the sugar canister and poured and stirred. Then he set a smoking spoon on the saucer. "I know exactly what you mean. Of course there were plenty of nigras to pick our cotton last year but I had to go after a number of them and take them home in the evening. They can't walk that single mile. No they can't, I tell you," he said and laughed heartily. "I sure am tired of catering to the nigras, but you got to love them if you want them to work for you. When I pick them up, I say 'Good morning' and when I drop them off I wave to beat the band and they wave back." And he waved his hand quickly to illustrate.

"Like you eat at the same table," said the sheriff.

"And during their breaks I take them out a bucket of ice water," said Mr. Ardor. "That's the way it's gonna be from now on. We might as well face it."

"All courtesy of TV," said the sheriff. "Plenty are getting TVs and it's giving them ideas. After what happened at Little Rock. Eisenhower—that damn bridge player—didn't have the balls to stop it. Now it wouldn't be practical to send them back to Africa. They wouldn't want to go. They got it too good here."

"Wouldn't be what I wanted either," said Burl Magee, "if I was one of them."

The sheriff cast Mr. Magee a look of amusement.

"You going soft on us, Burl?"

"No, I was just trying to picture it, that's all."

"Well, it wouldn't be any way you could get them back anyway," continued the sheriff. "They'd be hiding out and wailing and pitching. They got it too good."

"And it wasn't so many of them then," said Mr. Ardor.

"Or TVs," warned the sheriff. And then he turned slightly, toward the men, lowered his voice just a bit, not enough to keep me from hearing him, but enough to acknowledge, perhaps, that the company was mixed. "No, you know why they're gonna stay here. They're gonna stay here where they can go north and look for white girls."

And Sikes Daughtry said, "Yeah."

Then Sikes Daughtry winked at Mr. Ardor. "Y'all know what they call ABC." The two men knew the joke. They looked toward it like the last bite of pie on a shared plate.

Mr. Ardor forked it up. "ABC is All the Best Communists. NBC is Nothing But Communists. And CBS is the Communist Broadcasting System."

There was laughter down the counter.

"Speaking of TV," said Mr. Ardor, "y'all see that story today? About that boy? Over in Pearl? Two seventy-five. Bench-press four hundred. And do the forty in four-four."

And Mr. Magee said, "Must be a recess in heaven, God setting down a boy like that."

And Mr. Ardor said, "Well, tell you the truth, he's gonna be a minister, he told Coach Vaught."

And Sheriff Wade said, "Save us."

And Mr. Magee said, "Carry that pigskin for the Lord."

And Mr. Ardor said, "Hemingway Stadium won't ever get integrated."

And Sikes Daughtry said, "Yeah."

Yeah, I thought, here we go, as the chuckle started back around. Knowing what I know now, it's odd to evoke one of these conversations. Perhaps it should have been a pinprick on the time map, but I only did what I always did. I stood mute. I poured coffee. Then I watched the way the men reached for their cups. I had often thought it was funny, the way they reached for their coffee in the same instant. The crumpled murmur and blue smoke immersed their faces like something in an aquarium. A cigarette in one hand and a cup in the other. The pause and the sip and the cups back down to the saucers. The simultaneous clink. Then suddenly, from the other end of the counter, a loud *slurp*, as Clarice Lytle reached the bottom of her shake and pulled her straw from the glass and dropped her thumb off the top and let milk shake slide onto her tongue. She twirled the straw, the red and white swirls. Licked the sides real slow. Then she dropped the straw back in the glass and dropped change on the counter. As she slid off the stool I saw a change in the men. Their sentences burned off like fog in sunlight. She walked past. Trail of Ambush cologne. Eyes tracing buttocks and the back slit of hem. The door to the LADIES opening and closing. The men holding in the mind what they had lost with the eye.

There wasn't a sound for half a minute. Mr. Ardor's acned cheeks sank, and the sack under Mr. Magee's chin quivered, and the sound of Sikes Daughtry's asthma could be plainly heard, and Sheriff Wade just sat, his yellow eyes taking it in, and I held the pot of coffee. For nobody budged, nobody thought to swallow spit until the bathroom door *clicked* through the silence.

Then Sikes Daughtry caught me looking at him and dropped his eyes. And Mr. Magee, shaking like a dog emerging from a pond, said, "Go-o-odawmighty. I'm getting old."

"That's—"

"The Lytle girl," said Mr. Magee. "Harry's girl."

And Mr. Ardor said, "That ugly cuss. How'd he hatch her?"

And Sheriff Wade said, "You girls ain't girls anymore." But it sounded again like a certain kind of warning, and now all of them turned. They stared at me. Finally Mr. Magee seemed to recognize me. He bared his teeth, smiled all over his watery eyes, and said, "But I do remember this one."

"Cute." Mr. Ardor nodded.

"Not much cuter," said Mr. Magee.

"Keep a brick on your head," said Sheriff Wade.

Now they were all smiles. I was sprouting pigtails again, scabs on my knees and elbows.

"Yeah," said Sikes Daughtry.

"Oh yeah." Mr. Magee grinned.

"Sure," said Mr. Ardor.

There was an air of ownership around the counter, almost a note of congratulations. I thought they might raise their cups and toast. It was the way they held their families, their fields, their town in their skins. Moving from the back parts of their minds toward their daughters. I even pictured Clarice Lytle then, her teeth glinting in braces, her hair no longer teased into a lump. Making us back into little girls, they could relax again.

That night I carried leftovers home for supper. Macaroni and cheese, snap beans, mint biscuits. I went into the kitchen and opened the cabinet and got plates and glasses and went to the icebox and got out tea and filled the glasses. I opened the packages of tinfoil and let steam escape and spooned out food onto plates and carried them to the table.

"He came by earlier," Mama said.

"Don't call him he."

"Will."

"All right."

We sat down to the table.

"Did he say anything?"

"About what?"

"About anything."

"Well no. He didn't specify. And I didn't ask. Beatrice Ardor was here and I was rather busy. I've been hired to sew six dresses for next spring's pilgrimage. Silk and lace hoopskirts; the Magnolia Club's already bought fabric."

"The Magnolia Club."

"Yes."

I watched her. “You hadn’t got any business letting them take advantage of you,” I said.

Mama pursed her lips and looked up. “When I come around asking you how to run my business, you’ll know you’re big enough to tell me.”

“Yessum.”

She watched me. “So what all did y’all talk about today?”

“The usual.”

“Which was?”

“Women, football, worries about nigras.”

“Don’t say nigra, Fannie. Say colored.”

“Colored.”

Then Mama looked at her plate. “Are these your day’s work?” She broke a warmed biscuit and studied the green mint flecks.

“Yessum. We served them with red pepper jelly. Just this morning we started putting up the last from the garden. And Eugenia’s got Amos putting in more cabinetry, for storage. It’s a real zoo.”

I peeled the skin of wax from the top of a fresh jar of jelly. Mama spooned a shivering mound onto a steaming crescent. She tasted. Finally she swallowed and rolled her eyes. “Oh,” she breathed. “For my dollar I’d serve these to Jackie Kennedy. The First Lady herself.”

“On a silver platter.”

“You’ve got it. As I’ve said before, if I had this creativity and were in your shoes, I’d get an education.”

“I am getting an education.”

“College, I mean. It’s not me I’m worried about. Can I say that?”

I speared macaroni with the prongs of my fork. “Yessum,” I said. “You can say that.”

Mama broke another biscuit in half and spread it with jelly. We ate. After a while I pushed back my plate and glanced into her workroom, heavy in its array of bolted fabrics, a basket of scraps, the sewing machine, the ironing board, a female mannequin with pointing cone breasts, and windows that were hard to open. Snips of thread confettied the bare wood floors. There was about the place the attempted properness and all the strained hopes of a used furniture store.

"Look, you can say whatever's on your mind. Hell's bells. You can fuss at me about Will if you want."

Mama didn't answer.

"You know you can."

"Yes. But don't cuss."

"You got the fabric for those dresses?"

"Tomorrow. But I'll have to go to Jackson. For the trim."

"Why don't we go Saturday?"

"If you haven't got anything else to do."

"I haven't got anything else to do."

Mama sipped her tea; I watched her.

"You don't have to if you don't want to."

"I want to."

"Eugenia could go."

"And I could."

"Well, maybe first thing."

"I'll be ready."

I nodded. I started up with the plates. Mama looked around. "I wonder what this place could do with a new coat of paint," she said.

It took two days to finish making up the red pepper jelly. On the second morning I was awakened early by the phone ringing, down the hall, and Mama got me up, and there was Mattie's voice saying, "It's about time you get here. Will called to inform you he got work on the pier and I told him her missyness had not managed to make it in."

"I'm up," I said.

"Well, jelly's hot."

I hung up the receiver very deliberately, walked into the kitchen and poured myself a cup of coffee, sipped, got dressed, and stood long enough to finish the cup, as though there weren't any reason in the world to hurry.

But there was a reason. And I went quick, once I started.

Mattie was standing in front of a tall pot, on the gas stove, with a hand stirring and steam swirling around her head of wild cut-off black hair.

"Well," she said, eyes watering from the stinging vapor of pepper, but I didn't answer. I walked straight past the form of Eugenia, who was leaving the kitchen, and kissed Mattie smack on the forehead before she could shove me off, which she did.

"You don't know why I did that," I said.

"I don't care, as long as it don't get to be a habit."

"Well don't cry," I said. "It's just cause you know how to pronounce his name and your name ain't Lytle."

"Your own name's gonna be mud if you don't get on the stick."

"Maybe I'll just quit. Maybe I'll elope," I said, and for a split second, with a surprising tug in my head, I thought maybe I would.

Mattie was about to say something when the pot spat and she sprang at it as though she'd assault it with bare hands, and snatched up the wooden spoon. My own eyes were stinging. And when Eugenia returned I was not even sure she could see me, for her glasses were fogging up in the steam.

I said, "Eugenia?"

And she said, "I see you, hon," and took off her glasses, which hung around her neck, on a chain, her face oozing a few drops of moisture, and her eyes blinked and looked at me. She wiped her glasses on the corner of her apron. Then she put her glasses back on and pushed out the swinging door, just as I heard Sikes Daughtry's voice saying, "Who's a fella got to see in this place to get a cup of coffee?"

After the coffee crowd she helped with the chopping, the vapor of pepper rising and marinating the café, leaving behind a residue that would curl the very paint on the walls, for in this way the red pepper is like vanilla: It is as much smell as taste. All of us surely felt overwhelmed by memories of smell in that room with its intensive steam, going back to crop dusters, melting tar on blacktop, that first secret swig of liquor from a bottle hidden, just out of reach from children's hands, as our eyes and noses ran and lips tingled and knives minced the red flesh and seed. This process was interrupted by the occasional ring of Christmas bells and a customer's cry of *"Whoah!"*; or the occasional swing of the back screen door, which let in three or four more flies to compete for the pot in a drunken spiral, until we swatted them away.

The screen door slammed. And Amos muttered something about hades as he came in and glanced at me over his toolbox. We had spent hours next to his hammering, his caulking, his planing, his sanding, though he never once mentioned Will. He did, however, manage to boast about the new cabinetry he'd also put in for Dr. and Mrs. Butler, heart of pine with copper hinging and jousts, and then he began to reminisce about Will's mother, Elvira. It was when things had begun to settle. Eugenia had come back into the kitchen and Mattie was stirring a mixture so stiff it seemed to be pure pepper, with a little cidery seasoning holding it together like glue. When Mattie stirred she stirred with her whole body. I lined up the Ball jars in rows. And Amos said:

"Well, mud was thick as that jelly. We had plenty of rain that year, and farmers wanted those woods cleared for pasture and the Choctaws were in the way. Folk say they all cleared out of this area, or were run out, so Elvira's parents must have been the last of the stragglers. They lived out in the sticks. Y'all know Tchula Gaze's shack? That patch of woods just north? They had a camp out there."

None of us said anything. We all worked with our eyes watering. Then I said, "I wish I could've seen them."

"You'd have recognized them," said Eugenia. "I saw the two of them once, at the general store, buying salt. This was back when Amos and I were kids. Law, Amos, how long ago was that—it was before we had the Piggly Wiggly, I do know that. Mr. Huit's granddaddy ran that store, you remember, Amos, how he always used to give us those leftover broken Jack's cookies, and sometimes, Mattie, he'd give those leftovers to the colored kids and *any*way, that day I saw Elvira's parents in the store, he sold them salt without them saying a word. Nary a word."

"They weren't real social," said Amos.

"No they weren't." Eugenia nodded. "And I tell you, you don't see cheekbones like that every day. Except in Elvira's face. And Will's, of course."

"Sometimes I wonder what I am," I said. "What we are, Eugenia."

"Blood's good on your mama's side," Mattie said. "But on your daddy's, I hear say, you part alligator and part snake."

"And who are you, the Queen of Sheba?"

"What if I was?"

Eugenia gestured as somebody tossing potato skins. "Oh go on, Mattie."

"You don't know everything," I said.

"I do remember the Choctaw word for queen," said Amos. "*Ohoyo minko*. And *nashoba*, for wolf, I think."

"*Nashoba.*" I repeated. "And *Ohoyo*-what?"

"*Minko.*"

"What's Choctaw for smart lip?"

"I don't rightly recall."

Then Eugenia said, "Tell Fannie about Elvira and the wolf."

Amos put the hammer down. He was a burly man, with Will's broad shoulders, though the freckles on the back of his hands gave him a fragile look. He wore long sleeves buttoned to the wrist, even in the heat, sweat leaking from armpits, his red hair slicked back, a toothpick in his pocket, which he pulled out and chewed and then made a sound, sucking his teeth.

"Well," he said, warming for a story. "Elvira's parents had their camp, like I said, and they kept to themselves. A man's got a right to his own company. When they died—folk say it was on the same day—they were found at their camp. With a baby. Some farmers notified the church.

"Now the preacher at that time was Theodore Silas. He lived out at that little church that used to be out on the bluff. He performed the funeral. There were few folk there, some church ladies, I believe, and he said a few words, a prayer. Before he closed, though, a howling started up. On the edge of the wood. And for a second they saw it. A *nashoba*. Way too big for canine, they said. Then it disappeared.

"Afterwards, Preacher Silas adopted that baby. There were plenty folk who didn't approve, but he did so anyway. He named her Elvira, and she grew up baptized and Christian. Right out there on that bluff. When I started courting her I had to do everything right and proper, I tell you.

"Anyway, it was during that time when we were courting I was out hunting one day. Out in those woods not far from that church, not far from that graveyard when I heard a howling."

Amos raised back his head.

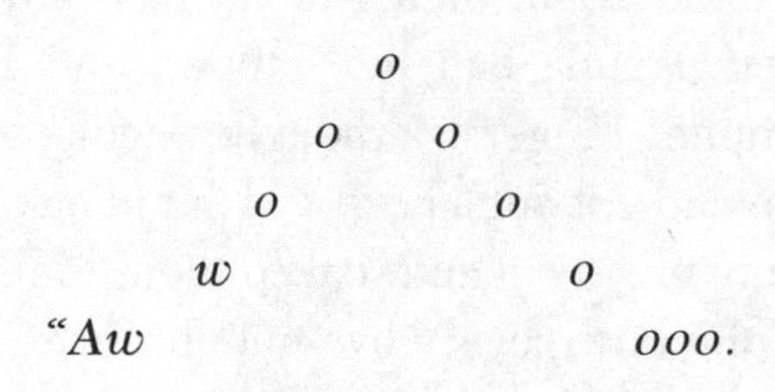

"In a clearing, I saw it. But it was come and gone so fast I didn't know whether it was flesh or spirit. Knowing that tale, I wondered. One second it was there, the next it wasn't. I do remember this. Silver eyes. It had silver eyes. Maybe it was a ghost, who knows? Or maybe it was just the mad howlings of the last wolf in Mississippi, lonely as hell."

A word of advice on putting up pepper jelly: Don't get it under your fingernails. By the end of the second day I put down the knife and held up my hands and blew on them. Eugenia took one look at my swollen fingers, made me drink a swig of her cooking sherry, and said, "Quitting time." All the way home I blew on my fingers. What they need, I thought, is baking soda. Then, while I was thinking of this I heard a dry, popping sound up toward the peninsula. Then silence. Then it came again. Then I figured out what it was. It was Tchula Gaze off shooting game with her old double-action Colt Lightning. She would watch for a squirrel or ducks from the west coming off the river, and reach into her pocket and start fingering the barrel, the handle, just walking rickety on her old bent legs with her faded blue cotton dress bagging around her drooping brown breasts and with the last rays of the evening sun whitening her already white hair. Then, all of a sudden, she would stop, and pull that piece from her pocket with her right hand, and aim—for in one brief startling motion she was no longer rickety—and the gun would go *bang*, and the squirrel would stop in its tracks or the duck would drop *thud* and feathers would fly in all directions. Or that's the way it was usually. Then Tchula would say, "Don't be messing with my eggs," and put the gun back in her pocket.

I heard the first pop, then the second, then I didn't hear any more. Which likely meant that Tchula had her supper, and I remembered it was time for mine. Fingers, I thought. I got on home and went into the kitchen and got out a bowl and put in baking soda and cold water. I put my fingers in and soaked them. And Mama dropped an ice cube in the bowl, every five minutes or so, as she heated the café leftovers.

We had a late supper of smoked ham, baked potatoes, and the last tomatoes from Eugenia's garden.

"How's the fingers?" Mama asked.

"I feel my heart beating in them."

"You'll survive."

"Is that the new fabric?" I asked. I motioned to the bolt on the side table, a long shimmer that seemed to refract light.

"Fortuny silk," Mama said. "Isn't the color wonderful?" She picked up a corner of it, let the pale green seep through her fingers onto the cinnamon-dark wood.

"It'd make a good dress," she said, "to feed the chickens in."

"For the Magnolia Club."

She nodded.

"Mrs. Ardor."

"Right."

"She's paying you enough."

"Right again. And I suggest you keep your fingers down in that water or you'll not be good for much else yourself."

"I saw Will on the way home. He's coming by later tonight. He's got some special salve that's better than baking soda. He said it'll take the sting out."

"Will take the sting out." But it sounded like a request of her own and Mama flushed and turned back to the stove. She dropped two potatoes onto the plates and shocked them open with her fingers.

She brought the plates to the table. Then she paused, turned, went into the other room and came back.

"Mail for you today. I almost forgot." She handed me a large packet and sat down to the table.

"Roosevelt Junior College. Spring registration. How'd this get here?"

"Burl Magee brought it."

I looked at her.

"Well? I know it's not a federal case if a girl of college age gets material in the mail about college." She pursed her lips and picked up the saltshaker. "All I'm saying is, if they want to send you material, it doesn't hurt to look, does it?"

"Mama."

"Now does it? You might consider going part-time. We never talked about that. That way you could still be at the café and not be worrying over Will. None of these little girls are gonna snatch him up." She sprinkled salt vigorously. "Not even that one you don't like."

"Who don't I like?"

"That Clarice Lytle."

"Why you say that?" I snapped, and in that testiness I lost, Mama triumphed.

"I might be getting older, but I'm not blind."

"In that case," I said, "you can see what I expect. I expect to make some decisions. The color of my wedding dress, for instance. Me, I gonna wear red when I get married."

"Red."

"A nice red dress. With a low V neck. Satin, maybe."

She looked at me.

"They wear it in China."

"This is hardly China."

"So?"

"So," she said, "we'll talk about this later." This was her way of curtailing a conversation; she would say, very quickly, "We'll talk about this later," and of course her intention was that the subject, whatever its importance, would be forgotten. We sat eating. I watched her. Mama finished her potato but hardly touched the rest and when she finished she dabbed the corners of her lips with her napkin.

"Aren't you gonna finish that?" I said.

"You want it?"

"No'm, I just thought you would."

"Well *you* can eat without gaining weight," she said. Then she took up the dishes and hauled them across the kitchen. She stood in front of the sink. "I'll just say one last thing. I wouldn't let him get the best of me."

She stoppered the sink and put in the dishes and soap and turned on the faucet.

"He's not worth it. None of them are."

I didn't answer for a while. Then I said, "Yes they are."

When Mama'd done with the dishes I got up from the table and dried them and put them up. Mama had drawn her bath and the house was quiet. I went to the icebox and opened it and pulled a Hershey's bar from a supply I kept there. Then I walked down the hallway.

I entered the living room and went to the desk by the sewing machine and turned on the lamp and sat in the old oak swivel chair. On the desk was a small purple velvet pincushion with pins sticking in it. The smell of spray starch. I pressed my fingers against the dampcool of the Hershey's wrapper and then I tore off the wrapper. I broke off squares and ate, and looked around the room. I noticed something different. Rodin's *The Kiss* embraced itself on the table. The record player probably assigned now to the bedroom. There was often some little change like that. I'd look around and wonder what it would be, for there had been a long procession of little changes in that room, each in turn finding its way toward a perfection. Mama was the first in town, for instance, to create the all-white living room. I knew that an important part of her well-being came from standing in that room, basking in these small changes, and that my acknowledgment of these talents was part of that well-being. She liked to look and circle, creating some illusion of escape, of refinement; she hung a little rug on the wall; she hung a scarf on the window of our front door. Much of the time I thought we were not estranged and yet we must have been, for whenever I acknowledged something she had done, my sense of relief came in the feeling that we were reconciled; for the moment, there was no division as she studied the arrangement, swiveling eyes around the room, taking a breath to celebrate the ideal.

For as far back as I can remember, Mama was torn between her desire to belong and to be alone, between admiration and loathing for what she called "putting on airs." In our town, for instance, the pockets of fakery for the tourists. Three Greek column houses and a bus all the way from Jackson and Mrs. Ardor and her Magnolia Club biddies parading around in hoopskirts: almost insulting. But the crimp of collar, pearl buttons, silk that carried riverlight into a room. I remember particularly the pleasure Mama took that year in making Mrs. Ardor's dress. For the spring pilgrimage, 1961. Each day she would tackle a new stage—the cutting, the pinning, the basting. She had to alter the pattern as she went along to allow for problems expected, such as the tight pull of a sleeve, the girth of Mrs. Ardor's figure. She even put a darker brocade in the middle to create the illusion of a waist. And there was Mrs. Ardor, in the wings, always questioning. In Persia there was always somebody lording over somebody and the change she made in Mama, actually, would remind me of Clarice Lytle. It isn't so different, in hindsight, the way one can seed doubt in another, just as Clarice, in her attentions to Will, could make me feel like the wrong answer to a child's sum in arithmetic.

After Mama finished that dress she saved several scraps of the fabric. Occasionally she would slide her finger along the pale green silk, a color that reminded me of pistachios. Or more particularly, a recipe I tried that was supposed to be the best dessert at the best restaurant in Paris. *Marquise au chocolat Taillevent.* Taillevent's chocolate cake in pistachio sauce. The cake is more a ripened chocolate mousse than a cake, and the sauce is actually a kind of cream sauce flavored with ground pistachios. You dip the ground nuts in a sieve into the warm, thickened cream, watching pale green threads of aroma spool into the sauce. The next time I tried the recipe I referred to a bit of that silk, returning it to Mama's scrap basket the minute I got home.

So that night I sat looking around the room. I finished the Hershey's bar and wadded up the wrapper. Then I turned out the little brass lamp and sat in the dark. Through the front-door window I could see the street light falling away down the street. I leaned back and crossed my feet on the desktop. The clock struck ten in the corner of the room.

Will came up on the porch and tapped lightly on the door. He was in a shirt and jeans and holding something in his hand. He looked at me through the window and tapped again.

"What you doing?" he whispered.

"Sitting."

We went out onto the porch. It was the tube of burn ointment he'd brought and we stood, looking out across the yard and down the street. We were aware of the quiet trees and looked up and through them. The sky thickened in the dark and stars flickered silver-blue, between the leaves, and down the street, a last window glowed yellow. Most of the houses were dark. There was a strained leftover sourness of cabbage and an owl *who-who?*ing and then the high peal, a baby's cry, all anger and discovery, which suddenly stopped and trailed into silence. Around us sky loomed over rooftops, stars swam down to the bushes, trees swished, the world turned alive and spawning, thick and silent at the same time.

As we stood on the porch there was a wild burst of music in the house, louder than the baby's crying, shaking the mildew out of the old woodwork. It was Mama's Mozart record.

Will looked toward the door and back at me. I gave him a look, which he understood. He took the tube of ointment and unscrewed the top and squeezed some out and rubbed it on my fingers. Then we walked to the edge of the porch. We tasted a long kiss good night, then parted.

By the time I went back inside, the record had finished and the house was quiet. I could hear the sound of the needle scratching through Mama's closed door. I undressed and got in my nightgown and got in bed. Then I pulled the sheet up. I had wanted it that way, to be in the dark, pulling under the sheet and retasting, a whisper, a press of bodies, a kiss.

There were the sounds of the house settling into itself. The scratching of the record needle. The oak rattling like so many years. I closed my eyes and opened them. I lay awake a long time, wondering what it would be like to be married to Will Leary.

The Entry

THE LAST TIME I DID endless experimenting with recipes I was working full-time, and I tore up that kitchen, and it was a long time ago—or at least several years, for it is now into 1964, but it seems like forever. But the first time I did the experimenting it was even longer ago, back in 1961, and I was a newlywed, living with Will upstairs above the café, in three high-ceilinged rooms with creaking wood floors and faded floral wallpaper and no furniture at first but a bed. You have to say this for the café: Smells curtained the place. Odors from one room climbed to another. Cinnamon. Frying bacon. Blackberry cobbler, serene as ink. There was a smell in our sheets like bread dough. There were nights when moonlight spilling along the river and through the window gave the wallpaper dimension. I thought I could pluck one of those flowers and lay it on my chest.

So there were nearly two months without interruption. Two months of fiery happiness. Then, on October 1, Burl Magee came into the café and delivered a letter, from the Southern Pecan Growers Association. On the upper left-hand corner, a tiny gold engraving of a tree. I stood at the café counter staring at it. It was an invitation to a cooking contest, winner take all: $1,000 and a weekend in New Orleans.

"Any letters for Eugenia?" I said.

"Nothing today," said Mr. Magee. "But that looks fancy enough—I'll take it."

"Yessir it does." I showed him the invitation.

Reading it, he said, "Well, when you win that prize and get famous, I'll be able to tell folk I handled your mail. Maybe you'll be in one of those magazines. Maybe a recipe book with your picture on the cover."

"That'd be something."

Getting that invitation started my experimenting hours into the evening. Exactly which recipe would I submit? I was back and forth to the kitchen, ideas darting over open cabinet doors and baskets of produce and the stacked shelves of the icebox. I turned the OPEN sign to CLOSED. I opened Mrs. Thistle's cookbooks and looked over the pictures. Then I started. I could feel some life flowing from my hands—sifting, adding, doubting, subtracting—into something I didn't know, and distances I could not imagine. There were nights I would be holding the edge of the oven door with a pot holder and I could hear Will heading out for a walk and smell the faintest boot leather as he passed. Later he'd guide me upstairs and walk behind me with his hands on my hips as we moved up and across the darkness and the squeak of a stairboard. Or I'd maneuver *him* up the stairs, pushing his waist, and his legs wobbled dangerously. It amazed me to see how much booze he could take in and remain quietly coherent. So I did not ask him where he spent every minute of his time. I did not ask him that. He, in turn, made no other sound as we walked, and this pleased me, was familiar and comforting. All those efforts tried and rejected: pecans roasted in barbecue sauce, pecans layered with goat cheese in a salad, pecans with eggs (don't ask), before settling on my entry. Catfish. Stuffed with squash, onion, bread crumbs, Swiss cheese, and pecans. The night I tried this, I knew Will was proud of me. I knew he was. Though later, on the night of November 9, 1961, when I first served the recipe at the café, he said, "At least I'm not married to a café." This revealed resentment I hadn't realized was there before. And when we fought about Clarice Lytle, it was perhaps the smell of this dish I remember most.

Four nights a week, then, I worked late. But the others were reserved for Will. For during weekends when he wasn't hunting, rising early for the deer stand, a duck marsh, woods that bred dove and quail, he and I would spend from late Friday through Monday morning together. And he would seldom sleep.

There was a popular night at the café, All-U-Can-Eat Night, as it came to be known, which was Friday. Will would sit, leaving occasionally for a walk. Mama would come before the crowd started in and join Will, Eugenia, and me at the counter. Amos came as well. That sometimes went nicely, particularly when Amos started reminiscing. He liked telling tales that began, "That reminds me, when I was a boy . . ." Or, "Eugenia, you remember when . . ." Night turned the windows to mirrors. Stray cats climbed the ledge to stare in. On all but the coolest nights, the glass gradually drew mist from the river and warmth from the kitchen, and the windows would turn to steam.

One time Amos winked at Mama and said, "When are you two gonna make us grandparents? Your mama doesn't look old enough, but I know I could play the part."

Will looked suddenly hard across the table. He said, "We hadn't thought on that, Daddy."

And Amos, as if recognizing some subtle shift in Will's mood, patted him with a heavy, nervously placating hand. "Aw, plenty of time," he said. "Plenty of time." Then cast me a look of apology. "You know how us old folk are." To Mama again, he smiled and said, "At least some of us," and I gazed at the tables, the stirring crowd. I smelled pecans from the kitchen. And remembered Amos's voice on another night, just before Will and I were married, filled with the same nervous solicitude: "Aw, Fannie, no need to look like that. I'm just saying Will has—this edge. And sometimes nightmares. After the accident, you know, the accident when he was a boy, but everything's gonna be fine. . . ." and there was something in what he said then too that bothered me, like an offstage noise or something seen out of the corner of an eye or an itch you cannot scratch because you are out in public. I gazed past Amos and Will at the rest of the tables and sensed that my lips were tingling. The recipe? I remembered my customers and moved on to work the crowd.

On this Friday night, then, November 9, 1961, the evening began as usual. There was a light fall drizzle at the windows and Will ate and got up and went out for a walk. Mama helped me and Eugenia wait tables. Amos sipped coffee as we jotted orders, fastened each slip with a clothespin to the string behind the counter. Mattie pulleyed the slip close enough to read it through the small order window and rifle plates, occasionally looking up at me, her face going into a gesture that was partly a nod and partly a shake of disagreement, the mustache of sweat on her upper lip. She added to a pile of scraps on the side table that would go to the stray cats. Toweling her lip with the dampness of her apron.

I maneuvered plates from the kitchen window, one at my waist, one high above my head, while Eugenia worked rounds with tea. Tables brushed her hips as she paused, her free hand riding over a baby's head, a man's shoulder, the shoulder of a Naugahyde booth. Sometimes when I tried one of my new dishes on customers, Eugenia liked to make a little show.

"Bon evenin'," she said, leading Burl and Mrs. Magee to a seat. When they came in, Amos got up from the counter and slid into their booth.

"You ordered yet?"

"Waiting on y'all."

Eugenia went over with another cup of coffee. "Now Mary Helen, I know what you want."

"Thank you, dear."

"And what'll you boys have?"

"Go ahead," said Amos.

He ordered a double serving of the new stuffed catfish with mashed potatoes and greens and biscuits. Amos ordered the same with a side order of corn pudding.

"You better load up good."

"You watch me," said Amos.

They sat with their elbows propped on the table and looked out the window west across the river to the distant foliage lying brown and flat under the evening drizzle.

"Ain't that a mess," said Amos.

Burl and Mrs. Magee nodded. They all drank their coffee. Eugenia and I brought out three supper specials. Then, stopping at their booth, Eugenia paused and held one of the plates under her nose and closed her eyes and inhaled dramatically.

"*Voilà!*" she announced, as she set it on the table. "Compliments of the chef!"

"Well I declare," said Mrs. Magee. And I took a little bow.

Now, Sheila Jones and her mother, Mrs. Adelia Jones, were as familiar with Eugenia's antics as most regulars. By the time they came in, I remember, the place was packed. It was a football night for Persia High, but the game had been called on account of the rain. Sheila ordered the new stuffed catfish. Mrs. Jones ordered chicken. In the year since her husband had died and she had returned with her daughter from California, Mrs. Jones had developed a reputation for anger. And when Eugenia lowered the plates, with the usual theatrics, Mrs. Jones said, "Damn it, Eugenia. I didn't ask for a dissertation."

Mrs. Jones's reply, which flew in the face of Eugenia's ceremonial humor, hushed the café to the last person.

"No ma'am, you didn't," Eugenia said, slapping the table. "And in that case, by golly, it's on the house."

In the silence that followed, Mrs. Jones was so flustered she could only sit in her seat. She touched her napkin and pulled it into her lap and looked toward her plate. Her full face was not soft; it was controlled, tightly, so even then you could tell she was Sheila's mother. She had the same girlish freckles and brown hair, only cut shorter; the same chin, only slightly thicker; yet there was already the age of widowhood in her, like some heavy liquid swallowed into the body and gelled.

Eugenia quickly moved to the next booth, where Amos and Burl and Mrs. Magee sat, and then she looked down at Amos's plate. He had peppered his mashed potatoes till they were black.

"Now there's a man who likes his pepper with potatoes," she announced, in a loud voice. I knew what she was trying to do. But the person I felt for was Sheila, who was staring at her stuffed catfish as though she wanted to crawl inside it. Even as Eugenia tried to jump-start another conversation and said "Yes ma'am" and said "Nosir" and glanced up and around the long room, which she knew better than any room in the world and which she knew was storing up this moment, no matter what she said. Sheila Jones's mother, after all, had left Persia. For California, of all places. And she had come back, but not because she wanted to. She was a branch without roots. A woman without appreciation. After her husband had died in a car accident, she had returned to Persia with her daughter. Her daughter had cried at the funeral, but she had not. Comfort and consolation had been offered, but she had refused it. To those neighbors who tried, she had replied, "What could you possibly do for me?"

Before Mrs. Jones had left for California, the older ladies said, she had been such a nice girl. She didn't pick her nose or cuss; she said "Great gardenseed" when she lost at bridge. What a shame, the ladies said, shaking their heads, and the men nodded; it was true. A few years earlier, when Jerry King had been sent home in a body bag from Korea, Mrs. King had stood up in church and slung an entire tray of communion grape juice into the faces of folk on the front pew. Nobody seemed surprised then, although Mrs. King had been known as a bashful thing, even sweet. But the town resented Mrs. Jones's anger. She had gone away. She had come back. She had decided to stay. But not because she wanted to.

"What was *that* all about?" Mrs. Magee said as Eugenia touched up her coffee. But Eugenia only shrugged. She looked a little sad, as if she were just remembering what becoming a widow involved.

November 9 turned out to be a long night. It was late after work, about ten o'clock, when Will and I walked upstairs. I had gone out and found him sitting on a pier bench, looking up at the stars. For it had stopped raining. The clouds were blowing off and the drops clung like bright metal beads on the blacktop as I walked across. In this weather he often found it hard to stay indoors at night. Most of the time he was on the levee by the pier, but he would stand up silently when he saw me cross the street. I was often the one made to feel I was finding him, near the headless statue of the Confederate soldier, upon whose stub of a neck birds liked to perch, bored and pecking until humans appeared. I would find him, this man who watched in darkness, who when drunk claimed he was descended from a family of bats.

The bedroom was at the top of the stairs. The bed in the middle of the room. It had an iron headboard and a loose-spring mattress. An overhead light, a cluster of fading candlelight bulbs on thin brass stems that rose and bent back like the broken necks of chickens.

There was an archway that opened into another big room, empty of all but Will's hunting equipment. A shotgun against the wall, a rifle, a revolver on the floor. A camouflage hat, a bird call, a hundred-pocketed vest. I passed this way to the door at the back of the room and started my bath. When I came back Will was sitting with two glasses of ice on the bed. He poured himself a glass of whiskey. "Up to it," he said. He would say this every time he took a drink. He knocked it back. "Have one?"

I nodded.

"Good," he said. "I got something to mention."

"Right now?" I said. I opened the side of my robe, flashed one breast, and quickly covered it.

"Yeah, in a minute," he said, pouring himself another drink. For a moment we stood opposite one another, he undressing, me pulling a comb through my wet hair. He dropped his clothes into a pile by his guns. He swirled the drink in his palm and stood by the unmade bed. The noise of the river, the breaking of the moon into silver fish prismed through the windowpanes. The moon was on him like this, that brief unbroken nickel sheen on a swimmer the instant he emerges from a pond. I sat on the bed and looked at him. I leaned against the headboard and held my drink and peered toward the face in this light—the eyes were just dark gleams—but I could tell that something was coming. Will stood beyond the opposite end.

"You'll take this how you like," he said. "Amos has hired Clarice Lytle to do our bookkeeping. One day a week. Every Thursday.

She's working one day a week for Mr. Ardor. One day at Piggly Wiggly. We needed somebody to come in."

I took this in without blinking. "This is Amos's idea or yours," I said finally.

"I don't know."

"That means it's yours."

"That means it's both."

I nodded. I sat there holding my drink. The moonlight was coming through the panes and I studied the pattern it made. I sat there a long time. The glass in my hand tinkled. There was the tinkling because of the ice. I took the glass and lifted it to my lips and drank. I was still looking toward the window, though there was nothing there really to see.

"You think she's pretty?"

"Hell, Fannie."

"You think she's pretty?"

"How do I know?" he demanded, peevish again. "She was good in math. She took bookkeeping in school. We thought it was a good idea."

"You think she's pretty?"

"For God's sake, forget it," he said.

He turned around, and came toward me holding his glass, walking on his knees over the sheets. He came up close to me and stopped. "Forget it?" I said, and looked back at him.

Then Will reached his free hand up and loosed my belt and peeled open the panels of my robe. He slid his hand under the small of my back and kneaded gently and leaned close to my face and whispered, "At least I'm not married to a café."

Right then I should have let the remark pass, arched my back toward him and let the whiskey loosen us both in the warmest way. But I looked at him and I looked toward the window again. I said, "You see that letter over there?"

"Yeah."

"You know what that is?"

"A bill, I figured."

"You figured. It's the details of the competition. The letter that came with the invitation from the Southern Pecan Growers. The winner not only goes to New Orleans for a weekend, but will be expected to devote a considerable time to promotions. On the road, with generous compensation. That could take weeks. If I'm able to get it, of course. Months, maybe."

Will rolled away from me. My skin, where his hands had been, felt suddenly cold. He got off the bed and sent a dark glance toward me and walked out of the bedroom though the archway to the next room. He picked up the invitation from the windowsill, held it to the moonlight, and read. Then he propped it back against the windowsill. Crossed to the other side of the room, just out of my sight. I heard a click and a spin. And then the upstairs thundered in gunfire—he fired one gunshot, piercing the invitation. My eardrums pounded.

"Hell's bells, Will! You've woke the dead!"

"What if I did."

I smelled gunpowder in the air. He carried the revolver in a way I didn't like, as if the weapon had been sewn into his palm and his long brown fingers.

"And half the town too! The sheriff already on his way. Just who I want to see. At this time of night. Feed him his supper and have him sniffing upstairs."

And then, before I could utter further protest, Will looked down at the floor, at his foot, almost casually, and with one eye squinted, aimed the gun at his big toe.

"Will!"

He cocked the hammer.

"Will!" And then, trying to put the panic out of my voice, "Well why don't you go ahead? Everybody's on their way."

"I doubt it," he said. Then with his thumb, he slowly let down the hammer. He put the gun down in the corner of the room. "Folk'll think it's Tchula Gaze firing off."

"Too far away."

"Well, Sikes Daughtry then, shooting possums."

"More likely, they'll think it's that crazy Indian. Gone out of his head."

He sat down on the bed and shrugged. "Gunshots make folk

think it's an ordinary night. Folk are turning in their beds right now saying, Yeah, Sikes Daughtry, possums."

"And what about the window?"

"What about it?"

"Who gets to tell Eugenia?"

"Eugenia, Eugenia. If it ain't Eugenia you're worrying over it's precious Mama."

"I expect somebody ought to worry. We got a disagreement and I don't get a word in edgewise when, in fact, I could say plenty. Just last May, who sent me a graduation invitation? Miss Lytle. And who received a recipe box, a fine graduation present from me? Again, Miss Lytle. But do I get a chance to mention this? *Nosir.* Do I get a word in edgewise before my husband turns it on me? I'll tell Eugenia, I'll just say, Eugenia, he picked up a gun like a child and used my personal mail for target practice."

I have to say, we ripped each other that night. Will drank with his bristles sticking out all over him and that faultless look on his face. I saw that and lifted my own hackles. He mumbled, and then his face, alternately flinching and reddening deeply, began to scare me a little, as he said, "So that's the way it is." The words came from deep within his throat, and he began to moan so the sound would be a barrier between us, a wall across which he could not be reached. By dawn he was into his second bottle and the longer version of his toast. "Up to it, down to it, son of a bitch who can't do it, should be hog-tied and made do it."

"Will."

"Leave me alone."

"Will, listen."

"No, you lishen." He closed one eye and looked at me through the amber curve of bottle. "Now you know what it's like to stay up all night."

"How about a hot bath? A hot bath then some sleep?"

Will raised himself, his head still down, then stood against me as if dragging himself away from the magnet of the bed.

Then he said, "I never been to New Orleans. Not at goddamned all."

I led him to the bathroom and drew bathwater. Then I got dressed and went downstairs. I made coffee and cooked all morning and talked to Amos that afternoon.

A hundred miles from Persia, somewhere along the highway that stretches east and west between Jackson and Pearl, there had been the building called Whitfield State Hospital with its locked front gate, an entranceway groomed with bright flowers, two damp orderlies in white and the overwhelming smell of cleaning fluid on the floors, and it was there, Amos told me that afternoon, that he took Will after Will tried to take his life by flinging himself over the bluff. This happened back in the summer of 1949, the day of the accident when Will collided with my uncle Lawrence while playing with his BB gun and Uncle Lawrence had fallen to his death. Afterwards, the sheriff took Will back to the original scene of the accident for questioning. Amos went along. And that's when it happened. On the edge of the bluff. Amos said he would have remembered the awful episode for many reasons, the lingering image of Eugenia's face, for example, but he would never be able to obliterate the main reason: the sudden raging strength of an eight-year-old boy (it took both the sheriff and Amos to subdue him), followed by what was for Will a complete reversal of behavior—a long silence.

When Amos described the outburst and told of what followed, I was of course reminded of Will's wild behavior, the pandemonium and gunfire from the night before. I was about to point out to Amos the similarities and question him about it, but by this time—devouring a huge steaming mound of black-eyed peas and a wedge of cornbread—he had become so totally absorbed in his story of their life together that I hesitated, then fell lumpishly silent. I considered the liquor. It was routine about Will and his drinking—the manner as much as the amount. For the fact is that the potent rotgut he often bought from a black fellow named Tomaine Tilden usually had little effect on his speech. At least this was true at first. Save for the night before, which was the first time he'd ever lost his temper with me, there were only two other changes I had seen.

It did occasionally turn him into a talker. As much as you could call Will that. Not that he had ever spoken directly about Uncle Lawrence or the accident or that particular part of the past. And the other thing the liquor did was quite enticing. Enticing, that is, in a maddeningly unpredictable way: It let loose any inhibitions Will had about places for sex. In the first days I felt mixed apprehension and delight as the possibilities were exhausted: upstairs and downstairs, the deer stand in the woods, and, on one particularly memorable evening, Avery Jones's barn.

But Amos's tone was almost funereal when he spoke of 1949; funereal, that is, and apologetic.

"You know, Fannie," he said a little hesitantly, "you know those doctors at Whitfield were giving Will drugs. I didn't know if you ever knew this or not. Anyway, I've not been quite honest with you. I could have mentioned it earlier, but I thought it was maybe Will's place to do that."

Drugs, I thought, *hell's bells*. For this had not occurred to me. In 1961 I was as surely innocent about drugs as were most of my neighbors. Our present-day drug culture had not seen, in backwater Mississippi, even the glimmerings of a dawn, and my notion of addiction was connected to the idea of "dope fiends." I envisioned Frankenstein mad scientists eyeing glass tubes of bubbling froth, zombies stalking the back alleys of New York City, comatose Chinese in smoky dens, and yes, straitjacketed madmen in podunk asylums. But that was not Will. As for drugs themselves, I knew nothing of types or substance. I wasn't sure I could name a single one. When Amos assured me it was true, and when finally I asked him what he had used, I heard for the first time the word *Darvon*. "A kind of sedative, you know. To ease the mind, the sleeplessness, the nightmares the boy was having. And I thought, well at least there's something. Something I can do. Take him to these doctors. And I tell you what, sometimes I wondered about them. Making their money picking over other folks' sores. And when I asked them about the boy's problem, they just said one thing. Sprinkling their explanations with Latin."

"How long was he on this?"

"Four years. Five."

"So that's over."

"Yeah, he got weaned of one thing."

"Then graduated to another."

"Yes ma'am. But I don't want you to get the wrong idea. Will's got—this edge, that's true, but he's come a long way, you know."

"You know?" he said.

"Yessir."

"And I still say it comes down to one thing." He held up one finger.

"One thing," he said.

"Which is?"

"Right here," he said, and put his hand over his heart. "Which brings me to the question I should have asked you. A long time ago . . ."

Amos pushed back his plate. Then he wadded his napkin and said, "How's your heart, Fannie?"

I looked at him.

"In that case," he said, "I'll give you the answer. Yours is stronger. Not better, but stronger."

"You think so?"

"Yes ma'am."

Then Amos gave me a smile. It was a smile with sadness in it. As though he were convinced of this one thing. As though somehow, in the face of this, I was Will's solution.

A coin spinning on the counter may fall to either side.

A few weeks later, after a big lunch crowd, after Eugenia'd taken off early and the afternoon gathering had dwindled, I made a vanilla shake for Sheila Jones. She came into the café carrying a loose-leaf binder and some schoolbooks. The wink of saddle oxfords; the tails of a white, button-down shirt fluttered along her hips.

She said as she slid onto the stool, "How are you?" as if she asked quite regularly.

I must have said something like "Fine."

"Nice day," she said.

I said yes.

"It is nice," she said again. She slid her books onto the counter. I could see a heart drawn on the corner of her blue loose-leaf notebook with a black felt-tip pen. A little arrow splitting through it. The ink had bled a bit into the fabric. I might have been peeking at her bra strap, her diary, the heart seemed so hopefully illicit, such a crooning curve. It made me want to smile, in spite of myself.

I scooped ice cream into the silver chrome cup, added milk, clipped it onto the lip of the mixer. The machine whirred. In the flash of chrome I saw Sheila's reflection and poured the shake into a glass.

"There you go," I said, and she put the straw to her lips. Her fingertips were small and pink and the edges of her nails jagged into her flesh as though she had just stopped biting them. Then she touched the side of the glass.

"Not long till Christmas break," she said.

I told her that she had just reminded me of how long ago school seemed to me.

She looked past me at the pictures on the wall. "What year d'you graduate?"

"In 'fifty-nine."

She nodded.

"You a sophomore, right?"

"And one more semester, I'll be a junior." She again looked at the pictures and back at me. "You in those pictures?"

"That's me, Will, Mama. And that's Uncle Lawrence. And Eugenia in her wedding dress."

"*That's* Mrs. Boatwright?"

"Yeah. Before my time."

"So Mr. Leary was your boyfriend?"

I set my elbows on the counter as though it were odd to do, this remembering. And I was also a little bewildered by her questions—did she really want to talk?—and so I said I supposed so.

She leaned over her straw. There was the sound of slurping and air bubbles from the bottom of the glass. "D'you go steady?" she said, as though making plans of her own.

"Well, yeah."
"So you always knew?"
"Hunh. That's one way of putting it."
That made her smile, her lip covering her upper teeth. Freckles on her cheeks, two shakes of paprika.
"And what about you?" I said. "You got a boyfriend?"
She shook her head. She wasn't saying. Then she reconsidered. "He had to help his nana. She's a weirdo. She's a nutcase. He helps her sell her eggs. He's got to help her. I guess I won't be seeing him till maybe later or something."
I understood then: She was bored, alone, without him. She was talking with me just to kill some time, maybe to keep from going home.
"So," she said, looking at me cautiously, "when you got married, was it kind of like going steady? Did he have to ask you?"
"He had to ask me."
"So what'd he say?"
"Actually he didn't."
"He didn't?"
"Not in so many words."
"But how'd you know?"
"I just did."
"What'd he say?"
"It wasn't so much what he said as what he did. It was kind of like a steamroller. A hammer on the head."
"That sounds like Mama. She used to say about Daddy, 'I ran real slow so he could catch me.' She would say this in front of Daddy and he would look at her over his glasses and say, 'Oh yeah?' " She dropped her chin, imitating her father's voice, then laughed.
I'd never actually talked with Sheila—certainly not for this long—and I don't know which I took in more, the way she looked or the way she saw me. As though I were within something. Maybe a painting. Some secure couple at a table. How many times must I have imagined this at her age, couples in their laziness of habit, with their friends over to dinner and grillsmoke and their matching sets of china. And something in me already questioning such a

view. Funny, I thought, what we expect. Then I remembered Will's ghastly all-nighter. For at some point the following afternoon after my long talk with Amos, had Will really come down and apologized the way he did? No, it was later, I realized, that his voice had come down through the ceiling, tentative, with the ponderous booted footfall on the stairs, his nose swollen, his face blue-whiskered and drawn and sickish, loosed from his entourage of demons, and said again, in the stuffed-head tones of someone who'd perhaps been crying, "Aw Fannie, I'm just an ass, just an ass!"

That voice had made me avert my eyes. But I was a person who wanted to trust in the notion that the blowup that night was a lamentable but rare exception in a world filled with hearts and flowers. After all, wasn't that what Amos had said? In so many words? And I could feel Sheila looking for the same thing. The same rosy light. Before me were the small sucking motions of her breath, her cheeks caving in over the straw. A single pimple on her forehead, almost hidden beneath her bangs.

She sat sipping the shake and looking at me. Then she fingered the straw.

"Yeah, Mama would always tell that story about Daddy," she said, and she may have looked a little sly as she continued, "but what my boyfriend and I have is different."

"How so?"

She thought for a moment. Then she rotated on her stool, turning outward so her profile was before me. I saw a grape-colored bruise, just under her collar: a love bite, a sure sign of the boyfriend.

"It just is." She bit the corner of her lip, as though to hold back a grin. Then she looked back at me. "I mean, I'm not like other girls. I've been through a lot and I know about things. I've seen it all. And when you've seen it you're not scared. I'm not even scared of dying. They showed a film in general health about CPR and it didn't even bother me."

There was something sullen in her voice, even a challenge. She said, "My daddy died, you know."

"I know," I said. "I'm sorry."

"Well, everybody does." She shrugged. "It happens to us all. I used to think, if my parents died, I'd just die too. But then afterwards I got to thinking, if a person's gone and you still got this feeling, he can't really be gone, can he. Can he? Because if he was really gone, kerplunk, *adios*, for good, that's it, wouldn't it be better if God made us something like—bugs? Something that can't think?"

"I suppose."

"Take my boyfriend. He lives a mile out in the country, so he's pretty cut off. He lives with nobody but his nana, and she's pretty touched. But now he's got me. I got him. So if anything happens to me he'd never forget me. Forgetting somebody, you know, is almost like they never been there."

I stood looking across the counter. I looked out the window and back at Sheila and finally back out the window. The light was darkening, but it was late light, without the grayness of fall. From the kitchen I heard a pot slam. Mattie's voice grumbled. A barge horn that had been blowing somewhere out over the river stopped. Then it started again.

"Is that somebody calling for you?" Sheila said.

"Probably."

"Well."

Then I looked at her.

"Well, first off you ought to know your boyfriend won't forget you. But you oughtn't be worried about that. You got your whole life in front of you. You know?"

"Yeah," she said. Then she smiled a little. She seemed to remember something.

"That's good. 'Cause you should."

A pot slammed. Mattie's voice grumbled again.

"Well, I better be going," she said.

She leaned back and reached into her pocket and dropped a warm quarter on the counter.

"You going to see him?"

She stood up and gathered her books and her notebook with the ink-drawn heart. "I'm already gone," she said.

Sheila and Earnest

FROM OVER HERE, WITH HINDSIGHT, you can see into every room on the streets in Persia. You can see through porch and window and curtain, down alley and backyard, along river and field, clear across cotton rows to the country houses, and if you look hard enough you'll see a mother returning from grocery shopping to check on her daughter home from school. She walks up the front porch steps, two brown paper bags propped on her hips. The station wagon by the front steps gives the house all the look of a place filled with children.

Mrs. Adelia Jones sets the bags on the kitchen counter and pads down the hall till she reaches the back bedroom. It's locked. She calls out to her daughter but there is no answer, though she hears an intake of breath from the other side of the door.

Now that it's all past, anybody can see the girl in the bed with her shirt unbuttoned. The sweat on her skin. Earnest March with his grocery apron strewn along the floor. You can smell the fear on their breaths, you get so close. So close, you hear the pumping in their swollen hearts. And out in the hall, you can feel the awful curdling in a mother's head, the anger, the half-comprehension she almost recognizes from memory.

The key is on the hook by the icebox. She gets it and returns. The door swings open and Sheila is on the bed, in her sock feet, a schoolbook propped against her knees. She looks up at her mother from under her bangs. She looks tough all of a sudden, grown-up, but her mother notices her shirt is buttoned crooked. Saddle oxfords on the floor, pigeon-toed. At the opened back window, the lace curtain trails out fluently on the breeze.

On May 14, 1962, a number of months after the first visit I had with Sheila, she came in again for a vanilla shake. She came late in the afternoon again; nobody in the café, except this time Eugenia was back in the kitchen with Mattie, taking inventory. Sheila walked in and took a seat on a stool. She looked like she wanted to talk but the phone rang and Eugenia came out of the kitchen to get it. Picking up the receiver, she looked over at Sheila and said, "Well hey, hon."

"How you been?" I asked her.

"Fine," she said.

I went over to dip ice cream.

"Y'all about out of school?"

"Yeah," she said, glumly.

The glumness in her voice made me turn around.

"What's the matter? Aren't you glad to be out?"

"Sure," she said. She sat there and reached for the jar of pickled peppers on the counter. She turned the jar around, looked at it, and repeated, "Sure."

I looked at her then. The face was a little fuller and the skin was pulled back so it looked almost transparent under the freckles. I thought about saying something about how slow things were getting now that summer was coming, but she was sitting there heavily and not paying attention and anyway, I had my own distractions. January, February, March, April, and no letter from the Southern Pecan Growers Association. No mention of Clarice Lytle, either, though she worked for Will and Amos every Thursday.

So I went about the business of making the shake. That very afternoon I had just gotten back from a walk over to Hardin Hardware, to order a new freezer. The old one was breaking down;

every time the door was opened the motor grunted; a layer of slush, the color of mold, had spawned and encrusted bags of berries, peas, shelled pecans; so Mr. Hardin had lent me the catalog to show Eugenia. The two of us had been studying it. There were floating illustrations of iceboxes and freezers. Some had the doors swung open. In one, a woman in an apron held open the door and looked inside it dreamily. The newest model, the Free-o'-Frost, was the one Mr. Hardin encouraged. That was who Eugenia was on the phone with now. Mr. Hardin had asked Mrs. Giddy, Persia's telephone operator, to put him through to the café as soon as she saw Eugenia's car.

In 1962, you see, we still didn't have the dial system. Back then you just picked up the phone and said, Mrs. Giddy, get me my mama or whoever. The telephone office was on the second floor of the courthouse, and Mrs. Giddy could see everything down Levee Road, including the café, Hardin Hardware, Huit Drugstore, the Piggly Wiggly, and Brother Works's parsonage by First Baptist. Whenever somebody died, she could tell you whether Brother Works's car was there or not.

Eugenia hung up the phone and turned on Sheila. "If it ain't one thing, it's another. And how you doing? What brings you out on this lazy day?"

"Fine," Sheila said cautiously. "I just thought I'd stop."

"Well, by golly, I'd have been mad's a wet hen if you hadn't stopped! Nothing like a cold shake on a hot day! Early enough too so's not to ruin your supper. Fannie'll get that fixed up for you in two shakes. Two shakes, hah, hah!"

Sheila still seemed slow and dull and oddly abstract. I don't think she looked Eugenia directly in the eye. She said, "Yessum."

"And how's your mama?"

"Fine."

"I know she's got plenty of work, this time of year, keeping up that garden. I was past there the other day, admiring. You got fine height on your corn. Fine. And what kind of peas you got out there, zipper creams?"

She nodded. I hooked the silver cup to the mixer and the machine whirred.

"Fine," Eugenia said again, pushing her glasses up on her nose. Then she reached down and opened Mr. Hardin's catalog and flipped pages with a flourish, licking her pointer finger each time afterward.

She stopped on a page. Put her finger to a paragraph and read, " 'Elimination of frost, even in freezers!' " Then looked up at Sheila. "That's what we're concerned about. Our own zipper creams not faring well in that breaking-down Methuselah. Listen to this." Then she read: " 'Refrigeration without visible frost may sound too good to be true, especially if you're still juggling pans of hot water and overflowing drip trays. This new feature has many names: Free-o'-Frost, Frostless, Frost Proof, No Frost, Frost-Freeze, Never Frost, Frost-Guard, Frost Clear, and Frost Gone. Whatever the name, it offers unbeatable advantages.'

"That's the Free-o'-Frost," she said, turning the catalog around toward Sheila. "That's what we're getting. Hardy says it's best. And just look at that girl posing by it. The way she's studying it. She looks pleased, doesn't she?"

Sheila was drinking her shake, but she kept her mouth on the straw and nodded politely. She had both hands wrapped around the glass. It was as though the cool of milk shake and Free-o'-Frosts was putting a lull into whatever was bothering her. Eugenia kept squinting through her glasses, and Sheila was drinking and drinking the shake, didn't put it down.

It was then that Mattie came in. Or rather, she pushed open the swinging door, took in the scene, and glanced at me.

"What's up?" I said, but apparently my tone was off. Or maybe she could already tell something was going on by sizing up the room, and if anybody could do that it'd be Mattie.

Anyway, she took in the scene and looked flat at me.

Then she said, "Nothing. Except milk delivery."

Sheila lifted her eyes from the straw by the time Mattie got out the words. They stopped, as Mattie held open the door; stopped, then jerked back like fingers from a hot skillet.

"Well what's eating her?" Mattie asked, as the swinging door closed.

"I don't know."

"She look like she snapped her garter belt in church."

I shrugged. I heard the crank and rumble of the Piggly Wiggly truck and through the back screen door I saw it pass. I picked up the receipt and began copying it in the ledger. "Perhaps it's the inimitable quality of my shakes."

"Mmm-hmmph."

"Mmm-hmmph? What's that supposed to mean?"

"Means what it means," Mattie said.

I could feel her turning her hot lamps on me but I filed the receipt. Then I went back out front. A quarter and an empty glass on the counter. And Eugenia, beetle-browed, said, "Sheila Jones, Sheila Jones." She picked up the quarter and carried it over to the cash register; punched the drawer open and dropped it inside. "That child's been through enough. Daddy in the grave and her mama halfway there. Come back here and holing up in that house. Every time I pass it just reminds me. Shutters all closed. I halfway expect to see Sheila Vaughn—that was Sheila's grandmama—sitting out there on the front porch. She used to sit out there every evening, and rock in that swing. But that was then. Before this." She swept her hand toward the door.

"So she left?"

"Say what, hon?"

"Sheila."

"Yeah, hon. Yeah she did." She took off her glasses and held them in front of her face and looked at them with the chain still around her neck. Then she reached for the corner of her apron and raised it up to clean them off, looked through them again, and put them back on. I watched the chain still swinging. Then she said, "Why Vaughn Jones had to go hauling them off, Lord knows. And to California, of all places."

"Maybe he wanted a little adventure."

"Maybe. But then, why do men do half what they do?"

"That's a wide guess."

"Yeah I know, hon—they a full bag. It's like I used to say to Lawrence, the natures of men and Mississippi are not for mortals to figure."

She looked at me. Then I looked down.

"If you say so."

"I say so."

She leaned back on the counter again. "It's a sticky issue," she said. "But a worthy one."

I looked up.

"Worthy of patience, I'd say, particularly for somebody your age."

"My age."

"Exactly."

I cocked my head toward Eugenia then, somewhat reluctantly, to let her know I got her tone. Eugenia watched me.

"Aw hon, all I'm saying is, you and Will are *young*. You don't appreciate that now but you will soon enough, believe you me. The two of you ought be standing in front of a mirror every night admiring yourselves. Just admiring. And you got plenty of time to make your choices."

"What choices you mean?" I wanted both to get out of this subject and get deeper into it.

"Choice of rooting for yourselves. A choice, when young folk got a little imagination, to see one day is not the whole picture. There's a day that asks questions. A day that answers. And others that make things come about in queer ways. There's a day you want to quit. A day you get surprised all over again."

"You making me tired."

"You telling me. Day to day to day. That's the way it goes. Yes indeedy. Let me tell you a story. And before I tell it let me make it clear so's we understand, this is not common knowledge, the town'd have a cow right here on this floor if they knew. That I'm no cook. Never was. Back when I was a bride, almost fifty years ago, the first meal I planned for Lawrence was his favorite. Fried shrimp. So I bought a pound, fried them so they'd be just right when he walked in the door. He ran in eagerly, smelling them. Then he spied what I was doing. He stopped cold. '*Eugenia*,' he said, 'what *are* you doing?' 'What you think I'm doing?' I said. 'I'm frying you shrimp for supper.' 'Aw Eugenia,' he said, 'you gotta *peel* them first, honey.' "

I watched Eugenia laughing. She laughed till there was a little damp at the corners of her eyes and she took off her glasses to dab them. I thought of how she had never intended to run the café, it was true. She took over it in the aftermath of Uncle Lawrence's stroke. Actually, for twenty years, Eugenia was a teacher. As a young woman she had gone to college at Mississippi Normal in Hattiesburg. She had taught fourth grade. She was midway through her twentieth year of teaching when Uncle Lawrence was stricken. The day she heard, she resigned her teaching position and took over the café. The only thing she kept from her teaching days was a row of grade-school annuals on her bookshelf.

At first Uncle Lawrence was unable to sit up or speak. The stroke had affected the right side of his body and his first words were garbled. The doctor from Jackson said that the amount of recovery was uncertain. "Those nerve wires aren't like heating coil or a radiator," Eugenia said, "where you get somebody to come in and replace them. But the doctor said anything can happen. Anything." With Mama's help, Eugenia nursed Uncle Lawrence around the clock. She fed him, blew on his soup, cut up his food for him. She changed his pajamas, his bedpans. As he regained speech, she put her teaching skills into practice. She made him read to her out loud. She made him say words over and over. Sometimes, in word exercises, she got up close to his face and shaped her own lips into vowel sounds, to demonstrate.

Eventually she set up a booth in the café where he stayed while she worked. She hired in a cook, Mattie Boyd, who it was said had run off with a man to New Orleans. It was the first thing I heard about her. They were supposed to have gotten married, but Mattie had returned—alone. Which did not sound at all like Mattie. She had made her way in the world up from fieldwork and the shack on the other side of the tracks by always figuring other folks' business and not letting you know hers. Her style was not to lead with the chin but to hit the ground running. And Mattie hit the ground running this time. Eugenia had said that somewhere way back inside of her there'd been the idea that Mattie would be the right mix, even before she learned of Mattie's cooking. And so that was the arrangement the café gradually came to, Mattie cooking, Mattie doing the dishes as Eugenia worked the counter and the cash register, taking orders, serving, all the while tending to Uncle Lawrence in the front booth.

Eugenia met Uncle Lawrence's temper, his flairs of frustration, with more books, more exercises. The right side of his mouth drooping as she asked him to count the number of napkins in a stack. The number of pickled banana-peppers in the jar on the table. When there were no customers she would help him get up on his walker and move back and forth across the room. Or she would read the dialogue of one character in a story and get him to read the other. She put a hot chicken-fried steak in front of him and handed him the knife and fork and walked away. "We'll get you there," she'd say. "We'll get you."

Up to the very moment he was stricken, when he was sixty-eight, Uncle Lawrence was a garrulous character in Persia. He was the first to open the café, where he presided as cook and host. He would holler "Howdy!" as you came in the door and point you to an empty seat. He had a habit of running out of order slips and writing a customer's order on his hand. His kitchen was slovenly. Blue ink thumbprinted his apron. But Uncle Lawrence could raise with one hand a tray the size of Moon Lake above his head, maneuver among crowded tables, and set it down, delicate as a doily. In my entire childhood memory of the café, whenever Mama'd take me, I do not recall a single broken dish.

Uncle Lawrence was a lanky man, with long sideburns shaped like boots. Eyes like two cracks of sky. He had fought in the world war and he liked to talk about France. It was the first I heard of it, even before I was old enough to read at Mrs. Thistle's library. Whenever I went into the café then, I'd walk slowly, and when I went inside I'd walk more slowly still, but with purpose, pausing a moment to watch the Christmas bells on the doorknob ring; then, without speaking, I'd step into the room and look up at the density of bodies. I'd look up the length of men at the counter and watch them tipping coffee in lordly manner, and breathe the blast of odor and sound, and hear Uncle Lawrence's voice, before I saw him, saying, "Well *there* she is!" I'd feel his hands under my armpits, and I'd be lifted, high, and seated on the counter, looking into a row of huge craggy and sun-reddened faces. The eyes of the men seated were interested and kind; some of the closest ones would smile; and then the farther ones, who at first just looked curious, would begin to smile. I'd smile back, and suddenly many of the men would laugh. I'd be taken aback by this and lose the smile a minute, before realizing it was friendly, and smile again; and again they'd laugh. Uncle Lawrence'd smile at me. Then he'd go into his imitation of Popeye, which thrilled me. "I tell you, matie, those Parisian women are some of the prettiest on earth, prettiest a man'd see anywheres. Except me little Fannie, of course, she's me Olive Oyl, she's me Olive. She's de reason I gets to de finage 'cause I eats me spinach. *UHguckuckuckucka!*"

Other times he liked to do Jimmy Stewart.

"Well, well, now, I tell you, Harvey is right over there. You see. You see. He's sitting there, next to Burl Magee."

And I would contemplate the empty seat next to Mr. Magee for some seconds before saying, "He is *not*." And the men would laugh again.

It is said that speech often returns to a stroke victim before physical mobility, but Uncle Lawrence was determined about both. After months of grueling practice, he graduated from the walker to leaning on Eugenia's arm. He learned to take steps. Then he got to the point where he could walk across the room. With the help of a cane he was eventually seen past Levee Road taking walks along the bluff by the river. "Lawrence, that big mule," Eugenia would say. "I don't know if he and that cane'll ever get to be friends." And then, of course, Will ran into Uncle Lawrence while playing with his BB gun. It is said that Will walked straight back to town and told Amos, and Amos took Will to the café. Sheriff Wade was already sitting at the counter when they told Eugenia the news.

Back to the day of Sheila Jones's visit. It was May 14, as I mentioned, Will's birthday.

Toward the end of the workday I started supper. I had planned Will's favorite. Smothered chicken and mashed potatoes. And a birthday cake that was an old recipe from Natchez, called "Love's

Delight," four layers of chocolate cake soaked in liquid chocolate, then filled and frosted with chocolate whipped cream and topped with toasted almonds. It was a recipe where the baking batter smelled rich and the wax paper you cut for the bottom of the cake pans was good enough to eat too. I stood there in the kitchen, inhaling. I looked out the screen door. And I waited for the cakes to cook, looking out at the lines of houses, their dark roofs brushed with the tinder light of evening.

There were stray cats out back, in their usual haunts. A yellow tom sitting by a garbage can, his tail rising and idly settling. I watched him. Breeze moving the telephone wires very slightly and picking up another smell from the fields. Crop dusters. A bitter taste, like citrus. This smell drifted; I heard mosquitoes whine, the start of crickets. Then there was a sound across the street, and a woman came onto her porch—a black woman, but I could not make out her face—and threw out a pan of dishwater, which flashed metallic. Then she went back inside. To what was the house. The floor of the house propped up on stilts. For this was the edge of colored town, just behind the café, and it went from here over to behind the railroad, where all the houses were propped on stilts, to keep out rain, and the walls were bleached thin and cracked, but you could not see inside. The woman closed the door, and all at once I tried to picture where she was heading, back to the kitchen, maybe, and her husband, coming in dusty-eyed from the fields. He'd be coming in soon. To whatever was inside.

This, in fact, made me think of where Will was now. He and Amos out on Mr. Ardor's place, where they had taken on the job to build the housing for a cotton gin. Up to now, the closest gin was twenty miles east. So when cotton was harvested, late September into October, it had to be hauled east by trailer and processed into bales before it was returned to Levee Road and loaded onto barges for shipment. This went on from Monday through Saturday. Field hands worked from dawn through dusk. When it got dark, farmers turned their truck headlights on the trailers so the cotton could be loaded. The harvest in the area might be thousands of bales, there being five hundred pounds to a bale. And since the process, as Will described it, was "bass ackwards," he and Amos were glad to get the work; the pay was at the rate of a dollar fifty an hour, with a bonus of a hundred dollars thrown in for completing the job before harvest.

Well, I thought, he'll be in soon.

Then the day came back into focus.

Cake, I thought.

I went over to the stove and almost burned my fingers touching the handle. I grabbed pot holders and opened the stove and touched a finger to the top of a cake and watched the brown skin gently rise. I took the pans from the oven and put them on wire racks to cool and went about getting supper. I iced the cake. Then I went upstairs and washed up. I put on a fresh dress. I came back downstairs and took a seat on a chair.

And waited. I sat there. It was getting dark.

Finally, Will came into the kitchen. He looked sealed up, mindful. Frankly, he looked like he needed a nap.

"It's your birthday," I said. "It's your birthday and you clear forgot I'd make cake, or you remembered, which is worse for your being late. You're impossible, Will. I made cake."

"Well, I'm here now, aren't I?"

"Yeah, and you look about as sorry as I expected you would."

Then Will went upstairs to the bath. And while he was up, I went upstairs and spread a quilt on the floor. Then I hauled up food to make it like a picnic. I laid out the smothered chicken platter, with all the necessary vegetables beside it: butter beans, sweet corn, black-eyed peas, cucumbers in ice water and vinegar, small crunchy fried okra, thick red tomato slices, green onions, Will's mashed potatoes, delicate hot crisp jalapeño corn sticks, and tall beaded glasses of ice tea. Two separate glasses, with more ice. A bottle of whiskey. And the Love's Delight cake, which I served up on Eugenia's burgundy rose-trimmed china cake stand and covered with candles and set in the middle.

I did all this while he was in the bath. I listened for the sound of him getting out of the tub and then the sucking sound of the pulled stopper. Then I lit the candles. He opened the door.

"Hellfire and damnation," he said, pretending surprise.

He looked over the spread and then he looked at me. "Well, you got to eat, birthday boy."

He stood there with his black hair wet and streaming and the steam coming off of him and the towel wrapped and knotted around his waist. He looked incredibly handsome but tired and drawn. I thought of his first all-nighter. He looked at me as though awaiting instruction.

"Well," I said. "First make a wish."

He did. He blew out the candles. Then he sat down on the edge of the blanket and crammed a hot stick of cornbread into his mouth.

He leaned toward the bottle and swung it around and poured into two glasses. It was dark and the café sign blinked on.

"Aw man," he said. Then we both fixed our plates. He plastered butter on the corn sticks, sprinkled the rest with salt and pepper, sliced the chicken in parallels, gave it a twist with the knife and sliced it crosswise.

"There's plenty more where that came from," I said.

"Got a plenty," he said, spearing a bite of chicken in peppery gravy and putting it in his mouth. "Thanks." He chewed and swallowed and speared more. "I bet that cake's good too," he said, lifting his fork.

By this time I was already picking off candles. "You eat," I said. I lifted the stubs of white, burned-down candles from their tiny holes in the chocolate icing and held them, and watched him eat. Because of the day, and the particular hour, the necessity for celebration and its interruptive detail, plus a kind of weariness that follows disappointment—my disappointment at his coming in late—neither of us said a whole lot. Will would realize I was watching him and look back, jaws busy. He was starting to look glutted but acted as though he'd finish it all if it was the last thing he did.

"Don't stuff, Will," I said.

"Hmm?"

"Don't eat more than you can hold."

"Don't worry," he said, spearing more. He was still chewing and then looked at me a certain way. He leaned over and kissed me on the cheek and pulled back. Then, as though acting on second thought, he leaned again and kissed me hard on the mouth.

"*Mnph,*" he said, leaning back.

There was far less on his plate than on mine, and I watched him glance at this. Then I sat for a moment eating and looking at the window. The light of the café sign blinked. Between blinks was the dark, and I listened to the sound of a car engine, which cranked somewhere down the street, its radio that blared forth news of arrests in two Mississippi towns where Negroes tried to register to vote, until the driver had a chance to turn it down.

"What you thinking?" Will said. I looked back at him.

"Just then? That I know what the men are gonna be talking about tomorrow."

"Those arrests."

"Yeah." Then I said, "You think they believed they could really get away with that?"

"With what?"

"Trying to vote."

"I don't know." Will shrugged. "Not much telling."

"Well, there'll be plenty of others happy to do it for you. The telling." Then I sighed. "Sometimes it seems like that's all we do around here."

Will watched me. After a moment he said, "What else were you thinking?"

"Before then? Aw, nothing."

"It had to be something."

"Well, yeah, actually. Something I read once. You know there's a restaurant in Paris where the ceiling is painted with angels, and the ceiling's got a mechanism built in so in pretty weather you can roll it back. And the folk dine under a blue sky and clouds. Or stars, depending on the time of day. And the chef is known to come out with a pair of doves in a cage and release them, right in the middle of the room."

"He just lets them go?"

"Yeah."

"Good eating doves?"

"Yeah. It's for drama. Atmosphere."

Then I said, "I wonder what they doing now."

Will chewed and swallowed. "Well," he said, "what time'd it'd be over there. Probably lunch. So probably having the finest time in the world. Probably picking out their caviar and all."

"Hell's bells," I said.

We ate.

"You ever get a funny feeling?" I said.

"Funny ha-ha or funny strange?"

"Funny strange."

"About what?"

"I don't know. About anything. Just a funny feeling."

He didn't say anything for a minute.

Then I said, "You know, suppose you had a funny feeling and you didn't quite know why. Would that mean you're almost thinking of something you're not supposed to but didn't know it?"

"What the hell's the matter with you?"

"I don't know."

"Well, you're not making a damn bit of sense."

"Forget it."

"Well you start to bait me, then you pull back."

I looked at him.

"Well first, then, I might ask what *you're* thinking."

"Me? Nothing. Money worries, I guess. Daddy and I got the gin coming, yeah, but folk owe us on work done in advance. I've got money worries."

"Yeah, and what with Clarice Lytle's salary."

"So that's what this is about."

I looked at him again.

He said, "Your funny feeling."

"No-no-actually. Did I say anything about that?"

Will shook his head.

"I thought I didn't."

"Look, all right, I'm sorry. Daddy broke his finger today. Dr. Butler fixed it, it's in a splint, but I didn't know anybody could break a finger tacking up a little dryboard. God Almighty, you put your hand wrong between hammer and nail and everything changes. What a stupid life this is. But anyway, what were you saying?"

"I don't know."

"I was hoping maybe now for a serenade."

I didn't say anything.

"Aw come on."

"I don't know." To which I added a tepid "But I hope Amos is all right."

Will nodded. After a minute I said, "And I suppose you'll be wanting cake."

"No supposing to it. And if you don't sing, I'll sing it myself."

"*Okay*, I'll sing it." Then I did. "Happy birthday to you. Happy birthday to you. Happy birthday, dear Will."

He ate some more. I finished the song. "What you think a monkey smells like?" I said.

"You got me."

We finished off the food and then I stacked the dirty plates and carried them downstairs and went back up. Soon Will hauled both the cake and the whiskey and put them up on the bed. He turned on the TV—our one newly acquired piece of furniture—and we both got up on the bed and leaned against the pillows. We lay there. Odd, but a fly that landed on the wall at this moment might have thought it was seeing an old married couple. One of those couples that faces no visible change, in fact, having already been led from the crazed stripping of two folks' clothing along the wood floors to the purchase of a TV so we could lie on the bed in our underwear and watch Ed Sullivan. We lay there awhile. In the single light of the TV, all the shapes of the room looked curiously gentle. The filigree of the bed making a shadow like rich houses' lace.

So we lay across the sheets with the cake on the bed and ate and sat thinking and watching the television. "I saw Sheila Jones today," I said.

"Mrs. Jones's daughter?"

"Yeah."

"Here at the café?"

"Yeah. She came in for a shake."

Will studied me across the bed. "And?"

"And she was acting pretty funny."

"Oh no, don't tell me. Funny strange?"

"Well, as a matter of fact. But if you don't want to talk about it—"

"No, no, I do." Will lay there chewing and sipping. "It's just, life at the café. A new surprise every day."

"Well, she was acting peculiar. Her features all fastened close together. Her eyes a little fuzzy. A while back she came in and talked up a blue streak, about her new boyfriend and how she wasn't getting to see him that day 'cause he had to help his nana sell her eggs. She was asking me all about romance and then she even talked about her daddy dying and went on and on."

"And what'd she talk about this time?"

"That's just it. She didn't say anything. Eugenia was there with her usual how-do and Sheila offered nothing to match her gladness."

"So Eugenia talked. This is not exactly unknown to man. And Sheila couldn't get a word in edgewise—"

"No, it was then."

"Then what?"

"She acted like she saw a ghost. But nobody was there."

"Another surprise. So-ooo, what color shirt d'she have on? What flavor shake d'she drink?"

"Will, what you talking about?"

"That you making me Perry Mason here."

"Aw well. I just—"

"Good *God*, all right, now I see. Sheila and the March boy."

"Hunh?" I said.

I looked at him. He held the glass between his thumb and forefinger and propped it down on the bed. "You remember that time I told you about," he said. "Time I saw them—remember—in the grocery store."

"And?"

"And Tchula Gaze sells eggs."

"Yeah, Tchula Gaze sells eggs. And what's that got to do with the price of tea in China?"

"Tchula Gaze is Earnest March's great-grandma. You said Sheila said her boyfriend's nana sells eggs."

"So does Laticia Wade. And Imogene Huit. Last time I checked both of them had a bumper crop of great-grandkids. Several in high school." I sat up on the bed. "I didn't know Tchula Gaze was his kin."

"Yes ma'am."

We considered this in the dark together. I could feel us beginning. It was true, too, that Will himself was dark-complected and took some teasing, enough that he was tender about it. It was still another of those circumstances having to do with the strict dividing line of the town, that I'd never heard him talk about his Choctaw side. A boy who was half Choctaw was considered white, after all, because he wasn't black. Yet in grade school once he'd beat up Jeffrey Shine, who'd said Choctaws were niggers anyway, that they didn't care who they married like white folk did.

"So that's it then," Will said softly but clearly. "Sheila and the March boy."

"You really think so?"

"You said she didn't mention his name?"

"Not once. Not at all."

"Then it is him. You can bet your bottom dollar on it."

Honorable Mention

ALL SUMMER, RIGHT UP TO the day in August, in fact, when Earnest March tried to run away with Sheila Jones, I spent the usual hours at the café. Though there was the summer slack-off of customers during the week, we had our Friday supper crowds and the work of harvest. Eugenia and Mattie and I did the shelling, canning, freezing. We made red pepper jelly. And we took the summer fruit and baked it in cobblers. These take advantage of the summer ooze, when the flies hover, when the fruit turns to liqueur in its skin and the bottoms of baskets seep amber, indigo, yellow. Peaches with ginger, or blackberries with lemon, honey-scented mixed-fruit cobbler. There is a narrow moment between ripeness and rot, but the clock ticks loudly.

In the evening hours Will and I also set up a usual pattern, after the café closed. We fell into it; then it went unspoken. It's odd, I suppose, that when I think back to what happened during that terrible summer, one of my sharpest memories would be of a routine in our evenings before everything began. Seemingly unconnected to much of what followed, it was the prelude—the brief, somber note I questioned but tried to disregard.

It was this: the moments of silence between us. The only sounds the noises of the café—the squeak of the oven door when I opened it, the drip of the pan under the icebox, and then the creak of the linoleum under Will's boots, and the ring of Christmas bells on the front door. I watched Will leave on his walks. And I drifted into experimenting in the kitchen. At first I merely looked forward to it, then came to rely on it, just not to be alone. Eugenia, who must have realized some change in Will and me, avoided the subject. After about the twentieth night in a row of finding new dishes in the icebox, she said, "So my kitchen's got you hypnotized, hunh?"

A particular evening I am thinking of was an evening in late July. A Monday. One of the slowest evenings was always Monday, after the congestion of weekend customers. And what I recall of that summer evening is that for some long moments in the kitchen I was suddenly aware of my *place*, in a way I wasn't often. That is, I was abruptly aware of all the tiny details surrounding me, all the details that connected me to what I called home, and yet feeling neither part of it nor truly separated from it. It was not unlike that feeling that perhaps you have had in a dream when you rise above your body and look down at yourself. Somehow impartial, detached—an observer. And yet aware of it all. But to no obvious purpose.

If I were trying to account for this feeling, I might say it had something to do with the way I kept thinking about the cooking contest, my entry to the Southern Pecan Growers Association, who the judges were, and what they might actually be thinking. I imagined them considering my work, lifting a fork and tasting. And on this evening in late July, as I imagined this, I stopped and looked slowly around the kitchen. Above through the open back screen door was the darkening sky, and now, the darting glint of lightning bugs. Everything quieted. In the air around me was the heavy scent of peaches. I breathed in. Then I picked a peach up and began to peel it. A layer of skin before me. Below, I could hear the steady *drip-drip* under the icebox.

As a result, perhaps, I felt suspended, waiting. Between all that was familiar and part of none of it.

We feel this way sometimes growing up; surely most of us can recall it. But then there's the impatience for the next thing to take shape, the big moment that will tell us who we will become. This was different: What if, I asked, there was no big moment?

I had also begun to feel this way, now and then, serving the customers, even as I took pride in my work, realizing I had done this many times before and could do so countless times again. A sense of being immediately there in the present moment, and yet looking from a great distance. Or during one of my conversations with Mama who, after a pause, would hint once again about my going to college. Or when the men, sitting at the counter, would worry about changes in a town that, it seemed to me, would never change. I had taken this kind of talk for granted. They would talk like this, then pause, then sip their coffee. Yet when they paused I would feel it again. A sense of being utterly present and, simultaneously, far, far away.

Now, on this evening, Will came into the kitchen with a bottle of liquor under his arm. He took two glasses from the cupboard, filled them, and handed me one.

And with that, as quickly as it had come over me, the moment ended. I could feel him trying to get me back in time.

"I think we should go up to bed," he said. "I'm sorry—or can we consider this bedtime?"

"I don't know."

"Well, think about it in your spare time. I know you're preoccupied with that concoction."

Will swallowed the last of his drink, then poured a second glass. "That smells good. What is it anyway?"

"A kind of peach cobbler."

"How long's that gonna take?"

"I don't know."

"You don't know how long, or you don't know whether you can get it right?"

"I don't know either, actually, and don't know what to tell you."

"A bit damn touchy, aren't we? Aw look, Fannie, come on, why don't you put that aside?"

As Will continued to look at me, I found myself wanting to tell him about my feeling but then not knowing what to call it. The shadow of it lingered with me, but I didn't say anything to him. He wouldn't understand it. Or he would misread it as some distance I wanted from him. So I simply said, "And if I put this aside, what are you gonna do? Take another walk?"

"Did I say I was?"

"No you didn't. But I never knew that to stop you."

"Well I'm here now, aren't I?" He looked at me again. Finally he said, "So, what are you gonna want to do then?"

"What I want to do is finish this."

"And what would you like me to do? Twiddle my thumbs. Whistle on an open bottle, *whoo, whoo, whoo,* or what?"

"There's TV. The paper."

"The paper, hunh. That's a joy ride."

"What you mean?"

"You might want to pull your head out of the recipes once in a while, Fannie. Those colored folk going to jail. Colored folk trying to register to vote, and getting beat up, though you don't get that part from the paper. God Almighty, all of a sudden this's all I'm hearing about. Just up in Greenwood. And to top it off, some colored boy's making noises about trying to get into Ole Miss."

"Well, you've got a new *Field and Stream*—"

"Are you hearing me?"

"Yes. And if you're referring to Sheila and the March boy, I'm hearing you loud and clear. All I'm saying is, there is other stuff to read, you know."

"All right, then. I'm more than content with that brainstorm. What a lot to pack into a night. A recipe, a bottle, *whoo, whoo, whoo*"—he blew high whispers on the bottle. "And then there's your very tough decision about where we'll sleep together. I look forward to resolving that. Well, we'll meet up somewhere, and you'll show me what you've made and I'll tell you what I've read. All right, Fannie, finish your recipe, and your drink there. And I'm about to get deep in my reading."

"You finish mine."

Will picked up my glass and carried it upstairs. I picked up the paring knife and turned back to the peaches.

I did not look in on Will, did not hear him upstairs. In an hour I had gotten started on a peach cobbler with ginger. This was for Imogene Huit, who was having a family reunion. The Huits had advanced me two dollars and would pay me another two on receipt of the cobbler. This was coming along well. It was best to keep at it. But Will came downstairs.

"We could start down here, and later move to the bed," he said from the bottom step. He was talking louder than necessary. "The bottle is empty and reading is hard work.

"Or we could start from the bed and end up who knows where. There's more choices than you might think, Fannie."

Will remained on the bottom step, watching me. He had on his jeans but was barefoot and shirtless. Finally he crossed the kitchen and opened the bottom cupboard. He got out a second bottle. Then he sat up on the table, facing away from me.

"All that reading hurt my eyes. Could you turn out that light? If you're through."

I took the peach cobbler from the oven and set it on the counter to cool. Then I turned off the light and went upstairs. I washed my face, brushed my teeth, carried my robe down to the kitchen, and undressed. I had never done that before, undressed in the kitchen. I hung my clothes over the stair rail, put on my robe, and walked over to Will. He took a long drink.

"Fannie," he said, his voice cracking softly. "I bet you think Persia is so small, whatever goes on, folk will hear of it. Sooner or later, but eventually."

"If you're referring to Sheila and the March boy, yeah, I do keep thinking about it."

"No—I meant *me*. Something about yours truly, Will Leary."

He began to cry, and there was something plaintive, childlike, in the voice, but breaking a little on the upper register. It just took me aback. It was such a powerful crying I could only look at him. I could only look at him, and Eugenia wasn't there. It was the only prop missing. That and a little boy with a thin brown face and black hair slopping over his forehead, sitting down on the kitchen floor and crying and holding his arms around himself, the day Eugenia slapped him. For that's how it was for me. All the years of knowing Will were jumbling into one picture.

"What's going on here?" I said. "I don't get it."

"No you don't." Then, "Fannie, do you know something I did, one time, before you came along?"

He turned up the bottle and grimaced.

"None of my business?" I said.

"That's right. But something you don't know can still affect you."

"Don't talk in riddles, Will."

I reached out to touch his shoulder, but he couldn't see me. I pulled my hand back.

Now, turning, he looked at me. "I mean *Eugenia's* way of treating me."

"Mama hasn't ever really liked you, I know, but I think Eugenia's been fair."

"Well, it's gotten worse for a reason in particular."

"What reason?"

"It was the time before you and I started up together. It happened back then." He wiped his face with the front of his arm.

"Will—listen carefully. If you're talking about the accident—the accident with my uncle Lawrence, well that's—"

He threw the bottle across the room, lay back on the table, rolled his head back and forth as though poisoned. As though the memory had poisoned him. "You're hopeless, Fannie. That's *not* what I'm talking about. And it's best I get out. I'm gonna get out now."

"Why don't you just go upstairs? Get some sleep."

"And get out of your way. Is that it?"

"No, I'll come on up."

" 'Cause you're not the only one with big career plans. You know that? And anyway, I'm working my way out of Persia, just like you are, eventually. Just like you are. . . ." and his voice trailed off. He rolled on his side, on the table, and was fast asleep.

I got two Hershey's bars from the icebox. I stayed up all night, not cooking.

The following morning Will was sick with a hangover, fever, vomiting. He awoke after dawn, had a few sips of juice, and went upstairs to bed. "Don't look at me," he said.

Eugenia and Mattie, of course, were soon starting breakfast rounds. I worked with them, looked in on Will to find him either in a fitful, sweating sleep or glaring at me. Before noon I carried up some chicken broth. "Don't watch me eat," he said.

Soon afterward he came down to the kitchen. He had taken a bath and put on fresh clothes, but he looked wretched and pale. As he reached the bottom of the stairs, everyone turned. I watched them. First, Mattie. Her eyes like a thornbush, sticking him all over. Then Eugenia. She oscillated her head, and hesitated. Then she decided.

"You want some coffee, hon? You look like you could use it."

"No thank you, ma'am," Will managed. "Thank you kindly, ma'am, but I got to get to work." And he left the café.

Several weeks later, Eugenia was standing by the kitchen table in one of Mattie's armhole aprons and leaning over a basket of peaches. Her hand rode their fuzzy skins. She lifted her palm to her nose and smiled.

"Zowie! Smell that?"

"Yessum," I said.

"We got enough to do one more?"

"I expect so," said Mattie.

Eugenia nodded to Mattie's back at the counter. "That is, if we got enough ginger."

"We got enough."

Eugenia looked toward the air conditioner. "This thing's supposed to have a cooler in it but it doesn't put out much."

"Feels fine to me."

Eugenia nodded at the window. "I might just do another, if you want."

Mattie nodded.

Then Eugenia looked at me.

"And as for you, young lady, there's something I got for you."

"What?"

"Well, I was gonna wait till the finish of work but I'm getting tired of walking around it, and anyway you look like you could use a break—and that goes for you too, Mattie."

She looked at me again. Then the Christmas bells rang.

"Well come on," she said. She took off her glasses and folded them on the chain and toweled the damp of her face with the apron. We went out.

It was Burl Magee and Mr. Ardor at the counter.

"Now what'll you boys have?"

She lifted the pot of coffee and I pulled out two cups and the men leaned their elbows on the counter. She was filling the cups as Mr. Ardor said, "Hey, Fannie."

"Hey, Mr. Ardor. Hey, Mr. Magee."

"Hey, little lady."

Eugenia slid the cups over. "Here you go, hon. Y'all want some peach cobbler to go with that?"

They looked at her. "Now you know you do, a little tide-over till supper. Mattie'll have y'all's warmed up in a jiffy."

"That sounds good," said Mr. Magee. Both men were nodding, and I went into the kitchen and told Mattie and came back out. But by that time Mr. Ardor had turned to Mr. Magee, and said:

"A nigra getting in? To my alma mater?"

"Maybe folk are just blowing it all up," Mr. Magee offered.

Mr. Ardor said, "Maybe."

"Or maybe he won't even try it."

"Or maybe," said Eugenia, as Mattie came through the door, "this kind of talk isn't good for the digestion." Mattie handed Eugenia the plates of cobbler, and Eugenia glanced at her hesitantly. Then Eugenia placed the plates in front of the two men. Then Mattie went back into the kitchen. I watched this. I watched Mr. Ardor pause, and frown. But even this kind of frown couldn't stand up to Eugenia, who turned to Mr. Ardor and gloated:

"Well, now, Fannie, I was just about to ask Aston here about his son. Not to change the subject on you boys, but since you were talking about school, these stories I been hearing about him sound a whole lot like his daddy. I hear tell he's up there making all those A's, gathering all the honors with that big incisive brain of his and impressing all those sorority girls in the process too, I bet, and I say Awww, Awww, that sounds like his daddy, nothing slow about him."

"Well the boy is—he is having a good time."

" 'Course everybody used to talk about you the same way."

"Did they, really?"

"—and of course I want to hear more about it, and see that boy if he gets back down here and has the time to stop by. That is"—and Eugenia poked his shoulder—"if he hadn't got too highbrow and smart for us. 'Course I know he's not a piker, I know that, I know that, he's got to keep his nose to the grindstone, but you need to tell him that doesn't keep us home folk from missing him. Particularly a boy like that."

Mr. Ardor basked.

"Yessiree, everybody's been telling me what a dandy fine fellow he is, just like his daddy, a scholar and an A-one gentleman. But then, we know quality, don't we, Burl?"

"Yes ma'am."

Eugenia inched down the counter and rested her hand on Mr. Magee's hand. She patted it in a way that was a little like the lead-them-on manner she must have used in the classroom. For the oldest of Mr. Magee's children had been her students. She said, "We know, don't we, especially when we got these kids to be proud of." She looked over at me. "I'd bet more than a little orphan nip of sherry on the skills of certain ones, I tell you. Oh, and by the way, Fannie, that reminds me, before I forget again, d'you get that letter Burl left for you?"

I looked at Mr. Magee. He said, "I left it for you earlier. By the cash register."

And Eugenia, innocently, "Now where was I?" And she set upon Mr. Magee, a whirlwind that whisked a question into my mind.

I walked to the end of the counter. The letter was propped between the side of the cash register and a cracked coffee mug that held fountain pens, toothpicks, and a folded check that Sikes Daughtry had asked me not to deposit until the end of the month when his disability came in. I reached for the envelope. It sprang up, almost by itself, and slid into my hand. The tiny gold engraving of a tree. Sure enough, the letterhead, unmistakable: the Southern Pecan Growers Association.

I held the envelope in front of me. In my chest, a fluttering. Beating wings in a chimney. I glanced to see if anybody was watching. They were doing a good job of acting like they weren't. I opened the letter and read:

> Dear Mrs. Leary:
>
> We are delighted to inform you that your entry, Stuffed Catfish, in the 1962 Southern Pecan Growers' Association Cookoff, has been awarded Honorable Mention by our selection committee. Congratulations!
>
> Our selection committee faced a truly daunting task of selecting from among an overwhelming array of fine recipes. Your delightful and unusual dish, indeed, is one of only two recipes to receive Honorable Mention. Mrs. Derik Esquivel, manager of The Peppers Grill, in Atlanta, was the other recipient. First prize went to Mr. Paul Dupree, a student at Opelousas High School, in Opelousas, Louisiana.
>
> Entries of the three recipients will be published, in November, in one thousand pamphlets, which will be circulated throughout the southern United States.
>
> Once again, my congratulations. If you have any questions, don't hesitate to contact me.
>
> Sincerely,
> Byram Betham Diggs
> President
> Southern Pecan Growers Association

Well, I stood there. Then I read it again. I held the letter quite daft, now soaring triumphant, now blackly longing. Had the contest been close? Had I lost first prize by, say, a couple of votes? One? What if I had worked harder on the recipe? Would it have made a difference? And who was this Dupree fellow anyway? And what was that phrase? Honorable Mention. Sounded like an oxymoron, if you ask me. Like jumbo shrimp. Honorable, so tall a word, so solid and fine and like old trees, lasting. But mention? Mention was brief as a hiccup, the flea a cow slaps from its hide with the flick of a tail. Wouldn't it be better if it were Honorable Statement? Honorable Prize? You mention you got a corn on your toe, you mention nice weather we're having, but mention a recipe that will appear in a thousand pamphlets? It didn't look right. It was too brief. The Big Hand snaps its fingers and the Honorable is done.

And then I thought: The recipe would go into a thousand pamphlets. With my name on it. A thousand folk would read it. Maybe more. Maybe they'd go into their kitchens. They'd say, this looks good, I think I'll try it. And they'd prepare the dish and serve it to their families and inhale the good smells and taste the good tastes that came straight out of my brain. And in a way all these folk I didn't even know would be sharing with me a moment well lived. They would in a way. For Honorable did mean good. It meant it was good. It meant I was good.

And wouldn't you know Eugenia and Mr. Magee were over there talking away. Like they weren't paying any attention. Mama'd be in soon to help with the Friday supper crowd and then Will, and I'd be able to tell him and he'd see, then, wouldn't he, how this could pay off, and Mattie, and Eugenia, Eugenia who sent my name in the first place, wouldn't she pretend to be surprised. I tried not to smile. And then I turned toward Eugenia and *there* was the surprise. Eugenia clutching her chest. Her eyes imploring me as though she had to ask a question. I stood and watched her and the letter drop in slow motion to the linoleum. I stood there for what seemed a long time, and then I was conscious of some motion coming from a great distance, Mr. Ardor and Mr. Magee around the counter and Mattie from the kitchen with a dishrag in her hand. She held Eugenia's head and put the dishrag on her forehead. I floated down to the floor. I couldn't take my eyes off her. *Eugenia.* I saw lipsticked lips and a trace of sour drool; the chain of the glasses askew and knotted at the neck; the fragile skin under the eyes veined and violet-shadowed; the pupils that shrank to twin pinpoints of light and went opaque.

None of us spoke. Mattie and Mr. Ardor did not move. Then Mr. Magee went to the phone and stopped the room from turning into a painting.

Right afterwards, I went outside. All I could think of was to tell Mama, but then I thought of Will and the fact that it was close to quitting time and walked out toward the river. I walked out the front door of the café and across the road. I paused there. I could hear the squealing of tires, which was probably Mr. Ardor in his Cadillac hightailing it to Brother Works' or Dr. Butler's. Then I walked down toward the pier. There was the headless Confederate statue that greeted you at the brow. As I went on, blackbirds swooped and cawed like messengers.

I went on down the pier, past a row of bass boats, past the occasional slick ski boat varnished with waves. Farther out I could see a barge that had dropped anchor. There was a smell of oil, fish, and muddy water, dock boards creaking dryly, chains of boats tied at the pier-posts and boats pulling at them like tangled necklaces. In the seat of one I noticed a tan-and-white package of Camels. Then several houseboats. The last was the *Elvira.* I went aboard. I opened the door to the cabin and there was Clarice Lytle sitting on the end of Amos's bed. Will was holding a bottle in one hand. A glass in the other. His back was to me, but when I walked in his eyes seemed to spin to the back of his head before he could wheel around. That's exaggeration, but you get what I mean.

Clarice had a shoe off. A long, high-heeled white pump. She looked at me, then at the other shoe, which she pried off with her toes. "There," she said. "Much better. I got blisters, you know."

I could have slapped her face. I could have slapped that damned pretty Barbie-doll blond thick-eyelinered face, which had smiled so nicely to thank me for the graduation present, bless her heart, and which was trying to smile now, but it was the color of strawberry and an insult to look into. Will glanced hastily over at her, and I could have slapped his face. He said, "We had some work to finish." He motioned to the stacks of paper on Amos's table. Irritated, he flattened his voice as if they had rehearsed the moment and neither of them could remember the first damned lie they had wished to tell me.

"On Friday?" I said.

"Yeah," Clarice said. " 'Course, I do normally come in on Thursdays, yeah, but Mr. Ardor had a backlog and by the time I finished I was running late so—"

"So we finished today," Will said, not looking at me.

"Yeah, we finished."

Clarice wore a pink sleeveless shell and a narrow, white short skirt over dark tan stockings. The stockings were about three shades darker than her arms. There was a little run beginning at the left big toe. Sitting on Amos's bed, she clenched and unclenched those toes; each time she did, the run grew. She said, "Well I guess I'll be going."

"Don't you move," I said.

"Fannie," said Will.

"Don't either of you move."

"Well I was just—" said Clarice.

"Shut up, Clarice," said Will. He sighed. He still didn't look at me.

"I just came to give you the news," I said. "I just came to give you the news that Eugenia died. In case you're not too busy to be interested."

Storming from the boat, I went up the pier and bypassed the café. I went down Levee Road, wincing in the sunlight. Somewhere down the road a truck honked. I wanted to get out of sight, so I cut to where the town road ended and the path turned to dirt and started toward the bluff and peninsula and Tchula Gaze's shack. A quarter mile out I passed Sheila and Mrs. Jones's house. Then the Ardor farm, with its caramel cattle in a green pasture, hardly moving, and at a great distance some field hands in dark pants and straw hats and bare brown shining backs were slowly walking a cotton field and using white shirts carried in their hands to wipe the backs of their necks. Just before you got to Tchula's shack, there was a narrow, naturally terraced drop that went down close to the river. It was rocky, it wasn't easy to get down, but the bottom had thick grass and a great willow tree and obscured the view of anyone who might be walking overhead. This had been a favorite refuge since childhood. I used to go there and lie under the tree and pretend it was someplace else. I loved to lie in its island of shade and watch the river. On a windy day, the river flashed and swelled silver to the Louisiana coast. Silver, then land. Over and over. Sometimes I would touch fingers to the water and say, "I am touching the Gulf of Mexico."

When I climbed down to the tree, I took a seat. There was velvet moss growing at the base of the tree, lush and tropical green. The green looked almost too bright to be natural, and now a redheaded woodpecker lit on a branch above and drilled its beak into wood. *Dahdahdahdahdah.* The beak bored farther. *Dahdahdahdahdah.* There was a wide space in my head where the thoughts should be. There were no words or notions under the words but only this sound. A redheaded woodpecker in my brain.

I sat there until the sun dropped, until the woodpecker gradually ceased its work and the last of its reverberations faded. Then silence. Then the sound of the river could be heard. Somewhere, intimate and very near, a cricket spoke and another answered. As the sun dropped, a breeze picked up, and, one by one, every strand on the willow moved.

I felt a strange coldness on my spine, and saw the glistening river as the great willow moved and tears sprang into my eyes.

The willow, the glistening; the swirl of bracken, minnows, cattail; and in the deep orange light of the sun, the silent swoop of the woodpecker, as it flew away; and then another sound, faint and farther off, the clankling cans of Tchula Gaze's scarecrow. A mosquito tickled my ankle; I looked down. Dewdrops crept haltingly down stems of clover. There were white clover blossoms and I started to pick some to make a necklace. It was a harried effort, though. I was killing time. I was starting to think about Eugenia. I was starting to think about Will. And I could not fathom what might come to me, except minute by minute. I stopped tying clover. I sat there until it got dark.

Finally, I returned to the café. From a distance I could see the blinking sign, the windows. As soon as I got to the door, Mrs. Butler led me in. It was strange walking in this way, half the town there, the women moving toward me, shocked mouths dripping question marks. They were all but blocking my way. Damp fawning hands as I tried to return each hug and made my way toward my mother. For a moment I joined in their hesitation and then made my way toward her, sitting against and within the bustle, counter to it, her mouth a straight line. Without saying a word I leaned down and put my arms around her so tightly I lifted her a little from the booth.

"Mama," I said, close to her ear. She sat in a kind of exaggerated helplessness, at once meek and sullen.

She said, "The entire town's been out looking for you."

"Have they."

"Will and the sheriff and Amos, and Burl. Lord knows who-all," she said, in a small cold voice. But I could tell she had been crying. Threads of red against the eye-white.

"Well I'm here," I said evenly. There was enough for her to handle this evening without worrying about me. And she would worry, if she knew the truth about Will, but her reaction would be more complicated than that. There'd be anger about what he'd done, but there'd also be disappointment.

"Well take a seat," she said. "Just don't stand there."

I took a seat.

"You want some tea?"

I shook my head.

"Well have some anyway." So I did. There was a significant amount of amber stuff in the glass that was not tea and I pursed my lips in a silent whistle and looked at her.

"Mattie gave it to me. And before you say anything take another sip. You look like you could use it."

"You might want to put some tea in here."

"It'll put hair on your chest."

I took another sip.

"I'd just like to know, if you don't mind, what in the Sam Hill you think you were doing? Running off."

Before I could answer, Mrs. Hardin came to the table and said, "You want some tea, hon?"

I nodded. And for a second wished I was back at the river. The air here so thickly human, the whole of town responding as if the sheriff had blandly announced a murder. At that very moment the Christmas bells rang and the sheriff walked in and took a bead on me and frowned and shook his head. Cigarette smoke rising so all the faces looked submerged. I had so much to consider, so much that could not get free for this thickness, and I found myself being borne along by them, without ever saying I would go. The sheriff came to the table and asked me if I was all right. Mrs. Hardin brought me ice tea, Mrs. Magee brought me a napkin, Mrs. Huit brought me silverware, and Mrs. Viola brought me a plate piled with enough food for two. Then Amos and Mr. Magee came through the door, came to the table, asked if I was all right, and took a seat with Mr. Ardor at the next table and talked about heart illness. Finally Brother Works came to the table, took my hand in his, and placed his other hand on top.

"We mighty sorry," he said. "We mighty sorry for you and Sister Bell."

He was still holding my hand between his, and now he squeezed it a little. In the reflection of the window I saw him doing this and felt a wave of claustrophobia. There was no doubt, though, that he'd be the star of this show, for the town greatly respected and admired him. But I had always had a certain prejudice, I admit, that perhaps had as much to do with the occupation as the man. Brother Works seemed the kind who had never done anything wrong, that he could think of. The kind who could find the implication of sin in the buttocks of a peach. I for one had often thanked the Lord that I did not have to listen to Brother Works's sermons as long as there was a pot of coffee and a pillowed bed, a newspaper, the loose-sheeted freedom of a Sunday morning.

Standing by the table, he was handed a dish of peach cobbler by Mrs. Viola and protested, "Bless you, dear, but I said a smidgeon.

I declare, you ladies have a generous idea of comfort." Then he turned back to our table and said, "You know, if there's anything I can do."

"Yes, thank you," Mama said, in a shut voice.

"Because if there's anything, you just let me know. Beyond the particulars, which we can get to tomorrow."

Mama nodded and sipped deliberately from her glass. Brother Works took that as his cue. "God comfort you," he said, and glanced at his plate. Then he moved to the next table.

I was just thinking how endless this was likely to become when I saw the kitchen door push to, and Mattie leaned out and looked around. I watched to catch her look at a customer, the way she did, straight in the eye like a dare. Some liked her, and those who didn't waited for her to do this, because there was reason to believe that when those black eyes looked at you, they could see where your next step would be planted. But Mattie didn't look that way. She just looked around, with her arm hanging straight down and dishwater damp glistening bronze on the hand and forearm, and with her eyes flinting a little as soon as she saw me. I got up and went toward her.

She said, "Will's in the kitchen."

I looked at her.

Then she said, "You want me to go out back?"

"No," I said, after a pause. "No, you stay."

She walked on ahead, returned to a sink full of dishes.

"Fannie," he said.

He was standing at an angle under the bitter overhead light with his chin down and his face partly in shadow. So I looked at red tomatoes on the windowsill. A fork upside down in a milky glass. I looked out the window but there was no help to be found there, either. Finally I looked back. Then I saw he had been crying. He had been crying and was mumbling something low to me that the noise of Mattie's banging pots tore apart as he waited for me to answer.

But I said, "I don't want to look at you."

He started to speak.

"I don't want to look at you. Not now. Not ever."

Then I walked back out front. I got a hug from Mrs. Daughtry, who had come in with some casserole and then I went back and sat down by Mama.

Mama said, "What have you been doing, Fannie? Rolling in the grass?"

I shrugged. She motioned to the yellow-green stains, which, now I realized, had streaked the behind of my dress.

"Not a lovely sight, I imagine." I picked up the ice tea and sipped it.

"You've stained a perfectly clean dress."

The funeral was held on August 3, 1962, late on Sunday morning. I stayed over at Mama's, ostensibly to keep her company. Will, as far as I knew, stayed with Amos on the *Elvira*. For the funeral Mama heavily powdered her face and covered the crown of her head with a black lace shawl. The shawl reminded me of the paramours of Spanish conquistadors in old movies.

"I chose the blue for Eugenia to wear," she said. "The sky blue, you remember?"

"The sky blue, sure." I had on my good dress and was brushing my hair. "Sure, I remember."

"Well, I thought she'd like that. A nice airy color. Nothing sad, you know."

We walked over to the church. Though it was still morning, the sun was strong, the sky deep and cloudless. When we got there, the pews were already filled. We walked down the aisle and took a seat at the front pew. Will and Amos sat next to us. I hadn't seen Mattie, though I figured she was somewhere in the back. Mourners stood inside along the back and down the sides by the stained-glass windows. They all watched us as if they were trying not to watch, as if there were a secret they were not supposed to tell. Mrs. Giddy, the town operator, was playing the organ. There was the most enormous spray of flowers, long and extravagantly bright red and yellow, starchy white, dark roses and white roses, ferns, carnations, some oily-looking palms, all running with black and gold curling ribbon, almost suffocating in their smell. Hidden below these flowers was Eugenia's coffin, which had been placed on two sawhorses in front of the elevated pulpit. Uncle Lawrence, I thought, and suddenly remembered, and saw in my mind's eye many rows of white stones and next to them green trees through which the wind blew light. I thought of the heap of flowers and how beneath the flowers, in the closed coffin, was Uncle Lawrence, and Eugenia standing there too, her face falling in pleats, but that was a long time ago.

Mrs. Giddy finished one song, then started another. There was a tinny scraping along the floor. I looked up to see, at the last moment, an unfolding of metal chairs down the side wall near the front of the church, and a dozen Amish took a seat. I did not know who gave them the news, but I was pleased so many had come. They moved together, a clump of black. Black netting covering the women's hair, broad black hats in the men's hands, and the children dressed the same. Among the Amish women was Mrs. Wiebe Schwietert. She had carried on a trade of clover honey with Eugenia for years from the small cluster of Amish farms outside of Persia. She looked somewhere in the vicinity of Eugenia's age, and she led the group. How hot they all looked in those clothes—how hot and wary and shy.

Just behind me sat Madeline Hanley, the undertaker's wife. At one point she tapped Mama on the shoulder and leaned up close and said, "I didn't know Eugenia knew the Amish."

"Know one, know all. The Amish, the Indian, the cook," said Deedee Hardin, in a faintly joking, resigned whisper. She sat in the pew directly behind me and now suddenly seemed to remember Will's and my presence. "Which speaks well of the deceased, of course."

Because of the heat and closed space, the crowd ripened past comfort, and all at once it seemed that Jesus fans alit on hands and fluttered down the pews. In the first thirty minutes Brother Works must have blotted his face ten times with his handkerchief. My attention detoured in the heat, though I do remember that in his eulogy he described Eugenia as "a spirited, caring Christian who not only reminds us what it means to be a lady, but also reminds us in generous example that love is eternal."

I wanted to like what Brother Works said, because it was for Eugenia, but I felt impatient to the point of taking offense. This is what all that preaching turns you into, I thought, a person who can generalize like that. I did not know all the reasons, but my tolerance then for Brother Works was quickly exhausting. I was beginning to feel a faintly sickening, familiar agitation. It did not help that I was forced next to—and within—a submerged dialogue with Will. Will's knee next to mine, holding my gaze straight ahead, while on the other side, Mama's knuckles whitely gripped her purse. Eternal, my eye. If love is eternal, it sure gets lost or covered up. I was relieved when Brother Works finally moved on to prayer in general.

"Dear heavenly Father, who is our hope and strength, a beacon of light in the darkest of our troubles, accept our prayers on behalf of thy servant Sister Eugenia Dare Mary Claire Boatwright, and grant her entrance into the land of light and joy, into the fellowship of saints, and all our dearly departed, through Jesus Christ thy son our Lord, who liveth and reigneth with thee, now and forever.

"Amen," he said.

"Amen."

Brother Works nodded to Mrs. Eliot, who was sitting across the aisle from us in the front pew. Mrs. Eliot was a tall, elegant woman in her forties. She rose gracefully—a butterfly of sweat stuck to the back of her dress—put down her fan, and walked up several steps to the organ. She wore her red hair coiled around her head in the old way, and her lips were reddened to match. She placed one hand on the organ. Mrs. Giddy began to play and Mrs. Eliot sang:

Shall we gather at the river,
Where bright angel feet have trod:
With its crystal tide forever
Flowing by the throne of God?

Mrs. Eliot was a soprano, and justifiably proud of her voice. It had the same lilt when you heard her talk. She lifted her chin and carried the song pure through in spite of all the heat and sadness.

When she finished she took her hand from the organ and returned to her seat. She picked up her fan.

In the dismissal that immediately followed, I stood and waited for Mama to rise so I could walk with her out of the church.

"I just think I'll sit here," she said, opening her purse and looking about wildly for something.

"Here," said Amos and Mr. Magee, each offering a handkerchief. She took Mr. Magee's, blew her nose, dried her eyes, and said, "Sit down, Burl."

"Why sure," Mr. Magee said, flushing pleased and embarrassed. He sat down.

"And Fannie y'all go on."

"You sure?"

Her face looked itchy and blotched where the powder had been.

"Yes I'm sure. I'll be just a minute. And anyway Burl's like family."

"Why, you know if there's anything I can do," said Mr. Magee.

"You want a Coke?" said Amos.

I went on out.

Will was behind me at the door and I skirted away from him and the crowd and got down to the side of the steps. Off a ways I spotted Mattie and she turned her head back squinting and nodded to me before she went off down the road. I stood and watched her, and, feeling suddenly thirsty myself, walked around back to the graveyard. The church was old—one of those toy white-painted boxes with a steeple and a church bell dating back to the time the town began. It and the parsonage were probably two of the oldest buildings. A house on the other side had been torn down to make a gravel parking lot where the cars pulled in. There were the still shade trees behind the parsonage, where chairs and lunch tables had been set up, and I walked that way. At the front of the tables were two red coolers and I reached into one and got a Cocola and opened it. Behind the first table I thought I saw a fox lying on the ground, grinning in the shade, but it turned into a dirty-marmalade dog that stood and ambled toward me, looked at me in a glazed, appraising way, sniffed my shoes, and ambled away. I drank my

Cocola from the bottle, tilting back my head and closing my eyes.

Then it all began. The crowd gathered at the graveyard. Eugenia was buried next to Uncle Lawrence. Then the crowd moved to the tables set up under the trees. At any point in the afternoon, I'd say—with the notable exception of Clarice Lytle—practically every man, woman, and child from the white side of Persia was in attendance, if only to pay respects, have a plate of dinner, and go home. Platters of fried chicken, sliced ham, potato salad, sliced tomatoes, cole slaw, pickled okra had been set up on one table. Varicolored sheet cakes, cupcakes, and cookies on another, along with the pitchers of sweet ice tea and the coolers of Coke. I fixed Mama a plate of food and took it to her. I passed Beatrice Ardor and heard her announce, "The Amish can eat this, yes, but they'll want to eat at a separate table." The Amish table was at the south end of the yard.

It kept on that way, or like that. The second helpings climbing onto plates, and the brass-and-shade afternoon, and the locusts singing, and the blacktop in front of the church glistening on its way to nowhere. I knew it was all there, but I couldn't pay attention to it. After a while, Brother Works stood and clinked his fork to a glass to signal the beginning of the testimonial, but talk at the tables was slow to settle down. All efforts looked slow through the stubborn, sticking density of air, like fish swimming through syrup, and the efforts seemed to pull against a growing magnetism of earth. The tables closest to Brother Works gradually quieted. Then he clinked his glass again and said, "This testimonial for Eugenia Boatwright has begun."

Mr. Magee pushed back his chair. He was dressed in his Sunday suit, which was a shade darker than his postal uniform. I recall looking at his collar, which was buttoned tightly to the top. He stood, his double chin quivering like rabbits toted in a sack. "I knew a little girl named Eugenia," he said, "and she's been my friend for sixty years."

He sat down. The Amish said "Amen" in unison.

"Is that it?" said Brother Works.

"Yessir," said Mr. Magee.

"Well, fine. Fine."

Apparently what Mr. Magee said was enough, because nobody else said anything. "Anything else?" Brother Works asked. "Anyone?" For an overlong moment Brother Works frowned and looked around. Then he sat down. Folk went back to their food. Gnats dive-bombed uncovered leftovers, women fanned, and Timmy Viola, whose mama had made him sit a minute too long, leaped from his seat with Boone Hardin and the two began heaving horse apples at one another. Off to the side, not far from them, stood Will. He stood for the better part of the afternoon. To look away from him I kept scanning the crowd. I was hoping it was about time for folk to head on, but few seemed to share my sentiment. Sikes Daughtry tottered on his cane toward Mr. Magee and patted him on the shoulder. Mrs. Adelia Jones and Mrs. Magee and Amos talked to Mama. Out near the road Mr. Ardor talked to the sheriff, then stopped, as a car filled with black folk passed. I watched the two men stop and turn and watch the car until it went off down the road; then they resumed their conversation. Then Brother Works approached Beatrice Ardor, pointing to the top of the church and raising his hands in an arching, expansive gesture. At the Amish table, a little girl held her mouth open in a dainty O as a father unwrapped a peppermint from its tiny crackling square of cellophane and slipped it onto her tongue. Then Sheila Jones walked up to me, with her smoothed bangs and her freckled shyness. She wore a gray plaid dress and black patent-leather flats. Faint brown hairs stirred on her arms as she stood.

"I'm sorry about Mrs. Boatwright," she said.

"Thanks."

We stood there by the Amish table. The tips of Sheila's bangs were damp and sticking to her forehead. Her gray-green eyes were heavy-lidded as she stared at the sun, and she seemed to be listening to something just behind me, the locusts in the trees.

"It's been—a nice turnout, hasn't it?" she said. "It's been—nice."

Shutting her eyes, she started to speak again, and stopped suddenly, and opened her mouth to breathe as divers do when they finally reach the surface for air. And then she fainted right in front of me. Her head cracked Mrs. Schwietert's plate. And she slipped to the ground as though she'd lost herself and become only her dress.

Mrs. Schwietert stood and gasped, "Child!"

"Dr. Butler?" I said.

"No!" said Mrs. Jones. She ran toward her daughter. The first up had been the Amish, and I saw the black clothes melt around us. But not all black, now that I looked. Dark blue, a touch of purple. I could see women's faces beneath the crowns of netting, men's beneath the beards.

"Mrs. Butler," I heard Mrs. Giddy say. "Where's your husband?"

"Out fishing," somebody said.

"This heat," said another.

"Purgatory," said another.

"He's inside," said another.

"Y'all clear back," hollered Amos. "Give her some room." And he pushed through the crowd. He blinked gravely at me.

I heard a woman's voice say, "Watch your language."

"A call of nature, then," growled Dr. Butler. "A call of nature."

"She's *fine*," Mrs. Jones said, lifting Sheila's bangs off her forehead as a host of Jesus fans fluttered around her face.

The Body

It was Monday morning, August 10. I had not slept for several nights. In fact, Mama and Mattie and I had agreed it'd be best to close the café for a week after the funeral, to give ourselves time to think. Yet this time off hadn't felt like time off, either. Mama hadn't said anything and I hadn't either, and I felt that even if I wanted to I oughtn't. Will apparently continued to stay with Amos. Then, on Sunday night, Mrs. Wade had brought over a Mississippi mud cake, which I ate without stopping. Yet I still didn't feel anything. I didn't even feel sorry for myself. I felt wooden as a puppet, and I remember being surprised to learn that my arms worked perfectly even if they were wooden, and my hands were lifting a slice to my mouth where my tongue, even if it were wooden, could taste the dark sweetness of chocolate and swallow it down. I ate without letting up, a binge unlike any I could remember. At dawn I made my way to the café. I had poured water into the coffeepot and measured coffee into the filter when Mattie walked in.

"The coffee bin don't go in the icebox," she said. "And cream don't go on the shelf."

"Sorry."

"You sure you want to work?"

"Yeah. Just keep an eye on the cream, I guess."

Mattie pulled on an apron and tied off the laces behind her back. Then she went to the sink and washed her hands and dried them on the dish towel. She pulled down the big stone-colored mixing bowl and sifted flour and baking powder and cut in shortening and rolled out the biscuit cloth and dashed flour and slid from the bowl the flesh of dough that spread soft as a sow's belly. I watched the motion of her hands. She said, "We getting low on shortening. Need to add that to the list."

"Yeah. And we need eggs too. I'll be heading out to Tchula Gaze's. Later, I guess." I thought for a second. "Flour's all right."

"Yeah," Mattie said. But her face was troubled with something else. "You stay this whole time at your mama's?"

"Yeah."

"She getting sleep?" she then said, as if not wanting to leave the first question standing alone and swelling in the silence.

"I guess."

"Lucky somebody can get some." She looked up through air clouded with flour. She looked at me. "You don't look so dandy either."

"I ate a whole chocolate cake last night."

The coffee crowd started in. Mr. Magee, Sheriff Wade, Mr. Ardor, Mr. Giddy. But Mrs. Ardor too, and Mrs. Magee, and Mrs. Hardin, with children in tow, Boone and the baby, and Mrs. Viola, with her grandson, Timmy, apparently to check on me. Women rarely came in at this hour, but each nodded and said "Good morning." The greeting itself was wishful, I realized. I was not without a severe pang, though, at the sight of Will as he came through the door and pulled himself to the counter and watched me. Well, let him. I got cups and put them on saucers. I got spoons and placed them down the counter. And I had the sense as I turned, with my back to the counter, and listened to the dry silence, and lifted the coffee from its warmer, and turned again, that for a moment everyone was looking for Eugenia, then remembering.

"Morning," Will said to me, under lowered lids. It was the same face I'd seen at the funeral, which was to say it was the face of a man who looked as though he owed somebody money. It was the face whiskered and drawn and damp-skinned and not quite purged of whatever demons and whatever it had swallowed the night before. I walked across the linoleum toward the face and the denim-shirted figure seated at the counter. Then I poured his coffee. For an instant I didn't say anything, but it seemed a long awkward time as others averted their looks, so I said, "Morning." I went on down the line touching up cups, moving through the crisp, cool room behind the sealed windows. There is nothing cooler than the café on a hot August morning, when folk have just come from outside and the air conditioner is working.

I went on down the line, but I could feel Will's eyes. Reaching. I knew their long effort and way. As I noticed the effort, the satisfaction I felt changed to a grim and prideful satisfaction. And it stayed that kind, as I saw from the tail of my eye Will's face, which showed a lowered chin and the tension of skin pulled over skull and the last days' changes. I took orders. I took his. I went in the back and got out the skillet as Mattie slid a tray of biscuits in the oven. I put on bacon and Mattie started pancake batter. I pulled two eggs from the basket and cracked them. Yellow eyes on the grill. Bacon strips on top like wrinkling eyebrows. I went back out and touched up coffee and returned. Mattie was pouring rounds of pancake batter; I carried out plates and handed Will his. He peppered his eggs and plastered butter on the pancakes, poured on syrup, sliced them in parallels, gave them a turn with the knife and fork and sliced them crosswise. By the time I came back he had just about finished it all and he looked up at me and said, as he always did, "It's good." He was waiting for me to speak and afterwards I would try to remember what it was I said. I only knew it made him ask for more and that had not been my intent. He turned and looked at the second helping I brought and poured syrup over it all steaming and started to slice and he looked back at me and down at the plate.

"Maybe a touch more," said Mr. Magee.

"Yeah, us too," called Mrs. Ardor, from the booth.

"Why don't we help you, hon," said Mrs. Viola.

"Well," said Mr. Giddy, "you know about Lee Hardin?"

"No," said the sheriff. "What about him?"

"Dr. Butler delivered his babies last night. After midnight, a boy and a girl."

"He's the proud father of twins."

"Poor bastard."

They kept on like that. And I hauled coffee around to the women, sitting together in a booth. Mrs. Viola was corraling Timmy, and Mrs. Hardin was shifting the baby on her hip, while Boone Hardin, who was such a little male, with his daddy's sharp features, sat as far from his mother as possible and blew bubbles in his milk. Now and then the women would pause and look at me. Every time I felt this, one of them would come over and gently touch my shoulder, and every time, I was more acutely aware of their pauses. Every time, I would get ready to answer, Thank you ma'am, I'm doing just fine. Mrs. Magee tried twice. Then Mrs. Viola rose and came behind the counter and with her kind, sad face, said, "You *sure* you don't need some help, hon?"

All of that.

Then there was a smell of smoke. I was speaking to Mrs. Viola when I caught it. Crust, I thought, flour, shortening, and something else, salt, an old burn. So I pushed into the kitchen. Sure enough, smoke. Sure enough, it came from the grill. And just beyond, there was Mattie. Opening the back door slowly, as though in hesitation. Holding a knife. And the back screen door groaned *aawwwww* and bounced against the door frame, once, twice, so that the framed picture of Mattie shivered like a last leaf in a winter blast.

"Mattie?" I said.

She stalked a few steps, hesitated, then ran headlong toward the back of a car. Stabbed the knife in the back tire. A black boy was driving, I could see that much; I could see a piece of his forehead just above the wheel. I had just missed some apparent scuffle, too, for when he peeled away, a white girl lay curled on the pavement.

Even now I can see it all, for it never ceases to be. I can see Sheila Jones getting up, pressing her hands into her thighs, staring with wild, wild eyes, crying *"Earn-ie!"* A scream so pure, so out of place on that quiet street that the very air seemed altered. I started toward her as the green station wagon shaved the curb and plumed exhaust down the road. I started toward her but remembered the smoke and ran back inside. Smoke was streaming from the grill. I could make out a pancake with its edge forced up by burn, and I slid a spatula under it and tossed it in the garbage.

Then I watched the men gathering outside. There was the sheriff, Mr. Magee, and Mr. Ardor. Mr. Giddy, the others. And Will.

"Will?" I whispered. I could hear the air being breathed in and out of his nostrils, quick and hard, against the bones. But he passed without looking at me and walked out the back door.

So I listened to footsteps all around the café, the engines starting. I could hear the women calling their husbands' names. It was a sound I had never heard coming from them, and as I went back outside there were trucks joining trucks—I could read them like name tags—fading down Levee Road.

I remember Mrs. Viola then, guiding Sheila inside. The rest of us fell silent. Already the sun was squeezing air from the sky. Now flies buzzed the lid of the garbage can as heat ripened the smell, frantic as they circled. Somewhere down the block, a chicken clucked. I looked toward the street.

In the distance, the sheriff turned on his siren.

And little Boone Hardin, standing by his mother, shaped his thumb and forefinger into a pistol, suddenly swung it toward my face, then swung it around, aimed it down the road, and said, "Bang! Bang!"

As he lowered his hand, I turned and saw that Mattie was shaken. She went back inside. I followed and watched as she went to the sink and washed her hands.

I said, "Mattie?" But she would not meet my eyes. She dried her hands on her apron and walked over to the remainder of biscuit dough and took the rolling pin and rolled. Then she took the biscuit cutter and plunged and lifted, hands fast against the dough.

So we went back inside the café, one hot morning in August 1962, the handful of women with their children, and Mattie and I, with Sheila Jones. And I remember feeling odd, alone, as if each of us were a separate island, in the expanding silence. Beatrice Ardor getting on the phone did not break the effect, as I thought it would; the women became more still. A church at midnight is earsplitting compared to the noise in a café if there's a particular kind of phone call being made. You stand there and pretend not to listen by looking around the room and looking anywhere but in the direction of the girl sitting alone in a booth and looking finally at the linoleum where there is a parallel trail of gritty sugar the old broom missed when first you cleaned up this morning. You pretend not to listen, though of course you do. So I stood and listened to the voice on the phone as beads of sweat burst out delicately on the upper lips of the women.

Beatrice Ardor was on the phone with Sheila Jones's mother. "I thought you should know," she said.

She spoke the hush. She spoke with a mayor's wife's authority.

"Oh, you do—" she said.

"Oh, he did—"

Now the rest of us were not even pretending not to listen.

"Well of course, we all are." She nodded grimly.

"Yes," she said. Then she hung up the phone. The rest of the women looked up. Mrs. Magee and Mrs. Hardin with the children, and Mrs. Viola who was going at Timmy with a napkin, one palm around his neck as she wiped his face hard, pinching down his nose to clear his nostrils.

I knew what I knew and now they knew too, and soon the rest would too, for while good news can travel at a glacial pace, the worst of news snaps like lightning. You could hear it as Mrs. Ardor replaced the receiver, with a tiny *click*, and turned and said, "Your mother's on her way." She said that with the hush. And waited.

Then, with the same hush but with satisfaction, she said, "She'll be here in a minute." And waited again.

And Mrs. Magee said, musingly, "It shouldn't take her long."

"At the most," said Mrs. Viola, "ten minutes."

Mrs. Magee looked at her wristwatch and said, "Five."

"Mm-hmmph," said Mrs. Ardor. And lacerated Sheila with a smile.

It was at this point that I finally looked at Sheila. She sat with her eyes caged, looking at nothing. So I went to the kitchen, where

Mattie stood with her back to me, and got a pitcher of tea from the icebox. I poured a glass. Then I went back out front. I carried it to Sheila's table. I noticed how her chest looked slack and her cheeks pinkish. The mouth slightly open and the breath through it heavy. It took me a moment to recognize the face. Certainly it was not the face of the girl in the white shirttail and jeans who had propped her schoolbooks on the counter last spring, sipping a cool vanilla shake and idly turning her straw, as she talked to me alone about her boyfriend. It was more the face of the last visit, the time she came in, sometime in July, in the middle of the afternoon. She had wanted to say something to me then, but Eugenia was there. I remembered that face, the way she was looking, the way you could feel thoughts running through the caves and tunnels of her mind but stopping just short of her mouth. Yeah, it was that face now. And I felt so sorry for it. I said, "Here," and put the glass of tea on the table.

I put down the glass of tea and tried to imagine how things would have been if she had run away with him. If that was what they were planning to do. Wasn't it? A love tryst that had fallen to a fight? And how did this get started in the first place? Hadn't she been scared? From the start? Had the thought of running away scared her? Or had the boy deceived her? Stolen the car? I could hear her breathing, and I wanted more than anything to know what was in her head, why she was sitting there and looking at nothing, while the silence seeped into her.

Then Brother Works pulled up. Through the front window we could see the Cadillac, we could make out the profile of Mrs. Jones in the passenger seat as she got out of the car. She walked to the front door. She pushed inside. And looked at her daughter for a long moment as though Sheila were a verse she had learned once, then forgotten.

"Come on," she said.

And when they left and rode away, there was the spreading silence. Mrs. Ardor turned to leave, and Mrs. Magee, and Mrs. Hardin with her children, and Mrs. Viola with her grandson, and their footsteps made no noise on the floor. Everyone had stopped making their customary motions and every voice was removed, and when I looked outside I understood that something had fallen. There was no particular thing that confirmed this. It was just the waiting, the dust motes in the window, that said *now*.

About twenty minutes after Sheila and her mother left, the Christmas bells on the door rang again and Amos walked in. His mouth open. That red head like a violated nerve. He too was quiet, and the noise of the Christmas bells was especially clear but seemed to come from a distance. He looked at me and said, "Will?"

"Yessir," I said.

He turned to leave. I said, "Wait a second," and picked up a white paper cup by the coffeepot. I poured it full and handed it to him.

"Thank you, hon," he said. He let out a long, tired, angry breath, and then he seemed to remember something. He looked at me and smiled the saddest smile imaginable. It was that smile with apology in it. It was that smile that showed what he had known from a long time back, ever since the days when Will and I were courting and he had opened the door on us that Saturday morning, in the cabin of the *Elvira*. That we had this in common, the Will who I had been with, the Will who at this moment was off somewhere, in the pickup, tailing the blue light of the sheriff's car and a string of other pickups, the Will who just minutes before had been sitting on this stool, at this counter, with his face bent over a plate, and who had not been with me then, either, but in some other place, inside himself, where something was crumbling dry and brittle like old leaves pressed in a book. We had this in common, so we paused there with the coffee between us, saying nothing. We had this in common: Will, who was what we didn't have.

Then Amos was gone. For maybe a minute again there was silence, until the phone rang and I picked up to Mrs. Butler, and listened to her questions. Sheila Jones with a colored boy? Did I think the girl was in a certain kind of trouble? Then Mrs. Works called and asked the same questions, and then Mama, and I tried to reassure her, and then Mr. Hardin, and I told him what I could, and then Mrs. Giddy, who said the town keyboard was lighting up like a Christmas tree and didn't I think the Jones girl and her mama would be heading back to Cali*for*nia?

After I hung up the phone I heard the whine of Sikes Daughtry's beagles. The pickup with dinted rusty fender, gun rack, fishing tackle, and three dogs bouncing off one another in the flatbed. He got out and closed the door and leaned on his cane. With his free hand he reached into his trouser pocket and fished around, pulled out a handkerchief, and coughed up a thick, asthmatic wad of phlegm. He crumpled the handkerchief, put it back in his pocket. Then he made it a few steps to the flatbed and reached out to scratch one of the dogs' heads. Across the street Mr. Shine ambled over to join him, and Mr. Curtis, and old man Huit, who was bench-sitting his son's drugstore. They opened the café door.

"Heard anything?" Sikes Daughtry asked, and old man Huit seemed to say something about getting what he deserved.

They started inside. Sikes Daughtry and the rest moved gradual as shadows, for a shadow does move, if you watch it long enough.

I watched and waited a spell and said, "Coffee?" And waited another spell as the question fell away and it was as though I hadn't said anything. I picked up coffee and poured. Then Sikes Daughtry said, "What time they leave?" His face like a runner-up in a beauty contest where somebody else got the prize.

And old man Huit: "Eight or so."

And Mr. Curtis: "No surprise, hear tell."

And Sikes Daughtry: "He ain't got a record."

And old man Huit: "He does now."

And Mr. Shine: "Yeah."

I looked out the window at the dogs and waited. And Sikes Daughtry raised a palsied, liver-spotted hand and counted on his fingers. "You got your car robbery. Assault. Attempted kidnapping. God knows what h'all."

Old man Huit wheezed a heavy breath and said, "Make a present of his balls." Their laughter was like a clap.

Then Mr. Huit Jr. came in with his wife and his children. They never came in at this time, with the store to run, but they sat in a booth and he got up and came over to the counter. Then the men repeated what they said, and looking to him for corroboration, heard his sudden snort. From the booth, his wife looked panicky and warned, "Beau!"; then, with her lips, "The *chil*dren."

"Oh, I'm sorry," and he too said with his lips—a whisper leaking, "I know, not in front of them."

"Well, if you don't keep your voices down they might make a c-o-n-n-e-c-t-i-o-n, between—between one thing and another."

Then somebody heard tell that the sheriff was on his way to the Joneses' house.

"To try to get it straight," said old man Huit.

"Plenty to get straight," said Mr. Shine.

"Well, I don't know how we didn't see it coming," said Mr. Huit Jr. He glanced at the others.

The men stirred with a kind of agreement.

I felt Mr. Huit Jr. glance at me. "Her getting herself," he said, "into that situation." He looked at the others. He said, "Yeah?"

From the booth Mrs. Huit then caught my eye and shook her head. What can you do for a girl like that?

"If she just had her daddy," Mr. Curtis offered, "none of this'd happened. Her daddy was here, he'd nipped it in the bud."

The men stirred again in agreement. And I thought of the story of Sheila's father. A car wreck in California. A funeral in Mississippi. Instantaneous, it was said. He had the wreck one morning as he headed to work, when a car ran a red light.

"I don't know," Mr. Huit Jr. said softly. "They keep after your daughter. What you gonna do? It's like Burl was saying—" He stopped abruptly, and looked down, and we all looked down at little Sissy Huit, who had just walked up to her father. Little Sissy, nicknamed "Tinfoil Teeth" because of her braces. She looked a little confused and frightened but pleased by this sudden attention, as if it were proof that the men might have to rally to protect her.

And Mr. Huit Jr. cupped his hand on the back of her head and said, "You get on back to the table, sugar."

And the rest of the men seemed either to continue to look at Mr. Huit Jr. with ill-concealed curiosity or to take special pains not to look anywhere except, rather fixedly and cheerfully, into his daughter's eyes. His daughter turned and walked back to the booth.

"As you was saying . . ." said Sikes Daughtry.

"As I was saying, you heard what Burl said. Just a few days back—he delivered a bill mailed to Adelia Jones—from a doctor in Jackson. An obstetrician." He waited a spell and let that sink in.

"There's no such thing as a part-white baby," said Sikes Daughtry.

"She wasn't too pretty," Mr. Curtis added, indicating Sheila with a nod. "Was she?"

The men seemed to consider this. They might have been remembering somebody from ancient history. And then one by one, they began to agree.

"Nope," said Mr. Shine.

"Not too very," said Mr. Huit Jr., as with regret.

"Ugly," old man Huit said.

"She wasn't ugly," I said suddenly. It was the first thing I said. All the men looked at me. They looked at me as though I had just come in the room.

Mr. Shine said, "Do tell."

Mr. Curtis stiffened.

And old man Huit said, "I didn't know you was a nigger-lover."

"Whoah, hoah," Sikes Daughtry said. He looked at them. He looked at me out of the sad watery eyes and said, "Hit's not what she's saying." Then he said, "You know, we mighty sorry about Eugenia and all."

I nodded my thanks, for I knew my place in this picture, and I touched up his coffee. Then I turned to old man Huit and said, "What's nigger-loving got to do with it? I like mine vanilla. All I'm saying is, she wasn't ugly. She wasn't even plain. She was cute, now that I think of it. Cute as a button."

Old Man Huit said, "You talked to her, didn't you?"

I shrugged.

Then he said, "They going to Cali*for*nia, ain't they?"

Which was the God's truth, I supposed, as I touched up their cups.

California.

Sure enough, they were packing that very day, as Brother Works later confirmed, and I wondered what heartache it caused them, fleeing home again. I wondered what disappointment Sheila's mother must have felt, in the two years since she lost her husband. Maybe she regretted leaving. Maybe she paused as she was closing a suitcase; or on her front porch as she turned to face the river and thought, How calm it all looks. How calm, in the distance, the roofs of the town with its courthouse and its church spire, and the fields, and the old house, the house of her mother, with its white paint and green shutters and front porch swing.

Or maybe when she rode away with her daughter she thought, How naive, our calm. A lot has been said about boredom in small towns, an awful lot, but I think boredom had something to do with the way we clung to Sheila's story. The way, for a long time afterward, we would ride by the Jones house, just to take a look.

The house would be empty by that evening. The shutters bolted. In the coming days Sheriff Wade would drive by to check on it, now and again. By the time school had started it became the ghost for children, the double dog dare. Spit on a grave. Let a black cat cross your path. Knock on Sheila's door, if you dare.

They were packing for California. We were sure of it. Naming that state like the final sin. Cali*for*nia. Hitting that third syllable, to sound like fornicate. Cali*for*nia. We would spend our entire lives in this town, in these houses, but we were sure that they would never, ever come back.

Yet I imagined the boy going for her. And when later, Sheriff Wade came in and said, "He got away," I might have sighed with relief. I imagined him combing the country, that green Buick station wagon crossing the river, eluding local yokels as far as the state line, maybe, then ditching the car, with its flat tire, and catching a ride on a truck, an empty train car, through Louisiana and the cowboy cactus, across mountain and sand, through grape arbors and cities, clear to the Pacific Ocean, if need be. I imagined him going till he found her, drawn forever on by that young girl's cry.

After lunch we closed down early, an hour or so early, actually, for Mattie said she had something to do. I asked her if she was all right. Her face looked a little caved-in, but her head jerked back like a bird flying into a glass door.

"Just don't say nothing," she said.

"Well I was just—"

"Just don't even start."

"*Look*, Mattie, I need to know what you saw."

"I didn't *know* it was him. Okay. You satisfied? I didn't *know* it was Earnie. And I thought that girl was getting hurt in some way."

Then she took off her apron and hung it on the meathook. She went out the back door.

So I tried to turn my thoughts to this. But there was also what the sheriff had said. And where was Will? I went out front and gave the counter and tables a wipe, dusted the booth seats, and swept the floor. The salt in the saltshakers was getting a little low so I took off the caps and refilled them. That done, I put up the broom and gave the place a final glance. I stood in the white-painted room, in the sour dress that itched, on the linoleum keen as lead on my feet. I lost one word of a question and then I lost another. I began again and forgot what I started.

"Hell's bells," I said, and decided to get out and take a walk.

I headed out Levee Road to the point where it dwindled to the dirt path that followed the river. And then on up toward the bluff. There were smells of cut grass and dust. A quarter mile out I passed the Joneses' house. Then the Ardor farm, caramel cattle in a pasture, hardly moving, and at a great distance field hands in straw hats and pants and bare brown shining backs were slowly swinging hoes over cotton rows. I headed on. For some reason, I went down the terraced drop in the bluff to my place by the willow tree on the river. There is a kind of relief that exists when you are alone. I felt that now. In a while, I'd head back and stop by the café and take Mama leftovers—ham, biscuits, corn pudding. There was a buzzard over the river. It had its wings outspread, hoarding the evening breeze. A pair of dragonflies, damping toes and soaring, making cursive writing on the air.

It was around six, I believe. I had been gazing for a time when a change registered with me. It was a change in noise, but it was more a hush than an increase. Lapping water. Tidal corduroy.

Something wriggling in the olive stew of algae. And then I saw, for the pulse of a moment, a shape in the cordgrass, against the water or painted onto it maybe, not quite discernible in the shadows of the marshy edge. I muttered something, but the shape, which could just be an evening shadow, did not move. A fallen sapling. A floating swimmer. I gasped and registered the arms and legs, strangled in riverweed. A high-top sneaker, still attached by a lace to the ankle, drifted to the side. Small waves slapped against Earnest March. He was faceup in the river.

Oh my God, I said. *Sweet-suffering Jesus*. Or I might not have said anything. I might have just thought it.

I stood. My vision going up and down like a well bucket. You might assume, seeing the body, I'd have thought of Eugenia. I could have. But what came to me was not Eugenia but a particular image from the woods, of the day last fall, of the day at dawn when Will and I were up in the deer stand, and he first told me about Sheila and Earnest. He was whispering the story of what he had seen, or what he'd thought he'd seen, at the Piggly Wiggly: Earnest bagging groceries, Sheila dropping the bag, Earnest reaching to help her, and touching her hair. And then the crackling from below, clash of dry leaves, and Will said, "Take the gun, take it! Look through the sight, look!" So I took the gun. The deer floated into the sight. Crosshairs on its heart. The shot rang out. The deer looked up, as though startled. And like a dream of itself the deer left its body and ran out and circled the meadow in one wide sweep then came back to the spot where it had been shot and, reentering its body, died.

And here. Oh. That mouth. It was the boy's mouth, grinning merrily. But not grinning, now that I looked. More like a grimace. *Fuck you* was what it looked like he was saying. *Fuck you* was maybe the last thing through his mouth. I could see it all on the yellowed teeth; flies mustaching the upper lip; I could see it on a hole in the forehead, big as a thumb, that minnows picked into strands of skin and vein. I ran behind the willow and threw up, splattering a sour burst of vomit on the base of the trunk.

As soon as I recovered, I was up the bluff. My heart was running. It seemed forever on the way up, my body sliding, as I clawed four-legged up the rock. It seemed forever down the length of dusty path that followed the edge of the bluff, and forever past cotton fields and the green pastures where cows browsed in clover. As soon as I got into town I went straight to the café. I went upstairs. I tore off my dress. I got in the tub. I plugged the stopper and turned on the faucets and sat in the rising water. And before the water could fill I saw the dress on the floor. In a little pile. I got out and stuffed it in the garbage. And cleaned up the bathroom like a murderer.

Who?

The mirror yelped from my scrubbing. The towel folded itself in a mute square. A loud CLANG downstairs and I jumped. I peeked out the window. In the parking lot, the cats playing. A loose garbage-can lid. I kept expecting something to happen, someone to come in and confront me with what I had seen. I tried to think. I tried to think what to do. And as I wiped up the bathroom floor, it struck me that I could tell somebody. There was Mama. Her long face would go taut, she would reach for the hem of her housecoat to wipe away the sweat along her hair, and then she would haul me to the courthouse to the sheriff's. Or I could go downstairs and call Mattie, and while I waited for her to speak, the greasy black phone would glow hot and slippery on my ear. Or I could tell nobody. Maybe nobody. Maybe the river had failed, but an act of God or the quick work of buzzards could still remove that body from the earth. Just a couple of days . . . No, I either tell somebody, or I don't. The act of cleaning the bathroom steadied me, gave me an almost lighthearted determination. The preacher, maybe. You can't have a death without a preacher. Or family. There was Mattie, who was his cousin, but not Mattie, but maybe—Tchula Gaze, Will said she was family, he said she was his great-grandma, didn't he? Tchula Gaze, who I was going to see; after all, I had just said this morning, I needed eggs, didn't I? But the answer to that receded. Because maybe, nobody. Maybe an act of God or the quick work of buzzards. No. All right. Either tell somebody, or don't. Yes, or no. Eeny-meany-miny-mo.

I did not know the answer.

But I found I did know it—it came to me. I got dressed. I

walked down the stairs. I walked out of the café. And I followed Levee Road again to where the path began, on feet in the dry dust, *shonk-shunk shonk-shunk*, with the land gradually rising above the river. A quarter mile out I passed the Jones house. Then the Ardor farm, the fields, the cattle. Everything stretched toward the bluff up and up higher over the water. Past the terraced drop to the willow tree, up the path to the narrow ledge.

My feet kept on. And at the end of forever I got to the highest edge. The sun was in the river. The sun was in the river, and there, with the bluff-high, cloud-drifted sky behind her, and the crucifix scarecrow, with its faint clinkling of cans, wearing that pale blue dress, her long brown breasts hanging down and loose under the gaping armholes of pale blue, and those eyes, those eyes blazing at me beneath the cloud of white hair, was Tchula Gaze. I could not look at her. I could not look directly into her face. For the entire day with all the speculation and the stories I had listened and looked straight into the faces with curiosity. I had then. It was true. But now I did not look into hers.

Then I looked into her face. She met my gaze head-on. I did not say anything. I did not need to. For, looking at me, she slowly nodded.

Tchula Gaze

AFTER MY VISIT TO TCHULA Gaze that evening, I headed back into town. I left her house and followed the path to Levee Road until it passed the café and set off toward the square. What now? I kept thinking, but the storefronts were sealed and quiet, and the trees on the courthouse lawn were still, and the quiet followed me up the steps and into the dark hall of the courthouse, where the ceiling fan whirred, and seemed to carry with it all the leftover hushed-up whispers, from this day and days before. I walked down the black oiled floor and passed paintings of old men, white-haired and somber, which were big as windows and hanging in thick gold frames. Voices drifted from the end of the hall. I got to the end. There was a window with painted letters with most of the paint peeled off. But it still said SHERIFF.

I walked into the room where Sheriff Wade was cocked back in his oak swivel chair behind the desk. On the other side, two men smoking. And as I opened the door, Sheriff Wade looked up. Then Mr. Ardor and Mr. Magee turned in their chairs.

"Fannie?"

"Hey."

"Hey, hon."

They started to stand but I motioned them to sit. I said, "I was out taking a walk and I got something"—I said *something* because it sounded important, then burst into tears—"I got something to tell you."

All the men were out of their chairs, a pair of arms gathered me in, and Mr. Magee said, "You just have a seat here, hon." He guided me to a split-bottom seat and I took it. Then he sat in the chair next to me. Then the sheriff and Mr. Ardor sat back down. On the rolltop desk a black fan stirred with little effect and wisped cigarette smoke toward the ceiling. I looked at them sitting with their legs crossed wide. On the desk was a calendar. An inkwell. A blotting pad. A pack of Camels. A wooden letter container tiered like jury boxes, and it occurred to me that I had never been in this office before.

"Now," said the sheriff, "you want to start over again?" Then he smiled at me. "No hurry, now, just take your time."

"I was out walking—"

"Thatta girl."

"—and I saw something in the river."

Then Mr. Magee said, "You want something to drink, hon?"

"Nosir."

"A Cocola?"

"Nosir."

"Well, we know what a blow this is." Mr. Magee looked at the others. He looked at me. "And you know how sorry I am—how sorry we all are—about Eugenia."

"We sure are," said Mr. Ardor.

"Mighty sorry," said Sheriff Wade.

"I didn't get a chance to say it," said Mr. Magee. "But you know how proud we are of you."

I sat looking at him.

"Winning honorable mention and all. Eugenia knew it was something good when I brought that letter in the mail. She said she just knew it."

I couldn't wait any longer, so I said, "Earnest March is lying dead in the river. He's shot dead."

"Who says?" asked Sheriff Wade.

I was so startled by the question that I snapped back, "I says." I tensed for him to rebuke me, but he did not. Instead, he stared at me, and I looked at a single drop of sweat sliding on top of his bald head. They all sat whitely. A minute, maybe, had passed, and I thought I might dissolve in the silent heat.

"A hole in his head, big as my thumb—and Tchula Gaze knew," I added finally, but I had not planned to tell them anything except that the boy was lying there. I had not planned to tell Sheriff Wade, or Mr. Magee, or Mr. Ardor, or anyone on God's earth that I saw that body, much less the boy's own great-grandmother. I had not planned to tell because I feared the next question.

"Old Tchula saw it?" Sheriff Wade worked himself forward in his chair and ground out his cigarette. Behind him, the bulletin board, with its newspaper clippings and tacked pictures, fluttered at the edges. "Don't be coy with us, hon."

The word *hon* bit this time like foil on a tooth. "I was taking a walk," I said, and I thought even the fan was suddenly quiet.

"And then?"

I started to cry again, and I said, "Yessir, I saw it. I was going walking and went down to the spot I used to go, that spot down the bluff before Tchula's, where the willow tree grows, and I saw something lying out in the grass in the marsh and then I realized that some*thing* was some*body* and I knew this was trouble."

"Old Tchula saw it?" Sheriff Wade said again.

"So I was up the bluff and back into town before I knew what to do or say or who to tell or not before I thought to go out and tell Tchula because she is his great-grandma, she is—she was, his family." Tchula was standing out on the bluff and I saw her face, saw her, slowly nodding. "So I went out to tell her but she already knew."

"What d'she know?" asked Sheriff Wade. He was sweating so much I could see the gray nest of hairs glisten above the V of his collar.

"She knew," I said. "She just—did. She just nodded her head—and I told her I was sorry—then she went into her house and I came here." Then I added, "I don't want to make any trouble."

"We know you don't, hon," said Mr. Magee, and he reached

over and patted my hand. But he would not look me in the eye, and as he reached, I realized I wanted none of it to be true. With all my heart, I wanted none of it. I had the sudden thought that I might have that drink of Cocola, and talk with them for a while and say I must have been mistaken, yeah, and then get up and go home.

But I had to know. Even as my thought of backing away receded, I knew I had to know the truth. I knew them all, and, sooner or later, I was going to have to find out. Because the truth is an awful thing. Because even if the buzzards ate the boy clean and nobody had missed him, not even his own flesh and blood, I knew Will, and I knew sooner or later, if Will had the remotest thing to do with this, he was going to walk in and turn himself in to the law, or to a sanatorium.

So I looked at Mr. Magee and liked him suddenly in a way I hadn't in years, his old shoulders and his patting hand, spotted as a bird dog. I was going to say something about Eugenia, and Will, and Mama, and the café, and the town that had been my whole life, but I knew I had to know.

So, as they waited—my thoughts must have invited a reading—the three traded looks. Then Mr. Magee looked at the sheriff and said, "We ought to—" but the sheriff raised his hand. Mr. Magee looked back at his lap.

I looked at Mr. Ardor. A fast question in his face. The flesh of his forehead bunched together like an angry exclamation point, but the sheriff nodded to him. Then, looking at me, the sheriff said, almost whispering, "Burl's right. We ought to let you know."

I looked at him.

"And first let me say, you've shed some light on this. You certainly have. Some of us tried to catch up with that boy, we did. We tried, but he got away. What maybe somebody tried—I'm not pointing any fingers now—broke every commandment but one. You understand what I'm saying?"

"Nosir."

"All but one. And that's history. History'll decide. You understand?"

"Nosir."

"Thatta girl. Now's we aired that, like Burl said, you ought to know. You don't know, do you," he asked, his voice still not much more than a whisper, "that Will is gone?"

The feeling that went through me was so strong. The room so still. I thought I had figured what was coming next, but I had not. When I spoke my voice felt lost.

"Gone?"

"Yes ma'am." And in the silence that followed he looked at me. He waited. Then said, shaking his head, "You know, he took out like a light this morning. And the last I heard, after we gave up chase for the March boy, was that Amos was out looking for him."

"Out looking for him *where?*" I turned toward Mr. Magee. "Mr. Magee? *You* want to tell me?"

But Mr. Magee dropped his face like a virgin bride. And the sheriff still shook his head as I turned toward him, very straight in the chair. The hook had found meat and he knew it.

"Now we don't know exactly, but we know Amos left on the *Elvira*."

"The *Elvira?*" I asked. A sense of loss as suffocating as actual bereavement welled up in me; I found I could say nothing.

"And of course, I'm not pointing any fingers," he continued, and I had, right then, such an overwhelmingly clear image of when I had first seen the sheriff twelve years before that the words "I'll have to ask you not to strike the witness" seemed to rush forward from that very day. He was standing at the kitchen door of the café, looking wide and hippy in his gun belt as he stepped in to look down at Will, who was on the kitchen floor, crying and rocking himself, because Eugenia had slapped him.

So I sat very straight in my chair, looked at the sheriff, and took it.

"Fannie," he said softly, "you know what we got to do next."

"I believe so."

"You remember where you saw it?"

"Yessir."

"Well, we better be heading on," he said, looking at his watch. "It's not getting any lighter."

"I'll go check on her mother," Mr. Magee offered. "So she won't—"

"Quite so, and I'm—" Mr. Ardor said.

"We can discuss—" the sheriff said.

Each sentence had been brought up short; immediately, everyone got out of their chairs and walked out.

This ain't happening, I thought, as I followed the sheriff to his car. Two pickups were parked alongside, and Mr. Magee went toward one of them. I watched him. He rushed to fumble his keys at the lock, opened the door, and turned his head in my direction, once again dropping his face. I looked away. Then the sheriff opened the door for me and I got in the front seat and Mr. Ardor got in the back and I rolled down the window. Even in the town air I could smell grass and manure and sweat.

"All right?" Sheriff Wade said above the cranking engine.

"All right," I answered.

"All right," he said again, and we rode like that with the engine purring under the metal hood.

I saw a flashlight stowed in the center of the front seat, in front of the CB radio, along with a toolbox, some fishing tackle. As soon as we were on Levee Road I wondered exactly what we would do with the boy's body, once we got out to the river. The backseat? And how would we get the body up the bluff? I was worried about this as I lowered my eyes to look at the fresh dirt still wedged in the sheriff's boot soles make black crust on the mat of the car.

At the edge of Levee Road the car stopped and the sheriff turned off the engine. He picked up the flashlight and got out. At once, a vast silence fell over the road and the bluff. Then the sound of water could be heard.

I got out of the car and looked at the river below me, visible as a broad silver motion, flecked with occasional shimmers. A denser darkness across the way, the Louisiana coast. Night was falling and a change was in the air. The dark sky looked liquid. Overhead thick gray clouds had begun to pile, except to the west, beyond the tree line, where the last light glowed through the break. The water was very still, and suddenly dark with evening, and away on out I could see green trees tingeing black. A river barge, hard at it. A smoking cigar on a mirror. The sheriff was walking beside me, and Mr. Ardor, a step behind.

"We better hurry," said the sheriff. "It's gonna blow."

"Pretty soon," said Mr. Ardor.

"Yeah." The sheriff hesitated and looked off at the sky.

"Are we close?" said Mr. Ardor.

"Not yet," I said. "About a quarter mile." Then I realized with a jolt that the two of them knew where Earnest was, knew as well as I did. But Mr. Ardor let my answer stand, and we walked on, scanning the sky, past the Jones house, cotton fields, and the posts that were all that was left of a duck blind on the edge of the Ardor farm.

"There," I said, and pointed to the terraced drop down the bluff. I climbed down ahead of them, wind lifting hot up my dress. It flapped a little; it was rising out of the west so the willow tree groaned and wrestled with it. Ridges of river nudged off, lapping a slapping sound. I walked ahead, maybe to see if the first of my wishes, act of God or bird or water, had removed the body from this earth. Then, as if to answer, it was not there; there was only the black water over the low, slippery bank. Was it underneath? I leaned forward. A figure loomed on the black, blurred like the moon under mackerel clouds, two figures, three.

"What?" I said.

"What?" said the sheriff.

"It was here."

"What was here?"

"The body."

There was still just enough light to see, but the sheriff turned on the flashlight and moved the cone of light over the water. "The body was here?"

"Right here."

"You sure?"

"I'm positive."

"You absolutely sure?"

"I told you. It was here. *Right here*."

"Right here?"

"Yessir. How many times I got to say it?"

The sheriff's face darkened. He looked past me. Mr. Ardor stood quietly to the side.

"What time you say you saw this?"

"Around five."

"Because it's been known, it's been known, that the water can play tricks on you. A bloated dog carcass. A deer."

"It wasn't a deer."

"Particularly somebody in your state. Your losses and all."

At that point I wanted to tell the sheriff what he was full of. I wanted to. But there was some border I was skirting and I was again besieged with such distracting questions and disloyalties that I prayed before I knew I was praying and I spoke sweetly before I knew why. "Yessir, I understand. I do. Really. But my eyes are fine."

The sheriff shook his head. He turned off the flashlight and set it down and pulled his cigarettes partway from his pocket without removing the pack. He got a lighter from his trousers and tried to light one, but the wind kept getting up. A sudden gust blew out the flame; he flicked it again. I stood waiting. I sniffed the air. Something seemed to move and swing in it, ready to slap us. Finally he got the cigarette lit with his hand cupped over it against the wind and put the lighter back in his pocket.

"Now you know what we want, hon. You know what we want. And if somebody did do this—I'm not pointing any fingers—he broke every commandment but one. It's history—" But before the sheriff could go any further a wall of wind hit and stirred water that lapped his boots and sent him backwards, sliding butt first on the marshy edge, and if it hadn't been for a lucky angle his head would have hit the willow tree with nothing to stop it but the hard thud of wood. Mr. Ardor jumped forward to help him. A dull howling began; the willow protested and groaned. A bug blew in my face as Mr. Ardor opened his mouth and shut it again. The wind bore over the river like a creature from another dimension, caged and screaming. The willow blew yellow and upward, like hair.

Mr. Ardor had his hands under the sheriff's elbows. "Go," he mouthed. "Let's *go*."

But the sheriff had a tough time hearing; he was shoving Mr. Ardor away, beet-faced and clutching for his cigarette in the grass, fighting the air that had worked its way inside.

"*—oddammit.*" The sheriff stood. Mr. Ardor pointed up the bluff. The very base of the willow began to shift, to move laterally and to complain.

Mr. Ardor pulled at the sheriff's sleeve.

"Stop. Go back.—is—*not safe*."

"The great-grandma," said the sheriff, poising his face like a divining rod, and started climbing back up the bluff.

We followed. We set out up the bluff and down the path. The air full of noises. There was a whining rippling, which I saw was the cotton branches whipping to and fro, tossing their froth of thorny twigs from earth to sky to earth. Lightning bugs sliced past our cheeks onto the cotton leaves, with a silver tapping, like rain. We hurried on, our cheeks whipped by flying leaves and streaking sap. A vague *cluck-cluck* of chickens. And then the empty, demented clankling, the cans on the crucifix scarecrow.

By this time night had fallen and swirled dark blue and touched at the edges with red dots and dashes that the sheriff's cigarette made as he walked, but beyond all this glimmered the flickering windows of the shack, and the dark ghostly figure of a woman, standing in the open door, silhouetted against the light.

I knew the figure. I said, "Mattie?"

Mattie looked up very slowly. She seemed hooded and dour and disoriented as she stood with her shoes planted, and her arms crossed. I looked into the face, which then drew in a breath harshly against the bridge of her nose, and, holding it there, she looked only at me. She said, "Tchula's dead."

I looked at her steady for thirty seconds, and there was not a sound but the sound of wind clankling cans on the bluff. I was listening to it.

Then I said, "Dead?"

"Flat on the bed," Mattie said, and leaned toward me with what seemed a barely veiled and poisonous triumph flickering in her eyes and in her voice. "She laid down flat on the bed and died. She was ready, poor thing."

"But I was just here."

"And I just found her."

"D'you talk to her?" said the sheriff, stepping up. He examined Mattie attentively with his small, yellow eyes.

"I didn't."

"What time you come?"

"After work."

"What for?"

"To check up on her," Mattie said slowly. "To see how she was."

The sheriff looked at her for a moment longer, like a child caught in the act. Then he said, "Where is she?"

So, in Tchula Gaze's shack, with that strange gathering of seekers and hunters, I walked inside, to candlelight, with the wind howling past, and the panes of the window rattling with flying debris as it raced off the bluff.

In the shack, I saw nothing at first but the guttering fire in the hearth. Then a table with a single candle, a wood bed with a woman lying on it. A lumpy pillow, a bare sheet crumpled to her chin. A basket of eggs by the door to the kitchen. Various tattered underclothes drying in front of the fire.

Sheriff Wade went straight toward the body. Mattie stood aside without a word. The sheriff stopped by the bed and lifted Tchula's hand. He felt for a pulse. Behind him, Mr. Ardor stood a step away, hesitated, then walked to the side of the bed. The sheriff looked up at him. He nodded. He said, again, without turning around, "You say you talked to her?"

"I didn't."

"What time you come?"

"A while after work. Six or so."

"What about?"

"What?"

"What'd you talk about?" The sheriff turned around.

Mattie shook her head. "I already said. She was dead. She was flat on the bed."

"You say she was ready?"

"Ready?"

"You said, 'She was ready, poor thing.' "

"She was."

"Why you say that?"

"She was ninety-two."

"Ninety-two?" The sheriff peered sideways at the body as he seemed to revise what he was about to say.

Then he walked into the kitchen. Mr. Ardor followed.

I stood in the hot silence. The candle flame and the image of the candle flame caught in the window, twisted and righted as the two men passed. The smell of smoke was choking. Mattie looked over at me and I came slowly forward. I stopped by the bed. I studied her age-crusted face. And this time I did think of Eugenia. The violet-papery lids closed, lying in the dark room, her nose the highest thing on her. That is not rest, I thought. That is not rest.

It was howling outside and hot and no sound of rain yet as I turned and walked into the kitchen. There was a frail moth smell mixing with the flavors of egg and old chicken, kerosene, the melting wax of candles. Earthenware dishes on a table. On the edge of a broken half of eggshell, its inner skin translucent and gleaming, a wasp pulsed, and I imagined the boy here with Tchula frying up supper, in the steaming saucepan, over the hearth, the black smoke of lard on the air. Just across the room was a cot made of two sawhorses and a slab of wood and a thin ticking mattress on top of that, a gray felt blanket. The bed was neatly made. There were some old books stacked on it. The top one said MATHEMATICS. Just above was one western window with a dark watery view of stubble-grass and the chicken pen on the bluff.

The sheriff said, "Who slept here?"

"The boy," Mattie said, appearing at the door.

"What's his name?"

"Earnest," she said, her face hardening suddenly. She looked out the window as though all her hate were there. Then the sheriff looked over the table. He picked up the books and flipped the pages. He hiked his britches on his thighs and squatted down. He looked under the bed. He slid an arm around and pulled out another book. He stood, opened it, and stopped. He said, "This is a library book." He peered at Mattie.

And Mattie said, "I don't know nothing about it."

And the sheriff said, "You kin, ain't you?"

"Cousins."

He looked over at Mr. Ardor. Mr. Ardor was standing slightly aback with his hands in his pockets. But he did nod at the sheriff.

The sheriff stood drumming his fingers on the cover of the book. His head did a massive quarter revolution from me to Mattie. He was apparently deciding something. He was deciding how to deal with the problem. Then he sighed. He had decided the answer to the problem was that there was not a problem. "You'll take care of this, then," he said to Mattie. "You'll get your preacher?"

"I'll get him."

"Well, all right then." He put the book down on the bed. He looked toward the window. Then he said, "Let's get on out of here. It's gonna blow."

We started out. Back through the front room where Mattie stopped by the bed and blew out the candle, back past the hearth with its smoldering embers, and out the front door. The weather was still sideways and the four of us pushed against it and I tried to push the hair from my eyes. The sheriff turned on his flashlight. Yards away the chickens in their pens made a frantic clucking, and in the beam of his light, briefly, we saw a mustard tomcat slinking his haunt along the bluff. Far below, the river roiled with wind and clankling cans, and his tail swished and languidly swayed; his glow-green eyes became slits.

A flash of lightning. Crack of drums and cymbals. Again the flash, whiting the river that rolled up to meet it, so that the world here seemed reversed too, silver water above rolling cloud. Still again, and the sudden snapshot of the sheriff and Mr. Ardor, and Mattie, against the river. I was still listening to this sound, and the great pervasive sound beneath it, which might have come equally from the rustling of water or of the fields. I was still listening when we got to the edge of town and the sheriff offered me a ride home, but I hollered that I needed to stop by the café. I needed to get up some leftovers for my mother, and couldn't Mattie come with me? She nodded. Then the sheriff hesitated and looked over at me with a question on his face so I nodded, real slow. He seemed satisfied with that and then he said some words that got lost on the wind. He and Mr. Ardor got in the car. They pulled away. By this time the rain had begun, big, hard, single spits that spotted the floury dust of the path. Then it was a driving rain, and the dust disappeared.

We took off running, with the rain whipping our skin, and reached the café, and got inside. Looking back out the window, Mattie stood, with her streaming black woolly hair loose, and her shoulders hunched as though she were about to shiver.

I said, "I'll get leftovers."

And Mattie said, "I'll get them."

We walked to the kitchen. Then Mattie surprised me as she walked to the cupboard, pulled out Eugenia's cooking sherry, and took a swig. She offered me the bottle.

I said, "Go-odawmighty no."

She didn't say anything to that and then she put down the bottle. She went to the icebox and pulled out two wrapped dishes and a pan. She unwrapped each on the drain board and got a smaller pan from the cupboard. She scooped biscuits, fried okra, sliced ham. She started for the drawer that held tinfoil. Then she said, leaning down, "Your mama's probably getting worried."

"She'll be all right."

"Well, it's best you get on."

She carried the tinfoil over to the drain board. She had her back to me as I said, "So, d'you tell them the truth?"

"You think it'd make any difference what I told them?"

I shrugged. "I don't know. I don't know a damn thing anymore."

"The truth is what happened. It ain't what comes out of folks' mouths. Tchula said that once."

We heard the water pan dripping in the icebox. Rain on the roof, like tambourines. I said, "I'm sorry about Tchula."

Mattie was pulling a sheet of tinfoil from the box. Then she stopped. I stood watching her.

"When I'd visit her in the old days," she said, "I'd see her standing on the bluff. Staring out at the river. Or more likely the sky. Watching for ducks. When it was a clear day out."

And then, as it is said when two people fall silent in a room, an angel passed.

"D'you see something?" I asked.

Mattie stopped pulling the sheet and said, "D'you?" and as I looked at her face now I didn't see her usual face, but another face under it, as though the first were a veil of glass and now I could see through to the other one. I looked at the second one and saw the full upper lip, and the purplish flex of muscle in the cheek where the jawbone hinges on.

I didn't answer her. Then Mattie said, "I thought so."

I turned slightly from her toward the stove and I didn't see any help there. Then I closed my eyes. I said, again, "Did you?"

"Did I see? Earnie gone. Tchula dead. White men with ants in their pants. A couple of white men a mile out in the country with nothing to keep us company but the wind. I got eyes. But I'm not stupid. And I ain't a fool."

"What you getting at?"

"What I'm getting at is," and Mattie crimped the tinfoil on the leftovers. "What I'm getting at is, I know what you gonna do."

"Oh really?"

"Really." And what struck me here, as much as what Mattie was saying, was the way she was saying it, in a voice that made you think of rubbing a cotton boll along your cheek, just as soft.

"Well, do enlighten me. How you come to know this? Another dream of yours?"

And Mattie said, "The Lord tears down the world every day and builds it back up by sunrise."

"Now what the hell, pray tell, is that supposed to mean?"

"Figure it out for yourself, Missy." Mattie rested the leftovers in my hand. She took the armhole apron off the hook and wrapped it over her head and shoulders like a shawl. She pushed open the screen door. Then she was off, blurred in the rain, nightrunning down Levee Road.

Chocolate

FIGURE IT OUT, FIGURE IT OUT, I kept hearing, but there was nobody else in the café. As I made my way out the door and down the road, it turned out that I was questioned only by my mother. The rain had slowed. I heard her voice before I got to the front porch.

"Fannie?"

"Yessum."

The rain drizzled in sheets over the edge of the roof. Mama stood in the doorway, holding the collar of the housecoat.

"Fannie, don't panic now. Are you all right? Now listen carefully. Burl told me. It's best we talk now. We'll sit down and talk and then we'll take things as they come." She forced a strict calm into her voice. "Right *now*."

I followed her into the house. Inside the hall small patches of vapor clung to the light, and several long wet footprints showed that a visitor had been there. Everything in this light seemed weighted with damp, the runnels of window and floorboard, the wallpaper that peeled back and scrolled near the ceiling, the housecoat that revealed beneath its hem a fluid ruffle of nightgown and furry hurried slippers. Mama padded down the hall. At the kitchen door I handed her the leftovers.

"Burl came when I was in the bath," she said. "He marched right into the house, imagine that. Imagine a neighbor doing that. Still, in this emergency, he remained discreet. He left the door open."

She set the leftovers on the counter. She got two mugs and poured coffee. I sat down at the kitchen table.

Then she placed a mug in front of me and sat down. I watched her hesitate. She said, in a lowered voice, "You thought you saw something."

"Yessum."

"And?"

"I saw—it. I saw *him*. Then I came back. Then I saw Tchula. One minute alive, and then the next one dead. Mattie was there. And Tchula. Flat on the bed."

"What time was this?"

"After work."

"At Tchula's?"

"No'm, the first time I went. To the river."

"And he was—"

"In the river."

Next to me, Mama had wrapped both hands tightly around the mug and brought it under her chin.

"And you went to, where then—Tchula's?"

"No'm, I came back to town. Then I went to Tchula's."

"After you thought you saw the body."

I took a deep breath. "I told you. I *did* see it."

Still holding her mug, Mama stood and walked toward the sink. "And would you say, at the river, anyone else saw this?"

"I don't think so."

"Think, Fannie. Think carefully. When you left the river did you notice anyone else?"

"At the river, no. Nobody else was there."

Mama looked away from me and out the window. Then she muttered softly to herself. "He could have gotten away. Ditched that car and headed on. Headed on . . . California . . . Or heading north . . . Like Burl said, he could be halfway to Chicago. . . ."

I tried to interrupt her. "Mama."

But her reverie continued. "Caught a ride? That wouldn't be hard. Caught a ride with some colored family. Caught a ride and headed on."

"Stop it, Mama."

She stood over the sink holding her coffee mug. She stood like that a long time, holding the mug and staring out at the night.

So I took advantage of the pause to ask, "Is this what Mr. Magee told you?" I wanted to know. I wanted to know, but she didn't answer.

I pushed a little harder. "Did he say—"

Mama cut me off. "Does anyone else know? Are you sure no one else saw him?"

"I didn't see anyone, but . . ."

"But what, Fannie?"

"Maybe Mattie saw him."

Mama pulled her face back as though she were dodging a fist. "Mattie?"

I nodded.

"Good Lord. Lord have mercy. Mattie saw."

"Maybe . . ."

"What makes you think Mattie saw?"

"She said . . . I don't know. She was acting funny. And after we got back from Tchula's she came with me to the café. She helped me get leftovers. I just think she might."

"Good Lord." She walked back to the table. She sat down. Then she said, "Okay now. Did you tell her what you saw?"

"No'm."

"So she might have been wondering."

"Yessum. I mean, no'm. I mean, she *knew*. She knew I saw the body. Or she knew I'd discovered something. She was out at Tchula's and here I come waltzing in with the sheriff and Mr. Ardor and, she just guessed, I guess."

Then Mama said, "Guessing isn't knowing."

"Hunh, you don't know Mattie."

"Still," she mused. "If that's so, well, then that doesn't change much. That doesn't change much at all."

"Maybe. Maybe Mattie wouldn't say anything. Maybe she wouldn't say a word. But she knows."

"Knows what?"

"She knows *I* know." I was close to tears. "She knows I know *something* about a *murder*. And there she'll be, day after day. With that look. I'm not gonna live with that look."

Mama placed her hands on the table, and I looked at them. In the flat brightness the first thing I noticed were the spots, just several, too big for freckles yet too soon for age, and the familiar squared nails, half-moon ghosts of cuticles, worn by years of laundering yet reliably creamed, and the thin white negative image of a watch patterned against her tanned wrist. I looked at them and wanted them to do something. I wanted them to take me in.

But Mama sighed and said, "Well, you don't have to decide anything right now." In the sigh I thought I heard both resignation and resentment, and so I got up to leave the room.

"Maybe just get some sleep," she said.

I stood with my hands dangling.

"Fannie?"

"Yessum."

"Is it true about Will?"

I held my face away so she could not see what I was doing. Then I wiped my eyes with the back of my hand and immediately wished I hadn't. "Is what true about Will?"

"Well—Burl said—that if anything happened to that boy that—"

"And I suppose you believe him."

"I'm asking you."

"It didn't sound like it."

"Look, I'm sorry," she said.

Back in my bedroom I looked out my window into the night. The day's tall green tree was dark and enclosing; across my window rivulets of rain branched and trickled. I could have shut my curtains against the rain but could not so much close out the strangeness outside. I put out the light and watched it all so gray, in the sudden dark of the room, in which the rain was more animated now, thicker and slower. I got my nightgown from my suitcase. I put it on and climbed into bed. The rain fell. I could just lie here. But now as I started to close my eyes I had a sense like the primitive infant fear of something coming up and striking me from under the bed. So I got up and went down the hall. I went to the kitchen, opened the icebox, and found a couple of Hershey's bars in the door. I unwrapped them one at a time while I paced and listened to rain patter and slide down the edge of the roof.

I got a good pace out of it. I broke off squares of chocolate, their sound soft as an easy conscience, and soon was no longer thinking of the things I had been thinking all night.

For instance. But there was not any one thing in particular. Not at first. I was pacing back through memory. And the pacing, and the rain, and something else, made it possible for me to put thinking on the back burner. Nothing uncertain in these memories, as I somehow identified my own movement with the measured trickle. Is uncertainty the worst of emotions, the one that can swing you between horrible hope and fear? And what is nostalgia but a forgetting of uncertainty, an amnesia of sorts, the attempt to attach meaning to one event without looking at the others? Well, I was doing that now. I was remembering and gently pacing. And if you ever have such a feeling I'd advise a quick cold shower, a jump in the river, a purge of hoodoo, or go to the nearest preacher and let yourself get saved.

But I was gently pacing, and the hands of someone big were lifting me gently to the bed. And the woman with the green eyes and brown hair and lines at her eyes faint as thread leaned over me and kissed me good night and left the faint smell of detergent through the dark. And the tall man in the armhole apron lifted over his head a platter big as Moon Lake as he walked across the café. And Eugenia leaned across the table with her glasses swinging from their chain and said, "Bon evenin'." And Mattie kneaded in a waltz of flour and bored black eyes through me so my twin reflections returned, tiny and pale on polished glass. And Tchula, with her white hair and her long brown breasts, said, "Don't be messing with my eggs." And Burl Magee, in his blue postal uniform, sucked in his stomach as he knocked on Mama's door. And I drifted on a river, while the birds flew to the sun, and barges carried hidden treasures to lands faraway. And always there was Will.

Little boys wear blue jeans that fray and floss over their scuffed knees, and they wear black high-topped sneakers with laces that keep coming undone, and their cowlicks are slicked down with Brylcreem on the first day of school but keep sprigging back up. That was Will and it was the first day of the first grade. And little boys climb the pier steps behind their father—following his example without being told to do so by holding their hands as he held his larger one, just an inch above the bleached wood rail of the pier. That was Will. Little boys are drawn like magnets to the STOP sign at the end of the street and they jump up to slap its metal face. That was Will. Little boys offer you a lunch bag at school and you open it to find a little garden snake, just a little garden snake, mind you, but before you know it you drop the bag and scream and the boys holler "Chicken!" And then one day you are alone, one Saturday when you are perfectly alone and fishing on the edge of the water, minding your own business, the boy walks up out of nowhere and doesn't holler "Chicken!" but just looks at you with big eyes coming out of a tan, smooth face, and you turn away and pretend to be concentrating on the fish. That was Will.

The first of my days were Will. And the first of my nights. I had a certain naive expectation and that was Will. In those days I could fall down a well and find a summer orchard full of peaches. Or catch a fishhook on the drowned booty of a pirate, that would ultimately pay for my trip to chef's school, and, somehow, that was Will too.

A day in high school, for instance. Early fall. I was coming out of PE and headed to the girls' showers and I was talking to Beverly Hardin. We were busy talking as I walked into Will. I walked right into him, without looking. I almost fell over him, and put up a hand to steady myself on his chest and he threw up a hand and clasped my waist under the damp of my sticky shirt.

And there it was, the electric jolt, like that emitted by a reading lamp when an unsuspecting child puts her finger in the empty socket. I got somehow back from him, briefly clutching the shoulder and then letting it go as though it stung. His hands were damp. He was certainly not now a little boy wearing black high-top sneakers and fraying jeans with a cowlick sticking up. He had on his gym clothes, which were damp, and baggy, and which did nothing in their bagginess but suggest the body underneath, and the hair, I saw, was damp too, running across his forehead, and seemed in its blackness to have a tinge of purple, like grape shadows. Purple shadow above his lip. Which I had never noticed before.

What was *that?* I wondered. Did he just give that shock, or did he feel it? But my body knew perfectly well he had felt it. When I looked up, his face flushed. Then he said, "Hey," huskily, and took off running across the court, speeding up enough to take a running leap at the basketball goal and swat the net with his hand, just as Beverly Hardin rolled her eyes and said, "Ooo-*woooo.*"

For a moment, after he left, the laces still swinging. In my chest, a high basketball net of happiness.

That had been in the fall. Our freshman year. That had been in the fall after the summer of the Saturday morning, the Saturday morning when I was perfectly alone and fishing on the edge of the water, and the boy walked up out of nowhere and I knew high school had begun.

It had begun. It had begun a time that wasn't like any other. Will and I were almost always together and my mind jumped across to another time. A time that had no particular connection to our childhood or passion, or anything whatsoever to do with innocence. What came to my mind, then, with increasing clarity was a day Will and I went to a birthday party. This time, summer. The year before we got married.

We had gone to a birthday party at the Ardors' house, or, rather, stopped by, I suppose, for Mrs. Ardor had ordered a cake. For her son, Ferrol, who was seven. A turtle. It was what he requested. Green icing, olive green, amber eyes, the shell of smooth ganache and piping sealed in clear syrup. I even put in an angry mouth, snipped licorice on the feet, for claws. I set this on a platter and covered it with cellophane. When we stopped by the house, I let Will carry it in.

By the time we got there, the party was in full form. Balloons quivered, and the chandelier had been dimmed to allow for the effect of hung bulbed strings of lights. There were books to the ceiling and an old smell like cheddar, a red Turkey rug that had on it, I believe, unicorns. Into the midst of all this walked Mr. Ardor, his face bookish too, and he stood as Mrs. Ardor spoke to mothers who had brought their children. She had on a dress the color of the rug and a girdle and high heels. She took a present and arranged it on the coffee table, then advanced around the room, her head bobbing. Her gaze went right over me.

They were royalty in this room, because of their name and what they'd built. They had the land of their farm and the mayorship and Ardor Department Store too, and here the old photographs in silver frames and coats of arms on the wall and geneaology charts to show who they were. They were aristocracy. Here too the threadworn chairs, never re-covered because Great-Granddaddy Ardor, who was the great-grandson of who-was-it?, sat there. Anyway, we arrived to see this, and, of course, the kids. They must have invited the whole class, I'll give them that. The Shines and the Butlers, the Hardins, Timmy Viola, and even that Daughtry kid, Melvin. I can remember, even now, how the other little kids looked clean and had on good clothes and shoes and the Daughtry kid didn't. I remember they each brought presents. Everyone's was nicely wrapped, except Melvin's. He'd brought something he'd just bought, from Piggly Wiggly, it looked like a cellophane bag of chocolate candies. I guess his mother or father gave him a nickel or a dime and he went in and picked something out. I guess that's what he would have liked for himself. His parents didn't have a whole lot; he couldn't have had too many toys. But it was a hot day and he'd been carrying it in his hand and by the time he gave it to Ferrol it was melted, just one nasty bag of goo, and the other kids laughed.

At that point Will and I were walking through the room. We were delivering the cake to the kitchen and then we were going to leave. But Will walked over to Melvin. "Aw," he said, "it's still good.

"Isn't it?" he said, looking at me. He nodded to the boy. He was holding the cake with one hand and he took the bag with the other, as we walked back into the kitchen.

"Man," he said, holding the bag with two fingers, at the corner. "Don't you think you could whip up something chocolate to go with the cake, so you could take it out there and say it was made out of Melvin's candy? That wouldn't be hard, would it?"

So you know what I did? I opened that bag of chocolates, melted the whole batch down in a pan, and poured it around the cake, to look like a mud puddle. And believe me, I'm telling the truth, did those kids love that cake.

I thought about that. I thought about that, as I was pacing in Mama's kitchen.

Could *this* man be connected, in any way, to a killing?

No.

I don't believe so.

Then I thought about what the sheriff had said. About Earnest March and all of it. The implications he made connecting Will to a murder spun me sideways and backwards. One minute I could almost shrug it off as another of the sheriff's lies. The next, the possibility of Will's involvement battered my senses. Why, after all, would he have run off? He had been with the men—surely he had seen the killing? Had he maybe tried to stop them in some way? That would explain the sheriff's anger. Or had he stood to the side and not done anything? Or had he run away because of his shame about Clarice Lytle? For this was the same Will who betrayed me, the same Will I found a week ago with Clarice on the *Elvira*. You try to attach meaning to one event and then you realize this is in vain. Getting ready for the weekend, for the promise of a Friday night, I had failed to imagine for Will, just as I had failed to imagine for my time at the café, any other life but the promising one I had presented myself, although even as I paced I was aware of the stunned naive fantasy through which I moved. Of time draining itself like a slow rain.

So this too was Will. Pacing there, I had what I thought was a refreshing perspective and saw that the boy I had married had not been true and fine but just a boy. I saw that he had not been mine but merely near, and though he had taken me in his arms he had not fallen for me, but had merely felt that mysterious jolt in the pulse. I was handy and love was a name for the mysterious jolt. And none of it mattered anyway, now, did it, for it had all come down to one thing: fleeing the town you were born in. And at the moment of thinking this, I especially clung to the word *flee*. I thought that word fit Will. That his life was a flight. And Sheila and Earnest, Sheila on a bus with her mother and Earnest floating in the river, and they too were gone. Long gone.

Who drops the path of crumbs that draws you? Toward this person here in your vision. The dreams of a girl, waking, mouth on her pillow, the O of wet there, like a grade-school morning, lipprints of breath on the bedspread chenille.

By this time I quit pacing. I dropped the tinfoil wrapper in the garbage. Then I stopped and looked around the kitchen. The faint, delicate tick of the clock; the dishes drying by the sink. Then I thought of Eugenia. All of a sudden I felt I could not bear to be alone. I walked down the hall, stopped at Mama's room, cracked the door and peeked in, but she was asleep. She was snoring a little, a fact that would embarrass her. Then I tiptoed on down the hall. I got into bed. I pulled up the sheet and mashed an ear to the pillow and listened to my beating heart, the way I will listen to pattering rain. Three A.M. Everyone asleep but me.

By five I had not yet accepted the thickening moss on my teeth and tongue and the green speck of pain in my head as a coming headache. I got up from the bed. I went into the bathroom and brushed my teeth. I took some aspirin and took a shower. I got dressed and put on coffee. Now instead of the headache I had a space in my head, a clear precarious space with a light buzz behind it. By six I walked out, just as Mama was stirring, into the deep morning shade of the front porch, and walked down the road, wincing in the sunlight, which was just breaking, ragtag blue through dissolving cloud. Out on the pier the *Elvira* was gone.

Then a car passed and honked, and I winced again. But I still lifted a hand to wave, without looking to see who it was, and unlocked the front door to the café as tires sizzled through leftover rain like something dropped in a hot skillet.

I went inside. *Tingaling* of Christmas bells and I turned the CLOSED sign to OPEN. I walked around the counter. I unlocked the cash register and put the keys on the shelf underneath. All quiet except the drone of air-conditioning and I pushed open the swinging door. Mattie and a black-clothed figure stood, waiting in the kitchen.

Her preacher. Something in me lurched a little, even before I recognized him. Mattie was putting on coffee and he stood peering at me. Certainly I had no reason to expect to find him in our kitchen.

Mattie said, "Fannie, this is Reverend Roberts. Reverend Roberts, Mrs. Fannie Leary."

"How do you do." He extended his hand. His voice deep and formal. I had seen him, a few times, perhaps at a distance, but often enough now for recognition to kick in. Certainly he was older than I remembered, the white patches of hair coiling cottonly at the temples, the steel-rimmed glasses recklessly loose on the nose and the brown eyes behind, the shoulders held and pulled back as though pulling against the balanced, growing, carefully held weight of the belly, as though it were a bag of flour or a sack of potatoes, carried by a buyer with a long walk ahead. The front of his jacket barely buttoned. His neck almost black against his white collar.

He stood, blinking gravely at me, for he too had apparently just come out of the early sunshine and into the dimmer light of the kitchen.

"How do you do," I said to Reverend Roberts. I took his hand.

"Just fine, thank you."

I looked over at Mattie. The question on my face. So she looked from Reverend Roberts to me.

Then she said, "I thought you'd like to talk," with a complicated mixture of satisfaction and accusation. She said it that way. I felt a huge irritability mounting inside me, compounded by my distress at hearing *tingaling* of bells and the sheriff's morning voice singing out my name.

"Fannie?"

"Yessir?"

"You back there?"

"Yessir, I'll be right out."

I glared at Mattie. Was it the alarms set off by the sheriff's voice? Or the fact the reverend was a stranger that allowed what was to happen?

Mattie said, "I'll take the coffee."

And I said, "Like hell you will."

Now it was Mattie's turn to glare at me. I said, "What you think you doing?"

"You know what I'm doing."

I sure as hell do, I wanted to say. There is a way to ambush a person and you say, "I thought you'd like to talk." You say it quick and sharp, and if you say it quick and sharp out of thin air, you may get an answer you'd never get otherwise. If the person you ask is off guard, the quick sharp remark may ambush the prey in the deep thicket, may surprise the words out of her before she can think.

But I dodged a little and said, "My, my. Well, I've seen it all now. Just barging at me when I'm trying to go about my business. We got a business to run here, in case you've forgotten. It's almost seven and I can't feed them air, but no, you got to bring the good reverend back here 'cause that's all we need to do. Stand around lolligagging because Mattie says, 'I thought you'd like to talk,' and just—what you want me to do? What you—*NNHhhh . . . aw God!*"

So Mattie stood, the reverend continued to peer at me. And the absorbent silence sucked up my sobbing groan like blotting paper.

Then I said, "I don't want anybody to get hurt."

Later, when I thought of this moment, I realized I was apologizing. To who? I wondered. For what? For rudeness to the reverend? For not stopping a murder? How could I have known? I was at work, where I was supposed to be. For finding the body? For telling Tchula? For reporting it to the sheriff? For staying in

Persia? For not going to college? For being married to Will, who hadn't or had done God-knows-what? Surely the Old Testament was wrong and we don't pay for sins of our families.

Maybe Mattie heard the tone in my voice, for she was looking at me strangely.

"No, Missy," she said. Her voice was queerly soft. "You don't have to do a thing." She picked up the coffeepot and handed it to me slowly, as though she was not sure I could handle its weight. "You can simply go through that door. Go ahead. Go on. Just go on."

The sheriff's voice sang again, "Fannie?"

Mattie said to the reverend, "What you think?"

By this point I noticed something else about the reverend. Though the sheriff's voice had no visible effect on him, this line of talk did. He looked almost embarrassed, as if he had intruded on a family quarrel. But *tingaling* again, and other men's voices, and he knew there was little time to waste. He looked at me. He said, "It's up to you."

I looked at the reverend, and then I stared back at Mattie. I stared waiting for her to say something more. When no other words were forthcoming, I said, "Aw, damn it. Just damn it all to hell." I thrust the coffeepot into her hands. "You want to know? You want to know? You want him to know, what Fannie saw? Well I'll tell you, Reverend, what Fannie saw—" And Mattie made a quick exit. And I lurched and blew like the lid on a pressure cooker boiling over and the steam whistling. I told him what I saw.

He stood and took it.

By this time Mattie had gone in and out of the swinging door several times. She emptied one pot and carried out another. Then she started kneading biscuit dough and made a point of looking busy. She reached one hand over and scooped congealed bacon drippings from an old coffee tin into the iron skillet. She put the skillet on the stove. She turned on the gas. The blue eye hissed. I turned on her and said, "You satisfied?"

She and the reverend exchanged a look and he nodded.

Then the sheriff's voice sang, a third time, "Fannie?"

I went through the door.

How to describe the feeling, checking my face, then walking out front, and into the bleary morning gaze of Sheriff Wade, and Mr. Magee, and Mr. Ardor, and Sikes Daughtry, who was just coming through the door. At first I was worried they might have overheard. Or that something in my face might tell of my betrayal. But I had a different sense altogether when I walked to the counter. It was much like the night before, when I walked down the courthouse hall and into the sheriff's office. I had the vague sense, rising from the depth of time, and from myself, of being a child, of walking into a room full of adults and knowing that *they* had just stopped talking because *I* had come into the room and *I* wasn't supposed to hear *them*. Had I? Had I almost overheard something? Overheard and forgotten? And if so, what?

The sheriff said, "Germany, girl, you mighty slow this morning."

And Mr. Ardor said, "Aw, you know by now . . ."

And Mr. Magee said, without looking up, "Morning, hon."

And Mr. Ardor said, "I'm not a betting man but I'd wager—"

And Sikes Daughtry said, "Aw, he's halfway to Chicago by now. . . ."

It was the coffee crowd, gathering. By all appearances your usual day. Reverend Roberts had vanished through the same door he came in through. Mattie slid biscuits and started bacon and poured pancake batter and cracked eggs. And me, I went back and forth and said how-do and took orders. I set down plates and poured coffee. I poured and I smiled. But I could smell the dead rat in the wall, the mold on the cheese, the silverfish that swims in the milk of an old bottle. The known had shifted a little, and I felt the flicker of uncertainty again. A kind of readiness. A kind of dread.

The Investigation

ONE DAY LATER, AT NOON, a black Ford pulled in front of the café. The car slid to a stop by Sikes Daughtry's pickup and its doors opened. Two men emerged in suits and ties. They shut their doors and took off sunglasses and looked at each other. One of them straightened his tie—he was way bigger than the other, and his sleeves were not long enough to cover part of his cuffs. *Tingaling* of Christmas bells; they came through the door. And closing the door, or rather just as they were closing it, I turned and saw sun reflect a flash over the room: the outline of the cash register; the milk-shake machine with its long cup that leaped, for a second, into silver life; and after the flash went out I saw the big man blink, as though some latent brightness were still teasing his eyes. He looked at me. He slipped sunglasses into his pocket. Then both men walked to the empty booth in the corner.

I got the pad from my apron pocket and walked over to the booth.

"Can I help you?"

The bigger of the two men turned to me, and nodded, with a slight motion of the head. "Ma'am," he said. "What's good?"

"Everything. We got burgers, fries, vanilla, chocolate, strawberry shakes, three kinds of pie. Breakfast is served till two. We got vegetable plates, and the lunch special today is two choices, ham or smothered chicken, with your choice of three vegetables, biscuits, or cornbread."

"I'll have the special. Chicken, and what's the vegetables?"

"Mashed potatoes, black-eyed peas, butterbeans, zipper creams, green beans, squash soufflé, glazed carrots, fried okra, fried green tomatoes, sliced tomatoes, plain or in a salad, and . . . coleslaw."

The big man nodded. He cocked his head a little to the side and rested his elbows on the table. As he listened he seemed on the verge of sleep; his eyes were like a basset hound's. Indeed, he seemed to be in reverie as he said, "Mashed potatoes. And you got gravy?"

"We got gravy."

"Mashed potatoes, then, and peas—zipper creams—and squash."

"Biscuits or cornbread?"

"Which is better?"

"Well, if I had to say one t'other, biscuits. Definitely, biscuits."

"Biscuits, then."

"And you, sir?" I looked to the little man.

"I'll have the same."

"Two tea?" Both men nodded. I took their orders back and kept moving. I noticed everyone watching. Then I turned and saw, through the window, in the back of Sikes Daughtry's pickup, the face of a hang-jowled, blue-freckled hound swooning in the heat of this moment—as my heart would not—while I made my way back through the room. Mrs. Wade was whispering to Mrs. Viola and staring at the two men. Mr. Giddy dropped his napkin, used that as an excuse to get up and walk past them, and ask me for another. At one point Mr. Ardor even got up and said something to them, and with dark doubt, turned and left the café, just as Sikes Daughtry addressed me: "Have you gone insane?"

"What?"

"I said: We could use that rain."

"We sure could."

"Who the undertakers?"

"Somebody passing through, I guess."

"You lie—they're not."

"Beg your pardon?"

"I say: It's still hot. You think it'd cool down. After that blow we got."

"You'd think."

"Yeap. Oh, and Fannie?"

"Yessir?"

"If you just hold my check. Till the end of the week."

"All righty." I watched Sikes Daughtry slowly rouse from the counter, take his cane, and leave. And wished I could have followed him, for at least an hour would elapse as the two strangers plunged through lunch and pecan pie and no less than three cups of coffee apiece. By the time they asked for the check the crowd had cleared. I asked if I could get them anything else.

"Actually, yes," announced the little man, turning up his squirt face. He produced a badge from his pocket. "Federal Bureau of Investigation. Are you Mrs. Fannie Leary?"

"That's me. Is there a problem?"

"That's what we're here to find out," said the big man. "But first my colleague's forgetting his manners. I'm Jimmy Nod. This is T. G. Wilson. And I want to thank you, ma'am, for a fine lunch. Outstanding. It's just that we've gotten report of a possible murder. We had a call from Reverend Roberts. He repeated a story you told him. So, you understand, we're gonna need to talk to you. We're gonna need to ask you a few questions."

Mr. Nod looked at me and waited. Then the little man, Wilson, rose from the table and said, "Is your cook by the name of Mattie Boyd?"

"Yessir."

"She here?"

"Yessir, she is. Back in the kitchen."

"Well fine, fine," said Mr. Nod soothingly. "This is just procedure, you understand. We're gonna need to have a little talk."

I looked at him.

"So you might just want to have a seat. First we're gonna go back and talk with her. Wilson, you might want to pull down these shades. Put that closed sign on the door." He started to rise and reached into his trousers pocket and dropped some folding bills on the table. "No need to be nervous, now, we're just gonna ask a few questions."

Within the next thirty minutes, the long black Ford with Louisiana license plates and the pulled shades and the CLOSED sign on the café door were enough to make Levee Road popular. A couple of knocks on the door, but I did not answer it. I figured with Eugenia's passing, they might think I'd gone home. That was one thing I figured, ridiculously. Another was that the men attached to the long black Ford with Louisiana license plates might be assumed to be elsewhere. Still another was the picture of myself sitting in a booth while those men were in the back with Mattie. The sound of voices made the faintest hum, and I wondered if that was anything like the sound the sheriff and others had heard yesterday, when Mattie had cornered me with the good reverend. I was pretty sure they hadn't heard enough to suspect—or had they? And that name, Nod, what was that? *Sailed off in a wooden shoe, sailed off on a river of crystal light, into a sea of dew . . .* I memorized that once, when I was a child. In a book from the Thistle library. The book was a hand-me-down, a donation from the Butlers. I remember Sharon Butler's name in it. I remember how she scribbled colors on the page, the picture of a sailboat, with a green sail, and pink sea, scribbling in a book being a thing rich kids did. Mama never would have let me put a mark in a book.

Anyway, I sat there for a time. I sat there, in the booth, listening to the hum from the kitchen, and the hum of air-conditioning, and the little crinkling noises that the plastic wrap over Naugahyde makes when you move, adjusting buns, stretching your leg, to keep your foot from going to sleep. Then someone knocked on the door. I sat very still. All I would do—all I would dare to do—would amount to looking at the drawn shade, which, when illumined from behind, was the goldcrisp color of fried potato. It was that color, with the afternoon sun on it. Then I looked at a brown mole made from a coffee spoon left in the sugar bowl, and moved my hand, and reached in, and picked it out, and held it between my thumb and finger, and sat very still, and listened, until the footsteps went away.

Or so I thought. Until I looked back at the drawn shade. On the other side a shadow, but what gave it away was the soft *clop-clop* of boots and the softer pause. The shadow stopped. The shadow lifted itself onto my shoulders. I was at the table. I was holding the speck of sugar between my thumb and finger and now I breathed in the leftover smells of lunch. I imagined I also breathed in the shadow.

Could whoever it was tell it was me? Could he translate the silence on the other side of the shade?

I heard the bootsteps, heard more gather, heard the silence of the men—heard them thinking, their profiles cocked toward me behind the shade.

Another knock on the door. And as if on cue, the FBI men came out of the kitchen. The little man was carrying a tape recorder. And the big man, Mr. Nod, said, "You want to me to get that?"

"Nosir. Where's Mattie?"

"She's gone for the day. If that's all right with you."

"Home?"

"Yes, she's been taken care of. She's gotten a ride."

Another knock. Mr. Nod looked at me and said, "You sure you don't want me to get it?"

"No, I better."

So I went to the door. I went so as to compose myself in a certain way. The way it's done, say, in the movies, when the man in military starches draws himself up and goes to a door to tell a family that their son has died. A family of strangers. So I drew myself up and opened the door and there was Sheriff Wade. But Sheriff Wade was no stranger. He liked his chicken crisp, his okra with pepper vinegar. His daughter, Christie, had been two grades ahead of me in school and his wife used to play bridge with Eugenia. I could hardly look at him, he was so still and frontal. He stood and stared at me.

I said, "Hey, Sheriff."

There was total blankness in his face, and then total murderousness. It was not a quick rise of fury. It was a pure and murderous certainty. It was as though the face had stilled in that instant of certainty. It looked like a face going back a hundred years, the face in an old painting—say, a painting in the hall of the courthouse—in which the painter has preserved that moment stilled in the light of the subject's eye as if all time had come to this, a contract broken, and it stares down at you from its thick gold frame.

I stood there for what felt like forever. I thought I knew what he was going to do. I thought I'd bought the farm.

Then the face wasn't there. It was just the sheriff's face with the mole on the nose under the balding dome and it took note of the FBI men and said, with uncling sweetness, "And just when do you think you're opening?"

I felt a nerve jump in my ankle. "Not long," I said. "Later today."

Then I closed the door.

I stood facing it. Finally I turned around. I looked at Mr. Nod. He walked over to the door and gently turned the lock. Then he gestured and said, "Won't you have a seat?"

"Yessir," I replied. Odd, but something in his politeness immediately consoled me. He didn't seem the least bit disconcerted by the sheriff's arrival; he inquired about how long I'd been at the café.

"Several years," I answered. "Longer than that, if you count earlier, when I was in school."

"Your great-aunt started the place, right?"

"Yessir," I said. "She and her husband."

"I heard she just passed on," he said. "My condolences."

"Thank you," I said, and for a moment I wondered if he would go on like this. He seemed nice enough, though now it struck me as a salesman's niceness—there was something hidden behind it—and I was ready for him to get on to whatever it was. Besides, the little man was over there waiting. Then I noticed that we were sitting at the booth with nothing in front of us, and it was nerves that made me ask, "You want some more coffee?"

“Oh no thank you, ma’am,” and as he declined the coffee his face turned serious. “Right now I’m just gonna be frank with you, Mrs. Leary. There’re certain steps we’re gonna have to take. A lot of it formality.” He reached into his jacket and took an envelope and handed it over. “This, for instance, is a warrant from the district judge. We gonna need to take a look around your place.”

I held the envelope between my hands but I did not try to open it. I said, “And why are y’all doing this?”

“As I said, we received the call from Reverend Roberts.”

“About Earnest March.”

“That’s what we’d like you to tell us.”

“But why are y’all going to this trouble?”

Then Mr. Nod looked at me in a different way. “For a colored boy, you mean.”

“Yessir.”

“Well, let’s just say the word was passed down.”

“The word?”

“Yes ma’am. Let’s just say, your Reverend Roberts has some influential ties. But now that’s getting ahead of ourselves. I want to hear what you have to say.”

I looked down at the envelope. Then I said, “I don’t believe he did it.”

“Who didn’t?”

“My husband.”

“Then you won’t mind us searching, now, will you?”

“What I mean is, there’s something *else* going on and—”

“Something else.” He nodded morosely. “And that’s precisely what I want you to tell me. Still, we’ll just take a look around,” and he looked over to the little man Wilson and nodded. Wilson moved behind the counter. He put on a pair of gloves. He perused a wooden salad fork in a jar. He opened a cabinet door and closed it. There were photographs on the wall and he ran his paws over those. He touched an ancient picture of a Persia Livestock Queen.

“Wilson. Get your eyes off the showgirl. And get that tape recorder over here.” Mr. Nod stretched his cuffs and set his elbows on the table. “Excuse me, ma’am. We had a call from Reverend Roberts. He repeated a story you told him and now that's what I'd like for you to do. Tell me the story."

Wilson went back into the kitchen. I could hear the stair boards creak. Then feet across the bedroom.

"This is procedure," he said apologetically. "We ask for your help."

Wilson came down the stairs with Will's shotgun in one hand and several boxes of shells in the other. "The guy's definitely armed," he said. "There's about ten more boxes up there."

"Put it all on the counter. Bag and tag everything."

Then Mr. Nod turned back to me. He pulled out a pack of Marlboros and set them on the table. He looked at the tape recorder, turned it around in his hands—tapered hands for such a big, bulky man—and punched a button. The machine began. Crack and spittle, a voice from the bottom, Mattie's voice, saying something about "bone" or "gone," until he punched a button—the tape skidded—he punched another. "Now"—he sighed—"Mrs. Leary. Would you just tell us what you saw."

The tape was spinning.

"Mrs. Leary?"

"Yessir."

"Would you tell us what you saw on the evening of August ten."

"Evening?"

"Yes."

He tapped out a cigarette.

Then, "Mrs. Leary," as he struck a light, but because of the movement of his hand, or a draft of air-conditioning, the flame illumined not his face but the drawn shade, which was still the goldcrisp color, but without the shadows.

"Yessir."

"There are reports of a boy missing. Your husband missing. An alleged murder. A woman dead. Can you shed light on these reports?"

"Nosir."

"No?"

"I mean, yes," I said, and looked to the goldcrisp shade, the smoke tusking from his nostrils. "But was it evening—no. It started before that. The story begins in my nose. . . ."

At midafternoon Mr. Nod, Wilson, and I walked out of the café door.

I had hoped for an hour's emptiness in the heat of the day, but I was squinted at by several dozen people and I saw Mrs. Butler drop a grocery bag by her opened car. There was the sheriff. The Huit boys. Mr. Ardor. Mrs. Viola and her grandson, Timmy. All watching me. They expected me to say something. And I didn't feel anything except a kind of numbness, a kind of numbness more than injury. I waited the way you wait for the pain to start after you've touched your hand to a hot stove. But the pain didn't come yet; it was still just numbness.

And then I saw Mr. Magee moving on the outer edge of the street and halting to glance back, walking without hurry and with great trepidation, as if this were punishment.

Mr. Nod was hulking toward the car in his dark suit, a pinch of Marlboro between his fingers, and sleepily hazing the group with his stare.

"Howdy," he said cordially. "Howdy, Sheriff." He opened the door for me, and I slid into the car. I waited for them to get in. Then the two men, in an identical sweep of gesture, put on their sunglasses and got in the front seat and I told them just go on down here, just go on, this is where Levee Road ends.

So the long black Ford eased down the road, past cotton rows where green leaves were uncurling fleshy, for the rain had come. We stopped where the road ended. We got out. The two men did a quick one-eighty at the sky and took off their jackets. Rolled their cuffs. Gun straps crossed shoulders, revolvers tucked under left arms, and I watched as Mr. Nod yanked off his tie and Wilson got a duffel bag from the trunk. Mr. Nod looked to me. And so I led them, up the muddy path, high on the bluff where it wound above the river, past the Jones house and the Ardor farm and down the drop to the willow. By putting geography in motion I did my best to give myself an impression of getting away. Yet all of this was seeming stranger to the eye. Beyond the willow, beyond the river, there was the slow suffusion of shimmering, the afternoon sun that for the moment revealed itself in a rim of liquid peeled-orange tinge on the edge of a remnant cloud, while the rest of the sky was losing its blue to heat, so the trees over in Louisiana seemed to melt in the white haze. The sun came out from behind the cloud. The river glittered. The willow advanced self-consciously and gave us a moment of blessed shade. Then I showed them where I saw the body. I went through all of it again.

"And tell me again," said Mr. Nod. "You saw it here?"

"Yessir."

"And what angle was the body?"

"Faceup. On his back, this way."

The willow rustled and I looked at Wilson, who was sliding his fingers along a branch. He had on his gloves and was feeling for something. He seemed in a throb of hunting pleasure. A catch of scent. Fingers paused on a branch. He scanned the clover bed beneath it, and his eyes stopped.

A Tootsie Roll dog turd.

"Hey!" he said to Mr. Nod.

Mr. Nod walked over. He looked down at it. Then we walked back over to me as Wilson pulled out a plastic bag.

"As I was saying," he continued.

"Yessir."

"Ma'am. If you would look this way. Just answer the question. What'd you see first?"

"First?"

"On the body."

"On the body? The face."

"Angled how?"

"Straight up."

"And you saw how many bullet holes?"

"One."

"Just one?"

"Yessir."

"Where was it?"

"Right here." I put my finger to the top of my forehead.

"There were no others?"

"Nosir. I mean, none I saw."

"Anything else?" he then said, and turned to the river, and squatted down, cupped his hand into the water. He lifted his hand and sieved water through his fingers.

"What you mean?"

"I mean, did you notice anything else? Anything unusual?"

"A body in the river is not my idea of usual."

Mr. Nod stiffened. He turned and looked at me. "I mean, around the neck, say? Any signs there, of demarcation?"

"I don't think so."

"Rope, anything like that?"

"No. I don't think—"

"Think, Mrs. Leary. Think carefully. After the face, what did you notice next? Work from there."

"The sneaker. That's what I saw next. The black high-top sneaker. It was off one foot but still attached by the laces. The laces were tangled on the foot. The foot was twisted a little."

"Right foot or left?"

"The right. To my left. I remember that 'cause it was floating slightly higher, like the face. The rest I couldn't make out. The water's dark, you see, and the minnows."

Mr. Nod swished his hand gently in the water to rinse it. Then he stood. He stood looking down at the river lapping its yellowish waters over the low, slippery bank. He said, "Is it, as you put it, within your idea of usual, that a body would be here one moment, and gone the next?"

"Nosir."

He fell silent. It was the hottest and stillest part of the day, and he seemed slowed by it. He looked out over the water. He looked at me. Then he looked back and over at Wilson, an acknowledgment that we would go now.

So the men had begun to place what I said beside the things they had seen and heard. And I wondered if they understood what locals had an inkling of. The river and rain were one thing, the power of story another, and there had been stories over the years, about bodies in the river. One winter a barge worker's body was recovered after three full months of immersion, and it was said that his skin resembled wax more than anything; he seemed a kind of paraffin. There was another who had been found one summer, facedown in shallow marsh, astonishingly intact beneath the waterline but eaten entirely—eaten to the bone by mosquitoes—wherever flesh lay exposed to air. I remember particularly the story of a woman on whose limbs the skin had peeled back like the detaching cocoon of a moth: Even the fingernails had come away. The body had traveled a hundred miles from the north; in spite of the peeling skin, authorities were able to make a positive identification, from the fingerprints.

And there were sightings. The earthquake of 1812, when the tides swelled and south turned north and the river flowed backwards. The summer of '48, when no less than a dozen Persia fishermen had sworn to have sighted an iridescent white feathered creature that was described as half goat, half swan, but with the glowing eyes of a beast. When several of the fisherman rowed out to get a closer look, the creature sank beneath the waters and disappeared.

There were other, private sightings.

Climbing back up the bluff. Huffs of breath. Clankling cans on a crucifix. The roof of Tchula's, in the distance. From up here, the sounds of the river reached us somewhat muted. That and the ammonia smells of an abandoned cow pasture. Now a pair of eyes beaded on us, one of Tchula's chickens—a dumb, long-throated rooster, standing on the roof of the henhouse—but the eyes burned at us as though his head were full of sun and boiling blood that spilled over on his bearded red comb and clotted. Other chickens in the pen, pecking dirt and stubble. Then Wilson reached into his pocket and pulled out his gloves and put them on, for a third time that day.

We walked to the front door. And when the men entered they looked slowly over the room, not unlike the way my mother looked over a room before rearranging the furniture. The empty bed. The mantel. I felt a moment of claustrophobia. The sheets pulled back. A dent in the pillow that, even as I looked, seemed to be losing shape where the head had been. I watched Wilson walk around the bed and look under it. He felt under the edge of ticking and his hand stopped. He lifted the ticking back. Then in one motion he pulled out Tchula's pistol and let out a long wolf whistle.

"It's an old one," he said.

He held the gun slightly above his face. His gloved hands touched nothing but the very bottom of the handle, and he held it upside down, dangling it between his thumb and forefinger. He put his nose near the chamber.

"Who you think she got this off of, General Grant?"

Mr. Nod shook his head. Wilson continued to dangle the pistol in front of him and he took a look. Then he turned and walked over to the bedside table and opened the drawer. "Here's casings," he said. "Powder. Everything for the bullets. Homemade." He turned back to Wilson and nodded. Then Wilson got out plastic bags.

They went into the back room. The table. The pieces of pottery and the cracked eggshell still in the sink. The boy's bed by the window. The whole place had that damp-salt odor characteristic of waiting. Now and then Mr. Nod would ask a question, but my mind kept flying off. That business with rope, Mattie's exit through the kitchen, the sheriff's face, Will walking out the door.

"And the sheriff," Mr. Nod said, "found these books under the bed?"

"Yessir. He asked Mattie how books from the library got to be there and she said she didn't know. Then he left them there. Right there on the top." *The Last of the Mohicans*. The night before I had been too fuzzy to notice titles other than his school math book, but now I wondered how Earnest might have gotten them. Books from the library. Surely not by himself, for black folk were not allowed to use the library. Or maybe Sheila checked them out for him; I could see how that might have happened, and how Tchula might have tolerated it. Wrongful possession of books. In the eyes of the law. But temporarily.

Was there a connection? Between thinking you could get away with a little thing and thinking you could get away with a careless move toward a girl that might put a bullet through your head?

There might be, there might be some connection. A matter of

attitude. And with her for a great-grandmother. Tchula was not one to take guff off anybody.

"After looking through the books," Mr. Nod said, "what did the sheriff do next?"

"He left," I said. "He nodded to Mr. Ardor and then we left."

Mr. Nod pinched the tip of his nose. He looked out the window with its watery view of chickens scratching in the dirt and stubble. He said, "Let's go over something one more time." Then we walked back outside.

He said, "You saw Tchula Gaze standing here."

"Yessir."

"And she didn't say anything."

"Nosir."

"And she was?"

"Just nodding."

"Just nodding."

"Yessir."

"And you said?"

"I'm sorry."

"And?"

"That's all."

"Look, ma'am, I know you're tired, but are you sure that's all?"

"That's all I said: I'm sorry."

So, returning to Mama's house that evening, I kept blundering through the strangeness of before and after. I went to the kitchen. Mama was standing there. There was a pile of laundry and a suitcase on the table. She stared, unmoving, by the table. I said, "Go ahead and say it."

But Mama didn't say anything. She just looked at me out of a face washed transparent and pure and when I looked into the eyes it was like falling down a well. Then she did a thing I didn't expect. She walked over to me and laid a hand on my shoulder. She let it lie there a moment, the way you might lay a hand to calm a skittish colt.

She said, "You do the best you can."

And stood there, with the hand still on my shoulder, and let that sink in. Then she said, "I just want you to know I know that."

She waited again. Then she took her hand off my shoulder and turned toward the suitcase. She paused, changed directions. She walked over to the laundry and began to fold it.

I said, "You going somewhere?"

"Oh, I've been thinking. Now that Eugenia's gone—I was thinking about the house. She's left it to us—it's paid for—free and clear just—sitting empty—and I've been thinking about—a change of scenery. A little break, you know. That sounds nice, doesn't it? A house in the country."

"What's happened?"

"Nothing."

"Mama. What's happened?"

She looked up at me with a labored motion as though I were the one who was supposed to answer. "What makes you ask?"

"Well, a lot's been happening."

"Well, and I'm moving."

"And when d'you decide this?"

"I just did," she said. Her hand in the laundry. From the pile she jerked a long sheet. She folded it in half, in fourths, decreasing squares. Each time she folded, she smoothed it hard against her stomach.

I pulled out a chair and sat. "Look, Mama, I reckon I know how you feel and I don't want to be dragging you into this, but—"

"You don't know a thing about how I feel."

"Some idea—maybe. But I came here to let you know what's happening."

"I thought you came because you're so fond of me."

"Actually, I do happen to be fond enough to come back and try to explain. And I'd also like to know, if you don't mind, exactly what—"

"Oh yes," she interrupted. "Everything's fine. Everybody getting along, Good Lord, just fine."

I waited while she finished the sheet and held her face away from me. She looked across to the window above the sink. There was a little sparrow in the windowsill and she looked at it, with that face washed transparent and pure like some martyr being led to the stake. Then the sparrow flew away, and I spoke very slowly. I said, "The colored preacher came to the café yesterday. Reverend Roberts? He was waiting in the kitchen, first thing in the morning. He was waiting with Mattie. And like I told you, Mattie already knows something. She knows I know something. She put two and two together, I guess, and then she sprung the good reverend on me, if you can imagine that. If you can imagine well—it just—took me aback. And what was I supposed to do, lie to the reverend?"

She didn't answer that. She didn't even seem to be listening to me. She was watching the clear air above the windowsill where the bird had been.

I hesitated, watching her face, then went on. "So I didn't tell the FBI. It wasn't me."

I waited again and watched her face.

"And I haven't heard anything about Will—in case you're interested—though they asked me enough questions. There were two of them—one asked me about Will and the sheriff and all the men who chased the boy out of town. Then he asked me where I found the body. We were at the café, they came in at lunch, and then we went out to the river and to Tchula's and I went over—it all."

I waited. Then, "So you want to tell me what happened?"

She seemed to be turning this over in her mind. If she had heard it, for I couldn't be sure.

"Do you?"

"I don't have any notion."

"No?"

"No," she said, "I don't. I didn't when I had a visitor come to my home and inform me of my desired departure."

"What?" I said. "What?" and came up out of my chair.

"Beatrice Ardor."

"I should have known."

"If you should have, why are you asking?"

And I hadn't. I hadn't known. So I stood near her and didn't dare touch her, even with the weight of my finger.

"Beatrice Ardor," she said again. "She came by to say that. She said that Mr. Ardor and she—had plans for the property—that they didn't care to rent it any longer—and when I asked her why, of course, she didn't say—the reason. She didn't breathe the word FBI. She didn't announce that my daughter had turned on her own people, no, she's too sophisticated for that. Nor did she say that courtesy of my daughter, half the town, including law enforcement, is being implicated in—a murder—"

"Mama—"

"Don't get me wrong, Fannie. You do the best you can. Just please don't pretend you couldn't expect—"

"But—"

"And Beatrice Ardor—in addition to not renting to me any longer, said that furthermore she had engaged—another seamstress. She said she spoke for the Magnolia Club and for Ardor Department Store—and the town—and another person to take care of her cleaning—she said all this politely."

"Damn her."

"As I said, she was polite. She said they had been considering this for some time—and anyway—I was thinking that old house of Eugenia's. You remember how we used to go out there when you were little—and Eugenia'd read to you—and then you'd be in the kitchen—you no bigger than a minute—wanting to climb up on a chair and fix dinner—oh Fannie—you remember?"

"I remember."

"Yes—and Lawrence was there—and they were so proud of you—and now—and now—" she whispered.

I looked at her.

"You do the best you can," she said, and lifted her chin in a way that suddenly made her look like Eugenia, that chin held at an angle to face the world, and I felt like bursting into tears. As if that was becoming my habit.

"Damn them," I said.

"It's done," Mama said.

"Damn them. Damn them all."

"Well, it's done. Besides, Eugenia's left the house. It's almost like she's—looking out for us."

"Damn them all," I said. "I hope they burn."

This was coming. This was coming, and I hadn't guessed it. And a part of my mind was saying: *See what you've done now, see what you've done, you've made it worse, by not leaving it alone,* while another part was shifting to the picture of Will walking out the door—all the while that part of my mind was saying: *Thanks a lot, Mattie.*

I thought that, as I began to help pack up, and later that evening, as I went to bed, and by the next morning I was ready to give it to Mattie. I was ready to give it to her, until I realized I had clear forgotten that she would not be in. For this was the day of Tchula Gaze's funeral. It was Persia's second funeral within a week. It would be quite different, I imagined, than the first. The first had been the funeral for Eugenia at First Baptist.

When I walked into the café the next morning, I said not a word. Not at first. For I had decided I would give it to Mattie in a different way. I was conscious of her eyes on my back and I turned toward her. We stared, in a tug-of-war. And I was not about to be the one to give in.

I pulled up the shades. Turned the CLOSED sign to OPEN. Meanwhile, Mattie stood with the flour scoop in her hands starting biscuits. Her face, above the white dress, didn't show a thing.

So I went through the door and stood behind the counter, waiting for customers to turn up. I waited for a while and stood listening to the silence. Normal silence is very different from the silence you get in a place like this when there are suddenly no customers. You stand there and think how cozy it was, with the clink of china cups and the haw-haw of visiting, and you look around the room, which seems suddenly larger than it actually is. The general impression is that there is a humming outside the walls, which is the sound of a place slipping away from you, and inside the walls you are absolutely alone. So I stood listening for the humming, and the slipping sounds of the coffee going to vinegar, and the dripping pan in the icebox, and the slipping of metal against metal as Mattie slid biscuits into the oven.

It went on like that. But I did think, not everybody. Wait a while. Wait and see. Wait till lunch.

So I watched the clock. I looked through the window. A band of sun hardening as it arched west. I paced back and forth and glanced at the phone. I thought I sensed some message coming and said to myself: *It's gonna ring.* Eventually I went back into the kitchen, started lunch. Mattie and I did not speak. I went back out and looked at the phone. I looked at the door. It was as if I almost had a hope even then that the moment would open out, that the phone or the Christmas bells would ring, in fact that perhaps all the changes would be wiped out, here in this place—my voice and Will and all those gone would be returned.

Still, no customers.

At half past noon I paced back into the kitchen and back out front. I watched the casseroles sink and the cornbread harden and the bacon fat coagulate in white skin on the green beans. Droplets of sweat exploding on the back of Mattie's neck. Ice melting belly-up in the top of the tea. Then I glared at her. I said, "You satisfied?" and walked out, slamming the back screen door.

I started walking. In which direction, I hadn't decided. The important thing was just to go, so I walked toward the railroad. Past the old depot, the Thistle library. Past Mama's place and the last of white folks' houses. I walked on. Across the street some loafer was swatting flies, and as I walked I hated colored town: the shabby shacks, the chicken coops in the yards, the women at the clotheslines in plump dresses and wet brown arms looking back at me with hatred. On the drooping front porches sat all the plodding old men with their dead eyes and sagging jaws. What you looking at? You think you so fine? You think you shit perfume? They all stared at me hatefully, and I glared back at each of them. Anger was like a mirror teaching me to hate the face that hated me.

Come to this. As I walked past the stoops of the pathetic, paint-thirsty shacks, I turned on the street I knew was Mattie's and passed her place and turned around. I headed back to the café. I returned the way I'd left and went in through the back and made a point of slamming the screen door, the second time that day.

"And folk on your side of town," I said to Mattie. "Looking at me like I'm something filthy."

Mattie was retying her apron with her hands behind her back, and she surprised me when she wheeled around and slapped my face. "They look at you the way you look at them," she said. "You don't know who those folk are. Maybe they're spiteful and mean and nasty. Maybe not. But you, of all people, don't know. You don't know what happens when they get up in the morning and what they call home and you don't know who they mamas are or who they children are or what they scared of. You think 'cause they colored and they watch you that they're mean and low and thinking awful things about you. Could be they looking at you sitting up here all high and mighty nibbling dandelion salad and looking at them like they the bottom of a pisspot—could be they jealous of you, wishing for what you got, scared of what you'd do if they ever set foot on your porch."

She walked over to the drawer and snapped out tinfoil. Her chopped-off black hair was wild and her face was plum-dark and the glint of tinfoil striking across it made her look like some rod of electricity. "Chef Madame Pompadour. You looking high but you seeing low. You make up one picture of yourself and one picture of another and that's the gist of it. They both made up."

I looked bitterly over at her and felt tears itch on my cheeks. "I hear you ran off with a man to New Orleans and then you came back by yourself. How come you never talk about that? You got so much to say, I'd like to hear. How come he didn't marry you?"

The tinfoil in Mattie's hand quivered. "You hear. You hear. Well, you hear this, Missy. I went off to New Orleans, yeah, but I didn't go for any man. I went for myself and I ain't never, ever wanted to marry nobody. I made my life, Missy, just the way I wanted. I made my life the way you gonna make yours—out of pride and blindness and too much anger.

"And let me tell you, you better think about who you mad at. You better think. 'Cause I need this from you like a hog needs a holiday. I'm so sick of this, sick to death. Your auntie dead and Tchula dead and now Earnie dead and me helping it along. *Me*. I didn't *know* it was the boy till I was already out the door. Till I stabbed the knife in the tire. I didn't *know* it was him, I just saw his back, that's all I saw. And on top of it all, *this*. This space in my head, all my days. Pushing back my thoughts to make room for *white* folks' thoughts in me. And let me tell you another thing . . ." and she went on like that. She spoke in tongues for five minutes straight.

A ring of Christmas bells, footsteps out front. And Mattie still going on until I threw up my hands. I hollered, "Hokay!"

"Fannie?"

It was Mama. She had pushed open the kitchen door.

I said, "Mama, what are you—"

"What on earth?"

"Nothing," I said, as Mattie put her back to us. "What are you—"

"Can't a mother come see her daughter? Can't a mother come for a visit, in the middle of the day?"

A second ring of the Christmas bells, and the two FBI men walked in. "Well," I said, "if it ain't Grand Central Station."

"Ma'am," Mr. Nod said, and bowed slightly to my mother, then to me, with an inclination of the head that twitched the memory of me standing with him by the willow on the river.

"I wondering if you could take a break," he said. "I'm gonna need to talk to you."

"Might as well," I said brightly. "As you can see, sir, we don't have any press of business."

He looked at me.

"But before we start, don't y'all want some chicken ham cornbread green beans? Mashed potatoes? How about twenty helpings? Thirty? Forty? On the house, might as well—it's all going untouched."

"That don't have to be the case," Mattie said, her back to me.

"Say what?"

"You heard me."

"No I didn't. Believe it or not, though it may defy the law of physics, for once I didn't. So what'd you say?"

"She said," Mama said, and she paused until her tentative silence caused everyone to look up. "She said, that doesn't have to be the case." Mama spoke out of the high pale face, her voice not much above a whisper. But Mattie had turned. It was one of only two times in my entire life I saw Mattie surprised. Mattie was staring at Mama, and so was I. And I did not find in Mama's face the conscious probity I expected.

"Uh-hunh," I said finally. "And I got real estate east of Florida I got to sell."

Mama warned, "Fannie."

And I said, "No, Mama."

And Mr. Nod said, "Mrs. Leary, if—"

And I said, "Just a minute."

And all the while, Wilson taking it in with his squirt face.

Mattie said, "You just don't get it, do you?" And waited a beat. She looked at Mama. She looked back at me. "You got customers, if you want them."

"You just don't get it," I mimicked. But her meaning was beginning to dawn. For a second I snickered but:

"Well do enlighten me."

Mattie didn't say anything. Nor did Mama. Mr. Nod stood at the door and the squirt face took it in.

Then I said, slowly, "Just how many you talking about?"

"As many as you want."

"You must have a big family."

"That's one way of putting it."

And Mr. Nod said, "Mrs. Leary?"

And I said, "Just a second, sir."

Thus for the moment of dizzy formulating; now hotter with doubt than the midday walk, now winning back the possibility of my own brand of revenge, for there comes a time when you hit bottom that you will try things you never considered.

I thought of the sheriff then, delivering me his message. As the sheriff's face had hovered in the last days between me and the boy, blocking vision of the body, so now Mama's and Mattie's faces waited before me, a veil across what had been the sheriff's warning:

"And just when do you think you're opening?"

I would be, perhaps, less naive when I had been working at the café for a few more years and could fully appreciate how the human heart can turn vile, its habits low, and what we are capable of, after all, in the name of loyalty. But I would try this too, and I was a hint of what I might become, a practical woman with a business to run.

So I looked at Mattie. I said, “You think they’d come?”

“Tomorrow,” she said.

“Well all right.”

Friday Night

"NEWS OF WILL LEARY MIGHT interest you," Mr. Nod said. Jacket removed, revolver holstered under his left arm, he ate ham, sliced tomatoes, turnip greens with pot liquor. It was after everyone had left. Mattie had gone to the kitchen, Mama to finish her packing, and Mr. Nod's colleague Wilson was off, he said, on reasons of business. He opened a biscuit and watched the steam escape. "Our sources keep us informed. Well, Amos and Will Leary were seen here in Persia, of course, where none of the leading citizens saw fit to stop them. Not that you could have, from what you tell me. And what you say about Amos Leary, by the way, about him not taking off with the rest on the chase that morning, well, that's been corroborated. Indeed, he's one of a few white males in the entire town confirmed not seen on the reported wagon train that day. Though a uniform attack of amnesia does set in when it comes to the question of who was in the group. But it still remains that Amos Leary was seen getting on the boat with Will Leary. Folk saw both father and son leave on the *Elvira*. They appeared to be in a bit of a hurry. After Persia, there were sightings in Natchez, and Black Hawk. We got a professional tracker out after them. He's done a good job for us in the past. He found an escapee in a tree house once. A tree house up in a cypress, in a Louisiana swamp. There were alligators out there."

"So, are y'all gonna start searching the river," I said, "for the body?"

"As a matter of fact, yes." He checked his watch. "That's where Wilson is now."

"Well, I was wondering. 'Cause that's where your focus ought to be."

"Why's that?"

"Because I just don't think . . ."

"You don't think your husband did it. Well, turning him up would turn up an answer, don't you agree? Which is what we're trying to do. Not to mention answering the strange question of what his father is doing with him. And we figure he and his father are well into Louisiana by now. Unless they're still on the river and haven't ditched the *Elvira* to head overland. I say that because Giles Thibodeaux, the sheriff of Black Hawk, was the last one to see it. Now, Mr. Thibodeaux was formerly in the bureau himself. I worked with him on a case when he was still in New Orleans. He left the FBI and took the sheriff's job as a kind of retirement. He left because the city got him too close to slimeball types who, shall we say, did not cotton with his nicer ideas of humanity. Which is no problem for our tracker. Anyway, Mr. Thibodeaux's still got good eyes and he saw the *Elvira*. Amos and Will Leary surely realize their visibility and might well be headed by now to dry ground."

"Well, thank you for telling me," I said. I was fixing important effort on pleating a napkin in fierce pinches. "And you'll be wanting dessert when you're finished? We got blackberry cobbler."

"That sounds good," Mr. Nod said, and I started toward the kitchen. A ring of Christmas bells, and Brother Works walked in.

"Fannie!" he said. And reached for Mr. Nod with his large, thick blanched hand. "And how are you, sir?"

"I'm fine."

"Glad to hear it!"

"And you?" said Mr. Nod.

"Couldn't be better! And I hope our talk was instructive."

"Can I get you some coffee?" I said to Brother Works.

"Oh, no, thank you."

"Anything else?"

"Oh no hon," he said, still peculiarly merry. Then he took a seat.

I went back to the kitchen for the cobbler.

"It's like I said before," Brother Works was saying, as I came back out. "Just a piece of advice, and I defer to you on this, sir—this is your territory—but being in my line of work I can tell you a thing or two about human nature. And before y'all go on this wild goose chase, you might want to check some of those honky-tonks up in Memphis? Or Chicago? Have you talked to the Jones girl yet—she might be able to point a finger in the right direction, for all we know, they might be planning to meet back up?"

Mr. Nod chewed a piece of ham and shoveled a fork into his turnip greens. Then Brother Works shook his head. "That was such a shame, Sheila Jones, a young girl like that, you'd have thought she'd think of her mother. Have a little consideration for her mother's feelings. There, poor Adelia, widowed and hardly a chance to recover from her loss when *this*." He paused and looked at me. "You were friends with her, weren't you?"

"What if I was?"

"Oh, nothing wrong, nothing wrong," said Brother Works. "Everybody can use a friend. Particularly a girl like that. Because, if she's carrying the March boy's child, there are curses that'll be put on her family for a thousand generations!"

"Brother Works," I said.

But Brother Works went on. "Therefore the Lord will smite with a scab the crown of the head of the daughters of Zion, and the Lord will discover their secret parts. In that day the Lord will take away the bravery of their tinkling ornaments about their feet, and their cauls, and their round tires like the moon, the chains and the bracelets and the mufflers, the bonnets and the ornaments of the legs and the headbands—"

I started to say something.

"—and the tablets and the earrings, the rings and nose jewels, the changeable suits of apparel and the mantles and the wimples and the crisping pins, the glasses—"

"Mrs. Leary," said Mr. Nod, "I wouldn't even bother."

"—and the fine linen and the hoods and the veils. And it shall come to pass, that instead of sweet smell there shall be stink; and instead of a girdle a rent; and instead of well-set hair baldness; and instead of a stomacher a girding of sackcloth; and burning instead of beauty. Isaiah 3:17 to 24. That applies to fornication! Lasciviousness! Illegitimacy! Adultery! Or the sin of deceit"—and here he paused significantly. His eyes pleaded to me with moist sympathy. "But I'm afraid you've been through enough yourself. The husband who departs. The wife who feels wronged. The wife who, understandably, might want a little revenge. And how does she do that? By up and seeing things? By calling in these fine men? By craving attention from the outside because, just maybe, it's lacking at home? I have to feel for you, Brother Nod, because that'd be deceit, just the same. Even if it is the imaginative creation of a woman scorned."

For a moment I looked at Brother Works. I just looked. And Mr. Nod reached toward his plate and took the last half of biscuit and sponged it in pot liquor, tinting the bread all the way to the crust a pale green. He chewed and swallowed it. He rubbed his mouth with his napkin. Then he looked around the room with his sleepy eyes. "I don't see any place named Zion around here, or any goddamned daughters of Zion." He turned to me. "Do you, ma'am?"

"Nosir."

Brother Works was overwhelmed and stood up. "A little respect, sir." Then, "I'd be a hypocrite to not look at all possibilities."

"Brother Works," Mr. Nod said. "We're establishing the nature of a missing boy and the possibility of murder, slow as the truth comes. We're conducting an investigation, not a Sunday school class. If you have some facts to add to those you offered in our earlier conversation, I would welcome any addition. But I don't need your conclusions."

"God concluded the first investigation. And God is here, sir."

"All right. God's here. You satisfied?"

"Why not go out to Sheila and Mrs. Jones's house," I said to Brother Works, "take the choir with you, throw open the windows, and sing at the top of your voice, 'I Love to Tell the Story,' the fine folk of Persia paying a price for the ticket?"

"A philandering and missing husband shouldn't draw out her sense of humor, now, should it, Brother Nod?"

"I'm out of here," said Mr. Nod. "Thank you for lunch, ma'am." He stood and put some folding bills on the counter. He walked out.

Brother Works watched him leave. Then he started toward the door and opened it, and with his hand on the doorknob, said, "Now the two of you look cozy, don't you?" And left the café.

So Brother Nod was our one customer that day. I moved through the rest of the afternoon, in the empty café, mopping an already clean floor and crouching over a blank table with the dishrag held as I thought. Now that the place was cleared of folk it seemed easier to pretend. My life was definitely like some train gaining speed, tall trees pressing in and then falling from square, slick windows. What was that Mr. Nod had said? That I'd been "corroborated"? So I would not think of going upstairs. I would not think of that now. Remnant smells from the closet, the bed half empty, hunting magazines listing on the shelf.

Each time I tried not to think of Will, he grew.

Is the man who flees the one? Or the man who stays, sleeping quietly in his bed?

Wondering, I felt I was guessing, piece by piece. But I thought, Go on, Fannie, just go on, or pull your head under the shell like a turtle in the road. A turtle's got to live, doesn't it?

But I did find out part of what Mattie knew.

It was Friday, the next morning, and already the hard white sunshine was heating the ground. Nickel light over the river. Chimney sweeps tossed along the pier.

It was that kind of morning, and I took my eyes off the river and went into the café. I found Mattie, who informed me that Reverend Roberts had called a meeting at Mount Sinai Church the night before. Reverend Roberts had passed on word of the café's decline in business and the church had decided to come. But not for breakfast or lunch, because men who worked the fields and women who worked as maids could not come. The only black folk with pocket change and spare daytime in August, as Mattie said, were the preachers and teachers. So it was agreed they would all come for supper, and in the course of the day say not a word to any white employer. They would all come. It was agreed. Friday night.

Mattie was simmering greens on the stove with a spoon in one hand. The black coils of hair were escaping at the nape of her neck, her face was damped, and the kitchen light striking across it made it more like the usual face. Except the face was back to a mask again, like the night when I found her out at Tchula's, and the eyes looking out of it were part of the mask. They were not aflame. They were not Mattie's.

"I was thinking," I said, "for tonight, Eugenia's fried shrimp."

She studied me for a second out of the unflamed eyes and said, "Fine."

"And egg custard?"

She shrugged and said, "Sure."

So I went over to the icebox and got eggs and milk. I got the big stone-colored bowl off the shelf and then I got sugar from the bin. I got vanilla and nutmeg from the cabinet. I cracked eggs over the bowl and measured in milk and vanilla.

"Mattie," I said, "you gonna talk to me?"

Mattie turned her head and gave me a long look. For an instant there was a flicker in her eyes, as when a match touches sandpaper. "Look here," she said, in a tired voice. "I think shrimp's fine. We got plenty to do."

"Yeah, but you gonna talk to me?"

"Shrimp's fine. Since the reverend called the meeting, that means the whole church is coming."

"Mattie," I said.

"What?"

I stood looking down at eggs swimming in the bowl.

"Would it help to say I'm a fourteen-karat gold-plated turnip-eating fool?"

"No argument from me."

"No argument from anybody, looks like."

We stood. After a while I looked up.

"All I'm saying is, I think we ought to talk—"

She didn't answer.

"—about what happened?"

She shook her head.

"Well? Well come on, let's get it aired, don't sull up on me—"

Mattie threw down the spoon. Then she jerked around and burst out in a voice that wasn't tired anymore but angry and wild, "Ain't you messed up enough in things? Why can't you leave me be?"

I stared into her eyes, which in the pained face had caught kindling and were crackling.

"Because I *am* messed up in things. I'm in it up to my ears and I'd just like to know. What it is I'm wading in."

I waited. Then, "You gonna tell me?"

She seemed to be turning the question over in her mind.

"Are you?"

She was shaking her head.

"What happened?" I demanded, more quietly than before—I was almost whispering—and took a step toward her.

"Why won't you tell me?"

"Why?" she repeated.

"Mattie, why?" I took another step.

"Because . . ." she began, and hesitated.

"Because?"

"Because," she said, and dropped the spoon on the stove, "Tchula saw it. Tchula saw the murder."

Tchula had seen. Tchula had seen. A familiar green acid was climbing from the back of my stomach toward my mouth, and I leaned back against the table. Mattie was standing there, and other than stare at her, I didn't know what to do.

I must have continued to stare, because she said, "So now you know." But she said that without the heat. She said that with a face drained of emotion, as though she was tired from the inside.

Then I heard my lips asking the question, as though to myself, "Who killed him?"

"All right," she said. "All right. Let's back up a minute. Back to before you got there. Before you and the others."

"Me and the sheriff."

"Yeah, you and Sherlock, and—"

"Mr. Ardor."

"Yeah. Before y'all got there. I had gone to check on her. I'd gone to tell her what happened. I needed to tell her, before she heard it another way. That I *didn't know*. I didn't know it was Earnie. I just saw his back, or I wouldn't have gone out and stabbed that knife in the tire, but how could I have known?"

Mattie looked at me as though desperately needing an answer. So I said, "You couldn't."

"How could I?"

"There was no way."

"So I went out to tell her," Mattie said. "And she already knew."

"About the murder?"

"Well, first of all about Earnie and the girl. She said she suspected. That he was seeing somebody. Though she did not suspect who. Which would sure fit Earnie, there was no telling him. Tchula hoped for a long time that something might shake a clear notion into that boy's head, or shake the stubbornness out, one and the same."

"So she didn't have any idea about them running off?"

She shook her head. "She didn't know the half of it. About how wrong I was. When I looked out that day I thought I saw a boy in a moving car dragging a girl along. *Hurting* her in some way. But as it turns out, it was just the opposite."

"How you know that?"

"From Mr. FBI. He talked to the girl—"

"To Sheila?"

"To Sheila—and she said that's the way it was. As it turns out, he'd knocked her up"—Mattie paused and let this sink in—"he'd knocked her up, and she'd wanted to run away with him. She told him so. It was *her* idea. So she told Earnie to meet her here, at the deserted parking lot behind the café, but at the last minute, when she got here, something went wrong. She got scared, she said, and hesitated. She got out of the car to talk to him and then I guess Earnie got mad. They fought. Then I guess it was *Earnie* who panicked. He grabbed the keys from her and got in the car and started to take off. Then she ran around the other side and opened the car door and was trying to get in. And that's when I saw. The car was moving and he had his right hand reached across the seat grabbing her arm and dragging her—*hurting* her in some way—at least that's what I thought. Only it wasn't. As it turns out, *he* was trying to push her away and *she* was holding on to him. That's what she said. And to top it off, I could just see the back of his head. I didn't *know* it was him."

I believe I thought about saying again I was sorry. But I said, half to myself, "What on earth were they thinking?"

"Maybe they didn't think." She sighed. "Maybe they were planning to run off to a new place. Maybe, to a city. Every plan's really half thought out, isn't it, because you can't know the finish. But I guess if he knocked her up, any plan's better than nothing."

"Maybe he was in love with her."

"He could be in love with her and still knock her up."

"Well I think Sheila was. In love. Or at least doing an awful good imitation of it, the times she talked to me."

"Well, that's neither here nor there now."

"But you were saying, about Tchula—"

"Well," said Mattie, "like I said, I went out there. And when I walked in, I didn't see anybody and I didn't think she was there. You remember, that night it rained and rained, and that evening the clouds were already moving in. It was darker outside than usual and darker in the house. I didn't hardly see her at first. Just a thatch of white hair on a pillow and then she came up partway off the bed and grabbed at my dress. My blood liked to froze, the look on her face. She said, 'They strung him up.' Then she let go and fell back. She laid there looking off at some imaginary spot on the ceiling. Her breath ratcheting. She just laid there. And then her eyes rolled back and looked inside herself. Where I guess we all go in the end."

I stood there with Mattie. The room so still. She'd hardly more than whispered now, yet I felt the stillness all around me and I stood there listening to the stillness underneath another sound, which was the sound of Mattie's breathing. I said, "That's what she said?"

"That's what she said."

"They strung him up."

"I don't," Mattie breathed, "have to hear it again."

"Sweet-suffering Jesus."

"Yeah," she breathed.

"But she didn't say who."

Mattie looked downward and sidelong; then, after a moment, peered up at me. "D'she have to?"

"No," I said, and felt my face flush all over. For when Mattie said that Tchula had not said who killed the boy, I felt suddenly glad. I did, for an instant. An instant of pure gladness. And then all over again, the familiar taste of something like green bile climbing up the throat from the back of my stomach.

I went over to the sink. Poured myself a glass of water. Drank it down. "Hokay," I said, and I looked up. Mattie was still looking downward and sidelong. Her face had altered in this stillness, and I remembered the night of Tchula's death; yes, it was the same face. I looked away.

"I'm sorry," I said, and put the glass down. "I'm sorry. D'she have a nice funeral?"

"Yeah. Yeah it was. We had the ceremony at the church but we didn't bury her there. We decided to put her up there in that old graveyard by her house. That one by the church ruins, overlooking the river. We thought she'd like that. And it turned out to be a clear day, and folk did turn out. But the strange thing was, who did folk want to speak to, other than me and my brother, of course. Earnie. Folk kept looking around for him. But then, folk at funerals always take comfort in the faces of the young."

After a minute, I said, "You know, I think I'm gonna go upstairs for a bit. If you don't mind. I'm more tired than I thought."

"You go on," Mattie said.

"If you don't mind."

"I'll go for a bit," I said, and remembered the big bowl, with milk and eggs and vanilla. I picked up the bowl and started for the icebox. "And I'll finish this when—"

"You go on," Mattie said.

So I put the custard in the icebox. I went up the stairs. It was the first time I'd been up there since the day Eugenia died. How long had it been? That was the same evening I had found Will with Clarice Lytle on the *Elvira*. In shame, I focused my eyes ahead, and doing so I felt suddenly hollowed out, as if a tooth had been pulled. I stood in the room. Then I breathed in the smells. Smells of him yawning from the closet. Opening the windows did not help; finally I lay across the bed. I fell into vague sleep, dozed, and woke again to the thing that troubled me. I got up. Went downstairs. Mattie was at the stove and Mama was wiping the counter.

"I thought I'd help out," Mama said. She was still wearing that sign around her neck that said Handle With Care. "Mattie said y'all could use the help. And when I came I was gonna check on you, but Mattie suggested I leave you be. She said it was good that somebody could get some sleep."

Folk started arriving around seven. They all came together. It was the time hunters call the duck hour, not quite bright, not quite dark, the faintest cast of gold film on the windows.

Tallow lighting.

Skin like coffee.

Eye sockets tinged with pink.

The white-painted walls of the café radicalized the darkness of the faces. Faces never before in this place. Yet now I felt I was within something, a painting, the black folk drawn into the background, from the beginning of my vision, so meeting them was at the same time a kind of memory. *Tingaling* of Christmas bells, and they came through the door.

None of them spoke, as they came in; yet it was as if they all spoke, as some men tightened hands gently on women's elbows, and women weighed hands on children's shoulders, or on top of their heads. They crossed the front porch, and children gaped at Mama and me with round eyes, and all entered the café, quiet as burglars, through the front door.

Reverend Roberts said, "Good evening," his glasses glinting silver. That voice full of deep stage and velvet curtains, the roll of accent, authority.

"Evening, Reverend."

Mrs. Roberts was standing with him, still huffing a bit from the walk. She was a soft dumpling of a woman in a nice red dress, with thick brown skin that fell in soft folds at the base of her neck.

By way of introduction he said, "My wife."

"Well hell-*o*," she said, a hill in her voice.

"Hello," I said. "Well, y'all just have a seat. Just anywhere you like."

The Reverend and Mrs. Roberts were walking in front of a younger man, who was standing with his hands in the pockets of his overalls, once blue but now covered with gray dust. His face looked angry, suspicious. He looked at me. He glanced sideways and quickly hunted the window. He walked to the counter and eyed a stool as though he were not sure whether he wanted to sit there. Then he decided.

I did not know anything about him, or most of the others. There was a shyness at first within each of us, made more evident by the fact that Mama was standing there, behind the counter, trying to look a certain way. Then the stillness was suddenly overcome. The couples and old folk and the loners and the kids—all took their seats and started talking. Gradually voices picked up. The reverend had just remarked on appetite, and in voices that sounded oddly gay in the heavy evening, they were asking about the Friday night special.

"Mattie said shrimp—all you can eat. Does that mean all I can eat, or all you can eat?"

The reverend laughed in a deep, practiced way that resembled him.

"All you can," I said.

"Is that true," laughed Mrs. Roberts.

"If it's all he can eat," said another woman, leaning from the next table, "you in trouble," and then she started to laugh, and then a man at the next table gave a snort of amusement and he too was caught in the contagion, so that the man and the woman, Reverend and Mrs. Roberts all laughed as though they would never stop. For a second they seemed to strain deliberately for more laughter, or to prolong it, until they began to settle down and were likely thinking what I was thinking, which was what a small joke they were laughing at, all out of proportion to this kind of release. Finally they quieted down, as though out of tiredness, and in this nervous silence I took orders.

Mama was sliding half-moons of lemon onto the rims of ice tea glasses and carrying them to the tables. I tried to hold my arms the way Eugenia did, acting normal and friendly. Sliding in at the next table was Mattie's brother. I could tell that much. Arthur Boyd was a long-faced mirror of Mattie and a saunterer who seemed to be in no hurry to get through a sentence. His wife, Henrietta, was no sound at all, with a wandering, blue, right eye that quivered gently, like a flame. Their itty-bitty daughter, Matilda, seemed plainly curious about everything in the room, including the salt and pepper shakers, as I walked up to their table.

"You Mattie's niece?" I said, and grinned.

She looked up at me.

"You want to shake my hand?"

"No," she said, and the salt and pepper shakers transformed into galloping horses. She made cloppeting noises with her tongue.

Her father said something about how, yeah, she's Mattie's niece, all right. Then he rolled his eyes comically. I asked them if they were ready to order and then I started through the menu. I took their orders. I moved to the next table. A man who looked married to a woman but whose rough dark hands moved bare of rings. An old man named Gatemouth whose smile bared, apparently, three teeth. A woman with twins, each in a white Sunday shirt. A man with a long vertical scar that rose from the right corner of his lips, so his lips looked like the letter L. A schoolteacher, Oleta Watson, who introduced herself, with an inwardly moving glance. Another woman, eyebrows working as she leaned toward her father to shout, "Shrimp!" at his deafness.

They were talking above the hum of air-conditioning. Yet because of the crowd the air felt damp and material. It would have been good not to be wearing any stockings.

So I went to the kitchen, through the swinging door, Mattie standing over the frying shrimp, the inch of hissing oil, the shrimp smelling like salt, like oily pink, like water. I went back out. Mama pouring tea, eyeing the level of glasses, Mama and I carrying plates. A burst of laughter and silence: all in fits and starts, our imaginations hugely elsewhere, so that time began to tick full and slow and spaces hung between what folk said, as the night put on flesh and thickness. Through the front windows the moon was round and near-seeming, with a line of crooked brown like the river. Lightning bugs on the panes. Then other lights as the sheriff's car pulled in front of the café and slid to a stop. For a moment he left his lights on. He left them shining on the faces. And then he turned them off and sat in his car, looking at the profiles bent over plates, now mute, lifting forks up and down, without raising their eyes to the waiting car.

A minute later, a man walked up to the café, alone. He had a square dark beard and a yellow face. He was an older man, but his body was still young, with muscles visible through his sagging overalls and shirt. He made a wide loop in back of the sheriff's car. He had apparently seen it as soon as he turned the corner and was making this detour on his way to my door.

But then the sheriff got out of his car. Everyone stopped eating. An expression of vast amusement gleamed for a moment in the sheriff's face. The sheriff approached the man and the talk became lively and suddenly the sheriff broke out in a deafening voice that twitched my memory of standing with him by the river. Without any forewarning, the man in overalls suddenly dropped his head like a child caught in the act. At another word from the sheriff, he took two steps back with the shuffling gait of a schoolboy and started back down the road.

At that moment, Reverend Roberts was out the door. He stepped into the road, faced the sheriff with folded hands. But his look was hard. He said something to the sheriff, and the sheriff continued in a voice that had become, for the moment, oddly harmonious. Everybody listened. When the sheriff had finished, no one stirred. Then he spoke again in an impatient voice. He said something else to the reverend, who shook his head. Whereupon the sheriff said a few words in the tone of a command. Reverend Roberts turned and called down the road, in the direction of the man in overalls, and then he turned around to face the café. He walked back toward us. He opened the door and took a step inside.

He said, "I'm going home with Eli Timber."

Mrs. Roberts stood up. "I'm going with you."

"No," he said.

"I am—"

"I am too," said Arthur Boyd, and stood. His wife, Henrietta, stood with him.

"Me too," said the man with the scar.

"Yeah, Reverend," someone else was saying.

I saw Mattie push through the kitchen door. The twins in white Sunday shirts pushed out from their mother then, and there was a ripple across the room. A shuffling, and everybody stood. The only light from the ceiling made violet, downward shadows of the faces.

"Wait," said Reverend Roberts, and held up his hands, and for a moment drew out the silence like fingers on the perfectly resined keys of an organ. He looked around the room. "Don't you know who wants you to do this? Don't you see?"

Mrs. Roberts stepped out from the table. She opened her purse and got out some folding bills and put them on the table. She walked toward him.

"I said—" said Reverend Roberts.

"I know what you said."

"Well"—he sighed—"the rest of you have a seat. Please." He kept his hands up. Then he nodded to his wife. Turning his back on the standing crowd, he followed her out, paused, and, looking back at me and with his hand still on the door, said, "We thank you for supper." And left.

Whereupon the rest of the crowd began to sit down. Slowly, one by one, they were staring at each other. They were staring at their plates. They were staring at their forks, like thin water moccasins on the table. The door had closed, and the sheriff got in his car and left. Finally they reached for their forks. Within the next ten minutes, they said not another word and managed to get through their food. They paid up. And damned if they didn't walk out of there, the same way they came.

Mattie went with them. Mama had followed her into the back and beat me to it: She told Mattie it was a good idea.

"Look," I added, by way of persuasion. "I slept half the afternoon, and now I'll clean up. I want you to go."

Mattie was hunkered at the sink and dropped in dirtied silverware with a hard cursing blow. "Then," she said, looking from Mama to me, "you go too."

"Well, excuse me, but I think spending the evening with you and yours is quite enough for the town to chew on without our going gallivanting down the sidewalk together."

Mattie stopped. She wiped the palms of her hands down the armhole apron and reached behind her waist and untied it and took it off. She hung it on the meathook by the cabinet.

I said, "I ain't telling you nothing you don't already know."

Then she left. She left with the rest, as Mama and I stood and watched. Then we started clearing tables as I glanced out the window. Down the street all was darkness. Not even a dog barked. I went back to the kitchen to help Mama start the dishes. Her mouth different from worry. But for whatever reason, because there was no help for it or the silence was working on each of us, we didn't say a thing. The clink of cups and the slide of crusted dishes sounded trustworthy, almost normal. Our hands pinked from heat, under the waltz of steam, as the dishwater went brown-gray, the suds bubbling a smell, like grapefruit.

Then the phone jolted my heart. A small pale animal, Mama's hand, leaped from the dishwater. It rang again. I went out front. On the third ring, I picked up.

"Bitch," a voice said, a man's voice. I hung up.

It rang again. I picked up and hollered, "What the hell you want?"

A listening silence, then click, the dial tone, a long hollow blowsy tunnel, spit and crackle, like frying eggs.

The Luna Moth

FROM AUGUST 26 TO SEPTEMBER 3, the FBI searched the river for the body. They also put out an advisory for Mrs. Adelia Jones's 1959 green Buick station wagon. Men scouted the area just down from Tchula Gaze's house on the bluff until they found, in a fissure on a branch of the willow tree, evidence of rope. Six microscopic strands of hemp, "fine as a baby's hair," Mr. Nod said. They had it sent to Forensics, he said. It all sounded so strange to me—evidence, Forensics—no doubt a mixture of the influence of crime television and my mind's effort to distance itself. Without consciously imitating the FBI's grisly fascination, I was perhaps becoming infected by it. Just as I was becoming equally cut off from anyone outside the café. Once in a while I'd hear *Bitch* whispered as I passed by, as though it were my epitaph before I had a gravestone. I heard the sheriff say it. Mrs. Viola said it. And all I could think was I would not listen. Nor would I try to serve the world's greater good. I would get up in the morning. I would wait on my customers. Then I decided to cut my hair. Before work, I went into the bathroom and picked up a pair of scissors and began to cut, not worried about style—I just cut it away. I cut what was left to the nape of my neck and went down to face my customers.

So the pattern of business changed, from weekdays to weekends, to Friday and Saturday nights. Reverend Roberts was a regular for lunch, and Mr. Nod would pop in to order a dozen lunches to go for his folk out working on the river. And then Mattie's niece Matilda would join us when her parents dropped her off on the way to work. The child wasn't much trouble anyway, so I said fine by me. She often sat drawing with paper and a box of crayons. She liked to draw her name, eat scraps of Mattie's biscuit dough, and ring Eugenia's Christmas bells on the door. Yet even Matilda offered little diversion, for when she was clever I expected it wearily, and when she was happy I regretted her innocence. The days went like that. Mr. Magee would leave mail on the front steps. When I would close up, I'd walk to Eugenia's house. I stayed with Mama there, until I went in one morning and found that someone had broken several café windows. There were shards of glass over the floor. Mama made me take one of Uncle Lawrence's old shotguns and I started spending nights at the café after that.

Then, on September 14, Mr. Nod paid his lunchtime visit. Reverend Roberts finished his lunch and Matilda was at a booth with her crayons. Mr. Nod took off his jacket, spoke to both of them, and set his sunglasses on the counter. "Home sweet home," he said. "I'll have whatever the special is."

I served him up fried chicken, acorn squash, mashed potatoes and gravy. I poured him a glass of ice tea. And I had two Hershey's bars, still cold from the icebox, as we spoke.

"So, anything?"

"Well, as a matter of fact," he said. "One nineteen fifty-nine green Buick station wagon. Parked in the back lot of a filling station, up in Batesville."

"Batesville?"

"Yes ma'am. Not two blocks from the train station."

"Which means?"

"Which means everything. Or nothing. Depending on how you look at it. Or don't want to look at it, as the case may be."

"Is there something you getting at?"

Mr. Nod looked at me. He looked at his tea. "What I'm getting at is, do you have any plans? For the near future?"

"Well, yessir, actually. I plan to unwrap this candy and let it nourish my body."

"I believe you're a woman with a dangerous will."

"Mama calls it mule-headed."

"Be that as it may, I suppose, you're in good company. But the fact remains I've been watching. And this kind of development just goes to show, a case like this can take on a life of its own. It can leave—how shall I say it—a legacy for a young woman of your kind."

I looked at him.

"It's just that, after all is said and done, sometimes a change of scenery can be a good thing."

"So you think I should leave?"

"I think you should do what you want to do."

"That's good to know."

He stopped and looked at me. I stood, lifting a small square of chocolate to my lips. He turned and looked out the window. After a while, he said, "As I was saying, the car turned up, not two blocks from the train station. Does that mean anything to you?"

"It means, I guess, somebody drove it up there."

"What it also means is that somebody's making an effort. That tire, which had surely gone flat when the boy fled, well, it'd been changed. Left in the back of the car with a piece of your cook's knife still in it. Free of all fingerprints, naturally. Considering this, and the placement of the car, it just goes to show you, ma'am, somebody's going to a lot of trouble."

"And why are y'all?"

"Why are we what?"

"Going to so much trouble."

Mr. Nod lifted the tea and was about to sip it, and then he stopped.

"You know," I said, "I asked about this before. You said Reverend Roberts—how did you put it—has some influential ties."

"Yes ma'am. He's got a friend in Birmingham who's got a bigger friend. So that's why I'm trying to tell you, ma'am. These things have a way of taking on a life of their own."

Mr. Nod said all of this a certain way. He said it almost like an apology. Then he reached and got his cigarettes out of his pocket and lit one and looked at me and looked out the window down the street again. "Well, look, anyway, to hell with my advice. After all, it's not my place to say.

"As for questions about the car, I'll be heading up to Batesville this afternoon. To ask a few questions. Though no one questioned thus far has any recollection of who took it there. Or when."

Mr. Nod sat and we talked a while longer. Finally he looked like he was about to get up, but he didn't.

"Well, I'm due up the road," he said. "I want to thank you for a fine lunch, ma'am." He stood and put his card on the counter. "That's my number, if you need it." Then he put on his jacket and sunglasses, opened the door, and set out.

As the investigation dragged on, I lost all enthusiasm for the cooking. While we were pulling in good business on Friday and Saturday nights, the customers on weekdays remained sparse. I even talked to Mattie about extending café hours to suppertime during the week, but she said it wouldn't work. Whatever their hours, most black folk simply couldn't spare pocket change for a restaurant meal during the week. So I went back to focusing on weekends. Then, at the lowest point in my profits and spirits, something occurred that proved to me I was indeed at a mercilessly low point. Brother Works came to see me.

I was behind the counter. It was Wednesday, September 27, and I remember the moment so clearly that I recall what Mattie was carrying. It was a small paring knife, old and nicked at the edges and slightly bent at the handle. At the ring of Christmas bells she came through the door and looked at Brother Works and led Matilda back into the kitchen.

"Afternoon, Fannie," said Brother Works.

"Brother Works."

"Fannie—" and he took a seat at the counter. He looked around as though he had mastered my situation at a glance. "Fannie, I know, perhaps more than you can realize, what you've been going through. That sometimes circumstances can get beyond your control. It's your story, but it's hardly new. Trouble's been a large force in the human dominion down through the ages! It's what we do with the trouble that counts! I have always tried to remember that, and in my professional capacity, I try to let that serve me from the pulpit.

"Be that as it may, we are all God's children, even though you think I am not on your side. God loves those we like and those we can't stand! I'll be direct: You have never attended church. You have offered no support in our direction. Yet I might be of service to you!

"This café has for years been a fine institution. Eugenia and Lawrence Boatwright before her, God rest their souls, offered a hot plate and a friendly hand and a worthy service to many a Persia citizen. This is undisputed. This is your family's history. But times do change. In addition, you're a person who of late has seen a decline in business. Those are the facts. Now let me add facts together. Let me make you an offer.

"The leadership in town would like to buy the café. I approached them with the idea that we should all have second chances! I suggested the purchase! And the deacons listened. They are good, patient men. I broached the idea of joint ownership, myself not part of that, mind you—this would be separate from the church. But the purchase might go a long way toward restoring peace in this town."

Brother Works took a breath, then continued: "For the most part this idea was carefully weighed. Why not let bygones be bygones? Why not let water flow under the bridge?

"Now, what are the advantages for you? A nest egg, a fresh start, for both you and your mother. Plus security for your cook, Mattie. Guaranteed! The deacons have agreed to keep her on and have even put that into the contract. One fine fellow in particular suggested leniency."

Brother Works pulled a folded piece of paper from his jacket and set it on the counter. I didn't pick the paper up.

Finally I said, "How generous."

"We try to be." His eyes glittered. "Clarice Lytle, as you know, is leaving us soon—oh, or did you? Trading in her bookkeeping duties for a move to Jackson and admittance to beauty school. That poor child, she has gone through her share of troubles, and you'll be happy to know—she has found her own repentance!"

"Well, in that case, I'll be especially happy to know another thing. You say that you can be of service to me. But now that I consider it, I believe my staying can be of service to you. Think of it. Sheila Jones has left town. Now, Clarice Lytle. Who would be left for you to pray over about if I leave? How in the world would you sermonize?

"Yessir, come to think of it, we're a lot alike, you and me. We both got our needs. Me, I cook. To use your kind of words, God gave me that desire for a reason. Actually, that was something old Mrs. Thistle said to me once. And maybe in turn God gave you this town, and on top of it all, He gave you me and the café. We can make your reputation, is how I see it."

Brother Works stood. "Your opinions don't interest me."

"But the café does."

"I would not, if I were you, take this proposition lightly."

"So, how much money you offering?"

"It says it all there, in black and white."

"And security for the cook, you say."

"Take a look for yourself."

"Well, I suppose I'll just show this to Mattie."

Brother Works' face hardened. "That's not for her consideration."

"And the café's not for sale."

"It's a wise woman," he said, "who knows when to throw in the towel."

"And it's a mo-ron," I said, "who takes advice from a horse's ass."

Then he took himself and the papers out my door. I felt that insults had been offered on both sides.

There was a wagging patch of shadow through the kitchen window: I knew, all the while, Mattie had been trying to listen. The shadow wagged on, the shape of it puzzling me until I put the pieces together.

"Well, you heard they wanted *you*," I told her, after Brother Works had left. But Mattie did not fly off at me as usual. Her lips compressed as though trying to hold inside the many facts she had to inspect. Or did she simply pity me my scrap of vanity?

It was true, as Brother Works had guessed, that I had not known about Clarice Lytle's departure. In my days with Will, in my old jealousy, I could recall how the very mention of her name brought that rush of feeling, like thorns in the feet. Odd too, for a moment when Brother Works told me the news, how I almost felt sorry for her. But I would try not to think of that now. I would not even wonder. I would head back into the kitchen again, where Mattie was. For Mattie was one of those left. And I was. And the silence too between us, not because there was nothing to say but because there might be too much and once you started you might break the strained balance we achieved. So we didn't make a move toward one another, even for a second; we didn't say a word.

We didn't say a word, but sometimes Mattie would talk to Matilda. She would pick her up and let her stand on a chair and show her how to sift, how to work the flour into shortening till it resembled small peas. It seemed a safe bet. Matilda never upset any balance. Though Mama was a different story. It had been a month, and Mama had weathered the town's rejection in her own way, yet sometimes such a bewildered look came into her eyes. When she came in to help us prepare for the Friday crowd, it was the same.

"Tell me about your day," she would say. She had just come from the dining room, where she had been decorating the tables. It was a thing she was starting to do, decorate each with some little bouquet. Then she came into the kitchen. She had been out at Eugenia's house alone all day, and Mattie and I were somebody to talk to.

"Won't you tell me anything?" she then said.

"There's not really anything to tell."

"With all this preparation going on."

"Mama, what you want me to say? Here's fifty pounds of catfish. Fifty of chicken. Those breastbones could use splitting."

"Well, would you like to talk about something else?"

"Like what?"

"Did you start any good books or see anything on TV or visit someone besides your mother lately?"

"What you want to know?"

"I want to know what you did today."

"What is this?" I said. I couldn't keep the sarcasm out of my voice.

"It's an attempt at civility," said Mattie.

"So shoot me," I said.

"Look," Mama said quickly. "I don't want to break your concentration. I won't say another word."

There was a long silence.

"No, I won't say another word."

She turned away suddenly and walked across the kitchen. She stopped in front of the back door, which was open, with the screen door latched. Through the screen fall air came into the room, with a smell different from the fish and chicken smell. It was a smell of harvested cotton and damp river and drying leaves falling from arched trees down the street. It was a smell that definitely did not belong here in this room. I heard the blue eye hiss on top of the stove. I saw red peppers on the kitchen sill and a fork and spoon upright in a milky glass. And suddenly Mama said, "Well would you look at that!" and then I turned and saw what she was looking at, a huge pale green moth, pale as a slice of evening sky—a luna moth, they're called, for they had come to Mattie's kitchen before. On a trace of air it drifted, silkily silent, an easy, easy floating. Now it landed on the screen door, where a luna moth definitely did not belong. I noticed Matilda then, and she walked toward the door. She had her paper and colors with her. She sat down on the floor and opened her little box. She pulled out a crayon. It was green, I saw that, I saw the way she was watching. Perhaps it's a good thing children's eyes are closed to the frailties of this world or else they'd have no cause to try at all.

I thought this. I thought this as I watched her.

Then I pushed out the door to the front. Mama followed. There was silverware that needed putting on the tables and I started to do that. And Mama said, "You miss him, don't you?"

"I just want things back to the way they were."

"I know," she said.

We were standing by the tables, outside the counter. I took my apron and touched my eyes with it. "The frypan makes my eyes sting. What about you?"

"It's the cayenne," she said.

I looked at her. "Mama."

"Aw honey," she said. Then she gave me a sad look and forced a smile. "You know, maybe things can turn out. It's like Eugenia used to say, take this day to day. So maybe all this—won't be like this forever."

I might have told her I was sorry, I really don't know. I was tired and confused and sick at heart. Mama kissed me on the cheek, then stood back and sighed. "You know," she said, "I've been meaning to say something about your new haircut."

"You don't like it."

"No, no, honey. I didn't say that. Did I say that? Maybe just, if you'd put a few curlers in your hair."

"Mama."

"Oh, all right, well, in that case," she said, clapping her hands together suddenly. "There's one other thing you can do."

I looked at her.

"The bou*quets*." She gestured. "The least you can do is notice my handiwork."

I looked around the room. I could tell how Mama was trying to make her mark. The plastic covers had come off the Naugahyde booths because Naugahyde and plastic, she said, were "redundant." She had taken her sewing machine out to Eugenia's and was talking about making some curtains. And now these bouquets on all the tables. The season for flowers was passing, so this time it was fall leaves, arranged artfully in empty fruit jars.

"It looks real nice," I said.

"Well, I thought about cotton bolls," she said to me now, reflectively. "So fluffy, so pretty, you know. But I figured that's the last thing *they*'d want to look at."

Folk started coming in around the usual time. And they came in their usual way, all together, watching. At first I'd felt ridiculous, plastic, unreal as a doll in my uniform and white skin. The black children who stared at me; the adults who would not. Some of the older ones would not even look at me when they ordered their supper. There was Eli Timber, the man the sheriff yelled at that first night on the street in front of the café. There was Gloria Tilden, a big, cinnamon-dark woman with six grown children. Gloria Tilden, I learned, had one son killed in Korea, one who died in jail, two daughters who'd left for Chicago, and two sons remaining in Persia. One, Tomaine Tilden, ran the local juke joint. The other, her youngest, Trey, the man with the L scar above his lip, had his face sliced by Mr. Shine for taking a long break from fieldwork and peeing against a tree.

But were those reasons not to look me in the eye?

And Henrietta Boyd, who dropped off Matilda on her way to work at the Ardor house. Henrietta had worked for the Ardors for years, as had her mother before her. Henrietta was there in the kitchen the day I delivered the turtle cake for the Ardor boy's birthday and the Daughtry boy's chocolates melted. When I told Henrietta of the idea of using the chocolates to decorate the cake, she had whipped out a pot to help me.

And Beatrice Ardor had once said she counted her silver punch cups, once a month, to make sure none of them was missing.

What would happen to all these black folk, now my customers, sitting here in plain view and letting white women wait on them? It all seemed the beginning of something bigger than us: I could see it in their faces—a constant fear and misgiving and at the same time an addictive excitement. You could look out and feel the world flickering beyond our walls.

Reverend Roberts was talking to Gloria Tilden. Oleta Watson was complimenting Mama on her leaf bouquets. Arthur and Henrietta Boyd were sliding Matilda between them in a booth, and Adele Shelby was tucking napkins into the Sunday collars of her twins. I stood and watched them all, and quite suddenly I did not want to be here. In the café, Mama and Mattie moved, already the assembly line, and I, glancing out the window myself, had the disquieting sense that I was continuing some mistake. The river was shrouded with darkness; even the winking blue light above the pier seemed foreign and unfriendly somehow.

"Damn it, Will," I said, under my breath.

As I came out with the Boyds' dinner, I saw Oleta Watson's mother starting a story, straightening very slowly, a spoon in her left hand. I recall taking a look at her plate. She'd made a gravy pond in her mashed potatoes with the back of her spoon. For her age, she had a remarkably strong voice and looked over at the Reverend and Mrs. Roberts as she spoke. "It was the early morning on New Year's Eve, nineteen forty-five," she said, "and I was taking a walk by the river. It was a cold day and foggy. I believe it was the coldest day of the year. And that's when I saw with my own eyes the face of Jesus in the fog. Well now, why was it so foggy and cold that nobody else was there to see this? I didn't know. I didn't even think of trying to explain any of this to this educated daughter of mine. And after giving it some thought I said to myself, who could I tell this to who'd believe me? Who'd understand? . . . Tchula Gaze. And up to now, she was only one to know my secret."

"Amen," said Reverend Roberts.

"Is that so?" said Oleta Watson, cocking her head, a bit embarrassedly, at her mother. That was the beginning of a talk, growing in volume, which would last through supper. I saw Mattie signal to me from kitchen door and I walked back.

"You get everybody?"

"Almost."

"Well, you better."

"I *will*." I stopped and looked at Mattie. She frowned at me, beside her the fillets, sizzling into buttery floats, and her buttery hands, which she held away from her now like a scrubbed surgeon waiting for gloves.

So the evening went. I went out front, then back to the kitchen.

There were stories that were open—like the one Oleta Watson's mother had told—and stories that were not, and I was learning to tell the difference. This time it was a reference to the sheriff, at Gloria Tilden's table, and I saw it. The drop of the eyes. A fullness poured into her features the minute I passed. She seemed used to trying and getting it wrong. She looked to the reverend; the reverend looked at me; I went back to the kitchen. It was what I'd come to expect. The secretiveness in the faces, the annoyance I felt.

So the conversations, for me, had gaps of story like fields flooded by rain, missing events.

Soon afterwards I went around asking, "Anything else?" At the next table I saw Matilda making a tepee out of fish bones. I saw Mama tip her pitcher and a tea glass flush amber. Eventually I saw the reverend push back his plate and I took it and then he reached into the pocket of his trousers. He paid up, like the rest. And they all went out together.

Later that night, I went upstairs and drew a hot bath. The windows were steaming. The air was heavily still. I stayed in the bath long enough to listen to the café settle into itself and the water to cool and pressure to slip from the soles of my feet. Then I got out and put on my nightgown. I was pulling a comb through my wet hair when I thought I heard a noise. I felt a strange prickling on the back of my neck. Through the window I saw the branches of trees. The stray cats crying around the garbage. I had given them the evening leftovers; for a moment I had stood holding the leftovers and watched them through the back screen door, their nostrils sniffing the meaty air. Then I had opened the door and set down the food and soft paws scurried, tiny white fangs tore at bones, backs arched and tails batoned and fur rose and brushed my ankles, making electric sparks. I had watched them. A dozen cats. Now they looked up at me standing in the window, glowgreen eyes, yellow and gold, their pupils narrowing to slits in the night.

I turned away from the window then and turned out the light. Then I shook my wet head a little and turned on the TV and got into bed. The picture on the screen looked familiar. *The Lost Weekend* and a crazed Ray Milland in quest of the salvation of his bottle. Poor bastard, I thought, which were the words Will—yes, Will—had said when he was watching this very movie. "Poor bastard," he had murmured. Now, with the bottle upended and the muscles of Milland's throat working, I was reminded of Will and thought: poor bastard. Which in itself would not be odd were it not for the fact that this was the first time since he left I'd experienced any emotion having to do with Will that resembled anything so clearly as pity. I could not stand pitying him. Or wondering what he'd done. Or wondering if he was okay. Or these sheets, for that matter, which reminded me of the old battlefields, and so I kicked them off. I got up abruptly. I turned off the TV. And thought, don't, Fannie, don't think of this.

Till morning.

I was pacing around, dropping my eyes in this direction and that, and I could hear something stirring, noticed it in the direction of the cats. I turned suddenly toward the back window and saw a flickering through the glass.

Torches. Near the edge of the parking lot. I saw the flickering and saw it reflect in the eyes of scattering cats. Then I saw who was carrying them: kluckers. In the dark, they seemed dropped from some great and ghostly height. It seemed the very window was flickering. There was light that darted and stuttered, sheets that worked to defamiliarize and floated in pools of yellow-orange as they came. Slits for eyeholes were purple-shadowed, and fixed on me at the window. There were nine, maybe ten of them. I stood there. Finally I reached up to the window and gave it a yank. But it was stuck. I yanked again. As fast as I did this it seemed agonizingly slow as they watched. The frame of the window made a groaning sound, and the sheets stopped. As I struggled with the ledge, the window flew open. Again they stopped, and the ensuing silence made me feel I was dreaming. I had an urge to shout and test my voice. I felt a rising panic in my throat.

Then Uncle Lawrence's shotgun gleamed in the half-light. It was leaning against the wall. I thought to pick it up and heard the little jingle of the squirrel load left inside and then everything happened all at once. The footsteps quickened. I was trying to get that gun up and in front of me and at the same time lean out the window. I got it up, I got it in front of my shoulder, but the other end butted against the wall. I took a step back and poked it against the screen. I pulled the trigger. In the blast and kick at my collar-bone the wind was blown out of me and I wondered—for an instant, Have I been shot?

But there was a sound under the sound . . . *Umph*, which was the sound of somebody getting the wind knocked out of him or, in this case, lead pumping its way in, and in the relief of torchlight I thought, *I got a piece of you, I did. I sure-God did.* I felt high and pure, for all notions of turn the other cheek tend to pass me by at such a moment: *You bet your ass I hope I got you, I got a piece of one of you, at least, where it counts, and I'll gladly do it again.*

I thought that to myself. I did.

And all over again, with all the same suddenness, there was nothing but the acid of green bile climbing my throat from the back of my stomach.

I slumped down with my back against the wall under the window and listened to the feet coming, or to what to my distorted hearing—both sharpened and dulled by the gun blast—sounded like coming. I raised the shotgun to try to pump another shell into the chamber, but there wasn't another, and the empty, ejected shell skittered across the bare wood floor. I watched the shell roll under the bed. I sat there. I tried not to breathe, hearing the sounds outside. In the wake of moving feet, there was an edge to the silence. Something coming. My blood moved at the thought of them deciding whether I could live or die.

I put my hand to my mouth. I was soaked through; I felt the sweat on my upper lip and through my nightgown. Where's that damned box of shells? I wondered as I stared blindly around the room, breathing gun smoke, my own voice leaving me in a small animal-like sound I couldn't stop, even as I kept my shaking hand over my mouth.

I didn't move. I sat there, perfectly still, trying to keep myself from crying. I felt sorry for anything I had ever done as I waited for them to return. And in the waiting I lost sense of myself as Fannie: I was just something panicked and breathing in the dark, crouched on the bare wood floor. When I lifted myself to peer over the window, I saw my own white hands outstretched as if to grasp something in the air before me. And I thought of Will, *Oh Will!* but he wasn't here he wasn't even near for he had walked out—why? Because he was a fool? Because of them? Or maybe just because he was gone, the way the boy was gone, the way Fannie soon would be—and then I dropped back down to the floor. I waited. Then the sounds of the river could be heard.

The sounds of the river, and I thought if I could ever sleep again, I might dream of this, the thin rolling surface silverleaf and then, say, I might see underneath. I might see to the riverbed floor. Say, Earnest March is standing there. And he stands there looking up at the surface of the river, which is no longer the thin rolling silverleaf but the brown lid of a coffin, which it was.

Is the pattern of our lives born within us? Or do we make our lives when we look up from them? Do we only look up when the eyes of the dead implore us?

A long time ago, way back, in some way that was beyond me, Will and I had grown quiet with one another, a change had started, and I could remember waking up one day with a deep sense that something was wrong and there was no coming back from it. There was a change in the air that left me with a tiredness so heavy that only my work seemed to lighten me. Up through this past summer I had worked, worked as hard as I ever had, as the days wore on and Will grew angry and sullen with me. I kept hoping for something, and Will knew it; something different, something grand as a prize in the cooking contest, but I did not care about that now. Not now, no, not ever since the day had come when I had found Earnest March, floating in the shadow of the willow, and I had become this person I was, clutching an emptied gun, sitting on the upstairs floor in the café in the middle of the night, wishing with all my heart it were some other time, some other place.

Somewhere, I thought, there must have been a point when Will moved up to me, was by me for a moment, when I could have looked at him, if I had known, taken his hand, and said hold on.

Well, I had not known. I had not known; how could I in this town where it seemed you could never really know another person? I was alone in the world, in a way that made me feel the dryness in my mouth and the deep ache in my breathing, and the darkness rising through the room, like smoke.

And yes, I could imagine Earnest March feeling a change in the air that drained his will and sapped the very breath from him, in that instant before he collided with folk who looked like me.

The Bayou Vista Tale

AFTER I FIGURED THE KLUCKERS were safely gone, after I'd crouched on the bedroom floor for I don't know how long and convinced myself that the silence meant they were going and not coming, I remembered Mama. I remembered her out there alone at Eugenia's and then I got downstairs and called her. She arrived at my door so fast I figured she must have flown. But when the door flung open, I might not have recognized the face I saw unless I had known it to be Mama's. It was white and ravaged above the housecoat and slippers and she was carrying Uncle Lawrence's deer rifle under her arm. She stood in the doorway. Then, just behind her, there was another sound, and she swung the rifle around. It was Mattie.

"Good Lord," Mama whispered. Then, "How'd you—" But Mattie only took a breath. Then she looked at me. Then the two women led me back upstairs, holding me up by the shoulders as you would hold a carefully pressed dress. Mattie drew a hot bath. Mama lifted the nightgown over my head. And I soaked in the tub a long while, for the second time that night.

Mattie's brother Arthur must have come in soon afterward, and also Reverend Roberts. Mattie'd apparently gotten on the phone to each of them, though I hadn't heard her. I don't remember hearing much of anything, as a matter of fact, and when I went downstairs I don't remember what was said. The words stopped when I came into the room. I was wearing a clean long nightgown and was barefoot and my hair was still wet.

All the faces arranged themselves as I took a seat. A bottle of Will's whiskey was on the counter. Mattie reached underneath and pulled up a glass and set it in front of me. Then Mama reached for the bottle and poured me a drink and the reverend didn't even blink. The brew was so strong that beads of it sweated through to the outside of the glass. Through the window I could see the lifting of the night, the room brightening as the river caught light and the window banded electric blue. It seemed oddly cozy in the room, the richness of morning surrounding the café.

So I sat at the counter. And somebody said something. And somebody said something else. I sipped the whiskey and felt its heat percolate through my bath-soaked body so I was suddenly exhausted. The voices of Mama and Mattie and Arthur and the reverend brought forth a dove-dull flutter as I nodded off. All those kluckers I knew, I had been thinking to myself, as I tried to catch my chin. Then Mama led me upstairs and put me in bed. I slept for twenty hours, clear through the Saturday supper crowd, the busiest day of the week.

Afterwards, I found out, Mama had gone looking for the sheriff. She had gone to his house at sunup and then over to the courthouse. She had let it be known she was looking for him. Then, a few hours later, he showed up at the café. He showed up as Mama and Mattie were preparing for Saturday night and Matilda was sitting at the counter. She was picking up peas with her fingers and the sheriff looked at her and said, "Doesn't that child know how to use a fork?"

"Only on strangers," Mattie said.

Then the sheriff asked Mattie to repeat herself.

"She said," replied my mother, and from there *she* launched into a diatribe that did everything from invoke the spirits of Eugenia and Lawrence Boatwright to warning the sheriff about the perils of parading around "like a bunch of douche bags." She said that if he ever touched so much as a hair on her child's head she'd be the one to pump so much buckshot between his legs he'd think it was pepper steak. Or something like that. Apparently I'd missed all the fun.

But you get tired. And then you get yourself in the bed. And when you get up, you feel like you've been over this before. Reverend Roberts had called Mr. Nod and when he returned for his round of questioning, he found no answers at all. There was no buckshot wound. No visitors to Hanley Funeral Home. Dr. Butler had treated no one. I had started to aim the gun, I thought, slightly up above the heads, but then I'd lowered it at the last second and there'd been that sound afterward, that *Uumph*, which was, maybe, I don't know, a trick of the wind, a trick of the mind? A syllable of my imagination? And then you get to where you try not to think of it anymore, you have thought of it so often. But that isn't the reason. It's just that those folk you knew then are the folk you know now. If it were absolutely either way, you could just close your eyes and figure it out. But the trouble is, you knew them before and you know them now, and in the end that is what paralyzes you. You wish you could explain this to someone, but that time is long past, and so you say as little as possible.

So I said as little as possible.

Except when Mr. Nod came in. He asked me to tell him what happened and I did. He raised his head to smell the coffee and I offered to brew a fresh pot. Over the counter we talked tentatively.

"Now what was it that gave them away?"

"What?" I said, and looked up from coffee I was pouring.

He reminded me. "You told me you know who they are."

I bowed my head, pouring.

And Mr. Nod looked around, sliding the sugar canister next to the pepper vinegar. He peered at the peppers layered on the bottom. Then he looked at me.

"Yes, you did," he said, "so I'm gonna ask you three questions."

He touched the rim of his cup and he asked me if I had heard a word any of the Klan had spoken. Then he asked did they come down the back street or from the alley by Ardor Department Store. Lastly he asked me if I had been able to focus on any shoes.

I told him they came down the back street and then I told him I couldn't give him anything else. Then I said again I knew.

"What do you know?"

"Well, I think it's a case of understood identity."

"Understood ain't proof. Intuition doesn't close a jail door." He sat and looked at me. He turned and looked out the window and then he turned back.

"Look," he said. "They might all be local, they might not. We got more than our share of night travelers. And if you hit anybody, since you say you started out aiming high, it might have got them in the arm or shoulder. It might have been a graze, a powder burn. Which would amount to no more than a discoloration of the skin. If that's the case, he's one lucky sonofabitch, whoever he is. Buckshot wounds are not usually—how shall I put it—modest. And as for you, Mrs. Leary, I'd like it a whole lot better if you'd try to get yourself killed in a more conventional way."

"What on earth does that mean?" Mama snapped. She had come through the kitchen door with a stack of napkins and she stopped and looked at him.

"Just a bad joke." He shrugged. "My apologies, ma'am."

"Apology accepted," Mama said, and went back through the kitchen door. Mr. Nod watched her walk back and then he leaned his forearms against the counter. He sipped his coffee.

"Well, is there anything else you can think of? Anything you might have left out?"

"Not that I can think of."

"Well, in the meantime, then, we're checking that car in Batesville. We got these pieces missing."

"Yessir. Everything's got a piece missing. And everybody. And when you try to find or make up for the missing piece, you make your worst mistake."

"Which is?"

"I don't know."

"There's something else, isn't it?"

"I don't know. I mean, nosir. I guess not."

"Well, if there is, let me know." He stood. "Is Mattie back there? I just need to ask her something."

I pushed through the kitchen door. Mama was pausing at the sink to counterpoise a cup and a dripping pan on the dish rack. Mattie was standing at the screen door, with her hand on the latch. I didn't see at first what she was staring at, but I heard the cough of an engine and saw the Piggly Wiggly truck pass. In the last months J. J. Shine had taken over the job of milk delivery for Earnest March. He never brought the bottles inside the way Earnest did but left them on the steps outside the screen door. He'd apparently been told not to come inside, though the bottles were so cold tiny beads of moisture clung to the outsides.

"Mattie," I said. "Mattie?"

I looked at her and then I wondered if this was what she was thinking of. We looked at the cold milk bottles.

In the week following, the town continued another part of its little game. My white neighbors continued to demand that their hired help not frequent the café. And my black customers continued to tell their employers that they would not come. Then they came anyway. Or they admitted they were coming and faced the consequences. Mrs. Butler fired Pearline Watson. Mrs. Lytle fired Adele Shelby. Then Mrs. Butler tried to hire Adele Shelby to replace Pearline Watson. Mrs. Ardor fired Henrietta Boyd and then hired her back, because, as Henrietta said, "She ain't gonna wash her own dirty drawers."

Meanwhile, at the café, Mama was making a habit of coming in every day. She would come in, she said, just to check on me, though this was half-truth. She'd comment on how thin I looked or what she said was my yellowish sheen, and then she'd ask me to come stay at Eugenia's. All of this before I had a chance to say I wanted to stay. Which was also half-truth. I'd go to bed at night and fall into a half-sleep, wake again sharply, to the thing that troubled me. I stared around the room that felt larger than it was, cavernous and resonant, and listened hard as though waiting for a signal. But there wasn't a sound except the hush that happens when there is not a breath of breeze and you are close enough to the river to get the whisper and stir, even when the water is quietest.

Nor did the coming of daylight bring things back to normal; the café, with Mama and Mattie and me, in the silence and pallor, seemed even emptier. The three of us in separate orbits, each in our separate gravitational pulls. For even when I was working I would feel the question tugging. Even when I was preoccupied, it would return.

Who killed Earnest March?

I could see the traces around me. A sentence. A word. Or from something as brief as the gesture in a face. I had walked into the sheriff's office that day, to tell what I had seen, and I had come to believe in nothing, to trust nothing. Their implications about Will. Burl Magee departing the courthouse to tell my mother. And that night, with the storm gathering as I led Mr. Ardor and the sheriff up the bluff and down to the willow by the river and the thing in their faces that told me what they had done.

It was sometime after this I considered talking about it to Mama. But I didn't see how I could. I did not even begin to acknowledge it when I saw her at the café or when I visited her at Eugenia's house, on Sunday mornings, over coffee. Visiting was a thing I did when I got cabin crazy. But I hadn't said a word.

Until the moment I had to ask.

So I was back in the parlor in the old brick house, among the mahogany furniture upholstered in burgundy, looking down at a vine in the carpet. Little had changed in that room, though Rodin's *The Kiss* now embraced itself by the door. She'd made a fresh pound cake that morning and insisted we take it all out into the parlor, on Eugenia's good china, and enjoy some "echo of civilization" for a change, for didn't we spend enough time in the kitchen?

I suppose she had a point. And I sat there with the coffee and cake balanced on my lap and looking at a vine in the carpet, or looking at Mama and back at the vine, as she glanced around in that abstracted way of a hostess enjoying company. And I said, "Mama, I'm gonna ask you one question. About—it. And if you don't want to talk about it, I won't ever bring it up again."

She looked at me without answering. She looked suddenly disappointed and tired. Then she glanced sideways toward the window.

So I said, "You told me—that night when Burl Magee came over to your place—that he told you that I was with the sheriff—and he told you about—"

"About the murder," she said, finishing the sentence on which I, for a moment, hesitated. She hadn't wavered. With this she seemed resigned.

I nodded.

"So?" she asked.

"Did he say anything about who did it?"

She thought for a moment. You could see her reaching back, and the curious shading of feeling on her face, too mixed for definition.

Then she shook her head. "No," she said, "he didn't say—except that it was—the boy." She hesitated. "And he said, we have a grave situation."

"He said, 'we'?"

"Then he said—something odd. He said on a day like this, the bushes have eyes."

"Did he say anything about a shooting, or a hanging?"

"No."

"Are you sure?"

"What do you mean, am I sure?" She bolted up from the chair. "For if you're implying—"

"I'm not implying—"

"—that *I'm* holding anything back."

"I'm not implying anything, Mama. I'm just wondering."

"Well, the fact is, you could at least exercise a little—common sense. If we're not willing—to sell the café—"

"Do you want to sell it?"

"I didn't say that."

" 'Cause if you do—"

"And give the local yokels satisfaction?" She drew herself up, as though breathing in high ocean air.

"Well, it'd be a neat solution. The white customers could have the café back. And we could be gone."

"Look, I didn't say that. Did I say that? All I'm saying is, I still think you ought to—come out here and stay."

"We've been over this, Mama."

"Well, there's plenty of room."

I didn't say anything for a moment.

"Oh, Lord." She started pacing. "Good Lord," she muttered again.

"Mama, don't."

Then she stopped. "You know, if Eugenia were here, *she* might be able to talk some sense into you. And you might think of someone else's feelings for a change. You ought to remember that all that's happened isn't—just your grief."

At that moment there was a knock on the door. Mama's head yanked around and in a single motion she went to the door and opened it to Mr. Nod and said, with a flourish of a hand, "Oh, *you* talk to her."

"Ma'am," he said. Then she went upstairs.

I closed my eyes and rubbed the lids and then I opened them. Mr. Nod had taken a seat on a chair. He had on the shirt with the white cuffs rolled back but no tie or jacket, and I could make out the outline of sunglasses in his pocket. For a moment he was quiet. Then he said, "I came by the café."

"Well, I came out here for a visit."

He nodded.

"A typical pleasant Sunday morning," I said. Then I offered him some of Mama's cake. He declined but took some coffee. We sat.

"Well, go ahead," I said. "Fire away."

"I'm not asking anything."

"Or is there some new stone unturned?"

"Well, actually."

"What is it? Don't tell me. A sudden confession? An attack of conscience?"

He looked at me.

"Or, no, could it be . . . a new strand of hemp, another dog turd?"

"Ma'am," he said, and put down the cup. "I just talked to Wilson. He's been up in Batesville. And what I was about to tell you is, we got a witness."

It seemed there was a postal route in Batesville on the same street as the back lot of the filling station where the green Buick station wagon was discovered, and the postman, one Jubal Sallis, on the job early, had noticed a young black boy fitting the description of Earnest March rushing across the back lot at 7:30 A.M., on August 18. The postman tried yelling at him, but he was too far away to be heard clearly, or the boy ignored him. The postman watched as the boy, wearing trousers but no shirt, ran across the back lot, through an alley to the train depot, and jumped a moving train. He hung on to the edge of a boxcar for maybe ten seconds. Then he pulled himself up and climbed inside. The postman wondered if he should alert someone, but before he could do anything, the train was gone. And because the postman had seen the boy not in the station wagon but near it, he said he did not realize the possibility of car theft involved.

"Hell's bells," I said quietly. "What next?"

Mr. Nod said nothing.

"This witness. He says he just happened to see him?"

Mr. Nod looked at me thoughtfully for a long moment. "I think he meant to see him, ma'am. I think the postman meant to see him."

"Has anybody else seen anything?"

"Outside Batesville? You mean your husband?"

I nodded.

"No, nothing. Sorry."

Then Mr. Nod left. I stood at the door while he went down the porch steps, watched him until he reached the car and then until he reached the road and let his hand up in something less than a wave. There was a sound on the stairs behind me; I turned; it was Mama, and I could tell by her face that she had heard.

And I thought, yeah. Soon everybody. By the next day, in fact, news of the witness had spread. At the café, for instance, I found Mattie working through the biscuit dough and an exchange with little Matilda, in which the usual "Hungry?" had been met with a nod. Then she turned and said, "A witness. Boy, ain't that ever like them."

I didn't say anything.

"So I guess that's the end of it," she then said.

"Maybe."

"Ain't no maybe about it."

"You almost sound pleased."

Mattie turned her head in my direction and gave me a long look. For an instant, the eyes embered. "What if I was?" she said. "What if I said, it's about time I had a rest?"

I looked at her.

"Why shouldn't I want to, after this? Big man come in here and flash a badge and think everybody's gonna sit up and say, Oh goody, goody, let's swap secrets. Coming in messing with folk who'd rather climb to the top of a tree to tell a lie than stand on the ground and tell the truth. Which is just as well, like I told him, I said, if folk ever did start swapping secrets you wouldn't get out of here with any ears. 'Cause they'd be clean burned off. I said, that goes for everyone till judgment day and that goes for you, too, Mr. FBI."

She stopped kneading the dough and looked at me. Then said, "And that goes for you too, Missy."

I didn't say anything to that. So she dropped back to the work, and into herself.

I got out the skillet and put on some bacon before I said, "Mattie, I've been meaning to ask you—about that night—when the kluckers came. How'd you know about that?"

I paused.

"I didn't call you to tell you, but you came here anyway."

I watched Mattie reach for the rolling pin. Then she shrugged. "I had a feeling."

"Some kind of a dream?"

"No, just a feeling."

Then I said, "Look, Mattie, I reckon I know how you feel—and I don't want to—be bringing up everything again, but—"

"You don't know how I feel."

"Well, I think I do. I think I got some idea. But what I was about to do—was, I was gonna ask you one more question."

"I thought what you're gonna do was a little work for a change."

"As a matter of fact, I am. That's one thing I'm not shy of and you know it. But that's not—"

"Yeah," she interrupted, "oh yeah. Work's a thing nobody's shy of and yet somehow it don't get done. There ain't gonna be no trial. No jury. No witnesses slapping their hands on the Book and swearing to tell a half-truth, a quarter-truth, anything but the truth."

I waited till she settled back down. Then I said, "You told me that day—you went out to see Tchula Gaze—and she told you about—"

Mattie didn't seem to be listening to me. She was quiet and rolling the dough. I hesitated, and then, watching her face, went on. "She told you about—what she saw."

I waited again and watched her face, but it didn't show a thing.

"I found out—one thing," I continued. "Burl Magee went to Mama's house that—night—to tell her that—I was at the sheriff's office. He said—a lot of things but—said, in particular, 'We got a grave situation.' Then he said—something else, he said—The bushes got eyes. As you can imagine, Mama was pretty flipped out at that point, but he stayed there with her for a while. That's the way he always was, though, trying to calm folk down."

"Yeah," Mattie said, not turning to me, "tell me about how well-meaning *Master* Magee is."

"I'm sorry," I said, and felt the blood rushing to my face. "I guess I did get off the point."

"I guess you did."

I waited. Then, " 'The bushes got eyes.' You got any—direct notion, what that is?"

Mattie seemed to be thinking for a minute. But if she heard me, I couldn't be sure.

"Do you?"

Mattie shrugged. "No, I don't."

"So you didn't—see anything."

"No, Missy," she said. "I can tell you no. Because, you see, I haven't *seen*." For an instant the voice rose, and then, just as suddenly, she seemed to have gone tired. She doubled the dough over. Then she punched it down and that seemed to restart her tongue. "You know how you feel about family."

"Well."

"I got a roof over my head. A home. And you know what old Tchula used to say? She said, folk get through things by being blind half the time. Taken me a while to learn that." She looked at me and pointed a flour-crusted finger at me. "You ain't got the hang of it either."

She slumped away from the counter and looked down at the floor. I thought about repeating the question. Or maybe I shouldn't. All right. I wouldn't. But Mattie began punching harshly at the dough.

"Long time ago," she said, "I wanted to say something to Tchula. I wanted to tell her, Don't let that boy run wild. Just 'cause you out there, high on the bluff, with nothing but cotton on one side of you and the river on the other, you think it don't matter. You think nobody's gonna care. But that boy's got to live in this place. Use a firm hand. Put the reins on him, but don't break him. But did I ever say it? Did I ever say a word?" Mattie jerked her head up as if she saw somebody else in the room. "And I tell you, if she was here, old Tchula could tell you a thing or two. . . ."

At that instant something dropped a long way, then landed. I saw her eyes going pink-rimmed; it was as if the eye-whites were smashed into a thousand fragments. In her eyes I felt something of the shock and energy that had radiated so strongly from the dead body. Did she know something else? She said she hadn't seen, but was there a distinction?

"Mattie," I whispered. I did not want to look into her eyes or ask. But I said, "Was there—something else? Was there something else Tchula told you, Mattie?"

Mattie turned away.

"You went out that day—you were last person to see her—was there—something else she said? She said, 'They strung him up.' Was there something else?"

"Auntie?"

It was Matilda, wandering into the kitchen, wrapping a stuffed doll in string. She variously amputated and strangled it, idly, while hugging it in the most gentle way. For her sake, I did not repeat the questions. And Mattie kept her face away from me, so I could no longer see her expression. Then she breathed out as if something had given way in her, and I could see she was gathering herself, trying not to show whatever it was that had just gone through her. She stood there. And when finally she put her hands to the dough again, she said, in the lowest voice, "Look after her. I'm gonna finish these biscuits."

I could find nothing to say to that. So I guided Matilda through the door and walked on out front, leaving Mattie to the silence of the back and with Matilda looked through the front window, down across the river, where coiled under gray branches bare now except for the last clinging leaves, the brown-curdled water was heavy with the tinge of algae, autumn, and darkness.

I had found out that Burl Magee had all but winked at Mama on his visit the night after the murder. I had also found out that Mattie indeed knew something else, and that she, too, was holding back, something about the details of Earnest March. But whatever she was holding back was for one reason. And the town's was for another. There was a vague and troubling vacuum created by the difference, which I could not fill with an answer, so muddled with my own questions about Will did I realize the answer would likely be, and anyway, I told myself there was nothing worth the look I saw on Mattie's face the day I asked her those questions. What I actually told myself was, Work. Just work, Fannie. That's the thing.

Then, on October 23, Reverend Roberts and Mr. Nod were eating lunch at the counter. They had come in separately, and they sat one seat apart. They both ordered the special, ham and acorn squash, black-eyed peas. Pausing between bites, they spoke in brief businesslike bursts, forks clinking their plates.

"Tell me, did the boy go to church?" Mr. Nod.

"Some of the time." The reverend.

"What about Tchula Gaze?"

"Oh, how shall I say this. . . . I believe Tchula had her own faith."

"So she kept to herself."

"For the most part."

"Would you say—while we're on the subject—that she could shoot a gun?"

"Everybody knows Tchula could. She used hers for food. To shoot ducks, mostly."

"From some distance, I imagine."

"Depends on the duck. Some are not very bright. You might say too trusting. Some don't use their natural skittishness to best advantage around people. Which was certainly, hunh, as far as I know, never true of Tchula."

"But ducks wouldn't fly right up to her door."

"Nosir. To shoot one, say, at twenty yards coming off the river over the bluff takes a steady hand and a good eye. Even for somebody younger."

"Particularly with that piece she had."

"It was, I believe, a double-action Colt Lightning. When I was a boy, she let me look at it once. Look at it, hunh, but not touch it."

"She ever say where she got that?"

"Not that I recall. But then, again, Tchula aimed discussion in her own direction."

"I got you. And while we're on the subject, you do any hunting yourself, Reverend?"

"When I was a boy. I had more time then. Once, I remember, I had a dream about a big gray-throated quail. And I said to myself, if I ever dreamed of a bird again, I wouldn't shoot it."

"Remind me, Reverend, not to invite you hunting."

"A practical man."

Both men chuckled then, and I watched them eating their food. They paid up and left. I had some leftovers myself and locked the front door and turned the OPEN sign to CLOSED. Then I went out back and tossed the garbage. The twilight shadows were lengthening. There was a hoot owl on the telephone wires, harbinger of nothing. Sighting an owl at nightfall meant that spirits would be finding you. At least that's what Mattie said. The owl called a few times, then, with a slight gust of wings, flew off, casting a faint shadow as it passed.

"Fannie—"

Hearing my own name caught me under the ribs, a stitch of breath there. I turned and saw a figure step from the side of the café.

"Fannie, it's me, Amos."

"Good God—Amos."

I had not seen Amos since he had left with Will. How long had it been? The better part of two months. Now his face was stubbled with red and gray beard. His eyes were flat. He was panting. But mainly he looked aged, an old man of sixty. As I took him by the arm and got him inside, he was wincing. And as I closed the kitchen door, I said, "Your arm. What's wrong?"

"It's not broken," he replied, "just a bad bruise."

"Oh," I said, then added, "where is he?"

"I'll tell you it all," he murmured. "Just first, if you could get me some water."

I went to the sink and got a glass and filled it. I handed it to Amos. He quickly gulped it down. Then he halted for an instant, and as he raised his left hand to return the glass I sensed something slightly unnatural in the gesture, wondering what it was, then realized he was favoring his right arm, which hung limply at his side. It was obviously causing him pain.

"What happened to your arm? And where—"

"Wait, Fannie. Another glass. And let's go sit down."

Sitting on a stool at the counter in the darkened front room, Amos watched as I pulled down the shades. He took another gulp from the glass. Then I joined him at the counter.

"You can't be too careful," I said. "Or maybe you know—"

"That the law's after me? In any other circumstances it'd be almost laughable, wouldn't it? Here, for the first time in his life, Amos Leary on the lam."

"How'd you get into town?"

"Wiebe Schwietert. The back of her buggy. I happened to see her on the outskirts of town and she said she was headed toward your street. She asked no questions. She's a good woman. Besides, I figured nobody'd bother the Amish."

"And Will?"

"Well, Fannie—he's in the hospital. Now wait—wait—" I had come up off the stool. He put his left hand on my arm. "He's gonna be all right. Just sit back down now, and I'll start at the beginning."

I could not see him all that clearly; in the darkening room his voice so closely resembled Will's it was difficult to tell the difference. Maybe Amos's was raspier, but that was all.

"You remember that last morning I saw you?"

I nodded.

"Well, I already knew then. I knew there was trouble. Before I came to the café, I was over at Mr. Ardor's place touching up the last of the dryboard for the gin, when Ivory Shine came by all in a tither and said everybody had chased a colored boy out of town. So I naturally drove first to the café. I had hoped to find Will here. Then I went out Levee Road in the direction everybody said they were heading. But by that time all the trucks were coming back and passing me and at the end of the road, nothing but hoof dust in the air. Then I saw Will. He was staggering a little. He had clearly been in a scuffle and had his platter cleaned and a knot on his head.

"As you can imagine, I was wondering when I saw Will, what on God's earth, as I know you must be wondering. Was there a killing? Had he got caught up in it? But when I tried to talk sense, he just said let's *go*. I said what's happened, and he said it again. He said *right now*. And when your son looks at you like that, you just do it. You go and ask questions later. So I got Will back to the truck and we drove to the pier and we got on the *Elvira*. I cranked her up and pulled out. I stood at the wheel and then I looked up at the bluff. I looked a long time. I looked up at the café and the spire of the courthouse. I looked up at Persia as it got smaller and smaller and the boat moved on and I thought, I am losing hold of my life.

"Fannie, there is news I must tell you and no better way of saying it, but Will was in a rough way. He was pretty broken up and when I tried to get anything out of him I instead got scraps and pieces. And from the look on his face I feared the worst. I thought he'd been in on it, but finally I got him to tell me *they* did it."

"Who?"

"You know who. The whole congregation. They killed the boy. And the thing was, Will had some wrongheaded notion that *he* could stop it."

"He tried to stop it?"

"Yes ma'am. As if you could stop a thing like that. When a herd of sheep get going they got no brains; they do not think, they can only follow the smell. You stick your nose into the butt in front of you and follow it wherever it goes."

"And you explained this to him?"

"Did I explain it!" Amos paused, and I could sense futility overpowering him, along with ugly guilt. "I should have explained better. And as soon as I realized he had not been in on the killing, I tried to get him to turn around. To come on back. But he just said he had caused the death of one man and was not able to stop another. He said this over and over. As if the two were actually connected."

"The *two*?"

"The two, yes, Fannie. Earnest March and Lawrence Boatwright. Your uncle Lawrence. You remember, of course, all those years after that accident when he was a boy, that accident on the bluff. I tried to help him back then, truly I did. I even took him, you know, to those doctors. But the fact was, Will was one to chew forever on what was eating him. Which is hardly news to you. And up to that last night, he seemed convinced that saving that boy would in some way have made up for your uncle." Amos paused again. "Not to mention how he'd hurt you."

I looked at him.

"But Uncle Lawrence was an accident."

"I know, but try telling him that."

"And you said, up to that last night—"

"Yeah, up to then, he kept talking about the two of us heading downriver. Out to the Gulf and maybe even south of the border—to Mexico."

"Mexico?"

"Yeah, he thought it was reasonable at the time."

"So let me get this straight. He was just gonna hightail it off. And he wasn't gonna tell me where he was going?"

"Fannie, Will was—not well. And he said he didn't want you to have that knowledge. If you didn't have it, you couldn't be responsible. In case somebody tried to point the finger at him. Besides, as I just mentioned, he said he'd already hurt you enough, and he didn't want to get you involved."

"Unh-hunh, yeah, right. Okay. Anyway, what happened then?"

"Well, like I said, I tried to talk him out of it. That the best way to make up for things was just to come on back. To tell all of it. And that seemed to calm him down. He sat in the corner of the boat, and I remember, we were around Bayou Vista, and it was so dark that night I could hear the river, but I couldn't really see it. Some fishermen on shore lit boat lanterns. It was a peaceful moment.

"Then I heard a jostling, a scraping, and I saw Will trying to go over the edge. Trying to throw himself into the water. I caught him just in time, but you know, Will's no weakling. That's how I got this arm. He put up quite a struggle, and to top things off, he was on his hoodoo in a bottle, as old Tchula likes to call it, as punishment. So after that I managed to get him to dry land, then to the hospital. To Whitfield. Then I came here. To let you know first." Amos fell silent.

I put my face down slowly and gently on the surface of the counter with its damp patina of cigarette ash and water rings, wanting to be overtaken by some form of unconsciousness. Then I raised my head and looked toward Amos, saying, "Amos, I'm sure that was the right thing. He had to be *confined*." I heard something gurgle up in my voice, vaguely glutinous. "Right *away*."

Amos looked away from me and when he looked back his eyes were wet. I could see them glint in the dark. "Well, maybe he *is* brainsick. Maybe he's got reason. Maybe so do I. When I think of what they done, these sons of bitches, well I can't tell you what comes to my mind. All I know is the one question that burns in my brain and that is the question of that day and what if I had gotten there sooner? One man can't stop a herd, but what about two? When a man's son takes on a conviction, however wrongheaded, he should be there to stand with him. And maybe Tchula's boy would be here and Will too and I would not be saying this to you. An old man's wondering. That is my cross to bear."

With his good hand Amos picked up the glass of water and finished it with a hefty gulp and then, turning again to me, said, "There's something else I didn't tell you. About that day."

"What?" I said.

"After Will came to? He said he saw the boy. Hanging from a tree. Hanging from the willow, just down the bluff."

"Oh shit," I said. "Shit, shit, shit." I heard myself murmur, "Shit, shit, shit, shit . . ."

"He said he saw Tchula too. Standing at the top of the bluff. He said he was sure she had seen."

I made a low, not entirely blasphemous whisper. "Sweet Jesus, have mercy."

But we couldn't just sit there bleeding all over each other's wounds. So I told Amos about Tchula's death. I told him about all I had seen and all that had happened since. I suggested he talk to Mr. Nod in the morning, but in the meantime, a meal, a hot bath; he would stay here for the night. I don't believe I'd ever so wanted anyone to stay. And he relented, I think, out of sheer exhaustion. Or the onset of numbness. At least that's what I was beginning to feel. When you're hit between the eyes by a bullet at close range you may fall back at first and then you don't feel a thing. Anyway, I was busy. Amos's supper and just overhead the bathwater running as I started on a Hershey's bar I'd opened and damned a fly that kept competing for the goodies on the tinfoil wrapper. It buzzed toward me and I waved it away as it kept going around and around.

So Will had not been in on it. That was one thing. And Amos came back to tell me. That was another. You reach toward the truth and find instead what is within your nature, which is often profoundly implicated in not knowing, in silence. Or you reach away from the truth and find it fanning, right in your hand, like a face deck of cards. A black boy dead. A great-grandmother dead. And Mattie, one of the few living relatives of both, who had run out behind the café that morning and stabbed a knife in the tire of a car and who had helped, by her single innocent act of justice, put a pistol to the boy's head. Or a rope around his neck, whatever the case may be, but we would not really know it all, would we, not from the boy, not from Tchula. And now, Lord knows what from Will either, who was not content to let the river lose one without trying to lose another, and who had managed to secure himself at the funny farm. And what had been his original plan anyway, to flee to Mexico, father and son, the open desert, the tequila cactus, the little towns and cantinas, a redheaded Scot and a lumbering Indian—what? In sombreros, incognito? Getting odd jobs, here and there? Or what else might have been in the grand plan, robbing banks?

The whole notion seemed so ridiculous and perversely logical that I burst out laughing and could hardly stop. Before I stopped, as a matter of fact, I realized I was not laughing but weeping and saying, over and over, "You stupid fool, you stupid fool." The tears broke and scalded like the end of summer drought. And summer had been long.

Return

In October 1962, the month Will was checked into Whitfield State Hospital, the FBI began to close down its investigation. This was because their search had produced no sign of a body, and I found myself paying close attention. I found myself stepping, the way you do, toe to toe, as targeters look back at the path you have taken. In their eyes are pieces of the past to aim at you, once they figure the story is over. But no story is ever over, and once the rest of time is discovered it will prove to have already been known.

The little game the town was playing was not over. But I'd almost forgotten that. I had almost forgotten that the story of Will, which seemed so complete in my talk with Amos, was a part of this bigger story, which was a question of murder and responsibility of a town.

I told Mr. Nod about Amos. He looked across the counter at me and said, "Well, I'll be damned."

I didn't say anything.

Then he said, "Where is he?"

"He's coming here soon. To talk to you."

Mr. Nod glanced up toward the ceiling. Then looked at me and said, "Am I being made a visiting fool of?"

I still didn't say anything.

"And you believe this?"

"What you mean?" I said.

"His story, I mean. It's just that sometimes, a father's loyalty, while commendable, can cause him to want to protect his son."

"I'm still not following you."

"And to protect his son, his father might say he's innocent."

"*Say* he's innocent?"

"Yes ma'am."

"Is *that* what you think?"

"What do you think?"

"Is *that* what you think?"

"I don't know," he said. "You believe it's true?"

"You already know that answer."

"Well, do you?"

"Goddamn it," I said, "of course, it's true. You think Amos'd make something like that up? You think he'd come all the way back here to *do* something like that to me?"

Suddenly I felt my lips press together and tremble. Instinctively, I turned around and clenched the coffeepot in order to turn my face away from him. I don't want to see it either, I thought. And when I turned back, Mr. Nod looked at me in a different way and reached across the counter. "I'm sorry," he said, and put his heavy hand on my shoulder.

I moved out from under the hand.

"I'm sorry," he repeated, "about your husband."

Then he sat back on the stool and fingered the rim of his coffee cup.

"There's still this story," he said, reflectively.

"Yeah, there's the story, but if you want anybody poormouthing Amos Leary or questioning his honesty, you better find some other face to talk to."

"In this town, wouldn't have to look far," he said, half to himself. I didn't respond to the hint of wryness in his tone.

"Look," he said, "I said I'm sorry. Really, I am. But there's a story you believe."

"And you don't."

"Well, you have to admit, there are impulses here that are pretty difficult to reconcile."

"Such as."

"Such as. For instance, why would Amos Leary run off with his son?"

"Because a father thought his son was in on a murder."

"The same father who urged his son to turn around and come back?"

"When he found out his son was innocent, yessir."

"Just like that?"

"Just like that."

"And this is, by the way, the same father who decides, once his son—excuse me, ma'am, Will—tries to do himself in, the same father who wishes that *he* never had to come back?"

"To *this* town?" I said. "Absolutely. Now *that* part I can understand easiest of all."

Mr. Nod stopped again. He was studying me drowsily under the drooping lids. "Mrs. Leary," he said then, "I know you've been through a lot. And I know you're gonna go through a whole lot more."

Then he said, "Don't you worry. Things'll end up working out."

"Yeah," I said sourly, "you'll be back in that nice office in New Orleans."

"I didn't mean that. I could be gone right now if that was all."

I looked at him.

"What you mean?"

He didn't answer for a moment, not even looking back at me but down at the half-inch of coffee and the fingers clasped around the cup. "Oh hell," he said, "just forget it." Suddenly, he set down the cup, so it clinked heavily on its saucer, and lunged off the stool. "It's like I said before, it's not my place to advise. I'm *not* your father and I'm *not* one of these preachers.

"But fact number one. No body: no case. It doesn't matter about a hundred eyewitnesses, living or dead. And fact number two. A case like this can have a life of its own, even after all is officially said and done. But like I said, it's not my place to advise. I know you got to do what you got to do. So do I. And they better not forget, either, by God, Judge Lynch is not the only law in this place."

He turned around toward the window, and said, half to himself, "So Amos Leary, now, Amos Leary."

Then he fell into a brooding silence, which, had Amos been able to see it, would have made him inclined to be anywhere other than right upstairs in my bedroom.

So the story of the aftermath of the murder, of which the story of Will was a part, went on, and I was paying close attention. What would become of Will I did not know. Nor did I know why Mr. Nod gave me a deepening sense that he was an accomplice in my trouble. As soon as I told him where Amos was, he was up the stairs. He was up there for quite a time. And as soon as the two men had spoken, they left for Whitfield to see Will. In the fight with the men of Persia who had purportedly caught Earnest March, it turned out, when Will had tried to stop them, he had received three broken ribs, a mild concussion, and a gash on his forehead that needed seven stitches. He was pretty battered up. Altogether, he would be in the sanatorium for four months. I would not visit him there. Mr. Nod found it within himself, however, to come back and explain the whys and wherefores of Will's condition. On the evening of November 3, he came through my door. "Is the coffee hot?" he said. He had four or five cups as we spoke.

"Fannie," he said somberly, "I've spoken extensively with your husband. Amos Leary is with his son now. He moved down near Whitfield. He found a room for the winter."

"As for your husband, he is—how shall I put it—in one of the gentler sections of Whitfield. He was a voluntary patient, checked in by Amos, so he's not locked up. It's not a prison. It's got doctors. More, it's for folk who—on whom life has knocked down hard, is how I'd put it. Knocked down hard and won't let up. You know how your husband's brain was fairly pickled in alcohol some days? Well, the doctors got their explanations. Now the gash on his forehead, the broken ribs are simple. Those are healing fine. Dizziness from the concussion should wear off eventually. He's got repeated nightmares that bring him up out of the bed and double him over. Whenever he does sleep, it's for a few hours at a time. The doctors are trying some sedatives for that. Still, given the story he and Amos swear to, if half true, it's a wonder he's alive.

"What the doctors do say pure and simple is that he's possibly too bull-headed to stop his drinking. That it might well be the thing that kills him, eats him inside out eventually. Of course he's not drinking in the hospital. But, like I said, it's not a prison. And when he gets out, well, he might line up every last bottle in Mississippi and invite himself to the party. That's what the doctors think. But Amos Leary insists you come to your own conclusions. He asked me to tell you that.

"As for your husband's claims about trying to save Earnest March, well, I'm considering the probability of his story. A man's testimony about a murder, after he fled on the day of the purported crime, is, on the face of it, to say the least, suspect. But sometimes there are other factors. You can look into a man's face and tell whether he's lying. When he lies, he becomes the lie. And panic and poor judgment are first cousins—so the things a man will do when he's in a panic are inevitably stupid. Which, by the way, applies equally to Amos Leary—the parent out to protect his young. That story's as old as the hills. And sometimes a story's too crazy *not* to be true. So let's say, for the sake of argument, Will Leary tried to save the March boy. And Amos Leary took his son and ran because he thought his son was in on it. And when he discovered to the contrary he got his son to come back. Let's grant all of that, but the fact remains, what we got is the story of your husband, Will, who, as a resident of Whitfield, is—excuse me, ma'am—not exactly an unimpeachable witness. We got your testimony about the body. We got a few strands of rope from a tree. We got the deathbed hearsay from one Mattie Boyd about what the old great-grandmother, Tchula Gaze, said she saw. But again, no body. No eyewitness to the actual murder, so the finger points to everybody and nobody. As for the rest of this town—and Batesville, for that matter—we got a whole barrelful of conflicting stories. The problem with liars is they never can remember what they said. Besides, at this point, it's useless—unless Earnest March decides to manifest his presence. And we've quit looking, because the bottom line is, ma'am, this is a colored boy. There it is, then."

It was Mr. Nod, too, who took a long look around the café and admitted that he felt partly responsible for the drop in my business. To his way of thinking, he could have handled the initial days of the investigation more discreetly by persuading me to be questioned someplace other than the café. "I shirked good judgment," he said. "I should have met you elsewhere. Preferably out of town. It's that simple."

Then he took it upon himself to bring back Will's shotgun. He surprised me further by making a donation to a collection taken up on Will's behalf, to defer medical expenses. It seemed Mr. Nod had his own turmoils with the case. He had his guilts. The collection was Mattie's idea, he told me, and Reverend Roberts confirmed this. She had brought up the idea at church. It seemed that while they were discussing the purchase of a headstone for Earnest March, the story of Will and Amos drew out a particularly strong sympathy for me. On top of it all, Mattie said not a word to me. Not a word. And I was still mad at her for being black and being my friend, two things that together she was never supposed to have been.

On yet another weekday, December 17, Mr. Nod paid me a lunchtime visit. He had barbecue ribs, baked sweet potatoes, greens, and biscuits. He had two glasses of ice tea and I watched him eat and push back his plate and I poured him coffee. I was pouring when he said, tentatively, "So Mrs. Leary, with all this wrapping up, your plans still the same?"

"My plans."

"You expect you're gonna stay."

I shook my head.

"I'm not expecting anything right now."

Then he said, "Well, I guess that's a fair answer."

He sipped his coffee. He sipped again and set down the cup and looked at me. He turned and looked out the window down the street. After a while, he said, "As I said before, I'm sorry about your husband. I've heard the story about when he was a boy, when he had that accident, circumstances I'm sure you remember, when he ran into your great-uncle out there on the bluff. It seems collisions are inevitably part of some folks' fate, hunh? Yet I admit that gets me to thinking about the past. I've seen a lot of strange things in my time, and I remember a case."

"Around here?"

"Not too far. In Magnolia. Just a few years back. Your obvious storybook case. Gunshot wound. Murder of old rich husband. Young wife. I was already in Magnolia, on another case—God, these small towns—so I got there as soon as the doctor. The doctor leaned forward to close the dead man's eyes, and the man opened them up and looked at his wife and sneered, 'Can't wait to have me dead? You heifer!' He sat up and swept off the blankets and lunged at his wife. So mad. You *heifer!* To die with that kind of anger. I guess I should've told Reverend Roberts that story. Till that moment, hunh, I never thought I'd see a resurrection."

Mr. Nod said that in a familiar way. He said it almost like an apology. Then he reached and got his cigarettes out of his pocket and lit one and looked at me and looked out the window again. "Look, anyway, I just came by to touch base before I head out. During all this you've been forthright and cooperative, and I appreciate that."

"So that's it."

"Well, I got a couple of other sources to check on, outside of town. They may shed a little light on your visit from the Klan. We'll see what we see."

Or we won't what we won't, I almost said. But before I could say anything else, Mr. Nod said, "Is there something else on your mind?"

"I don't know."

"In that case, I guess so."

"Maybe."

"What is it?"

"Something—I was wondering."

"Well, there's no time like the present."

"It's just—there's something that's kind of bothered me as all this has gone along. And now that you're finishing you act like—I'm in the right about everything and I don't feel that way."

I stood looking at a spillstain on the counter. I stood for a long time. Finally I looked up. "I just don't feel justified."

He nodded. "You haven't left anything out, have you?"

"Nosir. It's not that."

"What is it?"

"Well sir, Mama, for one thing."

"All right."

"She had her sewing and cleaning business in town and her place and she was awful good at it. Then—all hell broke loose and everybody decided to take their business away from her and whenever she's busy at the café she seems okay but half the time she sits out there overeager and the other half she sits on pins and needles, both from loneliness. And I was the one that brought this about. No one but me."

"You didn't tell folk to take their business away from her, did you?"

"Nosir. I didn't."

He nodded gravely. "Well," he said, "this town can take a crap without you being responsible."

"Yessir."

Mr. Nod sat watching me under the drooping lids. "Mrs. Leary," he said, "you impress me as being someone who maybe tends to be a little hard on herself. From what all I've heard you should be thankful to come through this with a whole hide. And I'm sorry about what your husband's going through, but maybe the best thing for you to do is to start trying to put this behind you."

"Behind me," I said. I stood there.

"It's all right to cry, you know."

I shook my head.

"Well, it is."

Mr. Nod waited.

I didn't say anything.

Then he said, "There's something else, isn't there?"

"Yessir."

"What is it?"

"It's just—that night, when the kluckers came? And I aimed the gun? When I took aim, I really took aim."

"Well, you had a little provocation."

"I know. But that doesn't—change things. I still keep thinking about it."

"And why's that?"

"Because. I don't know. I thought I—wanted one thing—and then I didn't—and then I wasn't sure who was supposed to be dead."

"You wouldn't want to be in law enforcement, would you?"

"Nosir."

"I didn't either."

"What you mean?"

"What I mean is, I think I know what you're saying. When I was growing up, my daddy was a sheriff and I swore as a result that I would never be one. Never be in anything related to law enforcement. Working odd hours for piss-poor pay in a forgotten podunk town. And then I got into a line of work where I thought the dividends were distinct. Where I found out later rather than sooner that I got plenty of colleagues who don't know their backsides from a hole in the wall but I thought I could make a difference. And then what'd I do? I shot down a boy of nineteen who was wanted for murder and ended up in the electric chair over in Birmingham. That was nineteen fifty-five. Was he supposed to be dead? I don't know. Would I do it again? Yes ma'am. But doesn't mean I don't think about it."

"I tried to a second time."

"Tried what?"

"Tried to shoot them."

"But you didn't."

"Nosir, I didn't. Not that second time."

I sat looking at him. The second hand on the clock ticked. Outside the window the last leaves were blowing and he was going to have to be heading out in it pretty soon.

"I tried to but the gun wasn't loaded. And when I fired the first shot I thought I'd made up my mind but I hadn't. I thought I was gonna aim high—and then I didn't."

"Look," he offered. "You were defending yourself. We've been over this. You were doing what you had to."

"No, you don't understand. It was what I wanted."

"What?"

"I wanted it for a moment. I wanted them to die."

"Well, some things are between you and the good Lord. And as I've said, some things are necessity. I expect you'll sort out the difference."

"So that's it," I said, after a moment.

"Well. As for what's going in my report, it's a case pending. Plenty'll interpret this as leave well enough alone, which is the motto, I know, for certain quarters in this town. But that's not the case. What that means is, pending more evidence.

"So as far as the report goes that is it, at least for now. But I will venture one prediction. I don't think they're gonna be bothering you."

"Oh you don't?"

"No ma'am. For two reasons. First of all, they can't burn down the café without the risk of burning down the department store next to it and half the town and ultimately half the source of leading citizens' pocket money. That seed's been planted. And second, even if they could light it up, I'm not sure they would, for after the way you shot out the window that night, they all think you're crazy. Which brings me also to the subject of your mama, who, appearances aside, is not always the delicate teacup you describe. The word is, the craziness must be genetic, and I'm not talking about your husband here, since your mama, you know, put on a pretty impressive display in front of the sheriff."

"Yessir."

"They think you're all touched."

"Well," I said, "we'll take our compliments where we can get them."

Mr. Nod picked up the cup and took a sip, a pained, ironic smile twisting his lips as if he had just swallowed lemon. Time for him to go. Who'd ever find these answers? He lit a cigarette and smoked it slowly, taking me in through the violet-gray spiral of smoke. Then he stood, shook my hand, put on sunglasses, and set out.

And it would be a long time before Mr. Nod came back through my door.

On the Monday morning following I was sitting on one of the customers' stools and drinking coffee and looking out the window. There was no one in the café except me and Mattie and Matilda. Matilda on the floor was tossing a napkin and after a while Mattie brought out some biscuits and set the child in the booth with a plate before her.

Then she looked up. "Well, Mr. FBI's gone now, ain't he. For a while there I wondered. I wondered if he was ever gonna leave. He sure seemed to be getting in a tizzy about you."

"Well," I said. "He's gone now. Him and all the rest of them."

"Yeah, they are."

"Well."

I got into the kitchen and we cooked, just enough for the small number of weekday customers, indoors past the days of dropping leaves and rain, and we said not a thing. Which was fine by me. That's what I told myself. Mattie didn't say anything else, and I didn't ask. Even the old questions I'd put to her didn't matter, for she had spoken her piece and I thought maybe that was where it should be left. So I told myself it did not matter anymore.

And that left the others in town. Those who had done it. And strangely, at first, there had been a bit of consolation in this knowledge. The sheriff had done it; I had seen him leading the procession. And Mr. Ardor, Mr. Magee, the Shine boys, Mr. Giddy. I could see them all, way over yonder, heading down the road. They were what I could measure myself against, for I was no longer bound to them. I was no longer bound to any of them, I said to myself, until the moment something suddenly happened. And when it happened it was like the moment I fired the shot from the gun out the window into the night, feeling so high and mighty until the purity backfired into the pit of my stomach.

This happened: I suddenly asked myself why, after a murder in this town, the sheriff had been so sure I would say nothing. And suddenly I saw the eyes of Mr. Magee and Mr. Ardor and the sheriff upon me, and all the eyes that looked at me that way, and suddenly I had realized if there'd been a hair's difference in the circumstance in the town's conspiracy, I might have had to look down and see blood on my own hands. It wasn't all I tried to say to Mr. Nod; it wasn't that. It was as though I were caught in something I could not fathom. It was as though I were in a place where waking forever moved toward sleep. The sleep contained the knowledge that all order in the world had failed and the sleep contained the faces of the men and the boy and Tchula Gaze as she stood there for the last time, nodding to me on the bluff. Would my dreams ever stop streaming? It was as though I could hear a deeper note, a composite vibration, of all the town said, and did not say. Persia's denial of responsibility, which went back farther than this, which went back a hundred years, actually, framed by the stone soldier by the pier and the flag by the courthouse and the streets named for Confederate generals who never came here. It was that near miss, no matter how brief or bloody, that added poignancy to lousy salaries and the drop in crop prices and the insults of drought or flood, and was something for the town to hold on to, in its latest death. The return for betrayal is betrayal, among all those who have walked down the back alleys of time and space beside you.

So I said to hell with you. And you and you and you. And I hated them all and I hated myself, for I was once part of them. And they were still part of me.

That's the way it was as the investigation ended.

I did not confront any of the old crowd. I did not say a word to Mr. Magee or Mr. Ardor or the sheriff. I did not want to see any of them. Outside at night there was the river washing down, over the old gray stones, and the frogs and the crickets, and the breaking-down pier, but I did not want to look at that. I clasped a hand around a coffee mug as long as there was warmth to be gotten from it. I cooked for the weekend crowd and visited Mama at Eugenia's house and sat upstairs in the café, watching television, admiring the easy retorts of old movies that reminded you of everything you could ever remember. And always, I was thinking of Will.

In an odd way, those weekdays at the café and wondering about Will began to remind me of growing up. The way time passed back then. The ticking space and late afternoon sliding and stillness.

When I was a child I used to visit Eugenia at the café after school and I would wander into the kitchen, climbing on a chair to watch as Mattie did her work and finished her creations. The kitchen seemed to me a time apart, a floating island, the place where I learned proportion. And then Eugenia would peel off her apron and promise me a walk. The walk was also for Mama's benefit, for we'd always end up at the house, though first we'd go by the river. And Eugenia would stand and look out and say, "Where'd the day go?" As though blame were everywhere and nowhere, an echo on the wind. "Where'd the day go?"

One of the saddest things is to love folk whose lives briefly cross your own.

So this was also the way I was thinking of Will. The way he was slightly beneath consciousness by day and beneath closed lids in sleep. Like a dead relative. Occasionally I fantasized about trying to escape this. Should I have put my name to that bill of sale that Brother Works offered and taken the money when I had the chance? I could have gone to another place far away, up north, maybe, to Maine, all the way to the top. And now, how was I supposed to think of Will? I tried to imagine him in a hospital bed, his growing quieter, something that, before we were married, I would have thought impossible, like a bat evolving into an animal that makes less noise. I didn't know if he was raging or merely resigned. Occasionally Amos Leary would call, so determined now to be positive that I only wanted to get off the phone. Mostly I wanted to sit still and wait. And though Will and I had not seen each other since the day of the murder, Amos, up from Whitfield, stopped by, the night of February 2, to say he was going to bring Will home.

"Thank you for telling me."

"I thought you'd want to know."

Three days later, Mattie called from the kitchen door as I walked through, "The boat's back." I walked to the front window. The *Elvira* had just tied up. Amos set the plank, went down to the bunk room to get Will. When Will looked up at the town, he disappeared back below. Amos apparently spoke with him a few moments, then came up the pier. I had busied myself behind the counter when Amos came through the door. "Fannie, we've just gotten in. We'd like to come for supper Friday night. That all right?"

"I'm here anyway."

"Good."

By six o'clock Friday evening, then, the café was crowded. A short time later, Will came across the street with Amos.

He was walking slowly, that was the first thing I noticed; and as I watched through the window, I took a good look at him. While he was handsome as ever, with all the right prominences and symmetries, there was something newly strange in his look—nothing visibly missing and not so much deficient as reassembled. And that was exactly *it*, I could see. The odd quality hinted itself through the skin. It had the sickish rubberiness of one who has suffered severe weight loss (along the jawline it was especially noticeable) and whose flesh is even now in the last stages of being restored. Also, I felt that beneath the brown skin was the pallor of a body not wholly rescued from terrible crisis. But none of this diminished, at this instant, at least, the casual but forthright way his pelvis moved as he walked, the tan suede of dust on his boots, the gush of black hair, combed back, freshly cut.

"Damn it, Fannie," I whispered. Then the Christmas bells rang. And as I looked away, I thought all over again, with all the old suddenness, of how dull and fumbling I can become when I'm in his presence.

A few moments later I started in the direction of their table. He and Amos had taken a seat in the booth in the corner. No one had gone over to their table but plenty of folk were looking and saying hello. As for myself, I reached for the pen behind my ear and focused on pulling the pad from my apron. Then I stood before them. The three of us were awkwardly close, here in this crowded room.

"Will," I said.

Then Will looked at me and said, "Coming here tonight was necessary for me, Fannie, even if it isn't for you."

"Good evening, Fannie," Amos said.

Catfish Pâté

Dear Earnest March,

This is your wollet. I kept the $4. It was pretty wet and wrinkled but it dried up ok. My friend says this is the wollet of a dead boy because I found it by the river. I hope that is not so, if so I am sorry. I knew I could sell the driver's license, but I felt bad in case you were dead. Your social security card fell apart when I took it out, so I did not send it.

MATTIE GOT THIS IN THE mail in March 1963, written in ink on the inside of brown paper wrapped around a leather wallet. The package had been forwarded from Tchula Gaze's old address, and she brought this to the café to show me. The wallet itself looked homemade, like one created, perhaps, in shop class: the two sides bound with leather laces, the hand-tooled initials, EM. As Mattie stood at the counter showing me this, I looked. Mattie was holding the wallet in one hand and the letter in the other, as I rested my arm on a pile of Mrs. Thistle's old cookbooks. A while earlier I'd had a visit from Mrs. Roberts, who had made a special request: a birthday cake for the reverend, whose fiftieth birthday was coming up. Mrs. Roberts said she wanted it to be a surprise.

In recent days, in fact, I'd already gotten out Mrs. Thistle's old cookbooks. I hadn't been doing any experimenting but it was something to do, to read without purpose, to let the mind drift. Then Mrs. Roberts had come through the door with her request for the cake. For March 31, she said. I remembered this again. A rhythm in my mind, like a dripping pot, and I looked at Mattie. I suggested she put down the letter and the wallet. Then I suggested she send it all to Mr. Nod, so I helped her wrap it up and she carried it to the post office and mailed it. Then I turned back to the cookbooks. A recipe for seven-minute icing. Slowly, I realized that for more than fifteen minutes I had been looking at the yellowed porousness of the page, the crease at the corner I had folded over as a mark. I bent back the page edge.

And now to greet us was the news of the ridiculous fate of Earnest March's wallet. All of it, everything from the moment the boy ran off to the news of Will's troubles, seemed freshly absurd. I decided just to focus on Mrs. Roberts's request for the cake, and anyway, it was a bit more cheerful than this recent correspondence.

A church, of course. The architecture of Mount Sinai Church, a cake replica. It was just before noon, Friday, and I thought of this idea again as Mattie and Mama and I got supper. I thought of this idea too as Will and Amos came in with the usual crowd, along with a fellow who came to dine with Billie Holiday. He was Adele Shelby's cousin, visiting from Atlanta, and he brought in a suitcase and took a seat in a booth. He removed a clay bust of Holiday and set it on the table while he ate. This did not bother me. I had just read a note from a thief who apologized to his victim in case he was dead. I fed the supper crowd and got on with my business.

By March 31, then, I made the cake. Then to decorate it I thought of the way the church looked, white-painted with a spire, rimmed with tangled grass and trees and the graveyard to the side. I used to pass it on my way fishing, the dusty dirt road, the stripe of grass down the middle. On the hottest days, steam would rise on the dew and hang in the roadside ditch and the church seemed to float like a little castle.

Mint leaves for roof shingles. A chocolate door. Melted Life Savers, maybe, for windows. And paint on the front steps, how to simulate that, it was the blue-gray of all faded front porches.

I was whipping cream to go between cake layers when Will came in. He nodded to Mattie, who excused herself. And when I looked at him, he didn't seem to know what to say. He needs help, I thought, doesn't he, standing there, backed up against the cabinetry.

"The cake's Mount Sinai," I said. "Only I'm making the windows nicer. The paint job better. So in a cake, you get to leave out the worst of the flaws, hunh."

"It's nice to see you, Fannie."

I kept my hand on the beater.

"And I've been meaning to tell you," he said, "I like your hair."

"Thank you. About the cake—it's for the reverend's birthday, in case you're wondering. I thought he'd like it."

"A nicer building holds out some hope for the future, is that it?"

"No, Will. I didn't think of it that way. It's just his church, that's all."

"I know the place better than you, and I know he'll approve."

"You make a pretty quick judgment."

"No, I been there a few nights already. In the middle of the night with my flashlight. I hardly sleep. Anyway, hunh! The reverend's congregation allowed in this café. That's a lark on this town.

"Speaking of that, as a matter of fact, Amos and I are back to doing repairs, courtesy of the reverend. Some on the rectory, and the church. It needs foundation work. So we got business, for now, at least. And I was thinking how odd it is, you learn to drive a nail and it makes you a living. I could take my work with me almost anywhere, I suppose. Maybe New Orleans—they got plenty of dock work down there. Or maybe Jackson, for construction."

"You just came from there."

"Yeah I did. But I can't highly recommend that."

He closed his eyes and appeared to sleep for a moment. "Fannie, when I was in the hospital I tried to put a name to everything that's happened to us. Everything that's happened in this town. All the funerals in so short a time. I don't know. I just don't know. But can I ask you something?"

"All right."

"Would you think about a stroll with me sometime? Not sitting down to supper. Not at a table together. Just, to talk."

"That's being out in public together, wouldn't you say?"

"Yeah, even if nobody saw, I'd know you'd risked that."

"You don't deserve it."

"I know that, too."

"Well, why not now?"

Will looked at me.

"Well? It's what you've been doing, isn't it? Talking?"

Will stood utterly still for a moment. He had looked so glad to be here—the kitchen—but also so ashamed, so conscious that what came next could determine everything. Then he said, "Hokay, I'll go ahead and say it. . . ." He took a breath. "Before I left, before I left town with Daddy—"

"Amos told me about that."

"No, before then, Clarice Lytle—" Then he blurted out, as though he couldn't bear to keep at this subject any longer, as though only the mention of this name could be expressed or taken in—one sentence, begun with an oddly formal introduction.

"*Allow me, Fannie, just to say* that was over before it started."

"Not for me it isn't."

"No, you don't understand."

"No I don't."

"I *didn't* sleep with her."

I looked up, thick-headed. Flowers on a windowsill in a jar. The green stems seemed to crack at the waterline and go milky on the way down. I looked at these and then I looked at Will. Then I turned off the beaters. "You didn't *what*?"

And here his whole face began to work, his eyes dry and brilliant, as though he were making some kind of grope, some kind of wild appeal.

"Look, I'm *sorry*. Sorry as I've ever been. But I *didn't*."

"You sure fooled me."

"No, it's not—"

"*Oh,* I get it. Fannie walks into the boat cabin at the wrong moment and interrupts an important business meeting."

"No, Fannie. It didn't happen like that. I thought about it—"

"You *thought* about it?"

"Yes, I mean no, what I thought about was getting your attention. Then I *wasn't* thinking. I was just—going through the motions. And then I *couldn't*. I couldn't go through with it. I didn't *want* to."

"How magnanimous of you."

I waited a moment. He said nothing.

"Are you saying to me you *never* slept with her?"

"No. Not then. Once. Back in high school. Before you and I were together."

"Well. That wouldn't be my business, I guess."

"Look, Fannie, I'm really sorry."

"And that's supposed to make it all right?"

"I don't know." Then, almost to himself, "I don't why I was so angry with you."

"Neither do I."

"Maybe for you not needing me to take care of you."

"I didn't—"

"Wait, let me finish. That's the reason I fell for you in the first place. I remember looking at you one night and thinking, God Almighty, this girl's going all the way with somebody just watching, and I couldn't stand for that to be anybody but me." And here his voice fell back like somebody who'd made the grope and held on for a moment, missed and knew there was little point in trying again.

Finally I said, "And why didn't you tell me about this earlier?"

"You never gave me a chance."

"Well you certainly got the town talking."

"Oh, the *town*. And we know that what the *town* says is always true."

I thought, at that moment, Will was surely using this as a reference to Earnest March, was surely using this as a last-ditch try for my sympathy. At that moment I also thought that even if he could have spoken more directly about all of it, even if he could have told the tale and I'd agreed with him that yes, what happened to Earnest March was murder and yes, in trying to save the boy, he did a good thing—after all that agreeing and sympathizing were over, I would have stood by the cake layers and the bowl of whipping cream, and from that distance turned and asked him, "So what does this have to do with Clarice Lytle?" And I understood that where the story for him was somehow all of a piece, for me it was two quite separate narratives, with separate meanings.

Now Will was fumbling to say something again, when I interrupted him.

"Okay, Will, you said you didn't sleep with her. So you didn't. But what a strange position you put me in. In effect to be grateful that you only thought about it. To be grateful that you changed your mind. To be grateful that you only came close to lying down with another woman and wrecking our marriage.

"And you will forgive me"—those were my words: *You will forgive me*—"if I can't do like Mattie and the reverend and all the customers and focus only on the March boy at this moment. I know what you tried to do, Will, but there's still this." I turned back to the mixing bowl of cream. I turned on the beaters. "Fuck it. That's how I feel. Fuck that."

Will left the café. Then Mr. Nod called to say that he'd received Earnest March's wallet and driver's license, which had apparently been mailed from Black Hawk, and was I okay? And by the time I got off the phone, the cream was past the stage of soft peaks and sticking to the side of the bowl a pale yellow. Butter. I had overwhipped this entire batch of cream and made it butter. Okay, so I'd make another batch but I would not waste this so I looked at the catfish that had just come in and hit upon the idea to smoke some and lit the smoker out back and put the butter in the icebox until the fish was ready. In the meantime, I finished up the cake and got the Life Savers to melt for tiny stained-glass windows by making molds out of chicken wire. Finally I finished the catfish concoction by puréeing smoked catfish with the butter and a touch of cream.

It was Mattie who stuck her head into the icebox later that day and looked in the bowl. She peeled back the plastic wrap and wrinkled her nose. "What is this, white Vaseline?"

"Look here," I said. "I overwhipped the cream and had all this extra butter and I was just finding a way to use it—"

She looked back at me and started to dip in her finger. She lifted the finger curved and put it in her mouth as her lips closed around; her cheeks caved in.

We stood, the vacuum-shaped silence between us. Finally, I said, "So, what you think?" It wasn't easy for me to say.

"Catfish," she said. "Smoked. The butter, salt, milk or cream. And . . . what else?"

"White pepper."

Mattie started to say something, thought better of it, and put the plastic wrap back over the bowl, and closed the icebox door.

Then we filleted catfish. Mama decorated the front of the café, and by the time folk came, the skillets were bubbling. Teenagers sat at the counter and I served them shakes and Cocolas. There was an air about them, particularly the girls, and I remembered it was spring. Their hair tamed prettily from effort, curls oiled, legs bare, brown and shining, fingers shyly touching the counter. The eyes of one girl beneath lowered lids were round and rich as plums. Some wore school clothes, white shirts and bobby socks, but others wore their Sunday dresses, every color. Peacock blue, mustard, orange, cherry red. I watched them watch a boy pass, the Chambers boy, who moved with such symmetry eyes had to follow. They sat with the boys or they didn't, they whispered and covered words with their hands while spinning slightly on the stools back and forth, back and forth—toward what? I felt suddenly underdressed in the white dress and apron and my hair cut short. I felt the bare nape of my neck. I picked up the opener and jacked the metal cap off a Coke. A little mist from the fizz sprayed the knuckles of my fingers, and I remembered sex.

I forged around the counter and looked over the expectant crowd. Mama's balloons tied with ivy bobbed at the ends of the tables. I looked at Will's table to check, the way I did, reflexively, and reached for the pen behind my ear. Since he'd returned, I would look to his table; even though I tried not to, I couldn't help but look.

Then I went back to the kitchen.

I had not noticed what Mattie was working over on the counter, not noticed what she was working over to the left of the cornmeal, with the catfish fillets bubbling in the skillet, and the corn pudding and squash and okra and greens and new potatoes warming in their sockets. Then, as Mattie turned, I croaked and startled.

As she turned, I had seen Mattie holding Eugenia's best china bowl. Filled with the catfish concoction. The bowl, bordered in fat burgundy roses and gold gilt, was set on a tray and surrounded with a fan of crackers. I stared. Apparently Mattie was planning on hauling it out in front of everybody. For an instant I felt hugely irritated but didn't know what to say; I didn't know whether to stop her, but I thought better of it, and anyway, she was holding the tray.

"Mattie, what you doing?"

"Let me by."

"But I don't know if that's—"

"Shhh," she hissed. Then she pushed at the swinging door, and stopped. She looked back at me. "What you call this, anyway?"

"I call it. I don't know. . . . I call it . . . catfish pâté."

Mattie cut me a look. She said, "All right, Eugenia." And went on out.

She carried out the tray and put it on the table in front of Reverend and Mrs. Roberts, and leaned over and murmured something to him.

A pause. Everyone waited. Their eyes went from the reverend to me in a way that made me doubly regret this presentation. The reverend picked up a cracker. He dipped it in the bowl and lifted. He bit and chewed and looked up at me.

Then he said, "I could eat this between tarpaulin." And after and for a long time to come I'd have reason to remember this moment and to think of the simple kindness that brought it, for it had a power like relief and it had a power to heal folk long after all else was exhausted.

When supper was under way, the reverend was talking to Mama.

Matilda was drawing squiggles in the condensation on the side of her ice tea. Then Tomaine Tilden pinched out a cigarette and stared at the very different contents of his glass. He had held it half-empty under the table to add spikery of his own distillation just as his mother held up a postcard from her youngest son, Trey, a photograph of the Chicago Montauk Building in her cinnamon-dark hands.

And Tomaine said to Will and Amos, at the next table, "You know, there's only two kinds of music." He looked up from his glass. "You got your blues. You got your zippety-doo-dah." Then he went back to staring at his glass.

Soon afterwards it was time to light the cake and it took Mattie and Mama and me all three to light the fifty candles, one of which I'd positioned at the top of the tiny church spire. The candlelight caught color and reflected in the little Life Saver stained-glass windows and when I went out everybody *ooh*ed and *aah*ed and the reverend took three breaths to blow them out and Mrs. Roberts scoffed that she'd never seen her husband short of breath before.

That's the way it all went until Mattie was setting down the serving plates and I was pulling off candles. Then a car turned on the street. It was the sheriff's car, I could tell that much. There was someone else in the front seat, but I couldn't tell who. What I could predict was the sudden stillness brought by the car lights even before they had shown on the window. The sound of the car engine hummed through the quiet dark and blended with the closeness and breathing of the room.

The candlewax ran down my hand and I let it harden as the car passed. I did not feel wax on my fingers but felt instead the nuance of happiness slip, in the faces, and the eyes empty. I was reminded of something seen as a child: the glazed, empty reaches of the field hands in the fields. It was as though they were looking not at the present way of the world but past the present toward something permanently lost. Mattie was looking this way, and so was the reverend. They were looking at one another as the car light fantailed over the room, quicksilvering Mattie's eyes, then passing over the reverend so that coils of his glasses seemed glowing and alive.

The room looked to the reverend as the light flattened, elongating on the wall, glinting the window, charging violet on faces, straining ears for the sound of the car vanishing down the street; so much waiting for one car to pass. And suddenly, the reverend raised his hands, clapped them together, and rubbed them over the cake.

"Now," he said, the first thorn in his voice, "where were we. . . ."

After the cake was cut, the room loosened back up, at least partway. Coffee was served and the cake was passed. Then folk paid up and started toward the door.

And wasn't this just delicious, they said, glancing out the window, their effort to return the end of this day to what it had been, to grasp some sense of the ordinary, reminding me of the way after dessert the children would lick their fingers for icing, searching for the remnant taste of what in substance was gone. Just as Mattie and Mama were already in the back, sloshing dishwater and rattling pots, proving in this final hour that the evening's interruption had been a paltry and passing disturbance.

The next morning, the first thing I heard were two voices. I heard two voices in the kitchen even before I came down the stairs.

"Isn't it splendid?"

"Oh yeah."

"Now it's my turn."

"Ah good. Real good."

"This is the greatest of inventions."

When I entered, I saw Mama and Mattie passing a jar of mayonnaise back and forth. Mama dipped in a spoon, then held the jar in front of her as she sampled. She beamed at Mattie, who seemed irritated that she did not have hold of it. Mattie hovered, spoon in one hand and reaching with the other, managing to pull the jar from Mama's hands.

"We have discovered a shared pleasure. Mattie and I. For both of us, growing up."

"You ever had mayonnaise cake?" Mattie asked.

I glanced back and forth between the two of them.

Mama peered at her empty spoon. "Uh*oooh*, I think we better stop," she said.

I watched Mattie screw the lid on the jar. She opened the door of the icebox. I looked back at Mama.

"Mattie and I are both local yokels—born in one place and wishing we'd lived elsewhere. Working to get away and then working just to work all our lives. That's why we get along just fine together.

"Which reminds me, last night, the conversation I had with Reverend Roberts. About the architecture of ascension, and how in the height of cathedrals, those tall ceilings and windows lead the eyes upward, toward heaven, while the architecture in these country churches reminds you of the here and now, in the small homelike buildings, as comfortable and intimate, he said, as this café." She smiled at Mattie. "I'll say this about Reverend Roberts, he is a gentleman. And what's his whole name?"

"Theopholus Philomene."

"Good Lord. That *is* a preacher's name. And where's he from?"

"From here."

"But his accent sounds, a little different."

"Well, he went off to preachers' school. To New York."

"I suppose that accounts for it."

At no point did either of them attempt to make me comfortable in their conversation. So when the Christmas bells rang, I went out front.

It was Will.

And what followed began, at the outset, at least, as one of those painfully childish dialogues.

"I was wondering, would you still think about taking that stroll?"

"I don't know."

"Well, you said you might."

"I said no such thing."

"And what does that mean?"

"I don't know."

"Or maybe you'd rather take a stroll with Mr. Nod."

"What if I did?"

Will looked at me.

"Well, I've heard plenty. From the horse's mouth itself. And from Daddy. And your mama talking about these phone calls and all."

There was a space of silence. I looked at him. Then I said, "Well. If this ain't the pot calling the kettle black."

"Fannie, I told you—nothing happened."

"It wasn't nothing."

"That's not what I meant," he said, and his eyes were so dark, suddenly.

Then he said, "What can I do, what can I say, to make things better?"

"That's the wrong question, Will. That's not how it works."

"How does it work, then?"

"It's something you have to *be*."

He was leaving the room. There was a short silence, and he stood in the doorway. He looked smaller, abruptly. Caved in. Then I said, "Will, why is it that I feel like the last person to hear about everything?"

He breathed heavily, once. I waited.

"And if I'd told you earlier. . . ." His voice was burred, and he cleared his throat. "If I'd told you earlier, would that have made any difference?"

I didn't say anything.

He was turning away.

Then I said, "Look, Will. I'm glad you're better and all."

But he had walked out the door.

"Hell's bells," I said. I went back to the kitchen.

Mama and Mattie stopped in midsentence and exchanged a look.

"Well?" Mama said.

"It was Will."

"And?"

"He wanted to take a stroll. Whatever that is of y'all's business."

"*And?*"

"And nothing. We'll see."

"We'll see what?" Mattie said.

"I *said*, we'll *see*."

One month later, on a Friday in May, I was serving the first teenagers of the afternoon at the counter. Cocolas and shakes. I jacked metal caps off bottles and dropped red-and-white-striped straws into glasses. The sunlight on the window was dropping, the air conditioner humming as they kidded and jostled, loosed and restless, the way they are at the end of school.

They sat there, sipping through straws in that vacuum of time that exists before everybody gets there for supper. Now and then they'd look back through the window at the smudge of sun on the heat-tingling horizon beyond the river and the pier. Then the Roberts and the Watsons came in, and Ulysses Watson joined the group at the counter. He had a book under his arm and placed it on the counter. Their high school annual. *The Persia Tigers*. They opened it and passed it among them, nodding, or simply stirring in agreement, as they looked at a page.

It was a photograph. Blown up to the size of the entire page. Then I read upside down in the middle of the facing page, blank except for the inscription:

To Earnest March,
in dedication

The annual lay open. I jacked the cap off a Nehi and handed it to Ulysses and then asked if I could take a look. He nodded and the whole group stilled as I turned the book around. I looked at the picture of Earnest March. The face, thin and dark against the white collar. His Adam's apple showed. The close-cropped hair, shine on the nose, cheekbones taut under the skin. All in all, a good focus, though the background was grainy, the edges blurred as though at the last moment, the face moved. And strange, but this too: The way his full lips bit in at one corner, as if suppressing a mocking laugh, seemed to me connected to his disappearance rather than his disrespect of the school photographer. There would always be, in that, I thought, a small measure of his own free will.

So I looked at the picture. And I felt the others still. And as I looked I began to turn up all the old images that were him, and not him. It was as if, slowly, a lens were being turned, another part of the picture was coming clear. Then I thought about Will. For Will, perhaps Earnest March had been some answer outside of him, some way to make amends. Perhaps this had been the way it was for him, at first. Perhaps he had thought of it all—his effort to rescue Earnest March— as a new answer, really. Something startling, something fresh about himself: Will could be, he might be, a person who could save someone. But then it had come muddled with the boy's death, with that time in Will's life he'd almost betrayed everything: me, our marriage. When he'd betrayed even Uncle Lawrence—he saw it that way, I knew—by living, when he'd died.

I thought about this. I imagined these confused equivalents merging in Will's mind. Then I looked back at the photograph.

I thought then about Sheila Jones, and all the times she had come in and sat at this very counter, after school, ordering a cold milk shake in the middle of the slow afternoons, and talked to me about her father and his death and coming with her mother all the way back to Persia from California, her freckles sprinkling like paprika and smiling under her bangs her small secret smile, for she had to go now, her boyfriend was waiting.

I remembered that. And that morning, the smell of smoke from the kitchen and Mattie running out back and stabbing the knife in the back tire of the green Buick station wagon, as Sheila Jones let out that scream, that scream that rang in my ears for so many months but was beginning now to fade, with the sound of the boy's name, the first hint of what perhaps she had already foreseen.

So now there was a picture in an annual, a high school dedication. With Earnest March dead, the investigation ended and his body not found, his absence was no longer something talked about, at least not openly, in the café, and the gift of his classmates' dedication was finally their gift to the ghost of Earnest March. It was a small gift dutifully offered, like a handful of flowers or a stone over an empty grave, to comfort the ghost so that it would trouble the living no longer.

And what of Sheila's comfort? I wondered too about that. For it was getting past nine months since the time of her and her mother's departure. Had she actually been carrying his child? Did she take to holding her hands over her stomach, the way women do in the last months? And before that, long before, did she draw from her mother not merely some sense of shame but a different kind of fear: when her period didn't come, when she found herself dizzy every morning and unable to eat her cereal, when she had to keep herself from imagining the smell of shakes, coffee, and fries that I slid across the counter?

And if she had been pregnant, when did she tell the boy? Did she tell him before, perhaps just before the morning she slipped out of the house with the keys to her mother's car and met him behind the café? Perhaps she thought of what she was setting in motion. Perhaps she did not. Perhaps only the speed of it all startled her. Perhaps she drove toward town, aware of the tenderness in her breasts, a certain tightness at her waist. Perhaps she began at her front porch and worked outward: not this, not this, nothing else matters. Or perhaps this was romantic. Perhaps she knew that the only thing for her to do was to disappear.

For what child could be hers, and what place? It was an echo of my own wondering. What it could be like. To be pregnant. As if this could somehow compensate. As if this would prove something, to see your face blend with his. There were times when I wondered if I'd wanted that with Will, deep in the center of the night.

I remembered the last time I saw Sheila, after the men had given chase, and after she was led back into the café, she'd looked weak and sodden. She had sat carefully on the edge of a booth. The sound of the women's voices as they spoke had made her look down at the floor. I had spoken to her once, and Sheila, in her thin summer shirt, in the air-conditioned room, had trembled. Trembled, perhaps, to think that the moment before, in argument with the boy, was the last time she would ever see him. Trembled, perhaps, fresh from her own father's death, to think of the last time she had seen him.

And that would have been the beginning.

So perhaps Sheila thought of all of these things as she and her mother took the long road back to California. Perhaps all her days would be an extension of this, of what had been taken away, and everything else to come after, no matter what, would be regret and waste and the clumsy sketch of half-truth like what a child draws with a pencil and looks upon and says, Erase that, do over.

Or perhaps Sheila held on to something that could never be taken away.

I stood there looking over the photograph in the annual, as all at the counter watched, breathing the odor of glossy paper and new ink, and turning these thoughts over in my mind. I finished getting them their shakes and Cocolas. Then I went back into the kitchen to help Mattie get supper.

It was the end of May when I saw the photograph of Earnest March in the annual. I continued with the way of life I had adopted, still retreating as much from the past as toward the awkwardness of my future. And in the end, months later, in August, in fact, the same old mix of feelings that tossed my mind sent Sikes Daughtry walking through my door. Now, at least, I can see that such was the case.

He came in a little before seven in the morning, on August 1. He pulled up in his pickup with his hounds in the back and got out and looked around. He pushed open the front door and the Christmas bells rang and he said, "No, you stay there" (to the hounds in his truck). Then he came inside, glancing again over his shoulder at the street, but there was nobody there. So he looked at me. He looked at me and waited.

And I said, "May I help you?"

So Sikes Daughtry was back in the café in front of the counter, looking around at the empty chairs and empty tables. So much had changed in that room, and had changed forever. But Sikes Daughtry had not changed at all. He was still as rickety and stain-toothed as one of his old hounds, leathered and leaning crooked on his cane with his bad arm held close to his side and his sad eyes watering. He took a seat at the counter as he looked at me and then again at the empty chairs, and my own glance strayed. He said he could sure do with a cup of coffee, and then he said something about the weather, but it was a strained and difficult line, completely empty.

You grow up in a small place seeing the same faces all your life. You see the faces so often that sometimes you forget they are there. Particularly the oldest of the old men who sit at certain times of the day at the café counter, liver-spotted hands on cups of coffee and the wrinkled sunburn going down into each of their collars. And after an eternity one looks up and says, Hey, little lady. And another says, It sure is hot. And another says, Yeah.

And you nod to each of them, and smile. And you look at the wrinkled sunburn going down into each of their collars, but the skin below is as pale and peeled as the skin of a spring onion. And you don't know whether inside they are happy or sad, and you don't know whether they were always this way, but gradually you begin to wonder if this is a town that eats its young and you begin to wonder when, when will life ever begin?

And then there is a time when the answer comes, but it will not be what you expect. It will be different than before. You will remember the old greeting, but you will forget the rhythm. You will remember the words, but they will die away as though nothing was said. So there you are.

Sikes Daughtry and I looked at one another across the counter. He had laid his cane along the row of empty stools beside him and held his coffee. And he sat there, as dust motes on the air caught the morning light and the noise of Mattie rummaging pots brought the faint *ding-ding* from the kitchen. Then he raised the cup slowly with a careful palsy and held it to his lips and took a sip and set it down. He set it down looking at it as though right then he might pick it back up, for drinking coffee was something to do. Nobody expects you to talk when your mouth is full of coffee.

In the end, though, he did say something. Perhaps having a cup of coffee on the counter in front of him, seeing me fill it, with what he knew was good coffee, as he and all the white men had once congregated at this counter and drunk coffee for years, made it possible for him to say something.

He said, "I see you getting on."

"I can't complain."

"It's been a while."

"Yeap," I said. And I thought of how long it had been, almost a year to the day since the café emptied and the men gave chase. That day, Sikes Daughtry had come in not twenty minutes afterward, his face dropping like the runner-up in a beauty contest, for he had gotten here too late and missed all the excitement.

He was silent for a moment, then said, "It's been a while, but I come here to tell you something."

I didn't make any answer.

He looked again back over his shoulder, through the window toward the street, and, thinking he might change his mind, I set the coffeepot back on the warmer and waited for him to leave. He looked ready to go. But he held his cup and said, almost commiserating, "Folk poking they fingers into everybody's business."

"And whose business is that?" I said.

"Them as is tending to it."

"Yeah right. But who's them?"

Sikes Daughtry's watery eyes blinked at me a couple of times, then he said, "Them who knows. Them who knows and talks about—about the way the café is—in your situation."

"Suits me," I said. "Talk all day. But you can tell them, as far as the café goes, there's not any situation."

Sikes Daughtry sat there, and out of the old face the watery eyes blinked. Maybe I hadn't said anything. Maybe I wasn't here at all.

"You can tell them," I said.

"In your situation," he said. "Folk sticking they fingers. And I say, I say I don't know nothing about that, but all I know is, she done right by me. She done right by me."

So that's it, I thought. So that's the reason he's here. And I thought of all the times the café had floated his debt, a habit begun by Eugenia, way back, and even before that, by Uncle Lawrence, who like Sikes Daughtry had been a war veteran and you had to respect that, so we'd stack up the uncashed checks in the chipped coffee mug by the cash register, waiting for his disability to come in. So that's it. Nostalgia for a free meal ticket.

The head nodded on the rickety stem of neck and said, "That's what I come here for to tell you. That's what I come here to say."

And having said that, he brightened. "And it's like I say, I say, I ain't a liberal, but there's a lot of them and less of us and she's got to make a living. She's got to make a living, I'll hand her that. I'll hand her that, her almost losing her husband and all—" and here he paused, and I thought with an instantaneous stab of what had happened to Will, and I hated the old rickety creature in front of me who said, "Folk sticking they fingers."

I thought to say something then. I thought to say a whole lot but maybe it was because he was old or maybe it was because it looked like the next gust of wind might get him, or maybe it was because of the way he kept looking back over his shoulder to see if there was anyone on the street. Or maybe it was because he said, You done right by me, even if what he was referring to was a free meal ticket and all the times he had never paid. But this time he did. He dipped a palsied liver-spotted hand down into the pocket of his trousers and pulled out a handkerchief and coughed up a thick wad of asthmatic phleghm. Then he reached back in again and pulled out and laid on the counter, a warm dime. He paused one last time and looked around the room.

"Well," he said. "I come here for to say it. And I did."

I must have given him a small nod.

"And you know," he said, more to himself than to me. "There's those of us who got good relations." He nodded to me. "We got good relations, we got good relations with our coloreds."

He stood and gathered his cane. At that instant the Christmas bells rang, and Arthur Boyd came in. He was dropping off Matilda. Sikes Daughtry saw him and called out, in a jocular tone, "Hey, boy." And went out my front door.

Thus Sikes Daughtry was able to pay me a final visit, admiring his own virtue and almost forgiving me.

Sikes Daughtry died of a stroke the following year, in 1964. And with his death he took the distinction of being the last of my old white customers. Indeed, he's the last to set foot in my place since the investigation of the murder of Earnest March. Another year has passed, another year, as I tell this story. Mr. Magee died of a massive heart attack in the spring. Mr. Ardor, who suffers from the onset of senility, stays kept up in his house, visible through the column-fronted window, wandering among his books. Brother Works, I hear tell, the new success story of the town, is moving to North Carolina to preach on TV. And Sheriff Wade? Well, Sheriff Wade—who is still here and is still, at least for now, sheriff—is what he is and cannot be named.

The day of Sikes Daughtry's final visit it was August. And somehow, I knew it would be his last. And because I knew that, I realized it was time for some decision. I did not come to realize this at the moment when I asked Mattie in the kitchen about the murder or when Amos told me the whole story of Will or when I looked at the photograph of Earnest March in the annual or when the Christmas bells jingled and I saw Sikes Daughtry come through my door. But because of those things—and all the other things that happened—I came in the end to realize it.

So one day at the end of summer, after I closed up the café, I took myself out for a walk. I walked across the street and down the pier. I walked out to the *Elvira*. Will and Amos were on deck, and I stopped at the boat's edge.

"Will," I said, "I'm ready for that stroll now."

Will was tying off some rope and he dropped his arms and looked at me. He looked up at me for a long moment.

From behind his mop, swabbing the deck, Amos jokingly said, "If you don't go, boy, I will."

"That's reason enough right there," Will said. Then he went down into the bunk room and when he came up I saw that he had his pocketed hunting vest under his arm. He had put on a clean white shirt and rolled the cuffs.

"What's in the vest?" I said.

"Rudiments of life."

"I thought the doctors warned you."

"Oh they did, Fannie, they did, not that it's any of this town's business. But for your interest, I will say, I take their advice—but in my own way. Since I been back, I hadn't had a drop."

"That true?"

"True. And I have to say, it's a hell of a note when you wake up first thing in the morning and think, This is the best I'm gonna feel all day."

We walked up the pier and up the steps. Then Will looked to me for some signal.

"Well, first you might say, lucky me. Lucky that this fine-looking woman has seen fit to stroll with me, so soon after our troubles."

"Fannie, I'm glad you came to the boat. Gladder yet that you want this stroll. And you do look fine."

Then we walked up Levee Road and up the bluff. We said very little. It was near dusk and a barge was easing slow on the river. We walked the path past Avery Jones's barn and the cemetery and cotton fields and then past Tchula Gaze's. Wiebe Schwietert's cattle browsed the pasture by the bluff.

"Over there," Will said, pointing to a grassy spot just back from the edge, next to a scrag of fence. We walked in that direction and he reached into a pocket of the vest and pulled out a pipe. He reached into another and pulled out a small drawstring bag.

"That's the nastiest looking thing I ever seen. And what's that?"

"Choctaw brain medicine. Old as Neanderthals, probably."

"Will."

"Look, I've changed, Fannie, but I ain't changed that much. Besides," he said, lifting a pinch of what looked like tobacco and tamping it in the pipe, "it was Elvira's, or Elvira's parents', I should say. Daddy gave it to me as a homecoming present. He said it'd help me sleep."

Will lit a match, put the pipe to his lips, and took a long draw. We sat then and he offered it to me and I declined and he smoked some more. We sat for quite a while and he smoked until he finished. Then he tamped in a second round and relit the pipe and said he had to tell me what happened.

He started to tell about Earnest March and about the men of the town and what they'd done. He said, "I followed them all out there, that day. Just like you saw. And that boy trying to drive on *that* tire. It was busted flat with the knife still in it. So, of course, everybody caught him, the minute he stopped the car. The minute he tried to run. And I told the sheriff he wasn't worth it. I tried that first. And I just kept thinking that if I could set this one thing right, well, then . . . But all I remember was going down. A swat from a paw. And the next thing I remember was the boy. By the time I came to and found him, they had him up. Hanging from the tree. With old Tchula looking on."

That was all he said. He looked down at the ground and picked up a rock. Then he pivoted his arm back and threw it hard over the bluff. We sat in silence. When he looked up, his eyes were red as noise.

"So," he said.

"You did your best."

"Yeah, that's what they said after your uncle Lawrence."

"Will, you weren't responsible."

"Responsible. Funny, hunh, how preachers and doctors like that word. They like to say that hurting makes you wise but the fact is, it doesn't, and so what good is it? And after that you ask the question, what to do next? Where to start again?"

I thought about this. I thought about how little Will had actually just told me, how he had spoken in bits and pieces. Perhaps sometime he would tell me about more of it, all of it, I said to myself. I didn't know who I'd live with if it weren't Will, who would understand the strangeness of our life. But I also feared that if I returned to him now, we might go on and on, we might come to a point where we looked back to find the relationship had disappeared.

All the same, I was sitting with him, and I felt myself about to say something. I felt myself about to say it and I fought against it. I warred against it, just as I still held on to some hardness in myself—a hardness, perhaps, even, I'd come to like a little—because it had gotten me through. I didn't know if this was the best thing to do, I didn't know if this was the smart thing to do, for Will had taken enough out of me, that was a fact, and maybe the problem with forgiveness is that there is rarely enough time. The green all around going black with a haze of purple, the silver glowing faces of cattle, crickets, the air at our feet blue as ink. I could hear breeze moving cotton leaves and the hard fertilized pods against branches. I could hear empty Vienna sausage cans clankle on the scarecrow crucifix. I could hear another sound too, massive and far down the bluff, lapping against the rocks, and the thing about remembering that was, it was still the two of us at the river, hearing the same light rumble I hadn't noticed in a while. It was still our lives.

And so I turned to Will. Then I made a gesture that expanded in a way that surprised us both. I unbuttoned a button of his shirt. I put my hand awkwardly onto his chest, on the scar where he had collided with my uncle Lawrence, when he was eight years old. Looking up at his face, I said, "You say you don't know what to do next. Well I'm not sure either. But maybe this is a good place to try again."

Then I kissed the scar.

So this is the story of a murder in a town, but it is also my story. It is the story of a girl who saw the world one way, and then saw it another. It is the story of a girl who grew up in a way of life and never thought to question such a basic thing. It is a story of a girl who did not look up from her own life until she had seen others dead. She had seen her aunt Eugenia dead. She had seen Earnest March dead. She had seen Tchula Gaze dead. She had seen all of these things but could not comprehend the change. She could not comprehend the change, but change did come.

The answer came in the night at the end of that summer when I took the walk with Will. I did not say why to myself at the moment when I walked with him for the first time in a long while out that dirt path on the bluff. Nor did I say why to myself when I parted with him and told him there was something I had to do. I followed my feet not back to the café but past the railroad, where the streetlights ended, and the blacktop turned to dirt and into the edge of colored town. It was a very hot, still night, heavy with the smells of vegetation, and the sky was thick with stars. The soles under my feet felt wobbly. The air where it touched under my clothes was still damp. Sore from unaccustomed lovemaking, I kept walking. I walked through colored town until I came to Mattie's house. There was a small light in the window. I looked at the house for a few minutes and then walked past the front-yard garden and up the steps.

The screen door was latched. But the door to the front room was open, and looking across the front room I could see down the hall to where a column of light stretched across the floor to what was likely the kitchen. I knocked on the screen door and waited.

In that moment Mattie appeared in the column of light down the hall.

"Who is it?" she hollered.

"It's me," I hollered back.

She came down the hall and across the front room toward me. Then she was at the door, a skinny, robe-covered figure in the darkness beyond the screen. I started to say Evening, but didn't. And she did not speak as she fiddled with the latch. Then the door was open, and I stepped inside.

I caught the trace of turnip smell, of vinegar and pot liquor.

"I didn't know whether you'd let me in," I said, trying to make it sound like a joke and trying to see her expression. But I could only see the shadow of her dark face, and the glint in her eyes through the darkness.

"I guess tonight's your lucky night," she said.

"Well, I didn't know," I said, and tried a kind of laugh.

"And why's that?"

"Oh, the way I've been."

I followed her down the hallway toward the column of light that turned out to be the kitchen. There were waxed wood floors and a pot on the stove. An oscillating fan, an oilcloth on the table, and Matilda's crayon drawings on the icebox. Mattie reached into the icebox and pulled out two Cokes. She jacked off the lids with an opener. Then I followed her back down the hall and out the screen door to the edge of the front porch.

"I think it's a little cooler out here," she said.

She sat down in one of the chairs on the porch and I sat down in the other. Then she said, "And just what way you been?"

I held the Coke without drinking it. "Aw, you know, the way I've been. It's just, for a long time, everything and everybody's looked the same and when I tried to move I couldn't seem to move. And when I made the effort I wondered what's the point. Or maybe you don't know."

She turned her head in my direction and gave me a long look. For an instant there was that flicker in the eyes as when a match touches sandpaper. "Or maybe I do," she said. "Maybe I know plenty and maybe I know most of all what it means to be tired."

"Yeah. It's like for me a long time there's a lot I couldn't do. I couldn't hardly even feel sorry for anybody."

"I never asked you to feel sorry for me," she said fiercely. "Not then and not ever."

"No," I said slowly, "I don't reckon you did."

"I never asked you that."

"I know," I said, and fell silent. I didn't say anything else and I didn't move.

I held the Coke a minute longer before I said, "Mattie, I reckon I know what you're saying and I don't mean to be bringing it all up again but—"

"You ain't got a clue what I'm saying."

"Some idea maybe, and that's why I came here to see you."

"Aw, I thought this was social."

"Well, as a matter of fact," I said, "maybe it is. We been together a long time and we always got on—"

"Oh yeah, we always got on."

"And I just think maybe it's time—"

"Don't!" Mattie burst out. "Don't start dragging this out again!"

"I haven't."

"I know you haven't," she said, and then she looked away and across the street, not facing anything, just sitting there, not looking at me or the porch, just somewhere out in the darkness.

And her face like that suddenly reminded me. The emptiness, the two of us together, not talking. It was the way it had been between us. It had been the very heart of it, and it was a hole. Only now some of the surfaces were gone: all the cooking and chores we held up around ourselves to cover the painful empty core. Mattie set the Coke on the porch, sweat gleaming on her forehead; then her arms hung. I waited while she settled back again into herself and continued to look out in the darkness. The sound of crickets and a pause. Then the crickets started again, and I said, "And you know the reason I haven't, I haven't, as you say, dragged anything out, is because . . ."

She didn't seem to be listening to me. She was watching somewhere in the darkness where the crickets were. I hesitated, and then, watching her face, went on. "Because you won't let me."

I waited and watched her face as I said this, but it didn't show a thing. It simply looked tired, tired and not giving a damn.

"I've been out with Will," I continued. "That's where I've been. And he was talking about everything—everything he saw though he didn't see—the actual murder. And now you say I'm the one dragging it out—well, maybe I am. For a long time after that day—that day of the murder—and Will disappeared and I didn't know if he was in on it or not. I couldn't quite imagine him being in on it but I didn't know. I didn't know and even worse, if it had boiled down to it, I didn't know if I was the kind of person who could deny it. To point the finger at your own kin. And then in the end when Amos came back and everything came out I guess I was sick of having a secret and I was almost glad not to have it any longer—"

"Yeah," Mattie said, not turning to me, "preach to me about keeping a secret."

"I'm sorry," I said, feeling the blood rush to my face. "I guess I did get off the point."

"I guess you did, all right."

I waited. Then, "The day y'all's boy—Earnest—got killed, do you got any notion who did it?"

She seemed to be turning the question over in her mind. If she had heard it, for I couldn't be sure.

"Do you?" I asked.

"I don't got any notion," she said.

"No?"

"No," she said, still not looking at me, "and I don't have to have any. Because, you see, I know."

"Who?" I said. "Who?" and came up out of the chair.

"The whole lot of them."

"I thought so."

"If you thought so," she said, "why you come around here messing with me?"

"Because. I had to be sure. Tchula saw it, didn't she? Didn't she? And did she see what they did to Will?"

"No, she didn't say nothing about Will."

"Well, she saw all the rest of it, didn't she, and then she told you. She told you who-all—" I stopped and stood there by her chair and stared down at the averted face, which the moonlight lay across. "You say you know who-all—so what about who shot him?"

"Damn you, Fannie Leary, damn you," she said in a tired voice, and turned her head to look up at me. Then, looking at me, she came forward in the chair and burst out in a voice that all at once wasn't tired but angry and wild. "Damn you, Fannie Leary, why can't you leave me alone? Why can't you let this be? Why you coming around and messing with things? Why?"

I stared down into the eyes, which in the pain-twisted face were fierce now and burning.

"Why won't you tell me?" I demanded softly.

"Damn you, Fannie Leary, damn you," she said again, using my actual name.

"Why won't you tell me?" I demanded, more softly than before—I was almost whispering—and leaned down toward her.

"Why won't you tell me?"

"Because . . ." she began, hesitated, and rolled her head around like one loosed on a decapitated body.

"Because?" I demanded.

"Because," she said, and let herself fall against the back of the chair, "Tchula did it. Tchula shot the boy."

That was it. That was it, and I would never have guessed it. The little porch seemed to shudder a bit as my knees slowly gave down, and I was back in the chair. There I was and there Mattie was, and I was looking at her as though I had never seen her before.

After a minute, she said, "Quit looking at me."

Then I heard my lips saying, as though to myself, "Tchula shot him."

"All right," she said, "all right, Tchula shot him. They were stringing him up and she heard the voices and then she saw it, from high up on the bluff. They were stringing him up on the willow tree, there by the river, and she saw it all. She'd been out squirrel hunting when she heard the ruckus and then she got to the edge of the bluff. And when she got to the edge there it was. There it was and she wanted to holler out but her voice wouldn't come. There was the Shine boys and old man Giddy and the rest of those men and the top of the sheriff's bald head. And the postman—*Master* Magee—standing off to the side in his blue uniform with his hands squirming around in his pockets, not taking part but not doing anything to stop it either. And the mayor, who would smile at me later that very night like he was practicing to be Jesus—and anyway, they were all there, stringing him up, not quick, mind you, but slow, slow and sure so that from where she was looking down at all this she started looking for one thing. One thing."

Mattie paused. "His feet," she said. "She was looking for the boy's feet, which she could see as they began to clear back and head out, his feet one minute on the ground and the next minute off and she could see he was still—and it's like she said to me, what could she do? What could she do? Then she remembered that gun in her pocket and that bullet in her gun and she asked me to understand—to understand, Lord Jesus!—and then like a flash she knew she'd shoot him."

"She shot the boy."

"Lord Jesus," she breathed. "Lord Jesus."

"She shot the boy," I repeated.

"Lord," she breathed, "and I helped. I helped do him in."

"No," I said, "we've been over that," and shook my head.

"Yes I did. And it's been like that. Ever since. I ain't the same as I was."

"You are inside. Inside, you are."

Mattie breathed. She stared ahead. "Inside," she said.

I had found out what I had come to find out. But I kept on sitting there. I didn't even drink the Coke.

After a while she said, “Come on over here. Slide your chair on over here.”

I got up and inched my chair over next to her, and waited. She didn’t look at me, but then she did an unfamiliar thing: She reached her hand out uncertainly in my direction. I took it and held it while she continued to stare into the night and the moonlight struck strange and pale across her face.

“Missy,” she said finally, still not looking at me.

“Yes?”

“I’m glad I told you,” she said. “I knew I had to tell somebody. Sometime.”

“But not the law.”

“Not the law. A colored woman putting a bullet in the flesh of her own kin? If that got out, you know how far this’d gone. It wouldn’t matter if half the town or half the state or the sheriff or the governor himself had his hand on the rope, you know who’d get the blame. So I’m glad I didn’t tell. I’m glad I didn’t tell the law but at least I told you. When you came through the door I thought I might. I’m glad I just told.”

I didn’t find much to say to that. So I continued to sit there for quite a while, holding Mattie’s hand, which she seemed to want, and looking out into the night, which coiled dampsweet and thick toward the river, in the direction of the café.

Epilogue

AND NOW WHERE DO I look as I remember? A year later. Leaves of time drop from the branches, coloring and sifting down so we have all changed before they touch the ground and still.

Where do I look in the café as I think once again I should get through stirring this egg custard and go back to the cabinet and sort out that old notebook of recipes? It is this café, this old wood frame on the bluff that triggers me back to the summer of 1962. Skin forms on the back of a wooden spoon, and memory twitches, for suddenly I am thinking of leaving the café. I am thinking of leaving, even as I continue to move in company different from the first. I have still not returned to the company I grew up with. For one thing, there is Reverend Roberts, who has been trying to persuade me to sell the café. And when Mattie said she would be willing to run it, what could I do but listen? For there was a time when I was not ready to talk about the café; I was not ready to talk about the future because I had no idea what or where it was. The present itself for so long had been uncertain, and we were trying to find our way. I tell Will of the idea in bits and pieces, and he tells me of his need to make a living. Amos, for similar reasons, is also considering a move. And the sale of the café would allow Mama to weigh her options. Then I think of Mattie and the time when the café almost went under and she was there. Half the town was there. The half I now wait on and listen to their stories as my feet get tired standing on linoleum.

And something this afternoon has tossed a leaf off the ground and allowed it to blow back in the air toward the summer of 1962. Perhaps it was a color in today's sky. Or the face of a white boy under a John Deere cap, who I saw through the window as a stranger. Or perhaps it was a conversation this afternoon with Reverend Roberts, when I remembered. In addition to talking to me of selling, the reverend has been trying to persuade Arthur Boyd to run for sheriff against Sheriff Wade, but we don't know if he will. It is rumored that electricity will soon be expanded to the farthest side of the tracks. Yet there remains something in this town, for me, that is irretrievably used up and old. I don't know how it would be if I do this. I don't know how it would be if I take off and try to get a starting job in some restaurant in a city, say, New Orleans. I am a woman whose love leaves out luck, and I don't know what the circumstances would be, and I don't know how Will and I would fare, and I don't know how I would hold my own jittery face if I were to set foot in a place where they serve food under silver domes, big as hubcaps.

But there could be this too. I was realizing it could come with a decision. I was realizing the possibility of it for the first time in a long while, and it was the relief of no longer having to wait and see what was going to happen.

I am a cook.

Just the other day I did run into Beatrice Ardor in the Piggly Wiggly. She was coming around the frozen vegetable section and I saw it coming, I saw it on her lips, she whispered, *"Bitch."* An arrowhead may forever point in the direction of the past, stones of the river may be old as God, and it may be that folk in a small town will forever be picking over your life for weevils.

Yet today I am thinking of leaving, and the world smells in some way different. A thunderstorm has rolled past. I see the remnant of it in the distance as I pause at the café door to look back toward the horizon to see how far the rain is from me. Here and there a flick of lightning, air scatters leaves and enters the sleeves of my shirt, though it is the smell that reaches me in bursts, the smell of those first days after the murder of Earnest March. I have never understood what-all it is about rain that smells, yet as I stand here I realize I am smelling the heart of the river. It is a smell not unlike the darkening of cut fruit. It is a smell torn from trees and woven in the bottom of kitchen baskets. It is that split-second sliding between ripeness and rot and I lift my face on the air, wondering.

And I still see Tchula Gaze, like a saddened ghost in her faded cotton dress, nodding to me on the bluff, spoken of and remembered, a story in my customers' mouths. Or spoken of and forgotten, by those not much younger than me, by those not old enough to know there are things that happen and leave without a trace, though it would be very wrong to say that the world turns on, unaltered, as though such things have never been.

The body of a boy turned up, on a fine June day, and opened Mattie's secret, and completed the story that only to her a great-grandmother had told. This is how it was.

There was a green riverbank, and all the flowers were blooming; black-eyed Susans, buttercups, fragile violets, clover, velvet moss closer to the bank where the ground was damper, cattail, deadly mushrooms, scattered rock, minnows swirling in mud eddies, and Jesus bugs, dragonflies, wings of translucent copper, gold, and blue, and round this border a higher climbing edge of sweet-smelling honeysuckle, and above this Queen Anne's lace, frothing whitely on a hill. It was blooming; it seemed it would go on forever. The birds called, and there were butterflies and bees, dipping from flower to flower.

There was a girl, moving along the river, wearing a clover necklace, humming to herself and skipping stones along the surface of the water.

There was a skull, smooth as stone and the same tinge, almost completely buried under a mildew of leaf and sod and moss, touched by the fingers of the girl as she made her discovery.

And so the final stage of the investigation that, once again, brought Mr. Nod through my door. He and another assistant, this time, different from before, who came to Persia and to another town seventy miles south, to investigate the discovery of a body, a skeleton, left astonishingly intact. The skeleton of a black male, five foot six or five seven, fifteen or sixteen years old, 115 to 125 pounds. This was the description. Authorities converged and completed a report that focused ultimately on two findings.

Two findings. The first involved the evidence of a gunshot wound to the forehead. The coroner's report revealed that while the bullet entered near the top of the forehead, it had exploded into fragments and lodged near the bottom of the skull in the back. Such a shot must have been fired from a distinct angle, the report said. Taking into account the two Persia eyewitnesses' sighting of the body—on the edge of the river near the willow tree at the base of the bluff, just outside of town—it was presumed that the shot was likely fired upon the boy from a height above, a considerable height, perhaps from the top of the bluff. As for the make of the bullet, the fragments lodged in the back of the skull were shown to match the content of homemade bullets fired from one ancient sidearm, a double-action Colt Lightning, belonging to one Tchula Gaze, and one side of town chalked up the whole thing to a family quarrel.

One inch below the bullet fragments, however, was evidence that dealt with the question of hanging. In the vertebrae of the spinal cord, there was no clean break that would prove a broken neck and instant death. Yet there was a strain in a fissure of the vertebrae that indicated the probability of another kind of hanging, the likelihood of a struggle. A smooth upward pull of rope, for instance, or the slight weight of the boy's body, each could have contributed to and drawn out a struggle at death, a slow suffocation, until the moment the bullet entered the skull.

This was the report. These were the possibilities, though no rope remained on the body and none was ever found.

And so by the summer of 1964, the investigation has officially ended.

I can't say I've spoken much of this, though we shall continue, no doubt, in the shadow of the story, the opening of the old secret, and the ability it confers, to remember what you cannot imagine. So perhaps this is the time Will and I should be leaving. And perhaps then there will come a day we can come back, sit in the café, visit Mattie and the reverend and the customers, lean on the counter bent by a thousand leaning elbows. And perhaps if that day comes we will speak of this again, but that will be some time from now, and for now I can imagine what Mattie wishes not to remember—holding the thing inside, looking inward even as she looked away. A story is a mirror you hold at an angle you choose. For so long we tried not to look.

Acknowledgments

I am grateful to my agent, Nina Graybill, who kept the faith; to Thomas Dunne, who took the manuscript and gave it a future; to Melissa Jacobs, who thoughtfully edited the book; to Nathalie Dupree, who understands the alchemy of red pepper jelly; to Jack Bass and Will Norton, who believed; to Eudora Welty, who gave me generous encouragement at a critical moment; to Jamie Moore Price and my mother, who predicted this would happen, a long time ago; and to Fred, who drank wine with me in the shadows of the San Gabriel Mountains, many an evening, as I read this story.